Blood Games

LIZ MISTRY

ONE PLACE. MANY STORIES

HQ
An imprint of HarperCollins*Publishers* Ltd
1 London Bridge Street
London SE1 9GF

www.harpercollins.co.uk

HarperCollins*Publishers*
1st Floor, Watermarque Building, Ringsend Road
Dublin 4, Ireland

This paperback edition 2022

1
First published in Great Britain by
HQ, an imprint of HarperCollins*Publishers* Ltd 2022

Emojis © shutterstock.com

Copyright © Liz Mistry 2022

Liz Mistry asserts the moral right to be
identified as the author of this work.
A catalogue record for this book is
available from the British Library.

ISBN: 9780008532468

MIX
Paper from
responsible sources
FSC™ C007454

This book is produced from independently certified FSC™ paper
to ensure responsible forest management.

For more information visit: www.harpercollins.co.uk/green

Printed and bound in the UK using 100%
renewable electricity at CPI Group (UK) Ltd

As always, to my family whose support means the world to me.

Prologue

THE ONE WITH THE GIRL AND THE ACID
POSTED BY BFDLASS#WWWTS JULY 28TH 14:08

Picture this – a sunny day at the start of the school holidays. What could be better? Six weeks of doing nothing but relaxing, exams are over and life is good. A girl, without a care in the world, swings the bag of summer clothes she's just bought from Primark in Broadway as she walks through town back to the Interchange. She's not frightened – why would she be? She's in a public place, surrounded by other shoppers and the sun has brought out the good in people. Ear buds in, she hums along to Justin Bieber and thinks ahead to her date with Taj later on. They're going to see a film at the Odeon. She doesn't know what film. Doesn't care – they won't see much of it anyway.

She doesn't know where they come from. Doesn't see them or hear them approaching in a rush.

The first thing she smells is the sourness as the liquid is thrown into her face. The first thing she hears is the phrase 'Allahu akbar'.

1

> The first thing she feels is the acidic burn on her skin and …
> The first thing she does is fall to the floor screaming!
>
> **#WhatsWrongWithThisShit?**

COMMENTS:

JakeK4292: *If the silly cow's listening to Bieber she deserves all she gets. LMAO* 😂😂😂

  Karryann3: *@JakeK4292 WTAF! Are you a psycho or something? This is terrorism! Her attackers should be shot!* 😠

  JakeK4292: *Chillax bitch. Can't take a joke, eh?* 😤

  ZainK: *Wanker! @JakeK4292*

  JakeK4292: *@ZainK LSR*

Jazzygirl3: *Poor girl! B*****ds. Why do they do this shit?*

  MH616: *@ Jazzygirl3 – by 'they' do you mean Muslims? No real Muslim would do this sort of crap. It's not what Islam is about – get your facts right.*

  Jazzygirl3: *@MH616 – PO. I meant the attackers – don't care what religion they are they're assholes.*

POSTED BY BFDLASS#WWWTS JULY 28TH 19:36

> Thanks for all the comments earlier – well not all of them – some were pure evil, but I let them be published. It's good to know what crap you're up against, right? By now you'll know that the acid attack earlier was actually a vinegar attack. Does that make this any less crappy? Does it make it less scary for the unnamed girl? Does it mean she'll be up and running about without a care tomorrow?

I THINK NOT.

She'll never wear her ear buds in public again. She'll never feel completely safe in her own city. She'll never trust crowded public spaces again and she'll see her attackers all around her.

#WhatsWrongWithThisShit?

Views: 107 Shares: 42

COMMENTS:

LazyJayz04: *She's not unnamed no more – she were Molly Cropper and she were shagging a Paki #servesherright #stick-withyourownkind #PakiLover*

> **MayLee:** *@LazyJayz04 you make me want to vomit. You racist AH. The girl can date who she wants!*

Jazzygirl3: *It's all gone to fuck! What about the machete attacks in Bradford? Not going to talk about them #WhatsWrongWithThisShit*

> **ILuvCurry:** *@Jazzygirl3: IK 2 dead ... FS! Reckon it's these honour fanatics?*

MH616: *@IluvCurry: Why do you whities all go down the Muslim honour killing route? #EducateYourself*

19TH OCTOBER

Chapter 1

'We welcome the senior officer leading the investigation into the increasing number of machete attacks involving young folk in the Bradford district. The most recent assaults on Shabana Hussain and Parminder Deol proved fatal and, with no suspects in custody, this continues to be a cause for concern. So, DCI Hegley, is this violence drug-related and what are the police doing to ensure the safety of our youth?'

'Bradford police are taking this matter seriously, as we do all violent crime in the area. We are exploring a range of enquiries and would ask that anyone with information regarding these attacks contact us on this num—'

DS Nikita Parekh switched the radio off and twanged the elastic band that circled her wrist. Her entire body was a quagmire of contradictions: rapid heartbeat, lethargy, dullness. She didn't know which of her physical reactions was worse. It was like she was pulling herself along a very brittle branch that was likely to snap at any moment, and she was unsure how to save herself. Inside her pocket, the latest postcard from Freddie Downey, her father, burned through the denim of her jeans and scorched her skin. Its contents, as usual, sent tremors of fear spiralling through her.

I'll be back. Your choice – who's next, you or your sister?

Couldn't Downey be content that her mum was dead? Why did he have to now target Nikki and Anika? It made her paranoid. Every time the letterbox clattered or when she couldn't get in touch with her sister, Nikki feared the worst. She should tell Marcus about these cards ... or even Sajid. But that would unleash a whole new can of worms. She just couldn't handle that at the moment. She shrugged. Downey would soon tire of tormenting his daughter and surely he wouldn't be stupid enough to return to the UK, never mind Bradford – would he? She shut down that niggle, but it could not be ignored completely. Nobody knew better than Nikki how conniving, brutal and vindictive that man was. There was no certainty that he'd remain at a distance, leaving it at merely taunting her, but that was a problem for another time. Right now, she had a crime scene to see to. Nikki forced herself to open the car door and step out into the potholed car park. This crime scene would be another victim to add to the list her boss had been talking about on Capital Radio News.

An oppressive, swirling mist swathed Chellow Dene and the lack of visibility was compounded by a persistent drizzle. Nikki stumbled her way to the crime scene. Her previous experiences at Chellow Dene were of day trips with the kids, walking around the reservoir to expend their energy in the fresh air. Set just outside Bradford's city centre, it was a popular place for romantic summer walks and free excursions during the school holidays.

Yet today, Nikki's thoughts couldn't be further away from such things because the autumn weather matched the purpose of her visit. Cursing the damp that seeped through her jacket and up through the soles of her DMs, Nikki trudged towards the glimmer that illuminated the area. Her bones ached, a dullness occupied her skull where her brain should have been, and her normal purposefulness evaded her. She longed to be back at home, huddled under her duvet, shutting the entire world out. But even *that* was a fantasy. Since her mother's death a few weeks previously, Nikki had developed insomnia, which made it harder for her to function. She had become sullen and unresponsive. Every day was a torture to be overcome, and some were just hardly worth the effort. Marcus, her partner, had expressed his concern on many occasions, but Nikki didn't know how to shake off the weight that dragged her a little further into its depths.

As she reached the perimeter of the crime site, she saw that DC Sajid Malik had beaten her there. Shoulders hunched, he stood out like a sore thumb in the floodlights. His designer Burberry raincoat, which, in the past, she had teased him about by referring to it as a Mac, and his equally designer-ish 'Young Farmers' green wellies, were more suitable for the weather than her attire. Even from this distance, the worry etched across his forehead was visible, and that knowledge drained her even more. What the hell was wrong with her? She was glad of his presence, because she had no energy to engage with the officers and crime scene investigators at the scene and, ever-dependable, Sajid would take up the slack, yet his fretful scrutiny made her feel like crap. She was letting everyone down, and she hated herself for it.

Almost without her realising it, her fingers wrapped round the elastic band she kept on her wrist for just these sorts of occasions and she snapped it three times, welcoming its smarting lash. She'd replaced her normal thin one with a more durable, thicker one. Still, sometimes even that wasn't enough. The thought of her kit stashed behind the towels in the bathroom and the frequency with which she used it nowadays had her stomach clenching. Was she going to be sick … again?

'Car trouble?' Sajid's grin didn't quite make it to his eyes, but Nikki appreciated the effort.

'Smartass. Just 'cause you ride around in an overpriced "look-at-me" heap.'

Some of his worry lifted, and the furrow on his brow lessened as he snorted. 'Don't see you moaning when you switch the heated seats on, do I?'

Waving his comment away, Nikki edged closer. The CSIs had erected a makeshift plastic covering using overhanging branches from the trees. It loomed eerily over the bundle that was halfway under the sodden foliage. With the CSIs at work, Nikki considered the scene. Had the victim met his killer in a pre-arranged meeting, or had it been a random attack? The secluded area inclined her to believe the former, but she wouldn't jump to judgement. The scene manager, Gracie Fells, noticed her presence and ordered her staff to move aside so Nikki could view the body in situ.

As she approached, Nikki got her first sight of the victim, and her mind exploded. She stumbled forward, her voice strangled as a single word left her mouth. 'Haqib …'

She fell to her knees in front of the body, and in a torrent of tears and hiccupping sobs that made catching her breath near impossible, she gathered the dead boy up in her arms.

Chapter 2

Sajid's heart thundered as he hesitated for a nano-second. His thoughts were all over the place. The shock of Nikki's behaviour had thrown him. She'd never been like this before, and he didn't know what to do. On the one hand, he ached to drag her away from the crime scene to avoid any further contamination whilst on the other, he wanted to kneel beside her, gather her to him and let her sob out her grief. As one of the CSIs took a step towards his partner, Sajid flung out his arm, blocking the tech's way.

'I'll deal with this, okay?' His tone was savage; unlike any he'd ever used to his colleagues before. 'Back off. Just back the fuck off.'

The CSI glanced at his own boss and Gracie too stepped forward, but whatever she saw flashing in Sajid's eyes made her pause.

'Sort it, Malik. Get this sorted pronto. She's fucked up the entire scene.'

Sajid, exhaling now the immediate threat to Nikki was past, nodded and moved towards her. He should have anticipated something like this. She'd been retreating more and more inside herself for weeks, and he'd shoved it to the back of his mind, assuming she'd get over it on her own. But she hadn't, had she? He'd let it drag on and had even persuaded the DCI to give her space. Shit, now she'd suffered this very public meltdown, the entire police station would know about it. This was so different from the usual prickly Nikki he viewed as his best friend, and he didn't know how to deal with her.

On her knees, unaware of the figures all around her, Nikki rocked back and forth, with the boy still in her arms, her tears dripping onto the lad's lifeless face. The keening sound coming from her lips pierced his soul, and sent prickles of fear up his spine. With the gentleness he would use with a child, Sajid gripped her and, his voice low and soothing, said, 'Come on, Nikki. You've got this all wrong. Let me help you up.'

As his fingers tightened on her arms, she flailed against him, her eyes wide and flashing, and in that second it was as if she didn't see him. In her confused state, she thought Sajid was the killer. Voice sharp now, he threw out his next words, staccato and quick. 'No, Nik. It's *not* Haqib. It's another kid. *Not* your nephew. *Not* Haqib. Look.'

Her thrashing subsided as his words penetrated her grief. 'Not Haqib?' Her voice was robotic, as if filtering through layers of thought processes.

'No, Nik. *Not* Haqib. Haqib's fine. He's at home playing stupid computer games with Sunni.' He had no idea where Haqib was, but he was desperate to inject a normal homely scene into Nikki's reality.

Whispering, as if no one else was there, Nikki repeated his words. 'Not Haqib. Haqib's fine.' She looked down at the boy, blinking like she'd just woken up from a trance. As if all her energy had drained from her body, she flopped against Sajid, dropping the dead boy back to the ground. She was hyperventilating now, and he imagined her heart thrumming erratically through his coat. Then she put her hand over her mouth and retched.

'Shit, Nik. You can't be sick. Not here at the crime scene.' Professionalism kicked in now that she seemed more normal and Sajid dragged her backwards, but Nikki had already swallowed the vomit and the immediate danger was over.

Chapter 3

As numbness returned and her drumming heart settled, Nikki noticed her surroundings and a darkness descended. She'd lost control and a combination of embarrassment, anxiety and pride forced her to wrap her armour around herself. She'd deal with her behaviour later – perhaps. Struggling to release herself from Sajid's grip, Nikki glowered at the CSIs, who had paused to observe the kerfuffle. With eyes downcast, they re-engaged with their interrupted tasks as Nikki, pale and trembling, stood up, her legs barely able to hold her weight as she peeked at the body.

He looked very much like Haqib. The lad was of a similar build and had his hair cut in the same daft style as her nephew. His head faced away from Nikki, which was why she'd so easily mistaken him for the nephew she thought of as her own son. That was where the similarity ended, though. This boy, only sixteen or seventeen years old, wore designer clothes. From his trendy camouflage Valentino trainers – a brand she only recognised because Haqib had been bemoaning the fact his mum couldn't afford to buy him a pair for his birthday – to his Armani Exchange hoodie, the victim shouted out 'money'. Nikki sighed. Such a damn waste. This lad could easily be a drug dealer – that's where the majority of job opportunities were for kids these days – but she couldn't presume that to be the case. Maybe his family was well-off. Contrary to public opinion, there were some rich kids in Bradford. As she bent over to study the wounds that she presumed caused his death, a surge of anger replaced Nikki's earlier desperation. She wanted to shake whoever had done this to the lad; whatever choices had brought him to his life's end in a wooded area by a reservoir, he didn't deserve to die like this.

With difficulty Nikki ignored the whispers all around her, and struggling to keep her voice from shaking, she focused on the murdered boy before her. Who cared what everyone thought about her? She wasn't important. Only this poor young boy was. Later on, she'd have to face the music for compromising the crime scene, but for now she'd move on and do her job. 'What do you reckon, Saj?'

There was a notable silence before her partner responded, and Nikki crossed her fingers, hoping that he'd let her deal with this in her own way; that he'd have her back and protect her from the wolves. His exhalation was noticeable, and she detected a tremor when he replied. 'Machete wounds.'

Soothed that he was allowing her this morsel of dignity – the chance to recoup some of the respect her breakdown had washed down the pan – she nodded. These types of wounds were familiar to most detectives in Bradford. However, recently there seemed to have been an upsurge in machete attacks, not just in the streets, but in some home invasions, too. 'Whoever did this was determined.' Her voice still shook, but at least the words were coherent. 'I can count a minimum of fifteen cuts. Why the hell do they do this crap to each other? Another life wasted, another family ruined by senseless violence.'

Sajid placed his hand on her shoulder and gave a light squeeze. 'It's very similar to those other two deaths, Nik. Let's head back to Trafalgar House, till they have something more to tell us. Plus, we can see if we can round up Springer. Not fair that she's always AWOL at the moment. If she wants to stay on the team

14

then she should pull her weight instead of disappearing off at a moment's notice.'

DS Felicity Springer was Nikki's nemesis. Although she'd grown to tolerate the detective a little more over the past year, she still held reservations about her, which was unfortunate as Nikki had become her child's godmother after saving Springer's partner and baby from certain death. Now the woman seemed to be included in every damn social gathering Nikki's small circle of friends arranged. Having to work with her constantly jostling to be the boss was hard for Nikki, but Nikki was the one with the experience and their boss DCI Archie Hegley had made it clear that Nikki was in charge. For now though, Saj had issued her with a getaway card – a chance to escape without doing any more damage and, more importantly, with a modicum of pride. Hmph, who was she kidding? Her fuck-up as SIO at the crime scene was unpardonable – she'd be lucky to retain her SIO position on the case and the thought of Springer's gloating face compounded her misery. Saj was right though. She needed to escape. The effort of trying to redeem herself for breaking down was just too much. 'Okay then. I'll head back to the station. You finish up here and I'll meet you there later.' With an attempt to lighten what she knew was an intolerable situation, she avoided meeting the concerned gazes of those around her and said, 'No doubt Springer's already swooping in on her broomstick to take over and I don't want her saying we didn't do things by the book.'

Aware that the CSIs who'd witnessed her earlier meltdown were whispering and casting shifty glances her way, Nikki forced her head up as she walked away, glad that the swirling mist would soon envelop her, making her invisible to them. Back in her car, she turned the ignition and switched the heater on. All the emotion she'd kept in check from the churning acid in her stomach to the exploding battle in her chest erupted from her mouth in a series of gulping sobs. Glad that the mist combined with condensation protected her from prying observers, Nikki flicked the engine on, then leaned her arms across the steering wheel and rested her head on them. It was only when she'd exhausted her last tear, that she realised that the drizzle had become a downpour, hammering against her windscreen, sending patterned rivulets of water down the glass and pummelling the roof of her car hard enough to lift the already patchy paintwork. The persistent drip from the leaky frame soaked her shoulders and found its way down her neck. She had to get a new vehicle. It was beyond time, yet the thought of letting this one go overwhelmed her. It was like losing another family member, and she still hadn't recovered from her most recent loss.

Looking at her wrist, she half-heartedly pinged the elastic, but it gave her little reprieve and her thoughts turned to her kit. What she'd give right now to retrieve it from its hiding place and here, in the cocoon of her rust heap of a car, use the blade on her thigh, or her belly. Anticipating the release that would bring was almost too much to bear, and she twanged the band again. Then, when that didn't do the job, she pummelled the steering wheel with her fists.

A peremptory rap of knuckles at the passenger window was too little warning for Nikki to cover up her distress before Sajid yanked the door open and, after checking the seat for remnants of food, inserted his dripping frame into the car. When he turned to look at her, his gasp was audible. He averted his gaze and together they sat in silence, staring at the river of water flowing down the pane despite the windscreen wipers working at double speed. The rain had slowed to a manageable drizzle and Nikki turned the wipers to a lower setting before Saj spoke. 'You need a new ride, Nik.'

'Yeah, Marcus is going to take me.'

Still looking straight ahead, he continued. 'You okay?'

Nikki hesitated before replying. After what had just happened, it was impossible for her to say yes. Yet her need to lick her wounds in private made it difficult to admit how out of control she felt. She refused to confide in Marcus, her partner, about her feelings since her mum's murder. So how could she speak to Sajid about it? He was her best friend, but she just wasn't the sort of person to share stuff like that. She'd never been *that* woman. Her childhood experiences had seen to that. Nikki suffered in solitude and worked her own way through things. That's what she did. It's what she always did, and there was nothing she could do about that now.

The silence became oppressive as Saj waited for her response, and she knew she owed him something. The trouble was, she couldn't give him what he deserved, so she shrugged. 'You know me, Saj. I'm always okay. Now get your ass back into your swanky car and I'll meet you at Trafalgar House.'

His jaw tightened, and Nikki wished she could offload everything onto him. How was that possible, though? She couldn't even verbalise her feelings to herself, so how could she share them with someone else?

'Right then.' Saj opened the door and swung his legs out. Before slamming it shut again, he popped his head back in and proffered one of his posh handkerchiefs. 'You might need this.'

As she took it, her brow furrowed in puzzlement. Saj slammed the door, leaving her alone, once more cocooned in her world of emotional turmoil. She assumed he'd given the hankie for her to mop up the drips on her shoulder, but as she caught sight of her face in the rear-view mirror, she started crying again. Mascara trailed down her cheeks in ugly long scars. She yanked the mirror for a better view. Her eyes were puffy. What was worse, though, were the black bags that hung under them and their hollowed-out aura of despair. Using a half-drunk bottle of water, she dampened Saj's hankie – for once seeing no humour in his desire to always carry pristine cotton or silk hankies with him – and wiped away the tracks of her tears, wishing she could eradicate the crow's feet that had sprung up next to her eyes and the deep furrows across her brow. She was turning into an old woman and her body, with all its aches and pains, protested against her every activity. Mascara wiped clean, she studied her reflection. 'You need to get a grip, Nikita Parekh. Too many people rely on you, so you can't lose it now.'

However, burrowing its way deeper and deeper into her soul was the desire to just give in … to let everything drift away.

Chapter 4

#WhatsWrongWithThisShit?

THE ONE WITH THE BOY AND THE MACHETE
POSTED BY BFDLASS#WWWTS OCTOBER 19TH 15:27

Picture this – a lad goes for a walk, maybe even a jog, in Chellow Dene. It's dark and foggy, but hell, maybe he needs the fresh air, maybe he needs the exercise, maybe he needs to relax or maybe he just wants to be outside. He's been in school all day long and his brain hurts with all the pressure to pass his exams. Maybe someday he'll be a doctor or a bin man, or an artist or a pop star or a nurse – it doesn't matter what he chooses to be, as long as he gets to be happy.

He won't stay too long. It's too cold and maybe a bit creepy in the dark, but he's not scared. He's done this walk/jog many times. He knows the reservoirs like the back of his hand …

Then, he hears the noise coming from behind him. For a moment he wonders if he's being followed, but dismisses that idea. Who the hell would follow him here?

It's only then as he shrugs and moves on that he feels the first sharp bite of pain – in his arm? Across his back? On his neck?

> I don't know but the sting of metal slicing his skin, warm blood dripping from the wound, the smell of cheap aftershave, the whooshing sound as the machete slices and dices again and again until he's dead …
>
> Over FIFTY stab wounds.
> #OverKill
> **#WhatsWrongWithThisShit?**

COMMENTS:

TheKhan: It's only the doggers who go down Chellow Dene at night. The guy should've been more careful IMHO.

RBP: OMFG! @TheKhan #VictimBlaming Not cool. We should be safe to go where the f**k we want no matter how dark it is!

TheKhan: @RBP STFU if I'd wanted your opinion I'd have asked.

AttiyaQ: It's his parents I feel sorry for. To lose a son like that they must be in bits RIP!

TheBossgal: I know. Such a waste. Is it even legal to own a machete …? #WhatsWrongWithThisShit. Let's get this trending. This crap needs to stop!

Chapter 5

'Parekh, Malik, get your proverbial arses in here, pronto!'

All that was visible of their boss, DCI Archie Hegley, was his head, but that was enough to make Sajid aware that he was in one of his moods, and that wasn't in the least surprising. Not after what had happened this morning. Sajid almost jumped out of his designer suit at Archie's rasping roar, yet when he glanced at his partner, Nikki was gazing at her computer screen as if she hadn't heard the boss's summons.

'Nik, come on. Get a bloody wriggle on. Didn't you hear? We've been summoned into the inner sanctum and Archie doesn't seem to be in the mood to be kept waiting.'

'Eh?' Nikki looked up at him, her eyes wide, as if he'd interrupted her sleep. He wanted to help her. He just didn't know what to do for the best, and he suspected that Archie's summons had everything to do with Nikki's meltdown at the crime scene earlier. Word would have reached Archie's ears. Gracie had agreed to keep quiet about Nikki's collapse, provided Sajid told Archie – but she'd been unable to guarantee the silence of her team. Still, Saj had hoped to have already worked out his strategy before they were dragged in and hauled over the coals. Not that it surprised him – not really. What Archie didn't know about what went down in Trafalgar House wasn't worth knowing.

Determined to remove the agitation from his voice, Sajid forced on a smile. 'Come on, Nik. Archie wants us in his office.'

Nikki stood up, exhaled and blinked once or twice to make her more alert. She had the air of a worn-out old barn owl with scrawny, defeated feathers, and Saj wanted to hug her close and tell her everything would be okay, but he couldn't bring himself to lie to her. He wasn't certain it would be. She'd really fucked up this morning, and he wasn't sure he would be able to protect her from whatever Archie had decided. Saj led the way to Archie's office, with Nikki shadowing him like an aimless waif. As they entered, the boss's phone rang, and with an impatient hand wave, Archie gestured to the two chairs positioned on the other side of his desk whilst he answered.

With her head bowed, Nikki seemed uninterested in the reason behind this impromptu meeting as if it was of no consequence although she must have realised the severity of her meltdown and the possible consequences of it. Archie generally left them to crack on with little interference from him. He trusted them to get the job done and Nikki was one of his best detectives – hell, her performance was second to none, which was why Archie turned a blind eye to her sometimes less-than-by-the-book methods. The fact that he'd dragged them in had Sajid worried, although from the way Nikki sat, hands clasped lightly on her lap, unmoving, she didn't seem concerned.

Archie's phone clattered onto the desk, as he leaned back in his chair and stretched, ignoring the ominous creaking sound that resulted from his actions. He'd put some of the weight he'd lost in his recent health scare back on, and although still loose on him, his office suits didn't hang quite so badly from his massive frame. 'Look. It's like this. My proverbials are tied in a knot, Parekh.'

He stood up, walked around the desk and leaned against it, arms folded over his middle as he studied Nikki. When she didn't

22

answer, he glanced at Sajid, whose only response was a resigned shake of the head.

'Parekh!' He barked her name out like a pellet from a handgun.

Nikki's head shot up, a slight frown puckering her forehead. 'Sorry, boss. I was miles away. What did you say?'

Archie closed his eyes, mumbled something that sounded very much to Sajid like, 'for cluck's sake', and massaged his brow. In a quieter tone, he addressed her again. 'Look, Parekh, you've had a crappy few months, and it's affecting yer work. Dammit, ye lost yer proverbials at the Chellow Dene crime scene this morning and that's just no' like you.'

He waited, but Nikki didn't respond.

Beside her, Sajid exchanged another glance with Archie, followed by a shrug. Neither of them knew how to deal with this, but at least they were both on the same page. An intervention was necessary or Nikki was going to lose it big time.

The previous day, Archie had agreed to give her one more week before intervening, but Sajid suspected that her behaviour earlier had changed Hegley's mind, and in all honesty, he couldn't blame the boss. Still, he was unsure how Nikki would take this. She was often unpredictable – volatile even, but the toll of her grief had left her reactions irrational, and Sajid had no idea how she'd react to what he suspected Archie was about to do.

'Look Parekh. It's wi' great reluctance I hae to dae this, but believe me when I tell ye I'm doing it for your sake, lass. Last year ye did something similar for me, when I was in denial aboot my heart issues, and noo *I'm* doing this for you. Because I rate you as an officer and because you're my friend, got it?'

Nikki's expression didn't deviate from her former mild interest. It looked as if she either couldn't anticipate or didn't care what Archie's next words would be. Sajid wanted to shake her, make her stand up and start strutting round the room, listing a hundred and one reasons why Archie shouldn't do this, protesting at the injustice of it, ranting about how short-staffed they were, but

Nikki did none of that. She stayed in her seat, detached from the proceedings.

'Aw, Parekh. Ye need to go haim, hen. Ye need to take a couple of months off. Get yersel back to normal. Maybe get checked over by the shrink – see a counsellor or something.'

Nikki remained immobile for a short time, then the furrow on her brow eased. She stood up, nodded at Archie, offered a tight smile to Saj and with a quiet, 'Thank you,' she left the room.

With Archie beside him, Sajid watched her go. She appeared so frail, as if every step required more energy than she had. Even her normally jaunty ponytail looked defeated. Nikki was flat. Flat and dejected, and Sajid's unspoken concern was that she would remain like this … or worse – but that didn't bear thinking about. None of this was good, and he only hoped their intervention was timely enough.

'Christ, Malik. That's no' the Parekh I ken.'

Exhaling, Sajid shook his head. 'No, she's not herself. She needs to be forced to take time for herself. I'll give Marcus a ring, so he knows to expect her home soon. Hopefully, he'll be able to convince her to get help.'

'Aye, well, I hope she gets what she needs. I can't lose mah best detective noo, can I?'

Sajid smiled. Beneath his boss's harsh words, the worry was evident as Archie collapsed into his chair and slurped from his water bottle before shaking his head. 'I need Parekh back – the old yin. She's a pain in mah proverbials, but she gets the job done.'

Chapter 6

Nikki couldn't work out how she felt about Archie forcing her to take time out. All she knew was that she wanted to escape from Trafalgar House as quickly as possible. Away from her colleagues, away from the too familiar smell, away from the hustle and bustle of people doing their jobs and most importantly away from the sensation of being physically present but not connected. For weeks she'd been in some sort of invisible bubble, with everyone around her getting on with their lives, oblivious of the gnawing ache that burned right through her. Marcus had told her she was dissociating because of her grief. He'd tried to get her to see someone, but Nikki knew it wasn't only grief that scorched her soul; it was anger and rage and regret that she hadn't been there for her mum. The last time her mum had needed her, she'd let her down. Instead of propelling her onwards, all the emotions just drained her, sapping her life, her energy, her confidence, wearing her down a little more each day – scraping away every healthy cell and replacing it with a venomous, self-destructive canker.

Nikki didn't know what to do with herself. Self-harming didn't ground her anymore. It didn't give her the release that allowed her to go on, and all she wanted was for this weight to lift, but it pressed down, squashing her more and more into submission.

25

Time stretched out before her – an interminable flatness, a never-ending darkness, an eternity of nothingness and each day the struggle to continue became harder.

When she pulled up in front of her house, she was surprised. She had no recollection of the drive over and for a second wondered what she was doing here. Marcus must have been looking out for her, because before she'd even opened the car door, he was there, bundling her up in his arms, holding her like he always did when she was overwhelmed. The difference this time was that she was numb. No emotions, no strength, just dullness. With faltering steps, she allowed Marcus to guide her into the house and through to the living room, where he sat her on the couch, yanked her boots off and covered her with a duvet. It was only then that she realised she was shivering. She dragged the duvet tightly around herself and stared at the blank TV screen.

'Shall I put something on? *Loose Women* will be starting shortly.'

Nikki turned towards him. His lips were moving; she could hear his words as they hit the air, but they made no sense. Rather than respond, she closed her eyes and lay there wondering if all this pain was worth living for as she planned her movements from the couch to the bathroom where she would retrieve her self-harm kit and end it, once and for all.

When she woke, it was dark, and she was in her bed with Marcus beside her. Had she fallen asleep? If so, it would be the first time in months. She couldn't have slept from midday right through till now? Surely she'd have wakened if Marcus carried her upstairs? The alarm clock told her it was three-thirty in the morning – no way she'd slept for over twelve hours. Maybe Marcus had sedated her. She exhaled and tried to attach her paranoid thoughts to something concrete. Marcus wouldn't do that. Marcus would never do something to her without her consent. The certainty of her partner's innate goodness should have made her smile. It *should* have made her feel cherished, yet that knowledge elicited little more than an acceptance of 'life before'. For that was how Nikki thought of it. 'Life before' had been replaced by this 'non-life'.

Grogginess abating, Nikki's thoughts drifted to her hidden kit. In it was everything she'd need to end her misery once and for all. A tear trickled down her cheek and soaked into her pillow. She pulled herself to her feet, but only managed to reach the window, where she stood, using the sill for support. A fox emerged from the shadows, tail swooping behind, sauntering as if he owned the land. A few seconds later a fox cub followed, and Nikki corrected her earlier assumption that the fox was male. Mummy fox waited for her baby to catch up, watching over it, and Nikki exhaled. The cub relied on its mum, but Nikki's own cubs would be fine without her. In fact, they'd probably be better off without her. All she contributed to the household was grief and anxiety; even through her fuggy, confused mind, the worry etched in their faces was clear. Sunni tried so hard to make her smile, nattering on incessantly until Nikki, sensing her head was about to explode, left the room in silence. Ruby's face was more often than not a worried frown as she skirted around her brother and sister, trying not to exacerbate things. As for Charlie, her eldest, she'd tried everything from cajoling, to pleading, to demanding that her mum join in with the family, but Nikki had shaken her head, gone upstairs and cocooned herself under her duvet where she lay in sleepless lethargy.

Turning away, she stumbled back to the bed and once there pulled the cover over her shivering body. The kit would have to wait for another day – one when she was strong enough to actually do it.

FOUR WEEKS LATER

24TH NOVEMBER

Chapter 7

Saj dragged himself out of bed when he got the call. It was five-fifteen and the central heating hadn't kicked in yet. His partner, Langley Campbell, opened one eye. 'Should I get up too?'

Saj leaned over and kissed Langley's forehead, then grabbed the clothes he'd laid out the previous night and got dressed. 'Nah. It's another machete killing. Reckon you've got an hour or so before we'll have the body to you.'

Langley was the pathologist, and he'd done the post-mortems on the previous three victims. Sajid paused. 'This victim's a white lad. Archie said he's the lord mayor's son, so it'll be high profile. Just what we need, especially with Nikki being off sick, Springer being flaky and the new DI still finding his feet.'

'Ah, the debonair DI Ahad. Has he taken over?'

'Yep, and Springer is well pissed. She thought with Nikki out of the picture that she'd get the SIO role, but thank God Archie knew she wasn't up to it. Besides, she's never here. Always sloping off in secret and turning up late. Jury's out on Ahad though.' He pulled his jumper on. 'He's second guessing and double checking every action we've completed to date. Questions all of Nikki's decisions as SIO.'

Langley sat up, and slotted Saj's pillow behind his back.

'Suppose he's covering his own back. He'll want to reassure himself that Nikki's decisions were solid.' He wafted his hand in the air 'You know, after her breakdown he's right to scrutinise her work. He'll take the can for any mistakes she's made.'

Saj glared at him. 'Nikki doesn't make mistakes, Langley.'

'Hey, don't shoot me. I'm only telling you what he'll be thinking. I know Nikki's great – but he doesn't. All he sees is an SIO who royally fucked up a crime scene and then went off sick.'

Mollified, Saj sniffed. 'Not sure he'll be the asset that Archie and DCS Clark thought he'd be. He's a bit of a pretty boy and I reserve judgement on whether he has any actual substance.'

With a snort, Langley stretched. 'Bit of competition for you on the fashion side, Saj?'

'Yeah right. Take more than a damn peacock like him to knock me off the number one position for best dressed man in Trafalgar House. Anyway, at least it's nearby. They found the lad in Lister Park.'

As Saj exited the flat he and Langley shared in Lister Mill, he was torn between walking down to the park and taking his Jaguar. In the end he opted to drive because who knew how quickly he'd need to be elsewhere once he'd seen the scene. He hated it when murders or attacks took place so close to his home. It made him feel even more emotionally invested – as if he was the sole officer responsible for catching the killer. As he slid behind the wheel, flicked the switch to start heating his seat and edged out of the parking slot, he grinned. It was Parekh's influence that had him feeling that way. Nikki took community and her responsibility to it very seriously and that attitude had worn off on him. His smile faded as he parked on North Park Road and saw the crime scene tape fluttering right round the park, with several officers guarding the perimeter. Although it was dry at present, a sharp wind had built up overnight and it was bitterly cold outside, but Saj's hesitance to leave his vehicle was more to do with dread at visiting yet another crime scene where the victim had been macheted to death, than reluctance to face the biting wind.

After the formalities of signing through the outer perimeter of the crime scene, donning his crime scene suit and signing himself into the inner cordon, Saj approached the bandstand which now had a crime scene tent positioned over the steps leading up to the main structure. The crime scene techs were already at work outside the tent, and as Saj neared, he saw the tall, slim figure of his new detective inspector, Zain Ahad, approaching from the Cartwright Hall entrance. The DI had only been on the job a few days and Saj had been unable to get the measure of him. Ahad had been work-focused and shot down any pleasantries with a surly stare. Saj didn't hold out much hope for a smooth relationship, but he would, at least, be professional. 'Morning, sir.'

Ahad glared at him as if he thought Saj had no business interacting with him. It was a toss-up whether that was because Saj was a lowly DC or because Ahad was a dick. Saj reckoned it was a bit of both, with the emphasis being on the 'dick' side.

With Ahad taking the lead, Sajid stood to one side before following him to the tent. He expected his DI to at the very least acknowledge Gracie, the crime scene manager, who was directing her team to prepare the body for transport, and was amazed when instead he thrust the tent opening aside and stepped through uninvited. Behind him, Saj waved at Gracie. 'We all right to come in and view the body before transportation?'

Hands on hips, eyes flashing, Gracie glared at Ahad. 'Good of you to ask, Saj, before marching onto the crime scene. We don't want another contaminated crime scene, do we?'

Ahad snorted, and his eyes lasered Gracie's. 'I'm the SIO and unlike that idiot Parekh, who, I've heard, didn't merely *contaminate* the last crime scene, but obliterated it, I'm more than capable of maintaining protocol. But thanks for your input.'

Saj had never seen Gracie speechless, but that's exactly what she was right then. Even under her mask, Saj could see the flush gathering on her exposed skin and his heart sank. Gracie would go the extra mile for you if you treated her well. She was happy to offer some assessments based on her vast experiences, but get on her wrong side and everything would be done by the book, which resulted in a slower turnover of results. Saj wanted to punch the DI. The machete murders investigation was already progressing too slowly and now his arrogance had just slowed it down even more. Besides, how could he dismiss Nikki so nastily? Saj feared there would be fireworks when Nikki returned.

With a hard swallow and a deep breath, Sajid cleared his mind of all negative thoughts and approached the body. The lad, identified as one Jamie Jacobs, looked younger than eighteen. He was a skinny little runt, with acne that even the liberal amount of blood spray hadn't been able to cover. He lay sprawled on his back on the concrete stairs, one leg bent to the side and his clothes sodden with blood, which had also pooled around him. Saj didn't want to consider how many wounds would be found. It was overkill – the lad would have bled out after a fraction of these slices.

Chapter 8

#WhatsWrongWithThisShit?

THE ONE WITH THE WEST YORKSHIRE MAYOR'S SON
POSTED BY BFDLASS#WWWTS NOVEMBER 24TH 14:08

> *Picture this – Jamie Jacobs – a bit of a lad, sometimes a tosser, but mostly just a clown. Now he's dead and that's not right.*
>
> *Imagine what went through his mind when he saw the machete in his attacker's hands. Wonder if he cried. Maybe he tried to run or talk his way out of it. Maybe he was too fucked to care. Still, high or not, dealer or not, did he deserve to die … like this?*
>
> **#WhatsWrongWithThisShit?**
>
> *Another machete attack and still no suspects. It's like we don't matter – maybe we don't. Maybe kids like us are expendable. Except he's not like us – not like the other victims.*
>
> *Maybe, now a white lad's been killed they'll wake up and take notice!*
>
> *Maybe, with all his money, his dad will pull some strings!*

Views: 1,322 Shares: 321

COMMENTS:

Ran98: You're dead right. Bet they up the police presence now a gora's been offed. This one deserved it as much as the others #killthedealers

> *Karryann3:* @Ran98 WTF. Are you for real? None of them deserve this. #RIPShabanaHussain 🙏 #RIPParminderDeol 🙏 #RIPLiaqatIlyas 🙏 #RIPJamieJacobs 🙏

> *ZainK:* Wanker! @Ran98

JakeK4292: Wrong place wrong time?

> *Jazzygirl3:* @jakeK4292 No place should be the wrong place. #Keepthestreetssafe

> *Jazzygirl3:* @Ran98 Really?

Jazzygirl3: We're all the same underneath #JusticeForAll

Chapter 9

Jamie Jacobs's home was a massive, detached house with acres of land around it, on the Bradford side of Ilkley. Ahad had insisted Saj accompany him to interview the parents, and Saj was interested to see how Ahad worked. DCS Clark had given the notification of death in the morning and Ahad had waited till after lunch to make his visit, using the time to conduct a team briefing and ensure all the bases were covered. Much to his chagrin, Saj couldn't fault him on that. Apart from a bit of a moan about Springer's absence, Ahad had got on with the job and ordered the uniforms to look for witnesses, although the likelihood of finding any in the park after dark were thin and the houses surrounding the park were distant from the bandstand. Sajid wondered if Jamie might have been meeting someone there, but Ahad had merely snorted.

The drive over had been uncomfortable. Ahad had insisted on driving a pool car, saying he needed to get to know the area, and Saj had been uncomfortably aware of the smell of fried food lingering in the vehicle. He hoped that whatever snack the previous occupants had indulged in hadn't made its way onto the passenger seat and from there onto his clothes. Ahad hadn't spoken, and after being on the receiving end of the DI's abrupt responses, Sajid looked out the window whilst mulling over the little they'd learned so far.

The woman that answered the doorbell had been crying, and Sajid initially wondered if she was the mayor's wife. However, she dispelled that assumption by taking them into a massive living room and introducing the two detectives to the mayor, 'Call-Me-Bob' Jacobs, and his wife Joyce. She must have been the maid or housekeeper or whatever these rich folk had.

Once seated, having refused coffee, Ahad began the interview with Sajid watching on. To give the DI his due, he covered all the bases and had replaced his usual bored expression with one of concern. Impressed by the way the senior officer teased information from Jamie's parents, Sajid made sure he watched for any non-verbal clues they might give off.

Joyce Jacobs sat separately from her husband, on an armchair that dwarfed her. Her feet were tucked under her, and her arms wrapped around her chest. Every so often a shudder hurtled through her body and she repeated the same words over and over. 'I can't believe it. This can't be happening.'

Her reaction was normal for those coming to terms with the loss of a loved one. However, it also meant that, for the time being at least, she could offer no pertinent information. Her husband, on the other hand, appeared almost bluff and breezy by comparison. As if he was on autopilot in his mayoral role and had to maintain a stiff upper lip. That was until Ahad started on the more piercing questions.

'So, was Jamie in any bother? Did he have anything on his mind? Girls? Boys? Drugs? Enemies? Anything like that?'

'Call-Me-Bob's demeanour changed in an instant. All bonhomie and niceties flew out the window and were replaced by hard anger and a harsh tone. 'My son's a victim here, Inspector. And you have the cheek to come here and treat him like a ... what? A petty criminal?'

'That's not at all what I'm doing, Mr Jacobs. I'm trying to find out who killed your son and in order to do *that*, I need to ask probing questions. If you want your son's killer caught, then it's best if you answer them.'

As Mr Jacobs stood and strode around the room, Saj's eyes turned to Mrs Jacobs. Her husband's agitation seemed to silence her muted pleas and her glazed look was dull but strangely observant as, with her eyes, she traced her husband's pacing. Sajid frowned, unable to interpret the dynamic at play. When she noticed him observing her, she closed her eyes and the low keening began once more. Not knowing what to do with that information, Saj stored it away to dissect later.

'We've had trouble with the lad.' Mr Jacobs sank back into the chair he'd vacated earlier. 'They're all at it, you know? It's hard to keep an eye on them all the time.'

Ahad nodded. 'We talking drugs?'

An abrupt nod confirmed what the detectives had already surmised. 'He got in with a bad lot. He was taking drugs, then he started dealing too. We got him help, but …' He swept a hand over his face, 'More than once in fact, but it never stuck. He always relapsed.'

'I'll need the names of any friends, dealers, drug contacts – any you know of.'

Bob nodded. 'I'll get that to you. It must have been one of them; they're a violent lot, those dealers – especially the Bradford ones.'

Sajid wondered if by Bradford ones, Jacobs meant the Pakistani lads. It was true that young Asian youths handled a hefty amount of the dealing and organised crime in Bradford, but there were many non-Asian criminals too and an upsurge in rival gangs from Eastern Europe made it more difficult to keep tabs on the gangs, but also to minimise the inter-gang warfare that, like in every other UK city, sometimes erupted onto the streets.

'Of course, it was one of them.' Joyce Jacobs leaned forward in her chair, her body rigid, her gaze focused. 'Who else could it be?'

Ahad smiled and shrugged. 'I'm sorry to have to ask this, but if I don't my boss will be mad. It's protocol, you know, and it has to be done – where were you both between eight o'clock last night and 5 a.m. this morning?'

Ahad had deliberately kept the parameters wide, as they had yet to receive a definitive time of death from Langley.

Sajid expected objections and indignant annoyance – he'd seen that before with victims' families – but that wasn't the response they got.

Joyce Jacobs sighed. 'We've both got an alibi, if that's what you're after. We were sleeping out in Bradford for charity for the homeless. We were in a huge group – about thirty of us in Centenary Square.'

Ahad smiled and stood up, extending his hand first to Mr, then to Mrs Jacobs. 'That's great. If you could give us a list—'

Before Ahad could finish his sentence, Bob Jacobs thrust a sheet of A4 paper at him. 'That's the names of the folk at the sleepout. You'll need that to confirm our alibi.'

To give him his due, Ahad's expression didn't alter as he accepted the list. 'Thanks for this. Now if we could just have a look at Jamie's room, then we'll get out of your way.'

The couple exchanged a glance before Bob rose and guided them out of the room. 'It's this way.'

Keen to examine Jamie's bedroom without the restricting presence of either parent, Saj put on his best smile. 'Don't worry, Mr Jacobs. We'll take it from here. You go and look after your wife.'

'Oh, okay. Top of the stairs, first on the right.' Left with little option, Bob sidled back into the living room and closed the door behind him with a bang.

'Excellent work, Malik. Last thing we need is the parents breathing down our necks. Let's see how Jamie lived, eh?' Ahad took the stairs two at a time, leaving Saj to follow, still basking in the unexpected compliment.

The first thing Saj noticed on entering Jamie's room was its neatness. It was orderly to the point of clinical. No posters, no books, no mess, no smelly teenage boy odours. Pulling on gloves, Sajid and Ahad wandered round the room in silence. As he opened the wardrobe door, Saj raised his eyebrows. It was almost empty – a couple of pairs of jeans and a hoodie were the only clothes inside. If he'd been in a poorer family's home he might have expected a dearth of clothing or, alternately, a wealth of cheap Primani tat, but here in such an affluent household, he expected to see a closet filled with designer brands. He closed the door and, eyes narrowed, considered the room with its neatly made bed and floral duvet. 'If the Jacobs hadn't said otherwise, you'd think Jamie didn't actually sleep here.'

Ahad wandered back through from the ensuite. 'Yeah, you're right. There's not so much as a shampoo bottle in there and the towels are pink. How many teen lads would choose pink towels and a floral duvet? Perhaps we need to have another brief chat with the Jacobs.'

Back downstairs, Ahad remained standing, his face unsmiling as he faced off with Jamie's parents. 'We looked at Jamie's room, which seems to suggest, contrary to your previous statement, Jamie doesn't live here and by the looks of it hasn't in a long time. Care to explain?'

Mrs Jacobs took refuge once more in closed eyes and keening, effectively leaving her husband to reply. He sat down on the sofa, not asking Saj and Ahad to sit down. This feeble attempt at a power play backfired, though, as both officers now towered above him. As if realising his mistake, he gestured to the chairs the detectives had occupied earlier, but Ahad shook his head, a slight twitch of his lips telling Saj that the DI was enjoying this. 'No, we're fine where we are.'

Ahad crossed his arms over his chest and stared at Mr Jacobs. 'We need the truth and it would be best for you if you tell us now rather than in a more formal setting at the station.'

Unable to maintain eye contact with the intimidating detective,

Jacobs jumped to his feet and resumed pacing round the room. 'Do I need to tell you who you're talking to, young man?'

Standing his ground, Ahad shook his head and kept his tone low and factual. 'No, you don't. You're a suspect in your son's murder until proven otherwise.'

Jacobs's face clouded over, a flush appearing on his cheekbones. But Ahad wasn't finished. 'I think *you* need reminding of who *you're* talking to. I'm Detective Inspector Ahad – *not* young man. Please address me as that ... or of course, sir, if you prefer.'

Sajid somehow managed to replace his smirk with a frown. Ahad's handling of the situation was almost worthy of Parekh.

Eyes narrowed, Jacobs marched over to Ahad and glared at him. 'I have a direct line to not only DCS Clark, but to her superior too. Perhaps you should bear that in mind, DI Ahad.' The last few words were spat at Ahad, but he didn't flinch.

'Just tell us why you lied about your son living with you and give us his actual address and we'll be on our way.'

Mrs Jacobs's keening had stopped as she cast anxious eyes at her husband. 'T-tell them, Bob. It'll come out anyway. Better it comes from us.'

With a curt nod, Jacobs returned to his previous chair and, head bowed, he addressed them. 'Jamie's not lived with us since he was fifteen. We've tried to get him back on track, but it's hard. He was, what I believe you call these days, a rough sleeper. We've no idea where he lived. Last we heard he slept under the arches in Forster Square in Bradford with the other down and outs. We've not seen him in over a year. He was ... troubled. We wanted to keep his troubles out of the public domain if we could.' With a spark of his previous anger, his head jerked up, and he glared at Ahad. 'Satisfied?'

Ahad smiled, not bothering to hide the sarcasm behind his words. 'Perfectly – for now, that is. A Family Liaison Officer will be along in a bit, but if you need to contact us with more information, here's my card.'

Once back in the drive, Saj exhaled. 'That was weird.'

Ahad shrugged. 'You mean Mrs Jacobs, the pre-written alibi list, or the lies about Jamie living with them? Who knows? Grief is a strange thing, and we can't judge or infer anything at this stage.'

'Guess not, but … well … the alibis are a bit handy, don't you think, especially with them being estranged from their son?'

Ahad laughed. The first time he'd done so in Saj's presence and Saj was taken aback. *So, the man can crack a smile?*

Still chortling, Ahad made his way to the car. 'Can't see Mrs J in her Louboutins wielding a machete though, can you?'

Saj had to admit he couldn't, but the fact they'd already misled them showed that the Jacobs could well be keeping additional information from them.

'Heard old man Jacobs has his sights set on more than Mayor of West Yorkshire. Apparently, he views it as a stepping stone to the House of Lords. He's got ambition, has that bloke. Folk will do a lot for ambition, and a wayward son might be an obstacle to his plans. What do you reckon, Malik?'

Eyes narrowed, Saj observed his boss as Ahad did a three-point turn in the Jacobs's drive. 'Yeah, you're right.' Then he added, 'You've only just moved to Bradford, so how the hell do you know all that about Jacobs's career trajectory?'

Ahad winked at Saj. 'I have my sources, Malik, and don't you forget it. There's not much gets past me, so be warned. I don't like secrets and I *always* make it my mission to expose them.'

Chapter 10

The Honourable Fixer

It made the morning news which means I can head to my 'day job' with a spring in my step, secure in the fact that the job has been well done. Before leaving though, I open my laptop, double check that all my encryptions and anonymity measures are in place and check my Swiss bank account. No point in doing the job if the clients don't pay up. Mind you, with the intel I have on the Jacobs, that's not really a danger. I make sure I have enough dirt on my clients before I do their dirty work. It's my guarantee that they won't double-cross me. Not that they could do much other than whinge. I've made sure there's no trail leading back to me. There's plenty of people out there who require the expertise of an efficient, anonymous and non-judgemental fixer to sort out their lives for them. Whilst I make it my business to know everything about them, from their shoe size down to their sexual peccadillos, they know nothing about me. Not a single thing, and that's how I like it.

I take a sip of coffee and lean back, savouring the aromatic fragrance. My security is in place and with all the dirt I have on various characters, I'm content. The network I've built up opens many doors for me to exploit and I'm satisfied knowing that my next big purchase is now within my reach. What an absolute joy when you hear the virtual *ping, ping, ping* of money entering your account, the result of a job well done. There's something so very satisfying about making other people's problems disappear. I laugh. And something so much *more* satisfying about getting paid big bucks to organise it. There's a lot to be said about employing minions to do the dirty work. I log off, grab my coat, and check my Rolex. Off to work – got to keep up appearances, after all.

Chapter 11

After lunch, in the semi-dark of the art supplies room at school, Haqib put his arm round his girlfriend. Fareena's family were very traditionally Muslim and any relationship with a boy, never mind a boy with one Muslim parent and one Hindu one, would be frowned upon. That was before you got into the fact that Haqib's parents weren't married, he followed no religion and his dad was in prison for child trafficking. This was the first time in ages they'd managed to sneak away without fear of the 'Evil Eyes' seeing them and reporting back to whoever their controllers were. What a bunch of dicks they were. It pissed Haqib off bigtime that a bunch of tossers with machetes could behave like dictators on the say so of an anonymous boss. God, some of them had been his friends before they got up their own arses and thought they had the right to control the area – and right under the nose of his Auntie Nik too. 'Eyes' – like summat out of that programme his mum was always on about where all the women were forced to wear them red coats. As if it wasn't bad enough that the 'Eyes' were making the Muslim girls cover up. Things didn't feel good and Haqib constantly felt on edge when he was out on his own. Charlie told him she did too. Haqib had even heard that there were different squads of Evil Eyes all over

46

Bradford – some of them not much older than he was. But that was a gripe for another time. For now, he was with Fareena and he was going to make the most of it.

The last thing on Haqib's mind was Fareena's middle sister, Attiya. But that was all Fareena talked about. Her face was all blotchy and swollen and although Haqib didn't mind that too much because she was the most beautiful girl he'd ever seen, he drew the line at her snotty sniffles. Despite his best efforts to maintain a slight physical distance between them, Fareena had buried her head in his chest, and now his T-shirt was all snotty and wet. It wouldn't have been so bad if it hadn't been clean on that day and it *was* his favourite Wiz Khalifa one. He'd taken full advantage of the relaxation of school uniform rules for sixth formers, but his clothes were supposed to do him for two days, cause his mum wasn't much good at keeping on top of the laundry. He'd worn it to impress Fareena today, but she hadn't even noticed. *Typical!*

Mind you, huddling in the school arts cupboard for their clandestine meeting wasn't really the way to impress a girl. At the back of his mind was the knowledge that his mate Ifty and his girlfriend, Shayleigh, had shagged in here only last week. That knowledge made Haqib conscious of avoiding any bodily fluids that might have escaped their union – mucky gits. Ifty could be a real tosser, but that was just gross. What if they'd been caught? Haqib grinned, imagining Mr Potter, the head of art, catching them at it. He wasn't sure who'd have been more embarrassed, Mr Potter or Ifty. One thing he was certain of was that it wouldn't faze that Shayleigh cow. She'd been at it with half of sixth form. Haqib's grin widened.

'You listening to me, Haqib?' Although Fareena's voice trembled and tears still filled her eyes, Haqib noted her frown and tried to look more concerned. He wasn't sure he'd succeeded, but Fareena seemed satisfied enough as she continued. 'It's all the secrets I hate. You'd think Attiya would have …'

Haqib resigned himself to a lengthy rant, exhaled and let his mind wander. Who the hell said men couldn't multi-task? Here he was doing just that – pretending to be fully absorbed in his girlfriend's angst whilst thinking about other stuff. He'd remember to tell his cousin Charlie of his achievement ...

When he'd first dumped his ex-girlfriend Michelle for Fareena before the summer, it had seemed romantic to skirt about, avoiding any of the snitches that kept track of the goings-on in school. Secret meetings, snatching time together, stolen kisses and surreptitious handholding had been exciting. It wasn't exciting anymore, though. Not now they'd been seen. They had made subtle threats. Some of the female 'Eyes' had visited Fareena in the girl's loos and he'd had a pointed note posted through his locker. They were everywhere, spying on everyone. Thing was, nobody knew who they reported to which made it even creepier. All he knew was that if the Eyes reported on you, you could expect some sort of punishment. One of his friends had been beaten up and another's dad's Merc had been scratched. He was sure Michelle had reported him and Fareena and now they had to wait for their punishment, and he had no idea how it would be meted out or who by. That silly cow, Michelle, had taken to wearing a hijab and saying she'd 'reverted' to Islam and banging on about how everyone was born Muslim. Haqib snorted at that. His next-door neighbour, Hafiz, had once told him that the convert/revert debate was immaterial as both were a commitment to the faith. As usual Michelle wanted to make a stir, make out she was better than everyone else. He'd bet she still fried up the sausages on a Sunday morning. Likes of her were all show and no substance. Well, that's what Charlie said anyway. The point was, Michelle was jealous of him and Fareena, and that worried Haqib. If she was an Eye, who knew what she'd get the others to do.

At first, he'd been full of bravado, telling Fareena to ignore it, but then his mate Taj had been beaten up for seeing a white lass and the girl had dumped him. Not surprising really, when some wanker in a balaclava had run up to her, shouting 'Allahu Akbar', and threw what she'd thought was acid in her face. *Poor cow!* Thankfully, it had only been white vinegar, which wasn't on her skin long enough to burn. Still, she'd been terrified. Last Haqib had heard, she'd been seeing a counsellor and couldn't leave her house. What was worse was that nobody knew who had ordered the attack and everyone felt that they could be next if they stepped over whatever invisible line the Evil Eyes and their bosses had drawn.

That was the last thing he wanted for Fareena. She had enough trouble getting out of her house as it was. The only place they could meet was at school. Since the attack on Taj's girlfriend, there had been tension in the school. A gulf between those who insisted Molly had asked for it and those, like Charlie, who said it was a 'reactionary infringement of individual rights'. Although Haqib was opposed to the barbarism of the attack, he wasn't about to start protesting like some of his friends. Not when it put Fareena at risk.

Now, here they were, alone at last, and all she wanted to go on about was Attiya. Haqib disliked Fareena's sister. She had a vicious streak in her and used her knowledge of his and Fareena's relationship to force her sister into doing most of the household chores. That was enough for Haqib to throw dark looks at Attiya, but Fareena put up with it and who was he to complain?

'Ouch.' He rubbed his ribs. 'What was that for? I'll have a bruise there, you know!'

Fareena rolled her eyes. 'I barely nudged you. And I only did it because you weren't listening.'

Truth was, Haqib hadn't multi-tasked at all. He'd found it hard to keep up with her snuffling explanation whilst he thought about the tense atmosphere at school, and had just offered the occasional 'really' or 'yeah' when he thought it appropriate.

Fareena pulled away, scrubbed her face with a sodden tissue and glared at him. 'You've not been listening. Didn't you hear?

49

Attiya's gone – disappeared and nobody will tell me what's going on. They've all pulled rank around me, shutting me out. Mum and Zara are whispering in corners and …' She snorted and gave another of her expressive eye rolls. 'As for the men? Closeted in the front room for hours and we've had weird visitors to the house. Summat's up, Haqib. Summat's up with Attiya.'

Haqib chewed on his lip, wondering if he should confide in Fareena. Tell her about the rumours he'd heard about her sister. It was a tough one. On the one hand, he wanted to help his girlfriend. He hated seeing her so distraught. Yet on the other, he didn't want to get involved in any family disputes. There was always more than enough drama kicking off at home with his mum and Auntie Nikki. All he wanted was a quiet life. His loyalty to Fareena won though and, decision made, he exhaled and came clean. 'There're rumours going round about your Attiya.'

He risked a glance at her. Fareena frowned, her forehead wrinkled in that cute, 'I'm not sure what you're on about' way, so he continued. 'I've heard she's got a boyfriend – some married bloke …'

Shuffling his feet, Haqib held his breath, waiting for her response, but when it came, he was surprised, for her entire face lit up and she laughed out loud. 'Get real, Haq. Attiya? Miss Goody-Two-Shoes? No chance.'

Haqib wasn't convinced. He shook his head. 'Fareena, I know you think she's a goody-two-shoes, but I'm not so sure. She's a sly one, is Attiya.' He shrugged, eyes down, wishing he didn't have to say his next words. 'Some folk are saying she's pregnant, like.'

Again, Fareena snorted, her eyes raking Haqib's face as she spoke in an urgent whisper. 'You're *serious*? You really think she's seeing a married man and is up the spout?'

'Dunno. That's what I've heard and …' He splayed his hands in front of him. 'With all this acid stuff and the Evil Eyes, well, it could be linked, couldn't it?'

Chapter 12

Nikki wasn't one for baring all, expressing her emotions and being all touchy bloody feely. According to the woman sitting opposite on a matching comfy chair – the sort that sucked you into its depths no matter how hard you resisted – that was what had 'landed her in the shit in the first place'.

Nikki was aware that her scowl – accompanied by a fleeting grin – was a massive improvement on her responses during her first visit to Dr Helen Mallory. Then, she'd barely heard the psychiatrist's words, never mind responded to them. Her head had been filled with heavy darkness and, for the first six sessions, she'd succumbed to the comfort offered by the predatory chair's cushioned upholstery and hadn't opened her mouth once. The cocoon effect, combined with the warmth of the fleece blanket that Mallory had tossed over her when her skinny frame had been wracked by bone clattering shivers, had soothed her.

Unperturbed by Nikki's silence, Dr Mallory had gone ahead with a series of breathing and mindfulness exercises, which as the sessions passed, Nikki found herself participating in involuntarily until one day, the dam broke and everything hurtled out of her mouth at breakneck speed. In *that* session, Dr Mallory was the one to remain silent as Nikki expunged all her rage and grief and fear and anger and … although drained and empty, somehow, she felt lighter, and that session was the turning point for her.

Recently, her daily sessions had been reduced to four in the second week, then three in the third week and now she and the doctor met up only twice a week. With a jolt, Nikki realised that soon they'd meet only once a week, then not at all. A flutter of panic shot through her body at the thought of losing this safety net. Then she breathed in and out slowly for a few breaths and grounded herself.

Nikki had come to respect the psychiatrist. She loved the other woman's triple ear-piercing and the septum ring that she hid when in 'professional mode'. She loved that she always wore black, purple and orange in some sort of combination and that her chunky jewellery looked like it weighed more than Nikki herself. The light purple walls and orange accessories amused her. Huge, flamboyant fabric chrysanthemums shared vase space with lilac and orange feathers on the windowsill, whilst a pen pot full of orange and purple pens with mini fluffy plumes sat ready next to her PC. All the paintings were in abstract shades of purple and orange with lilac frames to emphasise Mallory's dedication to her chosen colour scheme. It had become more of a pleasure than a chore to attend her sessions and Nikki was now at a stage where she could admit the benefits of them, not only to herself but to the doctor and her own family.

Nikki wasn't cured. 'You can't cure a lifetime of hurt in a few talking therapy sessions, but you sure as hell can kick its ass,' was a frequent Malloryism – as Nikki labelled them in her mind. One that she would carry with her as she continued her journey towards mental wellbeing. After struggling to release herself from the grips of the chair, Nikki finally wrestled herself to her feet and smiled. 'It'll be weird not seeing you so often, Doc.'

Mallory snorted. 'You've got my number, USE IT! That's why I gave it to you. You need me to kick your ass, then just call. I'll squeeze you in for a mini session at the very least.'

Nikki grinned again, but Mallory wasn't finished. 'Use all the things we've learned over the weeks to help yourself through tricky moments and talk that deliciously hunky Marcus's ass off when things get hard.'

How in the hell the quirky doctor had survived as a freelance police psychiatrist for so long puzzled Nikki. In her experience the police force leaned towards the prosaic and staid – Mallory was certainly not that. She was edgy, unpredictable, and good at her job. Some of her comments were risqué, to say the least, but she got results.

Nikki had once asked her how she survived and her cryptic response had been, 'I'm a chameleon, Nikki. I adapt and endure. That's me – a huge colourful lizard who prefers purple, orange and black to pretty pinks and grey, but that's not to say I can't be invisible when I choose.'

Goodbyes over for now, trepidation surged through Nikki and, as her heart skipped a beat, her legs wobbled. An entire week till her next session. Could she manage on her own till then? She pasted a smile to her lips and walked out to meet Marcus in the car park. Her fears that she couldn't cope with the slightly longer rope Mallory had given her faded when she saw not only Marcus, but Charlie, Ruby and Sunni, as well as her sister Anika and nephew Haqib waiting for her. A flicker of hope ignited and its flame got brighter as she walked towards them. 'Hope one of you lot is paying for lunch – baring my soul makes me hungry.'

Ruby guffawed. 'Thank God it's only your soul you bared. You NOT baring your ass is a major bonus for the rest of us.'

It wasn't that funny a joke, but they all laughed. Things were getting better.

Chapter 13

Maz leaned against the metal concertina door of the garage. The boss had asked him to lock up so he could drive his son, Amar, to his hospital check-up; although it was a few minutes earlier than usual, Maz reckoned he deserved it. He took out a pre-rolled ciggie and lit it, inhaling the smoke into his lungs before exhaling slowly, savouring the nicotine hit. After being on edge all day, he'd needed that. Since his boss left, he'd felt vulnerable on his own. Every customer, although there had been only two, seemed to be a possible threat. Each time a shadow appeared outside the garage, he'd dodged behind the car he was working on, until he was reassured there was no threat.

Now, under cover of dark, the persistent drizzle and the spooky fog, he relaxed. All day he'd gone over his options and at last he'd decided. He was in over his head, tempted by the propaganda of his mentors, but now he knew their agenda was wrong and there was only one way out. He needed help, and there was only one person he could trust to get him out of this mess in one piece. After he'd decided that, the headache that had sent flashing spasms over his forehead eased. As soon as he'd finished his fag, he would head over to the other side of Listerhills. That was where he'd get all the help he needed.

Muted voices drifted through the fog from his right. An empty pop can skittered over the pavement and Maz stood up straighter. Should he run? His entire body tensed as he froze, his back to the metal shutters, waiting to see who emerged from the shadows, made more threatening by the orange glow from the streetlights. Was it them? Had they sussed out he wanted to back out? Two figures emerged from the shadows, talking and laughing as they kicked the can to each other. Neither of them spared even a glance at Maz, and he took one last drag from his cig before tossing it into the gutter.

With his ear buds in, he hoisted his hood over his hair to combat the rain, and took off towards the Rec. The recreation ground, positioned between the two halves of the Listerhills estate, was locked up by this time. Parents had complained of it being misused overnight after finding syringes and used condoms in the children's play area and around the basketball courts, so the council had agreed that one of the park rangers would lock it up at 5 p.m. every night during winter hours. That didn't stop the people who wanted to make use of the meagre Rec facilities after dark and, although Maz didn't use the grounds for nefarious purposes, he knew how to access the area from both sides of the estate. Why would anyone want to walk around the Rec when there was a perfectly good shortcut? As he approached, he sent a cursory glance around him. The fencing could be prised back to allow access to those willing to risk getting their clothes caught on the soft metal. There was nobody there, so, head bopping to Wiz Khalifa, he squeezed through, not bothering if his overalls got caught in the process or not. The park was dark. It would be easy to imagine that no one else existed. Streetlights from the estate behind him faded as he walked deeper through the park, and the lights from the area ahead had yet to penetrate. Everything seemed unfamiliar and, in the muted light, a shiver spread up Maz's back. At a smarter pace, he headed deeper into the Rec, peering through the shadows, imagining the bushes were people curled up, ready to attack him. His heart sped up, pounding much faster than the rap he was listening to. As he passed the children's play area, the swings and slide expanded to ominous, hulking shapes that he could barely recognise. A slight breeze picked up, sending litter flurrying along the path, making him jump. *Come on, Maz, get real, will you? There's nobody there. Get a grip.*

The thud of his trainers on the concrete echoed back at him, taunting him for his cowardice. Sweat dappled his forehead as he trudged on. Almost collapsing with relief when he reached his exit point in one piece, he squeezed through. He was on the home run now and soon he'd have the help he needed and, more importantly, he'd be safe. God, how he longed to be safe. Not to jump at every noise, every sudden movement. He'd been a dick, and he was happy to own that. When he came clean, he'd be fine. Nobody messed with his dad after all. He picked up his pace to a light jog and turned into the back alleyway between the row of shops and the Rec fencing. The ginnel was peppered with potholes, but Maz was so familiar with this shortcut that he avoided them with ease. The huge wheelie bins lined up between the shops sent wafts of rotting vegetables and gone-off meat in his direction. He kept going, breathing through his mouth, hardly noticing when the shadows near the bins moved and formed into two figures, each brandishing a machete. The last thing he remembered before he collapsed in a sodden mess was the chuckle that harmonised with both Wiz Khalifa from his ear buds and the slash of the machete penetrating his skin.

Chapter 14

It was late and exhaustion pulled at Sajid's eyes. He was alone in the incident room. Even the Dark Knight – as he'd nicknamed the new DI – had scooted off to whatever dingy cave he called home. Yet Saj just couldn't pull himself away from the incident boards. Jamie Jacobs's death had changed things, and it irked him. Why should the murder of a white kid, albeit one whose dad was the West Yorkshire mayor, make the brass bring out additional resources? Why should the powers that be class Jamie Jacobs's death as more worthy of the extra resources the team had been crying out for since the first murder? It looked bad and stank a hell of a lot worse and he very much doubted the big bosses would succeed in making this more palatable for the previous victims' grieving families and friends. He sensed a shitstorm ahead and was relieved that, as a lowly DC, he'd be well out of the firing line on that one. That was one reason that, although he'd passed his sergeant's exams, he hadn't put in for any DS roles yet … that and not wanting to leave Nikki's team. He owed her big time. She'd trained him well, moulded him into a half-decent detective, whilst allowing him to be himself. Plus, he loved working with her. Life was never dull around Nikki Parekh.

With a sigh, he rolled his shoulders to ease the tension and again turned his attention to the crime boards. He was sure that something he'd missed lurked among the wealth of information they'd amassed, but it was just out of reach; if he could only see it, he'd crack the investigation wide open. The machete murders investigation hadn't progressed significantly since Nikki Parekh had gone on sick leave. In the initial aftermath of Nikki's breakdown, they had assigned him to work with DS Felicity Springer. He hadn't minded that too much. Springer was no Parekh, but she was organised and, when she had something to chew on, was a dogged investigator. However, over the past few weeks, Sajid had been left to take up more of the slack and her presence in the incident room was erratic at best. He'd been relieved when DI Ahad had taken up his post as DI earlier than everyone had expected. Now he had his doubts that he could work with the man.

The entire team was tense as hell, and Jamie Jacobs's death and the politicking around it, made everyone more stressed. And they were just waiting for another machete incident to occur. Jaime was the fourth machete victim and despite having four separate crime scenes to work on, and four different victims to cross-reference, they'd found damn all and it was so frustrating. He sighed and stood, arms folded across his chest, as he studied the crime scene boards. Any more victims and they'd need another brought in.

His eyes scanned the victims one by one: Shabana Hussain, seventeen years old, fifteen wounds, found in Northcliffe Park; Parminder Deol, sixteen years old, discovered in a kids' park in Wilsden, nineteen cuts. Then there was Liaqat Ilyas. This lad bore a marked resemblance to Nikki's nephew Haqib which was why she'd responded the way she had at the crime scene. Liaqat was seventeen and killed by fifty-three wounds in Chellow Dene. The most recent victim Jamie Jacobs was eighteen years old and had been found in Lister Park. Saj was awaiting the post-mortem report from Langley.

Thinking of Jamie took Saj back to his and Ahad's interview with his parents. He'd found it difficult to get a handle on them.

At first glance he'd have said Mrs Jacobs was desolate and almost dissociative, whilst Mr Jacobs, although upset, had been more in control of himself. However, Sajid couldn't quite get his head round the way Joyce Jacobs had sprung to life to recount their alibis. Not for the first time he wished he'd been privy to the initial interviews with the earlier victims' families. Those first interviews were often crucial in giving the detectives a feel for the dynamics of a family. Written notes, especially those scribed by Springer, lacked nuance and details of intuitive thoughts.

'You okay, DC Malik?'

Saj exhaled and spun round. DC Farah Anwar was looking at him, a small frown tugging at her perfectly shaped brows. As usual she was with DC Liam Williams. They had both recently been promoted to detective constable rank and although they lacked Saj's experience, they made up for it in enthusiasm and attention to detail. 'Saj is fine. Nikki's not one for formality, so let's stick to first names when it's just the team together ... I'm not sure how DI Ahad stands on that, so you should maintain formality around him still.' He gestured to the crime boards. 'Just trying to get my head round this.' He gestured first to the four names on the board in front of him, then to the smaller board that stood beside it with only one name on – Molly Cropper. Molly had been the victim of a fake acid attack in July and, despite Springer's disparaging remarks regarding his desire to consider the fake acid attack whilst investigating the machete attacks, Saj had insisted. He had yet to discover DI Ahad's thoughts on the matter.

'You're thinking they're related?' Williams said, his eyes sparking with interest. 'Even the fake acid attack and Jamie Jacobs's death? That makes sense to me. But forensics tells us the perpetrators were different in each attack ... that said, we don't know much about Molly's attackers. They took the eye off the ball with that one – poor lass.'

Saj agreed with Williams. They had let Molly down – poor girl was seeing a therapist and terrified of leaving her house. As for the other victims, guilt gnawed like acid in Sajid's stomach because they hadn't progressed the investigation. He sighed. 'We've got to keep all angles open.'

Their eagerness was apparent in the way their eyes scoured the data. He'd been like that once too. If Nikki had been there, they'd have been trained up, utilised and encouraged to contribute, but Nikki's absence and Springer's frequent disappearances meant that training the new DCs had gone by the by and Saj hated to see their enthusiasm and skills neglected. 'You got half an hour? We could brainstorm, if you like. See if we've missed anything. You never know, we might just kickstart a line of enquiry.'

Before he'd even finished, the two younger DCs had pulled up chairs, got their tablets out and settled down. Sajid grinned. He remembered being that eager. It felt like decades ago, mind you, but in fact, his eagerness had only waned when Nikki had her breakdown. Her breakdown wasn't directly responsible for the slump he was in. Saj was resilient and a team player and would happily work with anyone – if only Springer was consistently present and valued the team's contributions the way a DS should. Until Ahad had arrived, Saj felt he was driving the investigation forward on his own. It had been he who had authorised the re-interviewing of the victims' friends and families. He'd revisited every crime scene, gone over every piece of data available and was still no further forward. Meanwhile Springer was … who the hell knew where? Alongside lack of direction from Springer, he'd had to contend with Archie micro-managing, which led to lengthy conversations with the man and a shedload of extra reports when Saj's time would have been better spent doing other things. With Ahad around, Archie might back off. Saj might be jaded, but he was damned if these two officers would fall into that slump – not on his watch.

'Right then. I'll walk you through what we have and you two can butt in whenever you want.' Pausing, he looked at the photos of the victims, all lined up. Nikki always insisted on both a pre- and post-death photo. She reckoned it made it harder to forget the life that had been stolen from the victims. So, Saj had made sure that beside the smiling faces of each victim was a photo taken at the scene. Springer had objected, but Archie had weighed in on Sajid's side, thus both photos remained – a constant reminder of their failure.

'I know we have nothing to link the fake acid attack on Molly Cropper with the murders of the other four victims, but I keep coming back to it. It seems too coincidental that over the course of around three months we'd have a fake acid attack *and* four fatal machete attacks, all against kids between the ages of fifteen to eighteen. What's your thoughts?'

'Well, the fake attack on Molly was, we believe, perpetrated by a teen. Although we got little from CCTV, that was the consensus from the few witnesses who came forward. That's a link. Granted it's not solid, but it *is* a similarity, and we *are* grasping at straws. I've done a bit of research and …' Anwar consulted her tablet before continuing. 'Most of the machete attacks in Bradford are carried out by under-twenty-five-year-olds, so the perpetrators appear to come from the same age group as the victims.' She continued pulling at a strand of hair that had come loose from her ponytail.

'Mind you, most of the attacks cited are home invasions and don't result in death because the weapon was used only as a deterrent. Ninety-five per cent of the other incidents look like organised gang attacks meted out as warnings and, again, don't result in deaths – only mutilation. This "death by machete" is a recent local phenomenon. Plus …' Anwar shrugged and grimaced as if certain they would shoot her thoughts down in flames. She continued regardless, her voice animated. '*Most* murders of teens or young people are carried out by either a family member or someone from a similar age group and/or background. Also, family member killings aren't usually because of a machete attack – too gruesome, I suppose …' She paused for breath.

Saj clapped. 'Bloody hell, Anwar, if *The Chase* questions covered only criminal activity, you'd beat the lot of them hands down every time, including the Dark Destroyer. Brilliant research. Well done.'

Anwar's cheeks took on a rosy glow and some of Saj's fatigue drained away; it was proving useful that she and Williams had interrupted his solitary musings. 'So, what you're saying, Farah, is that because we excluded the machete victims' immediate families as suspects, we should focus on their peers?'

'It's just a thought, Saj.'

'You know something?' Williams sat up straight, his eyes eager as they scanned something on his tablet. He bit his lip and shook his head. 'Nah, forget it, it's probably …'

Anwar nudged him. 'Spit it out, Liam … We're brainstorming. No idea is too stupid.'

Uncertainty still clouding his face, Williams shrugged. 'I was just scanning the family alibis from each of the four victims and …' Again, the lad hesitated.

Sajid smiled at him. If he were Williams's mentor, he'd focus on building the lad's confidence. He was bright and creative and Sajid didn't want him to slip through the cracks. He'd make a damn good detective with the right guidance. 'Come on, out with it.'

'They're all a bit too pat. Their alibis, I mean. Surely not *every* family member can have a rock-solid provable alibi? Wouldn't it be more reasonable to expect a couple at least that were a bit …' He shrugged. 'You know … dodgy, like – I mean not so easily proven.'

At first it had been a relief to have so many suspects excluded from their investigation, yet, now Williams mentioned it, Saj realised it was unusual. His thoughts flicked to the Jacobs's alibis – rock solid. They'd been with many people on their charity sleepout and all had vouched for them. He sat down opposite the junior detectives.

'No.' Saj shook his head. 'On the contrary, it's one thing that all the victims have in common and that *is* a clue.' He laughed,

'Not sure where the hell it takes us, mind you, but it's worth bearing in mind.'

'Honour.' Anwar spat the word into the near-empty room, then raised her fingers to cover her lips. 'Sorry, that came out too loud. What I meant was, could there be some sort of honour motive?'

Williams swivelled to face his partner, frowning, 'But Molly Jones was white and so is our latest victim and one of them is Sikh. How can those be honour killings?'

Anwar smiled, but Sajid detected the flash of annoyance that flickered in her eyes. He understood she was pissed off by Williams's implication that only Muslims perpetrated so-called honour killings. He and Anwar faced these sorts of assumptions and prejudices every day and, like Williams, most folk didn't mean offence. Still, it hurt. Nikki's daughter, Charlie, would no doubt tag it #SignOfTheTimes.

Anwar rose in Sajid's estimation when she said, her tone mild, 'Honour comes in all shapes and sizes. Every culture has their own honour codes.' She shrugged. 'But I wasn't talking so much about the families being the perps. I wondered about vigilantism? Street honour?'

They'd been through these options before and had got nowhere. Williams's fingers drummed a beat on his knee, as he studied his tablet. Saj smiled at him. 'Liam?'

'We spend a lot of time on the street, me and Farah and well … summat's different from usual. I know the atmosphere changes when we see a spate of violent, random attacks like these – people are nervous, scared – and the longer we go on not solving them, they become antagonistic. But, this time, it just feels different.'

Anwar nodded. 'You're right. It's not so much with our older contacts – they seem as bemused as us – it's the kids. They're not talking and you usually get a few blabbermouths who want to big themselves up. Not this time. They look shifty when we approach and try to dodge us if they can.' Her laugh tinkled out, high and infectious. 'Sometimes the little fuckers even make a run for it ... idiots – I'm a sprinter so they've no chance.'

The contrast between the ever-efficient detective and this girlish response brought a smile to Saj's lips. 'Well, that's yours and Williams's jobs for tomorrow sorted. Get back on the streets and see if you can shake something up from the kids. Be real pains in their butts and take a couple of uniforms with you. Unless of course our new DI has other ideas at the morning briefing.'

The trio lapsed into silence, each lost in their own thoughts when Williams startled them from their reveries. 'Where's the fucking links?'

With uncharacteristic fervour, the lad jumped to his feet. 'There's *nothing* linking them – not a sodding thing. Different schools, different home areas, no social media crossover. Different social classes, different races ... we're back to the only two things they have in common – their youth and the way they died.'

Ever the pragmatist, Anwar exhaled, then said, 'Which brings us back to the evidence.'

Sajid snorted. 'What evidence is that? No CCTV, no sightings of blood-soaked perps marauding the streets of Bradford, no consistency with the wounds – some are more frenzied than others, each weapon used is a different make or type of machete, trace evidence in abundance, from fag butts to used condoms to footprints, but *nothing* that links one scene to any of the others. It's almost like we've got a different perp each time ... which brings us full circle back to vigilantism ... or not.'

He stood up and grabbed his coat. 'Don't know about you two, but I could do with a drink. You coming?'

Chapter 15

The Honourable Fixer

'Would you beeee-lieve it?'

I'm so flabbergasted that I say the words aloud. Sometimes just thinking indignantly isn't quite enough, instead you have to verbalise it. I grin and repeat myself to the empty room, a little louder this time. 'Would you bloody believe it?' I shake my head for good measure and scowl at the image on my screen. Some numpty has labelled the Porsche 718 Boxter as the best-looking car of the season. *Idiot.* That model is a Matchbox car – old-fashioned and dull. No way I'd waste my cash on that heap. No, my money's on the Chevrolet Corvette C8. It's a work of art that wouldn't be out of place in the Tate Modern. I scroll down till the Chevrolet is on view, then I zoom in, savouring it from every angle. Aw – there you are – all sharp and edgy. Making a statement. *Look at me … hear me 'rooooaaaar'.* Yep, she's the baby for me – not in red though – too obvious. Nah. Black – classy, ballsy and sexy – a lethal combo.

I lean back in my ergonomic chair and twist from side to side. So far, it's been a slow day in the office. One client this morning and another this afternoon – which is why I'm looking at sports cars now. I hate having nothing to do and I've still got an hour till my next appointment. Still, this morning was invigorating. Nothing more energising than the ker-ching of big bucks and the thrill of yet another problem fixed.

Yanking my desk drawer open, I glare at the four burner phones inside. With my most recent fix completed, I need a new project, but it's been a few days since any of the damn things were active and that's not good for business. I stride over to the window and scrutinise the proles bustling about below. It's too cold to go for a walk and besides it's not like Bradford city centre in the winter is very scenic. I could grab a cake from the Waterstones café though. That might be nice. There's always the Cake 'ole café too – they do a Turkish Delight cake. Yes, that's what I'll do. I'll brave the chill and grab a cake and coffee at the Cake 'ole.

That decided, I jump to my feet, but then an alert sounds from the drawer. I grin. Yes! In my haste to reach the phone I almost trip over the coffee table, bashing my shin on its hard edge. But when I see which phone has the alert, the pain on my leg is forgotten. It's the one that alerts me via my deep, dark and not so dingy incognito website. Another prospective client has DM'd me …

AntiVigilVirgil: *Don't know if this is your usual sort of job, but my organisation needs to create a disruption at a vigil in Bradford. Would this be something you could fix for us?*

Duh? Think the name answers that question, don't you, Mr AntiVigilVirgil? What a stupid name – somebody thinks they're a clever clog, don't they? Well, I suppose he's right. After all, he's been clever enough to reach out to the best fixer in the north.

TheFixer: *Tell me more. Here's a link to a secure communications hub: 8632GF169*&)572.*

Follow the instructions and we'll talk. In the meantime, I'm sure I'll be able to accommodate you, once you've paid the relevant fees. I require 75 per cent up front and the rest on completion.

AntiVigilVirgil: 👍

Idiot! Stupid damn emojis. Is he bloody twelve or something? Surprised he didn't add a smiley face too. Whilst AntiVigilVirgil follows all my pointless instructions, I gain more and more access to his digital footprint as my tracking system records his online activity. Won't be too long till AntiVigilVirgil reveals all his tawdry secrets to me. One of the cardinal rules is to know *exactly* who I'm entering into a contract with. I'm at a career point where I can pick and choose my projects, but this one has piqued my curiosity. I wonder what motivates AntiVigilVirgil to pay a shedload of money to disrupt what a quick Google search tells me is to be a peaceful vigil. His use of the pronoun 'we' makes me think my new client might be a group, which makes sense if my bill is to be paid in full with no need to bring in my debt collectors. If the 'we' extends beyond family, then my job might be harder. It's always easier to make a family toe the line, but controlling a discreet group might prove much harder. With a shrug, I add a zero onto the end of my quote – let's see if they have the money to make this worth my while.

Chapter 16

Archie was on the news again – this time on *Look North* and today he accompanied his boss, DCS Eva Clark. She stood shoulder to shoulder with a taller guy Nikki didn't recognise whilst Archie slouched behind them, looking like he wanted to crawl away. Drinking in his presence, Nikki studied Archie. She'd not set eyes on him since he'd sent her home to get help for her breakdown, and seeing him on the telly made her realise how much she missed his brusque, well-meaning nature and his stupid 'prover-bials'. His sunken cheeks and the slump of his shoulders told her how difficult he was finding this investigation and a nag of guilt pulled at her heart. She should be there. She had been the SIO on these machete killings and she'd let her team down. She inhaled, long and slow, forcing the tension from her body as she exhaled. She wasn't going down that route. Her lips quirked as another Malloryism sprung to mind; 'It is what it is, so let the fuck go'. Refocusing on Archie, she drank in his familiar reliable features. He'd be glad that he wasn't in the hot seat. Archie hated being on TV, which would account for some of his discomfort. Still, Nikki detected an underlying unease, and when his hand lifted to massage his chest, she frowned. *Is his heart troubling him again?*

The journalist droned on, her tone annoyingly nasal …

'*It's been over two months since the discovery of the first Machete Murder victim and now, the tally is up to four. Four deaths and there appears to be a significant lack of progress in the law enforcement investigation. Does Bradford have yet another serial killer on the loose, DCS Clark?*'

Archie tugged at his tie, and an indelicate beetroot bloom spread across his face as he shuffled from foot to foot. By contrast, DCS Clark was her usual unruffled self. Only those who knew her would notice the tightening of her shoulders, signifying her annoyance.

'*I find it unhelpful to label killers – it feeds into their narcissism and, quite frankly, for the press to bandy about unfounded suggestions that a serial killer is at work here is utterly ludicrous. Bradford police are pursuing many lines of enquiry. We have amassed an extensive amount of evidence and in due course will update the public on the outcome of this investigation.*'

In response to the rebuke, the journalist's smile tightened.

'*Yesterday's victim, Jamie Jacobs, the son of the West Yorkshire mayor, is high profile. His wife is a personal friend of yours, I believe. I wonder if this might influence how you investigate?*'

Ouch! Talk about a cutting question. It was DCS Clark's turn to tighten *her* lips. When she replied, her sharp tone could have sliced through an iceberg.

'*We treat every victim the same, high profile or not. All our available resources will be used to investigate all the tragic deaths.*'

'*Some might ask if bringing a new Detective Inspector from Manchester has anything to do with the fact that Jamie Jacobs is white …*'

Totally frigid now, the DCS's voice snapped across Archie to impale the reporter.

'*And … "some" would be wrong to ask.*'

With her legs pulled up under her bum, Nikki settled on the sofa and exhaled. The DCS was lying. They didn't have a Scooby. Even if Sajid hadn't kept her updated over the past couple of weeks, Nikki would have sussed it out from Clark's evasive replies. The reporter seemed determined to pin the DCS down and make the story her own, regardless of whether it might incite racial hatred along the way. Although Nikki admired her tenacity – after all, that was a trait she possessed and it had landed her in trouble on more than one occasion – she abhorred the blasé manner in which this woman fanned the flames that, prompted by fear, smouldered just beneath the city's surface.

'So, you maintain that these machete attacks, claiming the lives of four young people, are NOT the work of a serial killer? And that West Yorkshire Police are dedicating equal resources to all the investigations?'

Archie's beetroot face had eased a little, but his eyes darted about. To anyone else it would seem like he was scrutinising the studio crew, but Nikki detected the glazed expression and she bet his proverbials were in a twist. The tightening around Clark's shoulders seeped up to her jawline, lending her a pugnacious look as she replied.

'I'm saying that fruitless speculation is unhelpful at this juncture and as ever, we would welcome the public's help in this investigation. If you have any information regarding these murders, then please contact us using the number at the bottom of the screen. Thank you for your time, Ms Cray.'

Nikki smiled. That abrupt ending was typical of Clark. However, the reporter wasn't to be fobbed off and as the DCS left the seating area, she called after her, her words resulting in nothing more than a momentary falter in the DCS's steps as she marched on without a backward glance.

'... what would you say to the victims' familes and friends, DCS Clark?'

Archie had struggled to his feet and made to follow Clark off set, but he now hesitated and turned to glare into the nearest camera. His Scottish burr was strong and his honesty clear when he spoke.

'We'll get justice for all the friends and families o' the victims. Mark mah proverbials, we'll get justice and we'll put the clucker who did this away for a long time.'

Nikki snorted, almost choking on the sip of coffee she'd just taken. *Good for you, boss.* Only Archie would use the word 'clucker' on primetime TV. No doubt he'd get his proverbials slapped for that faux pas, but as far as Nikki was concerned, he deserved a medal. His sincerity shone through like an avenging beacon of determination and that alone took the sting from Clark's ultra-professional, yet very distant, interview. God, how she missed him. Her grin faded at the thought. Archie hadn't reached out to her since she'd been off work. According to Saj, he asked after her every day and it had been him who'd set up her treatment plan with Dr Mallory, but she'd heard nothing directly from him and it niggled her. Sure, he was busy; his TV performance told her that. But not even a sodding text, or a get well soon card?

Nikki suspected Archie was divesting himself of all responsibility for Nikki Parekh and she couldn't blame him. Over the years she'd caused him more hassle than she was worth, and after this last catastrophe – fuck, she'd contaminated an entire damn crime scene by having a very public meltdown … She wondered if she'd be pushed to the Cold Case Unit or worse, Archives, on her return to work. That was, *if* she was allowed to come back and, in her mind's eye, that 'IF' mocked her in huge flashing neon letters. Mindful of the slim line between melancholy and depressive thoughts, Nikki twanged her elastic band and focused on the next news article. Since she'd begun to feel better, it had become her thing to watch the news. She'd never had space before, and she savoured moments like this. Moments when she was doing ordinary things that normal people did. She used the time to focus on her breathing and, although not quite the mindfulness Doc Mallory had suggested, it worked for her.

'Both the Mahmood and Khatri families expect a huge turnout for the vigil tomorrow to commemorate Aqsa and Jusveer who were *murdered in London last month in a so-called honour killing that shook the nation. Local organisers in West Yorkshire have organised a series of vigils at various venues throughout the region to correspond with the larger one in Hyde Park and others around the country. The emphasis is on celebrating the lives of both the twenty-two-year-old Aqsa Mahmood and her boyfriend, twenty-three-year-old, Jusveer Khatri ...'*

Nikki switched the remote off. She'd promised Charlie that they would attend the vigil, and it pleased her that her daughter was growing into such a responsible person. Her heart went out to the young couple. Then a thought struck her; could there be some 'honour' link to the local machete murders? After all, there had been a fake acid attack a couple of months ago on a white lass. In her line of work, you couldn't avoid seeing this sort of stuff first-hand sometimes, and she hated that it still happened. Her suspicions might be wrong. Nevertheless, she made a mental note to speak to Saj about it. See if they'd progressed that investigation at all in her absence.

About to stroll through to the kitchen for a choccy biscuit, she was interrupted when Marcus walked in. 'Hey, Nik. You've got guests.'

Nikki plopped her mug on the coffee table and spun round, eager for a distraction. The only visitors Nikki usually had were her sister Anika, Haqib, and her late mum's ward, Isaac, or Sajid and his partner Langley. On occasion Stevie, Springer's wife, visited with Nikki's goddaughter, dragging a reluctant Springer in their wake. Everyone would be at school or work at this time of the day, so who could it be? Perhaps it was Archie? Maybe the interview had been pre-recorded, and he'd come to see if she was fit enough for work.

For the first time in forever, the thought of work didn't make Nikki's heart beat in trepidation. As her therapist had instructed her, she took a moment to note that small sign of progress before jumping to her feet. The flicker of disappointment when Marcus moved aside to reveal her visitors soon faded when she saw her friend Ali, whose sombre grin resembled someone who'd heard Nikki had died, only to discover she'd miraculously resurrected. Okay, it wasn't Archie, but Ali was nearly as good. His cousin Haris, who doubled as a bodyguard, accompanied him. Although Haris's expression was less exuberant than his cousin's, he deigned to acknowledge her with a single nod and a fleeting snarl, which Nikki interpreted as his attempt at a smile.

'Well, Parekh, you don't look like you're ready to do a flaky.' Ali, head to one side, scrutinised her for a while. 'Bit skinnier than usual and paler too. You got to take care of your mental health, you know? What am I always saying to the guys, Haris?'

Ali owned a flourishing taxi company near Bradford Royal Infirmary and from all accounts was a good boss. Haris, a man of few words, shrugged, but Ali seemed satisfied with that response, for he continued, regardless. 'Yeah, that's right. I tell them to look after their head space. Talk to their families about how they feel.' He peered at Nikki as if to push his point home. 'You know young men are most at risk of suffering from mental health issues? Well ...' He punched Haris hard enough to make his cousin wince. 'We say "not on our watch". Don't we, Haris? That's what we say, init? Not on our watch.'

Marcus exchanged a grin with Nikki, who frowned. Ali had never struck her as a New Man or of even being remotely 'in touch' with his emotions. You never could tell. Marcus had informed her closest friends of her breakdown and her subsequent three-week sojourn in Lynfield Mount, but she hadn't expected Ali to be so in tune with it all, and it flummoxed her. Although her suicidal thoughts had dissipated and she found her consultations with her therapist to be helpful, she wasn't ready to bare all to anyone other than Marcus and, to a lesser degree, Sajid. As usual, sensing her uncertainty, Marcus broke the silence. 'Cuppa?'

Chapter 17

#WhatsWrongWithThisShit?

THE ONE WITH THE RACIST COPS
POSTED BY BFDLASS#WWWTS NOVEMBER 24TH 14:08

Can you believe it?

Three Asian kids hacked to bits and guess what? Hardly a bloody peep from the press.

#WhatsWrongWithThisShit?

Now, a white kid's dead – not just any old white kid, but one whose dad's high profile – and they're all over it.

Press conferences with the police, uniformed officers all over Bradford, Detectives chasing kids to see what we know.

#WhatsWrongWithThisShit?
#Asiankidsmattertoo

Views: 124 Shares: 25

74

COMMENTS:

JakeK4292: *Aw get real. Who cares if a Paki gets offed. #NotMe I'm glad the 5-0 are going after Jamie's killer. Probably some Paki gangster anyway.*

   Karryann3: *@JakeK4292 WTAF! Racist scum #WhatsWrongWithThisShit? #Asiankidsmattertoo*

Northernlad: *@JakeK4292 Go F***k yourself*

JakeK4292: *Chillax AH. Can't take a joke, eh?* 😛

   ZainK: *Wanker! @JakeK4292*

   JakeK4292: *@ZainK LMAO!*

Jazzygirl3: *Is it a serial killer? They say after 3 it's a serial killer. Please NOT another Bradford serial killer!*

Chapter 18

Tea in front of them, a plate of biscuits within reach, Nikki waited. She suspected Ali's visit wasn't only a pastoral call. That wasn't Ali's style, and the fact he'd brought Haris with him confirmed that. 'Look, Parekh. I'm not only here to see how you are.' He flushed, his full cheeks wobbling as he grimaced, sensing that his words might appear insensitive. 'I mean, I've been getting updates from Marcus, and, well, erm, you got the bouquet?'

Nikki grinned. Since her breakdown, every week without fail, a massive bunch of flowers – probably arranged by Ali's ever-efficient business manager, Jane – had arrived with a card saying, 'Get well soon, Ali and the drivers x.' Although at first she'd been oblivious to their presence in her room at Lynfield Mount, she'd come to enjoy their sweet aroma and used the smell as part of her mindfulness programme, to ground her in the present.

'Aw, spit it out, Ali. Get on with it. What's up?'

Ali glanced at Marcus, who Nikki noticed nodded as if to grant permission for the favour Ali was about to ask. Marcus's protectiveness might have bothered her before, but now she was honest enough to admit that he was the staff that supported her. Whatever Ali wanted her to do, Nikki would do. No questions asked. She owed Ali too much. He always had her back and had helped rescue her daughter, Charlie, when she'd been kidnapped. Then, only the previous year, he and his drivers had helped to free a group of trafficked kids from a dire fate.

He reached into his jacket pocket and produced an A5 jiffy bag, which he pushed towards Nikki. 'I need your help with this, Nik.'

Nikki grabbed the pouch, unsealed it and upended the contents onto the table before Ali and Haris's combined 'NO!' registered.

With their yelped responses hanging in the air, Nikki stared at the object on the plastic tablecloth: a bloody ear. An ear that was detached from someone's head. An ear that now lay on her kitchen table where she and her family ate.

'For Allah's sake, Parekh, why'd you do that?' Ali raked his fingers through his hair, avoiding looking at the detached body part.

To give him his due, other than a strangled '*Yuck*', Marcus remained calm as he jumped to his feet and rummaged around in the cupboard under the sink before returning with a pair of gloves, some plastic evidence bags, anti-bacterial spray and kitchen towel. Meanwhile, Nikki's glare moved from the offending item to Ali, then to Haris, before resting once more on Ali's anguished face.

'Care to explain?'

Whilst Marcus donned the gloves and dealt with the contents of the jiffy bag, Ali hesitated before replying. 'It arrived this morning.'

'Okay. Do you know who it belongs to?'

Ali shook his head, but his moist eyes told Nikki the opposite. Ali swallowed hard a couple of times before responding. 'We think it's Jane's son's ear.'

'Jane?' Nikki expected Ali to name one of his drivers. Hell, Nikki hadn't known Jane was a mum. Thinking back, she realised she knew very little about Jane. The woman was a trusted friend to Ali and a brilliant manager. 'Didn't realise Jane had a son.'

'Yes. She's in bits. Will you help, Parekh?' Although Ali met her eyes, Nikki sensed he was keeping something significant from her. She exhaled, wondering exactly how she could help. 'You know I'm still off work?'

Ali nodded.

'You'd be better getting the police involved. I'll contact Saj for you, if you like. They have resources I don't have at present.'

Relief flooded Nikki when he agreed. She'd expected him to argue with her, but instead he said, 'Okay, get Sajid involved. Make it official, but you have to meet Jane. She asked for you. She trusts you and, well, he's her only child.'

Again, Nikki detected evasion. She raised a questioning eyebrow to Marcus, who nodded, his lips tightening. He, too, suspected Ali wasn't revealing everything.

'Marcus and I will come, but I won't interfere with the police investigation, okay?'

Chapter 19

It was easy for Sajid to see that Archie was pissed off because he stormed through the incident room, into his office and slammed the door shut, peppering the air with a series of 'clucks', 'effing clucks' and 'proverbials' as he went.

Through the partially open blinds, Sajid watched as his boss threw himself onto his chair, causing it to whirl with alarming rapidity in a semi-circle. Saj flinched, hoping the seat would withstand Archie's weight, and released a relieved sigh when it juddered to a halt with the large man frowning into the distance. With the 'collapsing chair' crisis avoided, Saj sank into his own seat, but continued to observe the older man. Archie had been out of sorts since Nikki went on sick leave. This, in turn, left the entire team on edge. He'd been short-tempered, shouting at everyone for no reason, and had begun to micro-manage them. Although Sajid understood that he was under pressure from 'Her Upstairs' – Archie's nickname for the DCS – it was hard not to want to snap back at him. The only thing that made Saj refrain was Archie's increasing breathlessness, the way he rubbed his chest when he thought no one was looking, and the scowl that had taken up permanent residence between his brows.

DS Felicity Springer was notable by her absence and DI Ahad

had schmoozed off to smooch with the big brass or, as he'd told Sajid not ten minutes previously, 'I've been invited to a strategizing meeting to discuss the rather lax investigative strategy used in this machete investigation.'

Despite an irrational desire to wipe the DI's self-satisfied smirk off his face, Saj had merely nodded. The bottom line was, they'd been banging their heads against a brick wall since before he'd joined the investigation. And with Springer disappearing without notice, the word 'lax', although not representative of the entire team, could certainly apply to her efforts. Yes, she was on top of the paperwork. What was missing, though, was an ability to think outside the box and the desire to listen to and run with other people's ideas. Until the Dark Knight had touched down, Saj had felt like he was the only one keeping the sinking ship afloat and that all the damn rats had run for cover elsewhere – bar Williams and Anwar, of course. Their contributions were consistently valuable.

Saj knew that he was being petty. Archie hadn't disappeared off anywhere. If anything, the boss was working longer hours than Sajid, but he was a manager these days, and often what Archie considered helpful only resulted in extra work for the team. As for Nikki – she'd not deserted anyone either. In fact, sometimes Sajid wondered if *he'd* abandoned her.

Still ruminating on the elusive Springer, he exhaled and opened up Jamie Jacobs's forensics report. Springer was the only person not pulling their weight. Her absence, combined with the abject lack of something concrete to investigate, was why progress was slow and why Archie's arse had been handed to him on a platter by the big boss on more than one occasion.

Forcing himself to focus, Saj scrolled through Langley's findings. The toxicology findings showed that, at the time of death, Jamie was out of his mind on cocaine and amphetamine. Enough to blow his head off if the numbers were anything to go by. The chances of him putting up a fight were slim, which made the number of machete slashes unnecessary. With the amount of blood at the crime scene, he'd expected the figure to be high, but it sickened him to discover that Jamie had been subjected to forty-three slices from a right-handed assailant. Maybe the attacker was also high on drugs. That might account for the barbarity of the attacks.

He scrolled down further, then closed the document. Jamie Jacobs, for all his family's wealth, was in a sorry state; malnourished with a low BMI, a failing liver and a weak heart, no doubt brought on by his addictions, the lad had been on a rapid downward spiral, with an inevitable end, which made his death no less tragic.

Saj leaned back and contemplated what he should do next. Conscious of Ahad breathing down his neck, he wanted to do something worthwhile, something to move them forward, but everything was being actioned. As expected, the Jacobs seniors' alibis were confirmed. Uniformed officers were still canvassing the local area and others were working through the rather short list of friends and enemies Bob Jacobs had provided. Of course, their efforts had yet to throw up a viable suspect, and Saj was champing at the bit to get someone in an interview room and grill them.

Williams and Anwar were doing as much as they could – taking up the slack, doing extra hours and generally working like little Yodas. Right now, they were trawling the streets, trying to convince some of their youth contacts to talk to them. He only hoped they'd come up with something concrete for he couldn't help thinking that things would improve dramatically if Nikki were back.

Although she was unaware of it, Nikki's doggedness inspired the other officers to do well. She wasn't touchy feely, but she *was* honest and hardworking and damn good at her job. The sooner she returned, the better. Not that he wanted her to return before she was ready. No way. The last thing he ever wanted to witness again was Nikki like she'd been when she'd suffered her breakdown. He'd been as scared as shit, and he wanted her fully recovered before she thought of returning to work. The job was too demanding for anyone with an empty battery.

As if he'd summoned her up, his phone rang and when he saw her name on the screen, he grinned, all concern for Archie forgotten. 'Whassup, Parekh? You lonely?'

The snort from down his mobile brought a grin to his lips. She sounded much better – chirpier. 'God's sake, Malik, don't you know that if I was bloody lonely, I'm more likely to phone a sex line than you …'

'Yeah, yeah, yeah. You say that, but I know you miss me.'

'Not you, Saj. Just your car. But I'm not here to stroke your fragile male ego, I'm phoning about Ali.'

By the time Nikki had explained about Jane's missing son and the nasty little gift she'd received, a frown furrowed Sajid's brow. Was this some sort of perversion of the machete attacks? He was unsure whether to hope or fear that they were linked. Either way, this wasn't a good sign. Fake acid attacks on a young lass, the four teen murders and now a young boy abducted and possibly mutilated, or possibly even dead. It was too much of a coincidence for the ear not to belong to Jane's lad – no one would send an ear to an unrelated address surely? What the fuck was happening? In DI Ahad's absence, Saj made the unilateral decision that, with everything going as planned with the Jacobs investigation, he'd check out this abduction to see if they could establish a link. 'Give me the address, Nik and I'll meet you there.'

After he'd finished jotting down Jane's details, he paused for a second. Nikki had sounded sparky, much more like her usual self and that lifted Saj's spirits. It was good that Marcus was accompanying her to Jane's home. Nobody wanted her to overdo it and impair her recovery. The very fact that Marcus hadn't dissuaded Nikki from helping Ali showed that he too thought Nikki was turning a corner. Marcus would make sure she was okay and, whilst glad that he didn't have responsibility for a still fragile Nikki, Saj was happy to have her involved.

Just about to grab his coat and march out to his car, Saj sent a final glance over to Archie's office. His boss sat exactly where he'd been before, staring into the distance, but what worried Saj was the way the older man massaged his chest with one hand. That was another thing Sajid would have to monitor. Hopefully, with the new DI in post, they could take more pressure off Hegley.

Chapter 20

#WhatsWrongWithThisShit?

THE ONE WITH THE DISMEMBERED COUPLE
POSTED BY BFDLASS#WWWTS NOVEMBER 24TH 15:27

*Picture this – a young couple are walking home from a lecture,
hand in hand. They're laughing – happy. Somebody, probably a few somebodies, grab them and drag them into a car.
They tie them up, they torture them, they kill them and they
dismember them before throwing them in a ditch to be found
by an eighty-year-old woman out walking her dog.*

How did they feel? How scared were they?

*So … meet Aqsa and Jusveer … they're in love. They met
at university, fell in love and planned to get married. Their
families took time to accept their love. Two very different
religions, different beliefs, different cultures … but over time,
Aqsa and Jusveer's parents blessed the upcoming marriage. So
far so good, you might think.*

You'd be wrong.

Somebody didn't like that Aqsa is Muslim and Jusveer is Sikh.

Somebody decided that Aqsa and Jusveer had dishonoured their families, their cultures and their religion …

Somebody plotted to end the lives of this couple …

Somebody out there took these young people from their families.

Somebody out there wanted to incite HATE

But that's not how Aqsa and Jusveer's families want them to be remembered

#AttendTheVigils

#LoveNotHate

COMMENTS:

FarrKMan: *WTAF! This is sooo wrong. I'm going to @Manchestervigil #LoveNotHate*

Karryann3: *Agree. I'm going @Bradfordvigil*

Ran98: *Sikhs and Muslims can't get married. Not unless he reverts to Islam. #ServesThemRight #StickToYourownKind*

Karryann3: *@Ran98 WTF! IMHO you're a Loser*

Ran98: *@Karryann3 Just cleaning up the crap*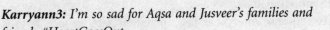

Karryann3: *I'm so sad for Aqsa and Jusveer's families and friends #HeartGoesOut*

Chapter 21

The Honourable Fixer

Venezuela looks good for this time of the year: warm, sunny, nice beaches and gorgeous hotels. Perhaps I should take some time off and hit the hot spots. Relax a bit, unwind from the day job. I could keep an eye out for a small property on the beach. A bolt hole in case I need to escape. After all, in the worst possible scenario, it's tricky to convince the Venezuelan government to agree to extradition. I've got to consider this sort of thing. It's as well that I plan for every probable scenario. I'm not arrogant enough to think my 'other career' will continue forever. Everything has an expiry date and the 'rent a kill' business is no exception. That's why I have plans in place to ensure my safety should a tricky situation arise.

My response interval is fast, incredibly fast, in fact. It took hardly any effort to infiltrate the back door police systems and because I was doing nothing other than setting up key word alerts, they've still not noticed. Soon as they have even an inkling that might lead them to one of the minions, I'll be aware of it. I made sure of that right at the start. All my documents are up to date. New identities created, historic financial and medical footprints in place and all with sufficient detail to convince the best detectives. With meticulous attention to detail, I've plotted various escape routes with guaranteed financial security in a range of exotic locations. Ensuring that, when the excrement hits the proverbial fan, the police will be too busy rounding up the disposable lowlifes, to bother about me. With a single press of a button on my keyboard all the breadcrumbs I've dropped will become active and will emblazon the links to all my paying clients not only on the dark web, but across all social media networks worldwide. Nobody will look for me and that's the beauty of it; I have the satisfaction of earning big bucks whilst my stupid clients continue, oblivious that should it all go tits up for me, it'll also go tits up for them.

With my ergonomic chair reclined, I put my feet up, allowing myself a few moments to daydream about my prospective Venezuelan purchase. It would have to be secluded, with optimal security and privacy. A five-bedroomed, sprawling two-storey with open lawns bordered by palm trees and an office space with a balcony over-looking the sea – sunshine guaranteed. What more could I want? An alert from my laptop rouses me. It's from one of my hidden, deep, dark and inglorious sites and the prospect of making more money makes me smile. Still, it's with reluctance that I position my chair upright. Time to deal with business – Venezuela can wait.

Veed32: *Got a job for you! Prepared to pay! Needs doing soon. You up for it or shall I go elsewhere?*

Arrogant sod – does he actually think he can take his project to someone else? *No one* is as good as me. Little does Veed32 realise, but his attitude has added a zero to his bill – and *that's* before he's even told me the details. Time to find out, though.

TheFixer: *Tell me more. Here's a link to a secure communications hub: 8632GF169*&)650.*

As he accesses the 'secure hub' – funny how none of these idiots realise that the only person guaranteed security is me – my fingers fly over my keyboard. Bit by bit, each of his sordid secrets spews onto an encrypted server. There we have it all: his dubious pornographic fetishes, his terrorist affiliations, his income from dealing crack and guns – that'll add another 5K onto the bill, he can afford it, his amateur attempts to hide his illicit earnings, his illegal marriages to three separate women; one in Syria, another in Pakistan, and the most recent in Bradford …

It's hilarious how little these people understand about covering their tracks, but their stupidity is my gain.

TheFixer: *How can I help?*

I've already worked out what he requires. He needs me to 'fix' a not so minor indiscretion. Unfortunately, my probing reveals that it's in the hands of the authorities as we speak. Still, it'll be an easy fix for me. Not that I'll tell him that. Best to keep them thinking it's all complicated. I could make it all go away in a flash, but let's see what he wants first. After all, the customer always comes first.

Veed32: *Delicate situation! Need you to off this bitch …*

Interesting. Veed32 is not a man of brains, for he hasn't even considered a less aggressive action. If he thinks killing this girl is his get-out-of-jail-free card, then so be it. I study the image he's sent along with her details. She's young! Late teens. Bit of a waste, but there's plenty more like her. If I do a good job, Veed32 will come running back to me next time he needs something fixing and I've no doubt he's the sort to always need stuff fixing.

Chapter 22

Nikki hadn't realised that Jane's home was on the Listerhills estate. She lived on what some referred to as the 'white' end of the estate. Nikki wasn't one of those people. She didn't see the need for areas to be defined by racial make-up. Besides, both sides of Listerhills were becoming more and more multi-racial as less-well-off European migrants flocked to the cheaper housing. Jane's street almost bordered the Rec, but not quite. To access the Rec from Jane's house was a five-minute walk through an alleyway between a line of shops and the play area.

From the outside, her house looked almost as Nikki would have imagined it, based on her knowledge of the other woman's attention to detail. Perennial plants edged a tiny square of lawn at the front. They seemed hacked off by the autumn chill and were in hibernation for winter. From the neat plant pots under the window, to the two-seater metal bench in the corner – positioned at a perfect angle to catch the afternoon sun – and the fenced-off wheelie bins, the property was cared for. Its tidiness contrasted sharply with many of the neighbouring houses, some of whose bins sprawled haphazardly blocking egress to their homes, whilst others had blitzed their lawns with tarmac which housed half-wrecked cars, broken fridges, and other trash. The house was a semi-detached, ex-metro build with a drive which currently housed a small, red car. No doubt Saj could tell her the vehicle's make and model, but Nikki neither knew nor cared. A car was a car – purely functional. Although, as the thought crossed her mind, she sighed; Saj's Jag was definitely a lot more than functional – it had heated seats!

As they followed Ali and Haris up the path, Marcus checked on Nikki yet again. 'You okay, Nik?'

For the first time in ages, adrenalin surged through her. That was another positive to add to her growing mental list. 'This'll be good for me, Marcus. I can monitor how I cope without the stress of it all. When I go back for real, the entire team will scrutinise me. Despite their best intentions, they'll analyse every move I make in case I flip again. I *have* to figure out if I'm strong enough to return to work.' She squeezed his arm tight. 'And you know what? I think I will be.'

Marcus grinned. 'I'm certain of it, Nik. It's too much in your blood for you to turn away from it. You just need to give yourself time to recover completely, to ensure all your coping strategies are in place.'

As he spoke, the door opened and Jane appeared. Her normally immaculately coiffed hair was pulled back in a raggle-taggle ponytail. Her oversized hoodie dwarfed her thin frame and her joggers had paint stains on them as if she'd used them when decorating. Worry rolled off the woman in waves and, with one glance, Nikki observed it in her pallid face and her red, swollen eyes. This level of nervous energy could mean that she was hiding something about what had happened to her son or, possibly, that she wasn't surprised by his disappearance. Nikki would have to discover if either of those scenarios were the case. Nikki smiled as she walked past Ali and Haris. 'Hi Jane. I'm here to help if I can. Shall we go into the living room and leave the men to make some coffee? I'm gasping.'

When she had settled in a chair opposite Jane, Nikki asked,

'Can you tell me what's been happening? What's your son's name and when did you last see him?'

With a scrunched-up tissue in her lap, Jane closed her eyes, took a deep breath, then told Nikki the details. 'Mazin. His name's Mazin, he's eighteen, and he's a good boy. He's on apprenticeship at Akhtar's garage on the other side of the Rec. Always tinkering about with cars and stuff, even when he was a nipper.'

She swallowed, then opened her eyes again. 'Last time I saw him was yesterday morning before we both headed to work. I was expecting him home at around six-ish last night.' She sniffed and grabbed a tissue from a box on the coffee table. 'He said he wanted to speak to his dad. Said it was serious – important. That he needed help. That's why I know something's happened to him.'

Nikki thought about Jane's words. Was she hinting that Mazin's dad was responsible for mutilating the lad? Was the boy's father on the police's 'keep an eye on' list? She'd make sure Saj checked that later, but for now, she needed more information about Maz's dad. In cases like these, the parents, followed closely by other family members, were the primary suspects. If Jane hadn't received that ear, Nikki wouldn't be quite so worried about the overnight disappearance of a teenager, but the ear made everything more urgent. It spoke of some sort of gang link, or vengeance. So, if Nikki was concerned, Jane would be too, which of course made it even more suspicious that, instead of it being Maz's dad being here offering help and support, it was Jane's boss. For a fraction of a second, Nikki considered waiting for Sajid to arrive. He was much better at the nuanced questioning of a victim's family. He always worded his questions so as not to provoke offence. On the other hand, Nikki was like a wrecking ball. Not because she didn't care, but because she was aware that, in these circumstances, speed was of the essence and she just wanted the answers. Still, she tried. 'Does his dad not live here with you?'

A flicker of something flitted across Jane's face, but was soon replaced by her earlier taut façade. Had the situation not been so dire, Nikki would have mistaken it for amusement. But there was nothing funny about a missing son and a dismembered ear. Still, that micro-expression irked Nikki. She sensed there was some undercurrent she was unaware of and although it might have nothing to do with the missing boy, her Spidey senses were on high alert.

'No. No, his dad and I get on well, but we don't live together. Mazin was going to speak to him after his tea last night.'

'And that was normal?'

'Yeah, sure. They spend a lot of time together. His dad's one of those hands-on types – always been there for both Mazin and me.'

Ali held the living-room door open for Marcus, who walked through carrying a tray filled with hot drinks, which he placed on a small squat coffee table between Nikki and Jane.

'Thanks guys.' Nikki's tone was dismissive, indicating that they should leave her and Jane to it.

The other woman interrupted. 'No, no. I want Ali here.' Jane looked from Ali to Marcus, then at Haris, who remained standing by the door, like a giant in a kids' playhouse. 'Sit down, please.'

Ali flicked a glance in Nikki's direction, then moved to claim the space beside Jane on the sofa. No sooner had he sat down than she intertwined her fingers through Ali's, and he responded by brushing a strand of hair off her forehead and whispering something Nikki couldn't quite catch. Mouth gawping, Nikki caught Marcus's eye and blinked. How could she have missed that they were an item? All the years she'd been friends with Ali, she'd dismissed the occasional rumours. Now, here was incontrovertible evidence that they were indeed in a relationship.

Marcus dropped onto a pouffe beside Nikki, muttering for her ears alone, 'You can shut your mouth now, Nik. I think everyone gets that you're astounded, no need to rub it in though.'

Nikki crossed her legs, making sure that she snagged Marcus with her heel as she did so, but she took his advice and replaced her surprised expression with what she hoped was an 'I'm in control – nothing fazes me' look. They couldn't have been together long, or he'd have told her, wouldn't he? 'Okay, so Maz wanted to meet with his dad? Can you give me his dad's address, Jane?'

Ali's head jerked up, his eyes dark and furious. 'You for real, Parekh? Who the hell do you think his dad is? *I'm* Maz's dad. That's why I want you involved, even if only unofficially.'

Ignoring Marcus's slight smirk, Nikki raised her hands to placate him. 'Shit. I'm sorry, Ali. *Really* sorry. I'm a little rusty – not putting two and two together. I thought you and Jane must be a recent thing since …' She had been going to say, 'Since you didn't tell me you were together', but left the sentence hanging. There would be time for her to tear a strip off Ali when this was sorted.

With a sniff, Ali took his phone out and sent a text. Nikki's phone pinged.

'That's the most recent photo of our lad that we've got. Find him, Nikki, before …'

Nikki nodded. He didn't need to finish his sentence; she was all too mindful of how it ended. After opening the image, Nikki smiled. The lad looked like his dad except, where Ali was solid muscle and balding head, Maz was all loose limbs and teenage gangly. She forwarded the image to Saj and continued with her questions. 'Can you think of anyone he didn't get on with? Enemies, people he might have had beef with?'

But before Nikki had even finished, both Jane and Ali were shaking their heads. 'No, not Maz. He is one of the popular kids. Nobody has a nasty word to say about him, do they, Ali?'

That was all fine and well, but it was inconclusive. Parents were rarely aware of the stupid things kids got up to. Who knew what had led to Maz's ear being shoved through his mum's letterbox in a jiffy bag – assuming of course it was *his* ear. She shuddered. *God, please don't let there be another kid out there missing his ear – one we're not aware of and not looking for.* No doubt Saj would get Langley onto that pronto. In her current status, Nikki couldn't send anything off for analysis, but Saj would sort that, along with all the neighbourhood interviews. Shame that this area of Listerhills had zilch in the way of home security. Chances were they'd gain little from a local canvas, but it would have to be done, anyway.

Jane's complexion had gone from pale to translucent, but despite her tears, it was she who answered first. 'He's been a bit moody – you know, the usual teen stuff? Snappy with me some-times. Nothing that would make me expect something like this.'

Her sobs choked her and for a second, Nikki expected Sajid to appear, proffering one of his pristine handkerchiefs – but of course, she wasn't here on official police duty and when Sajid arrived, Nikki would be side-lined from the investigation, so she needed to get whatever information she could before then.

'Have you received a ransom note?'

Jane shook her head, but leaned forward, her frown easing. 'You think he's still alive, then? If you're mentioning ransom, that means he's not dead, doesn't it?'

Ali pulled her back, placing his arm around her shoulders as Nikki replied. 'We don't know, Jane. It's early days. Did his boss expect him at work this morning?'

'Yes, Maz locked up last night and his boss, Mr Akhtar, expected him to open up this morning too. When he didn't turn up, he phoned me and I checked his room to see if he'd slept in, but his bed was still made. Then that … thing … arrived, pushed through the letter box. I almost didn't open it just then, but the writing on it was weird – a big black marker scrawl, so I ripped …' More tears flooded down her face as Ali tried to calm her down.

'Did Maz seem different at all recently? More introverted than usual? Secretive? Or did he have more money than you'd expect since he's only earning an apprentice's wage?'

'You're asking if he's doing drugs or, worse, dealing them, aren't you? That's what you're asking, Parekh, isn't it?' Ali's eyes flashed. His normally smiling demeanour was dark and threatening. 'He's not a druggie, nor is he dealing. He's a good kid, is our Maz.'

'I'm sure he is, Ali. But kids get caught up in shit. We've all seen it. There's so many gangs out there. Soon as we shut one down, another four spring up and we never catch the bosses. They know which triggers to press to get the kids to comply. It's not whether Maz is a good kid, it's whether he was targeted and, if so, how deeply he was involved.'

She gestured towards Jane. 'Jane's already told us that he wanted to talk to you about something. If I'm going to help you, Ali, I *have* to know what that was.'

Whilst she'd been speaking, she'd maintained eye contact with Ali. She had to break through his worry and convince him that he could trust her to be fair – no matter *what* Maz had done. The kid might not be involved in anything dodgy, but if they weren't to waste precious time, she needed to be sure of that. Nikki leaned forward and, lowering her voice, smiled first at Jane, then at Ali. 'I suspect you think that you've no real reason to trust the police, but for God's sake, Ali, I'm not police – not right now anyway. I'm your friend and I'm going to help, but I must have *all* the facts. Was he caught up in a gang, shoplifting or what? Did he want to talk to you about something dodgy he'd got himself into … maybe he was seeing someone?'

These were all bog-standard police questions that Sajid would no doubt repeat when he arrived, but Nikki still needed the answers. Maz was within the age range of the kids macheted to death and although the mutilated ear was a new phenomenon, she preferred to keep an open mind. The previous day's machete killing muddied the waters and made it unlikely the killings were related to Maz's disappearance. Even if the two incidents proved to be completely unrelated, until she'd eradicated that line of enquiry, she'd keep it on the back burner. The ear made everything much more serious than a teenager not coming home for one night.

Ali raked his fingers through his hair. 'I know you're doing your job, and I'm sorry for being a dick. I've no idea what he wanted to speak to me about.' He shrugged. 'Could've been about a lass, hell, maybe even a lad – we didn't talk about that stuff. Jane did that. Me and Maz talked about cars and football.'

His voice caught, and he exhaled. 'I'm sorry I don't have owt else, Nik. He's a good lad. We've tried our best to make sure he knew right from wrong.'

As the doorbell rang, Haris moved from his position near the door. 'That'll be the pigs, Ali. Just what we need. You'll have to go through all this again with them.'

Nikki shot him a look. 'Fuck off, Haris. We're doing our job and we'll do it the best we can, so answer the damn door.'

Growling under his breath, Haris left to let Sajid in, and Nikki and Marcus stood. 'I'll put out some feelers with my contacts, and Saj will get things moving at his end. Just ping me a list of his friends, will you? I'll see what I can come up with.'

Chapter 23

It was becoming a right habit of Fareena's – all the crying and stuff. And Haqib had no idea what to do about it. Sure, he wanted to help her, but what the hell did he know about all this emotional crap? They were back in the arts cupboard, but this time he'd enlisted Charlie to stand on guard nearby. Last thing he needed was for the Eyes to catch them. He'd seen Michelle giving him daggers yesterday, but she must have bunked off today, because she hadn't been in registration. He thought Michelle had her eye on some older guy. That's what Taj had said, anyway. Haqib hoped so. She could be a real scary cow when she got going.

'Two goras turned up at the house last night at teatime, Haqib. Can you believe it? At our door!' Fareena rubbed her eyes dry and sniffed.

Haqib wasn't sure why two white folk at your door was so surprising. At his house there was a near constant flow of people from all races. It wasn't a big deal. Half his mates were goras, and they hung out at his loads. Still, he shook his head as if equally surprised. Fareena's household was entirely different from his own, which was why they had to be so careful. No way would her parents approve of a half-Indian, half-Pakistani lad who wasn't even Muslim. Besides which, he suspected that even if they approved of him, they'd expect a ring on Fareena's finger before she could be alone with him. The very thought of that terrified Haqib. He loved her, of course he did. But no way was he ready to settle down with her or anybody else. There was a big wide world out there that he and Charlie were going to explore before they settled down. He wouldn't tell Fareena that though – not yet, anyway.

'Soon as my dad saw them, I was shuffled off upstairs like a kid. He was furious with them. His face went all red, and he swore at them. In *our* language like, not in English.'

Haqib wasn't sure that it mattered if they cursed in Urdu or English – the intent was there. The fact Fareena's dad did it in his mother tongue made Haqib wonder if the man was a coward. It seemed that way to him anyway, but what did he know?

Her lips tightened, drawing Haqib's attention to the shiny gloss on them. He'd much rather be kissing her than listening to whatever yarn she was telling, but mindful of Charlie telling him to act like a New Man, not a Neanderthal, he tried to look sympathetic. The trouble was she was so cute …

'Haqib!'

'I'm listening; you don't have to snap at me.' He took her hand in his and grinned. 'So, what did you do?'

'Eh?'

'After they sent you upstairs, what'd you do?'

'Oh, you *were* listening. I thought you'd drifted off again. You do that a lot, you know?' Not waiting for an answer, she went on. 'Well, I snuck back out and listened from the top of the stairs.' She looked at him, all smiling dimples and sparkly eyes that said, 'How smart am I?'

Haqib grinned and kissed her hair – it smelled so good, strawberries or summat – definitely fruity. 'And?'

'They were from the FMU … I googled it. It's the Forced Marriage Unit. It's a government thing, and it investigates—'

'Forced Marriages.' Fareena wasn't the only smart one in *this* cupboard.

Her smile faded a little as if he'd stolen her thunder, but then she perked up. 'Somebody from Safer Bradford – that organisation they're always going on about in PHSCE, it's there for all sorts of stuff – anyway, someone from there reported Attiya missing. Said she'd reported to Safer Bradford that she was being forced into a marriage with some bloke from Pakistan and hadn't kept up with her "I'm safe" calls.'

'Shit … was she?'

'Dunno. *They* don't tell me owt, but who knows, that's probs why she's gone AWOL.' Fareena's voice quivered and the tears started again. 'What if she's dead, like one of those kids? What if *she's* been hacked to death?'

She'd lost him now. Why would Fareena assume her sister might be dead? Why would she think somebody might machete Attiya? Surely it was her parents who'd be angry with her sister and they wouldn't kill their own daughter, would they? Haqib snorted. 'Can't see your dad brandishing a machete, Fareena.'

A juddering sob brought a fresh wave of tears, and it was a moment before she responded. 'But what about my brothers? Or my brother-in-law? That Naveed's a pig. Could you imagine *them* wielding one?'

Truth was, Haqib could well imagine Fareena's brothers and her brother-in-law with machetes. They were all big fuckers and never cracked a smile. Well, *he'd* never seen them looking anything other than tough as shit. However, Haqib's imagination didn't extend to thinking they'd actually use a machete on their own sister – no matter what she'd done. 'Nah, you're overthinking this. Why would they do that?'

Fareena lowered her head and Haqib had to lean in to hear her. 'Honour – that's why. My family's not like yours. It's all fucked up. It would be bad enough that Attiya has a boyfriend, but if she's pregnant like the rumours say, then …' She sniffled, but didn't finish her sentence.

Haqib's stomach flipped. The words she'd left unsaid were

chilling, and he hoped he'd misinterpreted her. 'What the fuck are you saying, Fareena?'

'My family takes their honour and standing in the community very seriously. If she's brought dishonour to us, then ...' She shrugged. 'That's why they'd want her to marry someone – some old smelly git – from a village in Pakistan or somewhere: to keep her in line.'

Haqib was lost for words. She must've got this all wrong. Her family wouldn't hurt Attiya, would they? Now the authorities were involved, surely they'd let the whole honour thing go. 'Attiya will be fine. You'll see. She's probably gone off with her boyfriend and she'll be safe.'

But Fareena shook her head, mascara trailing down her cheeks, her eyes reflecting the emptiest expression Haqib had ever witnessed. 'No, Haqib. If she's not already dead, it's only a matter of time. My sister will be discovered in some wooded area, like the others, and the Eyes will have done their jobs.'

Chapter 24

Maz came to slowly. Before his eyes were fully open, he was aware he was in deep shit. The attack the previous day had taken him by surprise and he remembered the machetes slashing his thighs and forearms as he'd curled over, trying to protect himself. The figures whooping around him like animals. Then the ultimate indignity. One of them, or was it two? That part was hazy – they had held him down in the muck. He'd thought that was it for him, but instead of ending it, they'd cut off his ear. He whimpered and raised shaking fingers to the area, but too afraid to touch the wound, he let his arms fall back to his side and focused on his situation.

The effort of prising his heavy eyelids apart was too much for him. A piercing pain emanated from his forehead, right to the back of his head where it ricocheted round his skull, before settling to a dull but persistent throb. There was no way any of this was good. Desperate to be pain-free, Maz kept his eyes closed and focused on using his other senses instead. He almost sobbed when he discovered that, despite only having one ear, he could still hear. That thought brought a hysterical giggle gurgling from his mouth. He was like one of the Weasley twins in Harry Potter. The one who *didn't* die – the one who lost his ear, but *didn't* die. Maybe he'd survive too.

His dad was always telling him to get his head out of the clouds and pay attention to what was going on around him. Thinking about his old man gave him a brief surge of hope. No matter what, his parents would never give up looking for him, and his dad had contacts all over Bradford. Whoever had done this had made a colossal mistake grabbing Maz, but that didn't change the threat of his current position.

His greatest fear was that his attackers might be nearby. He'd no idea how much time had elapsed since the shadowy figures erupted from the side of the bins, brandishing their weapons with a determination that soon had Maz unconscious on the ground. He wasn't even sure where he was. Whenever he attempted to look, the pain was too much for him. Was he back at home? In his own room? Had someone dragged him to his mum's house? Perhaps he was in his own bed, or in hospital? Hospital might be good – there was strong pain relief available in hospital and he had the feeling that he'd need plenty of it. He gave a tentative sniff – shit, even that hurt. Unless he'd pissed himself and nobody had cleaned him up yet, he could rule out being at either home or in hospital and that realisation sent his heart plummeting to the soles of his feet. Where was he? If he wasn't somewhere safe, and he didn't think he was, then his assailants probably *were* nearby.

He tried to picture his mum. She was brilliant – so was his dad. He kept a photo of the three of them in his wallet, but it could be anywhere now, couldn't it? The picture had been taken at Knowsley Safari Park. He'd been about ten years old. His mum held the largest ice cream he'd ever seen in one hand as his dad, holding a matching cone, grinned at her. He was snuggled between the two of them, ice cream all over his face, their free arms round him, like they'd never let go. He wished they hadn't. His stomach clenched at the thought of losing the photo, and a prick of tears stung his eyelids. *For goodness' sake, Maz, get a grip. The photo's the least of your worries right now, lad.* The voice he heard was his dad's. Strong and reassuring. It was only in his head, but that didn't matter. It gave him strength. He should focus on working out where he was, so, using his nose and remaining ear, he concentrated on what he could smell and hear.

He was indoors. That much was clear, because, despite the cold, it wasn't the freezing chill of being outdoors in the wind and sleet. Besides, he didn't feel wet, and surely he would if they'd dumped him outside somewhere. With small, localised movements that didn't involve jerking his head too much, he attempted to feel around him with his fingers. He was lying on something soft, like a mattress or bed. That didn't comfort him though, because this place smelled bad – piss, mould, dirt and stale weed; it convinced him that his assailants weren't done with him yet. His jeans and hoodie were crunchy with dried blood, and when he tugged at them, fresh blood oozed from his wounds. He couldn't count how many cuts he had, but though they stung like hell when he touched them, they didn't appear to be too deep. He wiggled his toes and realised he was barefoot. The bastards had taken his trainers. *Fuck's sake*. His Dior B22s had cost him nearly a grand. Bet they were going to sell them on – make a few quid. Then he grinned. They wouldn't be able to sell them because they were covered in his blood and he was glad he'd opted for the white trainers, instead of boring old black.

He strained his ear for any sounds in the room. Was that someone breathing? The creaking of a chair as someone moved? He held his breath, wishing for human comfort whilst also dreading his torturers' presence. When he recognised the familiar clunks of an aged central heating system kicking in, he exhaled. At least he'd be warmer. Maz braced himself against the resultant pain, then half-opened his eyes and studied the part of the room he could see. Without moving his head – an action he wasn't ready for yet – he saw the door with its lock and realised he was trapped.

His eyes drifted as far as they could around the room. It was a bedroom. Not one he'd been in before, and not one he wanted to remain in. The few bits of furniture were knackered – a door hanging off the wardrobe, scratches on the bedside table. But other than those items and the bed he lay on, there was nothing much. Nothing that would assist him in escaping, even if he could move. He presumed there would be a window on the wall behind him, but the slightest movement resulted in brain-splitting agony. He was sure now that his leg was badly injured. Even the slightest of movements seemed to have bones scraping against bone. Beads of sweat broke out across his forehead as his eyes fluttered back in his head, and he fell into blissful unconsciousness.

Chapter 25

As she and Marcus entered Akhtar and Sons Garage, the smell of engine oil, the rattle of tools and a vaguely familiar Bollywood song bombarded Nikki. This was strange for Nikki. She wasn't here in any sort of official capacity, which made her feel vulnerable. These were her streets and in all her time in the police, she'd always felt she knew her city. A brief flutter in her stomach warned her to take a few grounding breaths to settle herself. The other odd thing was that Marcus and not Sajid accompanied her. Although Marcus was reliable, resourceful and big enough to have her back in any situation, the dynamics were strange. Over the years, Sajid and Nikki had worked on instinct. They understood each other's strengths and weaknesses in the field. Not that she didn't trust Marcus – she did. With her life. It was just different – not inferior – just *different*.

The scene before her was familiar because Nikki had used Akhtar and Sons to delay the inevitable demise of her Zafira on many occasions. So far, they'd managed to cajole it back to life, but that wouldn't go on for much longer. Perhaps, whilst she was here, she'd have a look at some of the *For Sale* cars Mohsin kept behind the garage.

Nikki wasn't sure which Akhtar owned the garage because

there were four generations to choose from. In the office, watching something on a massive TV, whilst somehow keeping an eagle eye on proceedings out front, was the most senior Mr Akhtar, and he looked to be in his nineties. Wizened and hunched, with a trimmed, hennaed beard, and a Kashmiri shawl round his shoulders, he lifted a hand in greeting and turned back to the TV. On the table in front of him was a steaming cup of spicy Pakistani chai and, as Nikki waved back, his great-great-granddaughter, the one from Ruby's class, walked past, carrying a bag which emitted the tantalising smell of pakoras. Nikki's stomach gurgled and a glance at her watch told her it wasn't surprising, as it was after four o'clock and both she and Marcus had missed lunch.

'Grab a takeaway on the way home, eh?' Nikki's whispered tone was pleading. Marcus chortled and nodded.

Meanwhile, keeping guard on the workshop was the next most senior Mr Akhtar, who was in his seventies. He sat, knees crossed, in an armchair just outside the office, a mug of tea cooling by his feet, his arms folded and resting over his enormous belly. It always amused Nikki to consider the physical contrast between Mr Akhtars one and two. Mr Akhtar number three, Mohsin, was in his fifties and managed the practical garage activities. Nikki walked towards him. In a dark blue overall and a prayer hat, Mohsin spoke in a broad Yorkshire accent. 'Hey Marcus. You good, man?'

Marcus shook hands with Mohsin, then stepped back to emphasise that Nikki was in charge. Mohsin turned and grinned at Nikki. 'There's only two reasons you'd be visiting me, DS Parekh. Either that rust bucket of yours has departed this world and you're looking for a newer model or ...' He wiped his greasy hands on a rag, a frown pulling his brows together, 'You're here about Maz.'

Before replying, Nikki threw a wave towards Mohsin's son, Amar, whom she was familiar with from her school days when they were in the same form. He'd popped his head up from the belly of a car to greet her. Amar was awaiting a kidney transplant, which was why Mohsin had taken on an apprentice, especially since his older son had no interest in the family business. Nikki took a step closer to Mohsin. 'You're right. We're here about Maz. I take it Ali told you to expect us?'

'Yep, he did. He's a good lad, is Maz.' As he spoke, he led Nikki and Marcus over to a trio of plastic chairs that made up the waiting area. 'Sit down and you can ask your questions.'

Claiming a chair, Nikki sat down and began. 'I know already that you rate Maz. Ali told us you trusted him to lock up and such-like. Did you notice anything unusual about him recently? Did he seem distracted, anxious, scared? Was he socialising with a different crowd from usual? You see anybody hanging about outside the garage?'

'You think he was snatched from here?' Mohsin's eyes went wide and he shook his head. 'Surely not.'

'We're not sure yet. He didn't arrive home after locking up here, so we must assume that either he chose to go AWOL or someone took him between here and his house.' Nikki was glad she'd asked Ali to keep quiet about the ear. By holding something like that back, you could trip a suspect up. However, it was unlikely Mohsin would have had anything to do with Maz's disappearance. Still, she had to ask her questions.

'Maz sometimes snuck through the Rec to get home.' Mohsin tapped his finger on his bottom lip. 'Something distracted him yesterday, but …' He shrugged. 'The lad's just a kid and I put it down to girlfriend trouble or summat. Never expected owt like this. I wouldn't have left him on his own, if I'd thought he were in danger.'

'Look, you can't take this on your own shoulders. You're not to blame – no matter how this ends up, you are *not* to blame. Now, you mentioned girlfriend trouble. Did he have one?'

Mohsin grinned. 'He denied it, but we all saw the way she strutted past the doors, peering in, trying to catch his eye. Couple of times she was hanging about outside when I was locking up.' He raised his head and yelled over to Amar. 'Who was that lass who kept flirting with Maz?'

'Michelle … Michelle Glass. That's her name.'

Nikki exchanged a quick glance with Marcus. 'You sure, Amar?'

'I'm sure.' His face darkened as he squinted at Nikki. 'Weren't your Haqib going out with her a while ago? These lads certainly know how to pick them. Plenty of nice Muslim girls around and who do they fancy? The sister of a racist thug and an infidel to boot.' Amar shook his head, and muttering under his breath, ducked back under the bonnet to continue his tinkering.

Mohsin tutted. 'Thought you told me that Glass girl had reverted to Islam. She wears a hijab, doesn't she?'

'Yeah, like saying you're Muslim and wearing a hijab makes you one. Not even close. She'll be an infidel to me till she reverts proper like.' He snorted. 'And I reckon hell would freeze over in the meantime.'

With a head shake, Mohsin rolled his eyes, and turned to Nikki. 'Don't mind him, he doesn't mean it. A lot of youngsters are full of hot air at the moment. It seems like instead of getting easier as time goes by, it gets harder to live in harmony. In my day, we got on with stuff and things were fine.'

Nikki nodded, but she was unconvinced. For one thing, Mohsin was around the same age as Nikki's mum and it had been hard then too. For another, Amar wasn't a youngster. He was in his mid-thirties and she'd witnessed him being all judgemental at school about people not following *his* interpretation of Islam. Ironically, he had seen no conflict between his brand of Islam and his thieving, vandalism and shagging around. She suspected the family had gone easy on him because of his illness, but his inflated sense of righteousness grated.

An hour later, interview with Mohsin complete and the keys of a shiny used Touran in her hand, Nikki and Marcus said their goodbyes.

'Not bad for an afternoon's work. A name to pass on to Saj *and* a new car.'

With his arm wrapped round Nikki's shoulder, Marcus kissed her forehead. 'I'm just glad we no longer have to worry about the floor of your car collapsing and your arse landing on the fast lane of the M62.'

Nikki threw her head back and laughed. As she studied Marcus's face, she realised that some of the tension lines across his forehead had lightened and his eyes looked less worried. In a rare show of emotion, she spun around, wrapped her arms round his waist and buried her face into his chest. 'I love you, Marcus.'

Chapter 26

Both Ali and Jane looked exhausted when Sajid arrived so he opted to give them some recovery time between his and Nikki's interviews. Instead of sitting down with them, he asked permission to look at their son's bedroom. It was amazing what you could tell about someone from where they slept. As he took the stairs up to the second floor, he remembered Jamie Jacobs's room. If that kid had been his, no matter what he'd done or if they'd been estranged, he would still keep his bedroom for him. He couldn't get his head round how the Jacobs had all but obliterated their son's presence from their home. It didn't sit well with Saj.

After passing by Jane's room – a neat feminine room with a double bed facing the open door – Saj paused outside her son's room. He hoped that this lad's space would, unlike Jamie Jacobs', be a kid's room, like some of the ones Saj had seen in previous investigations.

He slipped on gloves and, pushing the door open, Saj smiled as the familiar tang of teen boy – stale sweat overpowered by lashings of body spray – greeted him. This alone spoke of a kid who lived at home and who had the freedom to keep his room as he chose. Once inside, Saj took a moment to absorb the chaos of Maz's room. Nikki had taught him that trick. It allowed him to get an overall picture of Maz's living space before exploring it in greater detail. A single bed was pushed up against the wall under the window. The dark duvet was spread lopsidedly over the mattress. A pile of dirty clothes lay on the carpet at the foot of the bed. The walls were covered in Bradford City memorabilia: programmes from memorable games, two or three different BCFC scarves – two hand-knitted, one extra-long – and a couple of signed glossy photos of the team. Alongside that were posters of rappers – not that Saj could identify any of them. God, he was getting old.

The chest of drawers and bedside cabinet were both adorned with an impressive array of empty crisp wrappers, pop cans, half-eaten chocolate bars and dirty plates and cups. Saj walked over and began yanking open the drawers next to the bed. The top one contained chewing gum wrappers, a few coins and notes and a Chris Ryan book. Boxers and socks filled the others. A quick sweep through the clothes was fruitless, but Saj spotted a photo of Maz and his parents in the snow with a snowman behind them on the chest of drawers. The lad looked like an awkward teen and he'd clearly been forced into the selfie by his folks – yet he'd kept it in his room. This was such a massive contrast to Jamie Jacobs's sterile room. The other drawers too revealed nothing more dubious than an ounce of weed hidden beneath his T-shirts.

Moving on to the wardrobe, Saj scanned the row of neatly lined-up and ironed clothes and, judging by the state of the rest of the bedroom, Saj bet that this was Jane's work. Under the hanging clothes, was a line of footwear: a couple of pairs of well-worn trainers, a pair of toe capped boots, presumably for his job at the garage, and a single pair of polished black shoes for special occasions.

When he pushed the shoes to the side, he found a box tucked right to the back of the cupboard. Saj pulled it out. It felt empty, but what had Saj's antennae twitching was the logo on the lid which he recognised because he owned three just like these himself – Dior. What the hell was Maz Khan doing with an empty Dior shoebox hidden in the back of his wardrobe? Saj opened the lid revealing scrunched-up tissue paper and a folded receipt. In trepidation Saj unfolded it. It was for a pair of B22 trainers in white and blue costing £940. How the hell could Maz afford such expensive trainers? Saj had scrimped and saved to afford his, so how could a lad on an apprentice's wage pay for them? Saj sank to the bed, box in hand and thought about it. It needn't be anything sinister. Perhaps Ali had bought the lad them for his birthday or for Eid. They could be an early Christmas present. There were endless possibilities, but none of them convinced Saj – not when the kid had been abducted and his sliced-off ear sent to his mum. No – this smacked of something dodgy. He took a photo of both the box and the receipt before slipping the latter into an evidence bag. Then he phoned Gracie Fells. 'Hi Gracie, wondered if you could send a tech round to the address I've just texted you. I need him to lift fingerprints from Mazin Khan's bedroom for possible elimination purposes and also to get a sample for DNA to cross-match to an amputated body part.'

That done, Saj exhaled before heading downstairs to join Ali and Jane. He held his phone so the couple could see the photograph of the shoebox. 'Know anything about this?'

Both Ali and Jane looked at Sajid with blank expressions. Ali frowned. 'A picture of a shoebox?'

Saj hated bursting people's bubbles at the best of times, but he needed to sort this out right from the start. 'I found it at the back of Maz's wardrobe. It's not just an ordinary shoebox. It's for a Dior brand of trainer – B22s to be precise. Does Maz own a pair of these?'

After finding an image of the shoes on his mobile, Saj once more held his phone to them across the table. 'Does he own a pair like this?'

Jane's face paled as she looked at the image, her mouth falling open for a moment before she spoke. 'But … But that price tag says they cost 940 quid …'

Eyes wide, she looked from Ali to Saj. 'He has a pair like these. He's right proud of them. I told him they weren't practical, and he'd have been better off with black ones, but he just laughed.' As she raked her fingers through her hair, a tear rolled down her cheek. 'They must be knock-offs. You know what kids are like always wanting nice things, so they go for big-brand knock-offs.'

With a nod, Ali patted her knee. 'Course they do, Jane. Don't worry. There'll be an explanation for this.' He turned to Saj, his eyes defying the younger man to contradict him. 'Don't get why you're bothering about my lad's trainers. You should be out catching whoever's got him.'

Saj held Ali's glare for a moment, before giving a slight nod. Ali was blowing off steam, his worry and helplessness coming across as anger. Saj sympathised, but he had a job to do. He turned his attention to Jane. This was the part he hated most. Jane had sounded hopeful, but now Saj had to burst that little spark. He flicked to another image and held it out to them. 'I found this receipt in the box. It says clearly that whoever bought them paid £940 in cash.' He waited for his words to sink in. 'I take it from your earlier surprise that neither of you purchased them for Maz?'

Jane lifted a listless hand only to let it drift back onto her lap, as she shook her head. Ali placed his arm round her shoulder and squeezed tight, mopping up the tears that flowed down his partner's cheeks, whilst ignoring the few that ran down his own. Saj felt like a dick, but he still had questions to ask. 'Could Maz have saved up for them from his wage at the garage?'

A snort erupted from Ali, catching Sajid unawares. 'Don't be daft. Do you know how much apprentices earn? Barely enough to keep the lad in crisps and chocolate. Never mind posh trainers. And we made him make do. We didn't charge him digs money, but still, there's no way he could've afforded these. And if he had saved up for them somehow, he'd have been up front with us.'

'You've no idea then how he could have earned extra cash?'

Looking straight at Saj, Ali growled. 'He wasn't a dealer. No way would Maz deal. He's seen too much heartache caused by drugs in his life already. He didn't get the money through dealing.'

Sensing that the pair were on the verge of closing down, Saj backed off. He hadn't anticipated kicking off like this, but there were still things he needed to ask about Maz and his routines and friends, so he smiled. 'Let's move on …'

Half an hour later, with the interview complete, Saj got up from his chair, caught Ali's eye and gestured towards the hallway. 'A word, Ali?'

On the assumption that he would follow, Sajid left the warmth of Jane's living room and headed out the front door and into her garden. Concern pricked at Sajid's stomach. For any parent, finding their son was a priority. However, Saj couldn't look at Maz's abduction and mutilation in isolation. The recent machete attacks, he was certain, were related to this incident and no matter how much Ali and Jane professed that Maz was a good kid, the expensive shoes told a different story. Sajid suspected that, like any other teen, the lad had his secrets. It was his job to work out if Maz's secrets impacted on the ongoing investigations. He wasn't sure yet if the lad was a victim like the other kids, or something worse. He'd logged the jiffy bag in for forensic analysis, along with the shoebox and the receipt. The ear had been sent over to Langley, complete with DNA samples from Maz's toothbrush for matching. Langley had been as sickened as Saj by the teen victims turning up in his morgue. Amputated ears appeared to be a departure in modus operandi from the machete murders; however, Sajid would keep an open mind. Although there were differences between the attacks, there were also some similarities and Saj's own gut feeling told him they were linked. The suspicion that Maz's ear had been sliced off by a machete lingered. No doubt, Langley would confirm that in due course.

Whilst Ali and Jane clung to the belief that Maz was still alive out there somewhere, Sajid was unconvinced. It was more than likely, if his suspicions regarding the machete killings and Maz's abduction were confirmed, that the lad would turn up dead like the other victims. In fact, it surprised him that he hadn't already done so.

He still had many questions though. What made Maz's attack different? Why the sudden need to torture the parents with a gruesome delivery? Were his instincts wrong, and the attack was personal to Ali and nothing to do with the other attacks? Although he didn't know previously that Ali was the father of Jane's son, Saj had to consider that others may have known Ali's secret. If someone wanted to get to Ali, his son Maz was an easy target. The amputated ear was personal and Saj hoped the killer wasn't evolving because, even after four deaths, the investigation hadn't moved forward that much. If the perpetrator had veered from their usual modus operandi, that was worrisome and Saj needed to keep all avenues of investigation open. He needed to catch a break and, although he wouldn't tell her so, having Nikki on the team, even unofficially, made him hopeful that they'd move things forward.

Ali, with Haris's looming presence tagging behind, walked over to where Saj waited in Jane's front garden. With a nod in Haris's direction, Sajid met Ali's gaze. 'I wanted a private word.'

Ali cadged a fag from Haris and lit up, inhaling deeply before blowing out a plume of smoke. 'Haris is my right-hand man, Saj. You know me well enough to be aware of that.'

Sajid stretched his neck till it cracked. The trouble was, Ali was a friend and the lines between friendship and professionalism were blurred. Okay, he wasn't as close to the man as Nikki was, but still. He glared at Haris who returned his glare with a grin that was halfway between insolence and sympathy.

'Okay, but nothing is to leak. I don't want the press hearing about your lad's ear. Keeping that sort of key information back will make it easier to weed out any pranksters who come forward – understood?'

Ali rubbed his chin, his fingers against his stubble making

a scraping sound. He was a big man – granted, not as huge as Haris, but imposing. Right now he looked as if a sudden gust of wind could floor him. His frailty seemed to come from within. Outwardly, his stature was the same, but whatever emotions seeped through to the outer layers diminished his presence. Ali was a man hollowed out by grief.

Ali raised dull eyes to Sajid. 'You think he's dead?'

Sajid hated this part of the job. It was best to be as honest as possible with the relatives of a missing person. Still, it was hard. He kicked a loose pebble before answering. 'Look, it's early days. We don't know, but there are various things to consider and I need your help. We have to work out whether it is actually Maz's ear – I'm not going to sugarcoat it, likely the ear will belong to your son, because why else would they post it to Jane?'

To give him his due, Ali's flinch was almost indiscernible. 'I heard that the kid they found yesterday in Lister Park was the son of some rich white dude. I want a promise that you won't prioritise the white kid over Maz.'

'You know I won't. I won't give up on your kid, Ali. I promise. Can you and Jane compile a list of Maz's mates?'

When Ali nodded, Saj continued. 'We also have to consider whether Maz's abduction is linked to the machete attacks. Maz is in the same age group, so we need to bear that in mind. If it's unrelated, then there must be another motive and *that* brings me on to …'

'Me?' Ali tossed the half-smoked cigarette onto the slabs and ground it out with his foot. 'You're wondering if I've pissed anybody off enough for them to abduct my kid?'

'Have you?' Sajid kept eye contact with Ali. He needed him to be upfront with him. Last thing he wanted was Ali calling up his lads from the taxi firm and exacting his own brand of justice. Sajid had first-hand experience of how efficient Ali's men were because Ali had unofficially helped the police out occasionally. Ali wasn't a gangster, but that didn't mean he had no enemies. He hated the gangs that preyed on the kids and was notorious for opposing organised crime in the area. Sajid and the other CID teams turned a blind eye to Ali's dealings, because they made their job easier and kept the streets a little cleaner. However, the man must have enemies.

Ali snapped his fingers in his cousin Haris's direction. 'Get a list of anyone with beef on me to DC Malik.' He turned back to the detective. 'Owt else?'

Without betraying his relief that Ali had decided to cooperate with the police rather than go rogue, Saj nodded. Had Nikki not been involved though, he reckoned it would be a different story. He doubted they would have been informed at all. Ali respected Nikki, and her presence in the investigation was key to keeping him onside. It was the only thing keeping Ali at home with Jane rather than out scouring the streets with his men. 'Can you gather your drivers together at your taxi firm and put out the word that they should cooperate with us? They have detailed knowledge of what's going down in the city and I want access to everything they know. I'll send a couple of my best officers to interview them.'

Again, Ali looked at Haris, but the big man was already walking away talking on his phone. A smile flashed over Ali's lips. 'Haris will get it sorted. Owt you need, go through him.'

'Appreciated, Ali. I'll leave you and Jane for now …'

Ali thrust his hands in his pockets and turned to go back indoors. Saj, taking it as a dismissal, walked down the path, but Ali's voice halted him.

'I'll give you forty-eight hours, Malik. Only because Parekh's on the case and if anyone can find my lad, it'll be her. But if he's not back alive by then, then all bets are off and I'll sort it myself.'

Sajid met Ali's gaze with unflinching eyes. Ali's eyes were the only part of him that had any energy right then. His shoulders were hunched and the pulsating vein at his temple told Sajid how much pressure he was under. Saj would allow him a little latitude because he was in shock, but no way could he condone him going off on his own.

'That's *not* gonna happen, Ali. You're not taking the law into your own hands – not on my watch.' And without a backward glance, he exited the small garden and walked to his car.

Chapter 27

The Honourable Fixer

It's a little annoying that Headhunter finds it impossible to keep up with activity on our secure communications channels. I've had to go low tech with him. Still, the benefits of having a compliant grunt work for me far outweigh his technological failings and, of course, it gives me a degree of deniability. I smile. Besides, sometimes it's good to slum it for a while. I've made sure that the burner phones we communicate with will corrupt if I need them to. The ability to obliterate the links between myself and my minions is why I'm the one in charge and they'll be the scapegoats when our luck turns.

'We've got a new job, Headhunter. Check the secure site for the details.' I wait whilst he tries to pull himself together. I don't know why, but as soon as he hears my voice he goes all stuttery and I know that's not his usual manner of speaking. Maybe he finds the distorted voice a tad disconcerting. All the more reason to employ it then, I say. Keeping the minions on their toes just adds that additional little pleasure to the working day.

'R-r-right. Yeah. R-right. I'll check it out.'

I roll my eyes and exhale down the line. 'You really need to keep on top of things, Headhunter. You know that, don't you? You've been a little lax recently and … well … there's always someone waiting to step up the ladder …' I leave the rest of the sentence hanging. Let him brood on that one for a while. Hopefully that'll make him up his game.

When he replies, his voice is low and in the background I can hear people talking. He's out and about, but he should have gone somewhere private to take my call. I tap my fingers on the desk as he speaks. 'Sorry B-b-boss. Won't happen again. What's the job?'

'Another machete attack, I think. Some bitch has spoken out of turn and needs to be punished for it.'

Headhunter's giggle is forced – uncertain. I have to force down my laughter. The idiot doesn't realise just how serious I am, but that's okay. It's good to keep them on the back foot. I hang up without another word.

Chapter 28

THE ONE WITH THE BOY AND THE EAR
POSTED BY BFDLASS#WWWTS NOVEMBER 25TH 22:08

> *Just heard this from a trusted source ...*
>
> *Picture this – a young lad's walking home from his work. Got his buds in, listening to Drake or Wiz Khalifa. It's pissing down and foggy, but he doesn't care. His mum's probably got his dinner ready for him.*
>
> *But ... he never reaches home!*
>
> *#WhereIsMaz? #NobodysSafe*
>
> *Next day his mum gets a gift posted through her letterbox. Somebody has sent her his bloody ear. Imagine how she feels. She must be gutted.*
>
> *#ThisIsSick #WhenWillThisStop?*
> ***#WhatsWrongWithThisShit?***

Views: 45 Shares: 6

121

COMMENTS:

Karryann3: *Yuuuck. This is Sick Sick Sick. His poor mum.*

    JakeK4292: *@Karryann3 Never mind his mum, he's the one minus an ear* 😛

ZainK: *Shit! Is this true?*

Jazzygirl3: *Why is this shit happening?*

LazyJayz04: *One more Paki down #WhoCares LMAO*

    Sal396: *@LazyJayz04 Sicko. You racist AH.*

Chapter 29

The phone call from the uniformed officers, telling Sajid they thought they'd found the abduction site, filled him with hope. Now, at least, they had something physical to work with. He was happy to leave the Akhtar's interviews to Nikki and Marcus, although he'd need to get a statement taken in order to cross the Ts, but an actual scene to work could prove crucial. Maz's attacker might have left vital clues.

The site was near his parking spot outside Jane's home, so he got out of the Jag and took off towards the ginnel. An outer cordon was in place and, as Saj approached from one end, the CSIs arrived from the other. Gracie Fells waved as she got into her crime suit, and within minutes they were processing the scene. Allowing them space to do their work, Saj observed from behind the tape, keeping an eye out for any looky-loos who might alert the media. So far, they'd kept the abduction from them, but they were like bloodhounds for sniffing out a story, and he suspected the press silence wouldn't last.

With her team busy, camera flashing, footprint casts being taken and debris tagged and bagged, Gracie approached him. As she neared, she pulled her mask down, revealing an enormous smile. Reluctant to get his hopes up, Saj tried not to wonder if that meant she brought good news with her. He didn't have long to wait. 'Well, aren't you a lucky boy today?'

Gracie's smile deepened and Saj released a breath he hadn't realised he was holding 'You found something?'

'A few somethings actually.' She laughed. 'I don't mean a map with a huge X marked, "Here I am". Still, it's a little more than we've had previously. There's a lot of blood which, as a formality, we'll need to match to Maz Khan. I'd estimate that in addition to the amputation, there were a series of slashes to the body. You can see blood spray on the bins and the walls – again, that's assuming this site belongs to your victim. I can't be sure without the victim that the weapon used was a machete. Langley will confirm that when we find him.'

Saj was glad she hadn't said corpse, but he wondered for how long they could assume Maz Khan was still alive. It was unlikely that this crime scene, with its proximity to Maz's home, belonged to another victim, and the blood spatter indicated a much more prolonged attack than the ear amputation. Sajid had hoped that the only injury Maz sustained would be to his ear. However, this added a decidedly more ominous shade – as if losing an ear wasn't bloody threatening enough.

Gracie interrupted Saj's thoughts. 'But we have blood samples from the other locations, too. Some scenes, depending on the weather, even had blood spray left intact. Unlike at the other scenes, there is evidence of at least two attackers. The spray released as they pulled the weapon backwards after cutting, before swiping again, indicates two attackers of different heights. This would be harder to prove if the assailants were of similar height. However, I'd guess there's almost a foot's difference between them. Get a good blood spatter analyst in and it'll pay off, in court, if you find the fuckers.'

Saj nodded. Langley would recommend someone, and it would get Archie off his back for five minutes. Archie loved that kind of liaison with experts; it added pages to any report, and showed that no stone was left unturned.

'The other little gem, is that the absence of rain overnight, gave us three sets of fresh footprints. One of them will be the victim's, the other two the perpetrators.'

As Gracie guided Saj over to the cast prints, he wondered if they could match the victim's shoe treads with Maz's expensive trainers.

Gracie pointed. 'The two sets we assume belong to the attackers, are again consistent with a height difference. This print looks like it's a size five, tops, indicating a short attacker. The other is a size nine or ten. We'll confirm at the lab. We've been able to obtain a couple of good prints from behind the industrial bins where no doubt they hid.' As she spoke, the CSI indicated the different areas. 'As you can see, the prints where the blood pooled are less clear, but we got a couple that, although not pristine, probably belong to the victim. We'll check out his shoe size and cross-match with his shoes from home.'

Saj's heart thrumped in excitement. This was the concrete evidence they'd needed, and now they might be able to confirm Maz's abduction site through his fancy trainers. 'There are trainers missing from his bedroom. I'll ping the details to you – maybe save you a bit of time trawling through the footprint data base.' The CSIs had produced excellent work, and Sajid could have kissed Gracie. He knew cases like this with multiple victims affected the CSIs as much as it did the police, and often their input went unpraised. 'You've done a grand job, Gracie. This is all top-notch work.'

Although he couldn't see her smile, the crinkle around her eyes told Saj that she appreciated his comments. 'I'll share your praise and thanks with the rest of the team, kind sir. Now, sod off, I've work to do.'

As he made his way back to his car, Sajid had much to consider. The crime scene had revealed a departure in MO. Whether the attacks were linked was unconfirmed, but at least now they had something to go on. He wondered if a seasoned machete wielder had brought a younger lad along with him to train up. Some gangs paired young kids with older ones for just that purpose. His phone buzzed and a quick glance told him it was a text from DI Ahad.

DI Ahad: *I don't expect DCs to make unilateral decisions regarding serious incidents without alerting their superior officer. Get back ASAP.*

Saj groaned. He should have updated Ahad before he left Trafalgar House, but he'd known the other man would break away from whatever he was doing to join him at the victim's home, and that would mean a bigger confrontation about Nikki's involvement. Everything would be so much easier if Parekh was back at work officially. Then he wouldn't have to work with the Dark Knight.

Chapter 30

After their meeting with the Akhtars, Marcus and Nikki headed to the Kashmir for a curry. The Kashmir was the oldest curry house in Bradford, having opened its doors in 1950 to cater for the textile workers encouraged to come to Bradford by the UK government. Because of its proximity to the Mannville Arms, where Nikki and Marcus had both nearly lost their lives during a previous serial killer investigation, neither had wanted to dine there again until now. As part of Nikki's 'getting back on track' programme – another Malloryism – they were attempting to put bad memories behind them by replacing them with good ones. Besides, the pub had closed and stood shuttered and desolate within sight of the window seat where they sat and, more importantly, its proprietors were now safely locked up. It would eventually reopen as a hairdresser's or something, and Nikki was glad of that. For the moment, though, she cherished the time with Marcus and savoured the aromatic chicken tikka masala she'd ordered, pleased that the need to twang her elastic band had abated after the first ten minutes of their visit.

'Don't know what to make of all this, Marcus. What's your take?'

Marcus hesitated before responding. 'I've no idea, Nik. It feels like there's something ...' He shrugged. 'I don't know – ominous?

Insidious? – going on in the city and it's kids who are on the receiving end. I worry about Ruby and Charlie – not so much Sunni because he's still at primary school, but definitely the girls.' He chewed on a chapatti before continuing, 'And Haqib, of course. That lad takes too much at face value and that leaves him vulnerable. We need to have a talk with them, Nik. Find out their take on it all. I mean, although they said they didn't know the murdered kids, they *will* know Maz – he attended their school, and he's only a little older than Haqib.'

With a sigh, Nikki pushed her half-eaten food away from her. She'd enjoyed it, but her appetite had all but disappeared and she'd lost weight despite Marcus's mission to fatten her up. 'I was thinking along those lines too.' She twanged her band hard twice, but when she caught Marcus's concerned gaze, she put her hands under her thighs and sat on them – that was one way of avoiding twanging. 'It makes me so damn angry – everything does, but kids being killed really does and …' She looked out of the rain-smeared window. 'I feel personally responsible because I screwed up Liaqat Ilyas's crime scene.'

'Aw, Nik. You got to let that go. You were grieving. You weren't yourself. You have to move on. What's that Malloryism? "I'm moving on up, moving on on, moving forward, nothing can stop me."'

Nikki grinned. Her psychiatrist had bastardised the lyrics to many songs in the name of helping her clients, and the Heather Small one was Nikki's favourite because she could sing it in her head with the new lyrics. Full up, Nikki tossed her napkin on her plate and stood. 'Let's get this bagged up in case I want a midnight feast and get "moving on home".'

*

Amid moans about not being included in the curry trip, Nikki and Marcus eventually convinced Haqib and their daughters to sit with them in the living room.

128

'What've we done *now*?' Charlie flounced in, threw herself on the couch, and glared at her parents.

Torn between tearing a strip off her older daughter and hugging her and telling her not to be so prickly – not so much like her mum – Nikki settled on raising an eyebrow. 'Guilty conscience, Charlie?'

Charlie's expressive tut drew a nudge from both Haqib and Ruby, who perched on either side of her. In deference to Nikki's mental health, and their shared pledge not to hassle her, it was followed by a sullen, 'Sorry.'

Nikki exchanged a glance with Marcus and sat down, leaving Marcus to kick off the conversation. 'Your mum got a visitor today. It was Mum's friend, Ali Khan. His son, Maz Khan, has been abducted, and they sent his amputated ear to his mum.'

Marcus allowed the moans and groans of disgust to subside before continuing. 'None of this leaves this room, though. I mean it. Anyway, Ali requested our assistance and in turn we need your help. With the murders and now Maz's abduction, we're concerned and thought you might know something that could assist us.'

Charlie kicked off. 'I didn't know Maz were Ali's son. Didn't know him except by sight. He's closer in age to Haqib.'

Haqib shrugged, and Nikki and Marcus allowed him to process. 'Maz is a stand-up dude. He were all right. You think he's dead like the others?' He spoke in a rush, each word rolling into the next, and accompanied by a concerned frown.

With Marcus reassuring the kids that the police were doing all they could, Nikki contemplated what 'stand-up' guy meant. Unbidden images of Jack Dee and Billy Connolly, her favourite comedians, sprung to mind – though she doubted Maz Khan had been a comedian, she got the gist. Now it was her chance to take over the questioning.

'Why do you look so worried, Haqib?' Despite her attempts to make her tone casual, she knew she hadn't quite covered up her interrogative style.

Squirming in his seat, Haqib glanced at Charlie for support, but Charlie had averted her eyes as if hoping that in doing so, her mum wouldn't call her to question. Nikki focused on Haqib. He was easier to break than Charlie, and Nikki was positive that any leads would come from the older teens. 'Haqib?'

'Shit, Auntie Nik, why d'you always pick on me?'

Haqib resembled a petulant toddler and Nikki wanted to smooth his hair and tell him it would be all right. He wore that expression a lot and Nikki was certain it was because, apart from Marcus, the key influencers in his life were very vocal females who often spoke over him. She waited him out and as expected, he succumbed to her probing stare and the silence.

'There's some shit going down around school. That's all I know. Some kids being dicks and that. But that's got nowt to do with the killings. The dead kids all attended other schools, anyway. Only Maz went to our school but he's left now, innit? He's doing an apprenticeship or summat.'

'What sort of shit?'

The lad shrugged. 'Dunno, just "stuff". Nowt serious.' Eyes wide, he met his aunt's gaze, but only for a second. 'I'm not doing owt wrong, Auntie. I'm not involved in owt. Honest.'

For a moment, Nikki studied her nephew. She couldn't quite shake the feeling that he was holding out on her. It wouldn't be the first time Haqib had done that. She made a mental note to talk with him again. The thought that her nephew, and possibly even Charlie, knew more than they let on, persisted.

'What about you, Charlie? What's going on in school?'

'Aw, Mum, it's nothing for you to worry about. It really isn't – it's just some of the older kids flexing their muscles.' She glanced at Haqib and gave a slight nod, which Nikki suspected her daughter didn't want her to see. 'There's been some taunting and crap, but the teachers are on top of it.'

'Taunting?' The conspiratorial glances between Charlie and Haqib had her senses on high alert and she wasn't ready to let it go yet. If necessary, she'd get Sajid to pay a visit to the school. He'd have reason to, now that Maz was missing – that was standard procedure. The schools attended by the other victims had also been visited.

'God!' Charlie elongated the word and accompanied it with an eye roll – her speciality. 'Remember that fake acid attack in the summer?' When Nikki nodded, Charlie continued. 'Well, that lass Molly was seeing Haqib's mate Taj. That's why they did it. A group of them didn't like that she weren't Mulsim and so they got together and ordered it.' Charlie's lips tightened. 'The A-holes thought it would be funny to terrorise that poor girl. Molly's not been back at school since then.'

Nikki was pleased that her daughter realised the severity of the attack, fake or not. 'We've not found the perpetrators, yet.'

Charlie shook her head. 'No, you've not. It's not good letting them think they've got away with it, is it? Some kids are scared and most of them in interracial or cross-religious relationships have split up.' She raised her eyes to glare at her mum. 'It's the same old, same old racist crap.'

The resignation in her daughter's words engulfed Nikki with rage. It took five hard twangs of her elastic band to calm her down. She'd had her share of hatred flung at her as a kid because she was of dual heritage, but she'd hoped to hell that this sort of prejudice was on the wane. Seemed not!

With her hand resting on her mother's smarting wrist, Charlie prevented her from adding any more pings. 'The bad guys won, Mum, and nobody's doing anything about that. I think it's time you returned to work.'

Chapter 31

The Honourable Fixer

The *Stolen Art – The Real Crime* documentary is a fascinating, if incredibly biased take on collectors who buy stolen works of art only to keep them hidden. The presenter's a bald, mincing whiner with a chip on his shoulder and a condescending attitude to boot. Who the hell is he to lecture art collectors? I'd bought a couple of Warhols on the dark web and, unlike the sanctimonious dick who's being all 'isn't it tragic' and 'art is for sharing and appreciating not for hiding away', I wasn't going to share *my* treasure trove with the great unwashed. I detest public art galleries and am more than happy to secrete my ill-gotten gems in a secure location, under a different identity. After all, they are *mine*. I worked hard to afford them and I'm not about to share them. My indignation grows as the idiot drawls on and on and when the pressure along my back gets too much, I take a swig of my St Emilion Grand Cru and, glass deposited back on the coffee table, I roll my shoulders, taking them right up to my ears, breathing in deeply as I do so – a tried and tested relaxation technique – and it works. The tension eases and the whiner's drone fades away.

I'm just about to surf channels when my mobile, the one I've nicknamed Headhunter, rings. 'What the hell does he want?' He annoys me almost as much as the damn whiner on the box does.

Resigning myself to bad news, I have another sip of my wine, savouring the rich fruity base with silky undertones of vanilla and nutmeg that roll over my palate. Let the moaner wait. It's good to show him who's in charge, after all. The ringing stops only to restart moments later and, with a slight smile, I pick it up and inject a cold annoyance into my tone – not that I'm one hundred per cent sure that it comes across as such. I've installed voice distortion devices on each of my phones so there's no danger of my contacts recognising me. Although they don't realise it, I've met each one of them prior to our little contract. Mind you, if they were familiar with the *Die Hard* films they might recognise the borrowed voice.

'Speak.' I leave the words, 'You idiot!' unsaid, but the implication is clear and the sharp inhale that rushes down the line sends a delightful shiver up my spine. I enjoy 'shitting them up' as the youngsters say these days.

'That you, Boss?'

For goodness' sake, who the hell else is it likely to be – your grandma? Again, the words remain unspoken, allowing the silence to work its magic, and it does. When he speaks again, his voice is all stuttery and ingratiating.

'Really s-s-s-s-sorry, Boss. Hate to bother you with this but, erm, well, erm …'

I want to tell him to spit it out, but I can sense his fear. His panting breaths inform me he's pacing up and down, and I imagine his flabby jowls swinging as he moves.

'G-g-g-got a bit of, well, whatya call it … bad news and …'

I replace the silent treatment with a single word explosion that will no doubt have him falling into the nearest chair – weak bastard that he is. Hard to believe he's an adult male. 'WHAT?'

His breathing's even faster now and the rattle in his chest doesn't sound too healthy. I hope to hell his heart holds out till

133

he's told me what's gone on. On the hoof, I rethink my strategy and soften my tone to a caramel smoothness; maybe it'll conjure up images of Mars bars and calm him down. 'Let's deal with this dreadful news together. What's happened? I'm sure we can navigate a solution.'

My change of tactic is working. His breathing seems less laboured and so, giving him time to settle himself further, I sip my drink – ah soooo smooth, would definitely buy that one again.

'Two of the Eyes kidnapped a lad. One of ours like. Another Eye. He was, like a bit … you know, erm well … unsure, like?' His words erupt like a runaway steam train rattling over the tracks.

I almost choke on the wine. Unsure? Unsure of what? Then it dawns. The lad had been questioning his role. What the hell? I'd imagined he'd say he couldn't find enough Eyes to manage the job for AntiVigilVirgil. Last thing I expected was that the Eyes would go rogue on one of their own, albeit a rebellious one. This was bad news … terrible news. I'd chosen the Eyes for one reason and one reason only – their inability to think for themselves. Seems I'd been mistaken. Of course, their raging hormones had probably factored into their stupidity. That and vying to impress in order to grab a toehold of power. 'Which two Eyes?'

'Just two of the younger ones …'

The way his voice tailed off at the end hinted there was more. 'And?'

'Shit. Boss. I'm sorry. Didn't expect them to do this. They … well … they chopped off the fucker's ear and, well there's more …'

I shake my head. What more could there be? 'Go on.'

'They sent it to his mum.'

It takes a moment to digest the words. They sent it to his mum? The idiots! What were they thinking? That's the point though. They weren't damn well thinking. Now I'll have to clear up their mess without jeopardising my ongoing work. I pace round the room. What would possess them to kidnap a recruit? To go off-script? Bloody gnat brains. That's exactly why *I'm* the one making the decisions, not the damn hired help. I fire a question into the phone 'Why?' If that single word was a laser, it would draw blood and I can almost feel the tremor of fear quivering down the line and Headhunter's stammering's back.

'Erm – w-w-well – they thought he w-w-w-were going to tell his old man about us.'

'And they couldn't just report their suspicions to you?'

'That's what they sh-sh-should've done.'

'Precisely. Who's this boy, anyway?'

'M-m-m-maz – Maz Khan. His dad owns a taxi firm on Toller Lane. He's a bit of a do-gooder. Like a community leader or summat. He dun't like drugs and gangs and stuff and he has a whole load of heavies who like to use their fists against the drug dealers.'

Shit! This is getting worse by the second. I know Ali Khan, and if these idiots have taken his son, then all hell will let loose. Khan might even be tempted to involve Nikki Parekh – she may not be back at work after having her flaky, but ... This is bad news and needs sorting straightaway. I think for a moment, weighing up the choices. I could just have the lad killed – what's another Bradford teen macheted to death? Hell, half the city was expecting more attacks, anyway. Might be beneficial to give them what they want. On the downside, is there any benefit to drawing Khan into the fray? Not really. All my research into key 'policing' figures in the district told me that Khan would be a pain in the arse in his desire to avenge his kid's death.

'Did he see their faces?'

'They're not sure ...' Headhunter's voice lowers to a whisper. 'They think he might have heard them speak though ...'

Bloody hell – it's impossible to get a damn decent criminal these days, they're all brainless. I release a long, calming breath. What a fucking quandary. The stupid brats have left me with few options. Headhunter's too useful, but I'm too angry to let him off lightly. He needs to suffer for not controlling his goons. With my eyes closed, I imagine myself tightening ball-screws round his droopy sack. That would give him a reason to squeal, wouldn't it? It focuses me and I'm ready to proceed with the punishment.

'Who's responsible for the Eyes' actions?' Like acid, the accusation burns away the last of his composure and the blubbering begins. For God's sake, has he left his balls in Tesco or something? Oh no, I forgot, I've already pulverised them. 'Shut. Up!'

When his whimpering fades to the odd choked gurgle, I continue. 'Let the lad go … dump him somewhere, but not till after the vigil.'

Headhunter might have thought his relieved gasp went unnoticed, but it didn't. I wait a beat before delivering the ultimate punishment. 'Then *you* kill the Eyes who acted out. Got it?'

I hang up, cutting off his half-hearted protests, and pour myself another glass of wine. Well, it has been a stressful evening, after all.

Chapter 32

By the time Sajid appeared at her door that evening, Nikki was on tenterhooks. Her partner had brought bottles of craft beer and hard copies of the files from the machete deaths.

'You know I risk instant dismissal bringing you these, Nik? The new DI is a stickler and I've already had it in the neck from him for interviewing Ali and Jane without clearing it with him first.'

Nikki laughed. She'd yet to meet the DI and wasn't looking forward to it. She hated meeting new people who were neither witnesses nor suspects. Still, she'd cross that bridge when she came to it. 'Don't be a wuss, Saj, just have a drink and once Sunni's settled upstairs, we'll crack on.'

At that point a whooping Sunni tornadoed into the room and made a mad dive towards Sajid, which sent him sprawling onto the couch with a 'Hey, big man. You okay?'

Sunni succumbed to Saj's tickling for a while. Then, extricating himself, Sunni frowned. He looked for all the world like he'd aged three years between the capering and the serious question he was about to pose. 'Saj, you gonna take my mum back to work now, eh?'

Sajid glanced at Nikki, eyebrow raised.

'Don't look at me. I don't know what he's on about.' Nikki

had long since given up trying to work out her son's complicated thought processes. 'You're on your own.'

'Thanks for nothing, Nik.' Saj turned to the boy. 'Eh, well, Sunni. When your mum's ready she'll come back to Trafalgar House.'

Sunni's skinny shoulders slumped. 'When the hell will that be? She's getting on everybody's nerves here at home.'

Nikki snorted. Really? Nerves? Bloody cheeky little imp *and* he'd used the word 'hell' when she'd expressly told him he not to. 'Language, Sunni.'

Not quite managing to hide his smirk, Sajid winked at the lad. 'Now you know how we feel at work, eh, champ?'

'I am here, you know?' Nikki placed her hands on her hips and glowered at them. 'Bedtime, Sunni. Tell Ruby to get on with her homework and Daddy will be up to read you a story after you've tidied everything off your bedroom floor – and I mean everything. I want to see the carpet.'

Sunni exchanged a look with Sajid. 'See what I mean? When she's working, I can leave my stuff on my floor. Dad doesn't mind. It's just her – she's got too much time on her hands.'

Sunni said the last phrase in the exact same tone that Nikki's mum had used when she was alive. Nikki tensed, waiting for the immobilising panic and the dart of pain to slice across her head – but it didn't come.

*

A little later, kids in bed, Nikki sipped her cool beer, with Sajid and Marcus beside her at the kitchen table. She'd hardly drunk alcohol over the past weeks but she deserved a treat. Marcus had made sure he wasn't sitting where Maz's bloody ear had landed on the table earlier. Oblivious, Sajid leaned his designer Armani jumper sleeves right on the spot where it had lain, and Nikki grinned. Saj would be fuming if he knew about that.

Before discussing Maz's abduction, Sajid updated them on the

Jamie Jacobs investigation, including the fact that the lad was sleeping rough and was far from the golden boy the Jacobs had portrayed in a sneaky interview with *Calendar News* earlier that evening. Ahad had been pissed off about that and Sajid was glad that the DI's annoyance was diverted away from his decision to unilaterally interview Ali and Jane.

'What's new on the Maz front? Charlie mentioned the fake acid attack in the summer – you think that's linked with Maz's abduction and the machete killings? Both the girl and her boyfriend attended Charlie's school. Reckon it could be racially or religiously motivated?' Nikki didn't believe in coincidences, and it seemed unrealistic for the machete attacks, a possible kidnapping with torture and a fake acid attack, to be unrelated.

'Funny you should say that. Just last night I discussed this with Anwar and Williams. We agree that it would be stupid to discount a link between that and the current attacks. But – drum roll please – we found Maz's abduction site …'

Nikki listened as Saj updated her on the site and the clues it had given them. His relief at having some lines of investigation to cover was palpable, and Nikki wanted to hug him. He was doing an outstanding job under such difficult circumstances, and she was glad he'd caught a break.

She pulled the files towards her and flicked the top one open. 'Let's go through everything. Langley confirm the ear belongs to Maz, yet?'

Saj nodded. 'Yeah, he says it looks like it – it's a blood match and he's sure the DNA will confirm that.' Saj paused. 'Of course, whether we'll *need* the DNA confirmation is another matter.'

DNA analysis took time, and the chances were Maz might be dead before they got it back. 'So, what gems did the abduction site throw up?'

With a snort, Saj began. 'Before I go onto the abduction scene, I want to tell you what I discovered in the lad's bedroom.'

Nikki's heart sank. Ali had been certain that Maz wasn't a

dealer, but this sounded ominous. After Sajid revealed all the information about Maz's Dior trainers, Nikki was unsure what to think. That Maz had access to sizeable sums of money that his parents couldn't account for was troublesome. Poor Ali – he and Jane must be going through hell. 'That's a turn-up. Bet Ali didn't take that very well?'

'You got that right, he ricocheted from furious to confused and back to furious in ten seconds flat. But now let me tell you about the abduction site.' Saj's grin was wide as he shared his findings. 'The abduction site was a ginnel only a stone's throw from his home. Another couple of minutes and he'd have been safe. Then again, if he was targeted and, because of the ear situation, we're working on that assumption, they'd probably have got to him eventually, anyway. On the bright side, we got prints.'

Eyes widening, Nikki waited for more. This was exactly what they needed.

'Shoe treads though, not fingerprints. However, Gracie reckons that we're dealing with two attackers. She estimates one was almost six feet tall and the other barely five foot.' He shrugged. 'It needs to be confirmed, but I've got an expert in blood spatter analysis coming in tomorrow. Anwar and Williams have taken over the neighbourhood canvas. I wonder how they moved the lad and to where.' He took a swig of beer. 'What about you? What did the Akhtars tell you?'

Nikki revealed the snippet of information about Michelle Glass hanging around, mooning over Maz. She had moaned to Saj about the girl when Haqib had been seeing her, so Saj was familiar with her. 'Haqib's been going on about kids at his school. He wasn't specific, neither was Charlie, but they both indicated something was "off".'

'That gels with Anwar and Williams's thoughts. They reckon their usual youth sources are being obstructive and keeping stuff from them. I'll make certain they visit the school – see if the teachers know anything.'

There was little else they could do to progress Maz's investigation, but Nikki was interested in brainstorming. Often that was how a case was broken. 'Tell me about these machete attacks, Saj.'

Sajid peeled the label off his beer bottle before answering. 'You sure? I mean, you were at Liaqat Ilyas's scene, you know when … well.' He dragged his fingers through his hair, and his face scrunched up as if he'd rather do anything other than have this conversation with Nikki.

'When I freaked out? When I lost it big time, fucked up an entire crime scene, had the biggest breakdown possible in the most public of arenas surrounded by my work colleagues, some of whom were, no doubt, *thrilled* to see me disintegrate like that? Is that what you mean?'

'Hmm? Well, I wouldn't put it *precisely* like that …' He grinned. 'But close enough.'

Nikki prodded a bony finger into his soft jumper. 'Watch it, Malik. I'll be back lording it over you soonish and you better just be careful what you say.'

Sajid took a drink. 'You catch Archie on the TV earlier? He bossed it big time. Mind you, Clark's pissed off with him. Gave him a right old telling off. We could all hear it. Said it hadn't been his place to add to the interview after she'd vacated the set.'

'Oops!'

'Exactly! The proverbial "clucking" oops, to be precise. Archie was livid. His proverbials swung round the incident room and I'm quite surprised he didn't decapitate anyone.'

Marcus snorted his beer out all over the table and whilst he spluttered and coughed, Nikki grabbed a cloth from the sink and cleaned up. 'I thought the machete investigation was Springer's?'

'Yeah, well, that's another thing. When the shit seeps through the hierarchical cracks, it ultimately lands on those at the bottom and Springer's proverbials were verbally mangled by DCS Clark, too.' Head bowed, Sajid, in a tone that was all too readable, continued, 'We're seriously short-staffed, particularly in the DS department … and well, Archie's—' With a yelp, Sajid stopped speaking, rubbed his shin and grimaced at Marcus. 'Shit, Marcus!'

'I warned you not to pressurise her. It's still early days.' Marcus's voice was a threatening growl that had Sajid flinching in response before offering a sheepish smile. 'My bad – sorry mate.'

Hands on hips, Nikki jumped up, glowering at them. 'For God's sake, stop talking over me, like I need protecting.' It was Marcus's turn for her prodding finger. 'I'm perfectly capable of making my own decisions. You can't wrap me in …' She exhaled with a frown. 'You know, that fluffy white stuff? What's it called?'

'Cotton wool?' Sajid's tone irked Nikki more. She hated the fact that she sometimes lost track of her words. Those minor memory lapses reminded her that although she was getting better, she wasn't quite there yet. Her fingers strayed to the ever-present band round her wrist, but she resisted the urge to twang it. Instead, she imagined banging Sajid and Marcus's head together, which, for now at least, served a similar purpose. 'Thanks, mastermind – helpful as usual.'

Her sarcasm wasn't lost on Sajid, who, grinning widely, raised his bottle towards her before taking a swig. 'Sorry, Nik. I'll try not to do that.'

'Yeah, yeah, yeah – you're full of shi … I mean promises, Saj. However, I think you were going to mention that Archie's health is troubling you? I noticed him rubbing his chest during the interview. It worried me.'

'Aw, he's all right, Nik. I'm monitoring him, but at the risk of gaining a matching bruise on my other shin, we are short-staffed and even when Springer comes back, well, she's not you, Nik. Anwar and Williams are doing a top-notch job though. If they weren't around, I think I'd top …' Seeing Marcus's narrowed eyes, Saj didn't finish his sentence. Only he and Marcus knew of Nikki's suicidal thoughts, and neither would betray her privacy. Putting his foot in it like that was insensitive.

'Top yourself …? That what you were going to say?'

After Saj's sheepish nod, Nikki shook her head. 'You two can't censor yourselves all the time. I'm getting better and part of that process is confronting my ideations. You've got to stop pussy-footing about. If and when I'm ready, I'll come back to work.'

She flopped onto her chair and took a sip of her beer, savouring it, because with her meds, she wouldn't risk taking another bottle. The thing was, Nikki wasn't the same person. Since her break-down, she'd divided her life into three parts. Pre her mum's death, pre-breakdown … then, NOW. The word loomed in big balloon letters and she couldn't tell if the 'NOW Nikki' should or, more to the point, could work as a police officer again. Some days she thought she should, but at other times she plummeted and had to escape. At those times she covered her head with the duvet and blocked everyone out. Sometimes the urge to sneak to the shops to restock her self-harm kit was overwhelming. At others, she could scarcely string two sentences together. Although less frequent when the dark tide of hopeless guilt engulfed her, she doubted she would ever work again. But NOW she was enjoying her involvement in the investigation. There was something to be said for being involved but not responsible.

'I can't think about returning yet, Saj. I need to prove to myself that I can still do the job …' In a rare moment of self-revelation, she added, 'I'm not the same Parekh as before. But hey, enough about me.'

Chapter 33

Although his throbbing head had eased, the wound where his ear had been was a pulsating mass of gore. Maz didn't dare touch it. Every time he thought about it, he wanted to retch. Bastards! His leg ached like fuck when he moved it. However, if he kept it still, the pain reduced to a numb throb. Why the hell would they do this? Stupid question. He *knew* why. These were sick fuckers, and *that* was why he'd needed to tell his dad. It was too late, and now he was stuck in this dingy cesspit with no idea what his fate would be. Tears seeped through his lashes and turning his cheek into the pillow, he allowed himself the release of a full-on blubbing episode, welcoming the misery that each wracking sob brought with it.

When he was spent, he thought back to the previous evening. During the night, three figures in balaclavas and oversized hoodies unlocked the door, flicked the light on, and entered the room. He'd been sure that was the end for him and at that point, despite the pain suffusing *his entire body*, he almost didn't care. Had it not been for worry about his parents, he'd have given into it all. He'd pulled through the agony and made a feeble lunge for the open door, hoping that he'd take them by surprise. He hadn't. Instead, he'd landed on the stinking carpet, squealing like a pig being slaughtered.

With ease, the larger two figures hooked their arms under his shoulders before he fell to the floor, and dragged him back to the bed, where they laid him down, making sure his wound was clear of the pillow. Despite his confusion, Maz wondered what they were playing at? Was it their way of protracting his misery? If they asked for a ransom, his dad would pay it. Maz was certain of that. Then, he'd hunt his son's torturers and make them suffer … but that might still be too late for Maz.

His captors had remained silent, but one of them cleaned up his injuries. Maz had the vague sense that he was older than the others. He was certainly bigger. Each touch had sent electric shocks shooting into Maz's skull and at some point he must have passed out, for when he woke up, he was alone. However, he was warm – covered by a fresh-smelling duvet. What was going on? First, they beat him to a pulp, cut off his ear and abduct him, and now this? Maz closed his eyes and thought back to the previous evening's visit. He was positive that only two people had attacked him near the Rec. He had been unable to see clearly in the dark, and everything happened so fast. He could have been wrong, but the third bloke – the one who'd dressed his wounds – was big; he'd have noticed him if he'd been there at the Rec. That caused him to consider the others. He thought that they were familiar to him, but he couldn't put his finger on it. His brain was too fuzzy, and waves of dizziness made it hard to concentrate. Before he'd fainted again, he'd attempted to take note of their appearance. His old man would expect nothing less from him, and if he escaped or was released, he wanted to be able to catch the fuckers. He'd help his dad cut off each of their ears. They didn't speak, not to him, not to each other, and that was creepy. He realised that was to prevent him from identifying their voices. But hadn't they yelled at him at the Rec, whilst they were letting loose with the machetes? He was positive they had. Flashes of metal, moving shadows and laughing taunts were a hazy memory – but that was all, just a vague recollection.

One was larger than the other, quite a lot bigger, but not as hefty as the fat dude. The other was skinny. Mind you, their exact builds were difficult to judge because of the hoodies. He'd glimpsed their hands though, and he was fairly sure that the chubby bloke had brown skin like the big guy. He thought the skinny boy was white, but he'd kept his distance from him, as if worried that Maz would recognise him. Funny that, if only he could focus more, he might be able to work out who the scrawny kid was.

With a hesitant glance around the room, he spotted three Morrisons bags on the bedside cabinet. Maz edged closer to the side of the bed and forced himself into a sitting position, grimacing against the tenderness in his leg. He reached over and dragged them towards him. The first revealed a pile of garments – joggers, a hoodie and a T-shirt. *Weird.* He stored that thought for later. Much as he'd like to change his clothes, because boy, did he stink, he had neither the energy nor the pain threshold to consider it.

Not sure what to expect, he opened the next one. It contained sandwiches, biscuits, crisps, drinks … Maz didn't know what to make of it all. But when his stomach rumbled, he grabbed a can of Pepsi and guzzled it. Inside the third, he discovered painkillers and gauze. There were packets of Ibuprofen and Paracetamol as well as prescription medicine with the patient's name label torn off: Naproxen and Diclofenac – strong ones. His dad had taken Diclofenac when he did his back in last year.

Thank God! The prospect of escaping the relentless agony was bliss. About to take a couple from their blister packs, a plan occurred to him. His captors had no reason to keep him alive – none at all. They'd had no qualms about killing the other kids, so why was *he* different? In fact, he was more of a problem for them. He had some inside gen. He knew things about the organisation. Okay, some was only rumour and most just basic stuff, nevertheless they wouldn't want it getting out. Whoever headed up the

Eyes would be wary of any risk to their operation, so regardless of food and pain relief, Maz wasn't stupid enough to think they'd free him. No chance! He was a threat to them. The only answer he could come up with was that they were only keeping him alive till his dad paid a ransom. If they needed funds, this was a simple way to get them. Once they got their money, they'd kill him. He was convinced of that. He was only alive now because they had to provide – what was it they said in the films? Yeah, that was it – proof of life.

Maz was certain his fate was sealed – however, they had provided him with the potential for one last act of defiance. If his dad didn't find him in time, he could take matters into his own hands. He popped a large handful of pills from each of the blister packs and, decision made, stuffed them between the mattress and the bed. Maz wasn't about to give those bastards the chance to off him. Instead, he'd wait till tonight and if he hadn't been rescued, then he'd sort things out himself.

Chapter 34

Insomnia plagued Nikki. Her mind churned over everything she'd discussed with Sajid earlier. None of the sleep techniques she'd learned from Mallory worked. Careful not to wake Marcus, she crept back downstairs and settled herself at the kitchen table, allowing the house to settle around her before opening the files Sajid had left.

With Sajid and Marcus present, Nikki had kept a tight control of herself, determined not to give them a moment's cause for concern. She didn't want to be excluded from this investigation. After all, she was inextricably linked to one of the machete victims. It had been the discovery of Liaqat Ilyas's corpse that had been the final catalyst for her breakdown. Now, studying both the images taken from that crime scene and those provided by his family, Nikki realised that the boy bore only a passing similarity to her nephew. A flashback of falling to her knees and cradling him pierced through her, transporting her back to that scene. The circle of shocked faces, her piercing cries, her hammering heart and shaking limbs replayed in a cacophony of images and sounds. This had been the third of the four attacks – five if Maz's abduction was included – and she was responsible for compromising it. Yet, even this limited contribution to an active case gave her a buzz. But could she meet her self-imposed standards or indeed the expectations of her close colleagues – the ones who had such faith in her? She couldn't silence the fear of letting them down, revealing herself to be a useless imposter. The tightness in her heart made her gasp for air, and dizziness overcame her. As a twist of anxiety approached, she focused on her relaxation techniques. In time with her slow breaths, she listed all the things Isaac and Sunni loved about Jodie Whittaker's Dr Who. She reached number five – 'She's kick-ass, like my mummy' – before her chest loosened and the danger was over. Another panic attack averted. She was good to go.

An hour and a half later, fatigue pulled at Nikki's eyes. She'd read through the files and found nothing that she would have done differently from Springer. Although she would have implemented various actions more speedily than the other detective. Springer had been methodical, if tardy, in her pursuance of associations between the victims. She'd interviewed and tried to cross-reference relationships between them, but to no avail. Both Springer and Ahad had pondered the discrepancy in victim type – a white male, two Asian males, one of Pakistani Muslim descent, the other a Sikh and a girl of Bengali descent – and had eventually been forced to retrace her investigative steps to find a link. Unfortunately, the re-interviews of friends and family were similar – too similar to the originals and scouring over the forensic findings had been futile. This attacker was ghost-like, invisible. Nikki agreed with Sajid that they might be looking for multiple assailants. But if so, what was their motive?

A while ago, when she was first a detective, the team she'd been with had investigated a series of muggings – each mugging was perpetrated by a different person, but when the case was solved, it turned out that the attackers were part of one gang who had made their attacks into a game. Could the current ones be similar? With their lack of leads, it was worth mentioning to Saj.

She looked at the folder containing details of Maz's mutilation and abduction. With the amount of forensic detail, it was the more extensive, so she set it aside for now and reached for the other folders. The first victim, seventeen-year-old Shabana Hussain, was discovered in Northcliffe Park. She'd been dragged, post-mortem, into the undergrowth. Cause of death was a frenzied machete attack, but due to the adverse conditions, swathes of evidence retrieved from the park had proved worthless. Even without factoring in weather, evidence obtained from such a public area was usually cumbersome to deal with due to the quantity of often irrelevant matter. Nonetheless, they had to trawl through it all and hope that they could find relevant clues to link to their investigation.

From the crime scene photos, it was difficult to make out the girl's features. Nikki was thankful Saj had included another image. The girl was pretty and laughing in that photo, and Nikki identified Peel Park easily. Shabana had been there for the Mela and was tucking into a samosa. She had a glittery butterfly painted high on her cheekbone. What a waste. What a fucking waste! Placing the photograph aside, Nikki frowned as she read Saj's summary of the household interviews – alibied to the hilt and with nothing to contribute, Shabana's family had contributed zilch worth following up on. It was so sad and Nikki's thoughts drifted to her own two girls – if something so awful happened to them, Nikki would walk through hell's fire to get justice for them. Closing Shabana's file, Nikki picked up the next one.

The more she learned of each murder, the more Nikki realised why this investigation was so difficult. No matter what leads they had followed, the police had come to a dead end, the forensic evidence was sparse, and the usual sources – friends, family, acquaintances, teachers – none of them had contributed anything resembling a lead. The cynic in Nikki snorted. Someone had information, and the question remained: were they deliberately withholding or did they not realise the importance of whatever little snippet they knew? Not for the first time during her reading, Nikki wished she'd been present for the interviews. Reading the demeanour of the interviewee always revealed something, and Nikki hated relying on officers who weren't from her team.

In investigations involving multiple victims, victimology normally gave the detectives a solid starting point, but not in this instance. Thinking aloud, Nikki pressed her fingers into her shoulder muscles and asked the empty room. 'What the hell links these kids? Maybe their attackers aren't targeting a specific target. Do they just grab anybody they come across? What am I missing? What is their motivation?'

A voice disturbed her, making her jump. 'Knew you'd be back down here.'

Marcus wiped the sleep from his eyes whilst scratching his bare belly at the juncture where it met the waistband of his pyjamas. A flash of desire cut through Nikki's concentration, but fizzled away almost as fast. Would she ever want to have sex again? Marcus was incredibly patient with her, and she didn't deserve him. He moved over and flicked the kettle switch and set about preparing teas. 'Chamomile for you, Nik.'

Yuck. Nikki didn't *hate* chamomile, and she had agreed to reduce her caffeine intake. Still, a strong espresso was more desirable when she had work to do. One look at Marcus's implacable expression told her that was not an option. Tea made, he sat down opposite. 'Okay, share your findings. I'll give you an hour, then I'm off back to bed.'

With the fragrant tea filling her nostrils, Nikki put her thoughts in order. 'None of this makes sense, Marcus. I mean, look at this. Liaqat …' She stumbled over saying his name aloud, but moved on regardless. 'He's not from the Chellow Dene area. He's got no links with the area and neither do contacts – he went to school over in Thornbury. Then we have Shabana – similar age, loads of friends in Bradford nine where she was killed, talk of a mysterious Sikh boyfriend, but nothing confirmed.'

Nikki pointed to a third picture. 'Parminder Deol, sixteen, hacked to death by a machete in Wilsden – not Shabana's Sikh boyfriend, according to family and friends. Again, no known links to the others.'

She exhaled and plucked up another image. 'Lastly, if we don't count Maz, the most recent victim Jamie Jacobs, same cause of death, discovered in Lister Park. He was eighteen – a bit of a wild kid by all accounts – minor arrests for distributing weed, and according to Saj he's been estranged from his parents since he was fifteen. Bet that isn't something Mr West Yorkshire mayor Jacobs wants going public.'

Spreading the photos on the table, Nikki and Marcus studied them. 'Springer looked at a possible drug angle, but found nothing. Only Jamie is a user. The thing is, unless they are random attacks, and I'm not convinced they are, there *must* be a link – there has to be.'

'So, you think it's the same killer?'

A small frown puckered her brow, and Nikki sighed and bit her lip. 'I considered that and initially thought it was inconclusive. However, forensic reports indicate that the wound marks were non-identical, which points to more than one killer. In one attack, Langley is sure a left-handed assailant delivered the wounds, whilst in the others, it was a right-handed attacker. Also, according to Langley, wound length and shape indicate the use of four different machetes.'

Wafting her hand at the pile of files, she continued. 'The data's in there – blade width, curvature and length are all inconsistent.' She exhaled and glanced at Marcus. 'Of course, we all know that machetes are ten-a-penny in Bradford. I read a report that said the weapon most used in knife attacks in the city last year were machetes. So overall, the limited evidence we have points to multiple attackers, but it doesn't seem plausible to me. I mean, these are frenzied passionate attacks – would different perpetrators have the same passion?'

'Passionate …?' Marcus rolled the word around his mouth. 'What sort of passionate fervour could provoke such violence?'

Nikki studied him. The way he chewed on his cheek when he was thinking was adorable. He had piqued her interest with his question. 'Jilted boyfriend or girlfriend ...'

After another sip of tea, Marcus dropped in his suggestion. 'Theft of something important ...? Drugs, but they've already ruled that out ...'

'... or perceived betrayal or insult ...?'

'Religious fervour ...?'

'Yep, it could be any of those, couldn't it? But which one ...?' asked Nikki.

'Could it be pretend passion or just sheer enjoyment?' Marcus didn't look convinced.

Nikki shuddered. '*That's* what worries me the most. If enjoyment is a factor, then that doesn't bode well, does it? I mean forensics points to at least two killers and if they're each enjoying their jobs, there's no incentive for them to stop. You know, hearing Amar Akhtar's talk of infidels and his dislike of mixed marriages makes me wonder. Could the attackers have a shared common cause ...? I was going to speak with Saj about this, but what do you think?'

Marcus took his time to reply. 'You mean punishing anyone who does something they disapprove of ... vigilantism?'

When Nikki nodded, he went on. 'It fits ... but wouldn't they need someone to coordinate things? Besides, I'm not sure that enjoyment and excitement alone would be a good enough incentive. That implies a personality disorder, and it's unrealistic to suppose we have a raft of sociopaths roaming the streets.'

'Hmm, you're right. It could be nothing. Still, I might pay Amar Akhtar another visit tomorrow – apply the corkscrews.'

'Screws will do, Nikki – let's leave the corkscrews for that bottle of red I've got in the cupboard, eh?'

Nikki grinned. 'I *knew* that, smartass. But no matter what type of screw I use, that fucker is going to talk to me tomorrow.'

Marcus yawned and placed his cup in the sink. 'I'm knackered, so on that ominous note … I'm going back to bed. You coming?'

But Nikki, already absorbed in her own thoughts, waved her hand in a vague 'later' gesture and, picking up the photo of Maz, recommenced her earlier monologue. 'So, Maz, are you part of the elusive pattern or not? Why have you disappeared? Maybe you're the machete killer's fifth victim.'

She shuddered at the thought. 'No, of course you're not. If you were already dead, there would be no need for the ear stunt, would there? Perhaps that was a warning – but to whom? To you or your parents? They could have killed you already and are just taunting us … I hope not, for the sake of everyone.'

Three hours later, Nikki was more tired, but not one inch closer to a conclusion, when Charlie flounced into the kitchen in a waft of Arianne Grande's Sweet like Candy perfume. 'What the fu … I mean, what the hell, Mum? You been up all night? You gave me a fright.'

Ignoring her eldest daughter's near swear miss, Nikki leaned back and stretched her arms above her head, grimacing when her neck clicked. If she was a good mum, she'd jump up and pour a bowl of cereal for her daughter. Instead, she gathered together the file she'd spent half the night perusing and said, 'Make us a coffee, Charlie, hon.'

With an eye roll that spoke volumes, Charlie flicked the switch, grabbed a mug, coffee, and milk, and pushed it across the table to her mum before sorting out her own breakfast. 'You've not forgotten the vigil tonight, have you?'

Nikki yawned. 'Course not.' She was lying, and she suspected Charlie knew it, too. However, now that Charlie had reminded her – she'd be there. The series of vigils had been organised to take place throughout the country to commemorate the brutal murder of Aqsa Mahmood and Jusveer Khatri the previous month. In a so-called honour killing, lads from the Mahmood family's mosque had strangled the teenagers before throwing them onto train tracks near the murder scene. The Mahmoods had joined with the Khatris to condemn the killings and had worked together to arrange this evening's vigil. Nikki was determined to take the entire household with her. The sort of vitriolic hatred that had been spouted on social media during the investigation had taken her breath away. She hoped that her children would be more open minded.

26TH NOVEMBER

Chapter 35

Despite the rain bouncing off the road, Haqib stood outside his house rather than take shelter indoors. His excuse was that he was waiting for Charlie to go to school, but in reality, he wanted to check on Fareena. He'd been on edge all last night and she hadn't been answering his texts, which really had him freaking out. They wouldn't be able to talk because her dad usually shepherded her into the car, but if he was lucky, she'd manage a wink. That would be all he'd see of her because whenever she left home, she had to wear the niqab, which left only her eyes visible. As soon as she got to school, like the other girls who only wore the niqab to please their parents, she'd bundle it in her locker and scuttle off to the loos to put on her make-up. When she returned, she always looked like a different person. When wearing the niqab she walked different – more hunched like. Eyes down, like she was petrified. She'd told him it was because she preferred to make herself as small as possible to avoid any hassle from the racist bastards out there. Once, two white girls in the bus queue had pulled her mum to the ground and snatched her veil off. The world was crazy, and it was no surprise she was scared. Her sister Attiya, on the other hand, wore the niqab as if it was armour and she didn't give a damn what anybody thought of her – like she was invincible.

He wiped the rain from his face. Attiya wasn't so invincible now, was she? Haqib had half a mind to talk to his auntie about it. She always knew what to do, but he didn't want to give her anything else to deal with. Not when she was recovering so well. Haqib had been distraught when he'd learned that she'd thought he was the dead kid. Charlie told him it wasn't his fault, but still guilt gnawed at him. If he hadn't been so much of an idiot for the past couple of years, then Auntie Nikki wouldn't have even considered it could be him. Indirectly he felt responsible, and so he'd do anything to avoid upsetting her like that again.

The front door opposite opened and Fareena, sandwiched between her brothers as if they were her bodyguards, walked down the stairs. Haqib averted his eyes. No way did he want to get on the wrong side of Kam and Farooq – not after what Fareena had said yesterday. Shit, they were muscly. Mind you, if they were handy with a machete, it wouldn't matter if they were built or not.

He snuck furtive glances in her direction, but Fareena did not try to engage with him at all. The things she'd told him the previous day about forced marriages and her sister made him view her family entirely differently. He couldn't dismiss her conviction that her brothers could be violent. It was all more than he could get his head round. Haqib's own dad was a bastard, but even he, despite all the really fucked-up crimes he'd committed, wouldn't hurt any of his *own* kids – other folks' kids were a different matter – but he refused to think about that now. Which parents or brothers could hurt their own family? It would be like Haqib hurting Charlie or Ruby and that would just never ever happen – no matter what they did.

A yell from the doorstep attracted Haqib's attention. It was Fareena's brother-in-law, Naveed. 'Wait up, you three. I'll join you today. Nowt else to do. You don't mind, do you, Fareena?'

Fareena's steps faltered, but behind her niqab, Haqib couldn't see her expression. He didn't need to, her body language said it all. She gave a single nod and slid into the back of the gleaming Mercedes.

Naveed was of slighter build than both his brothers-in-law, yet there was something about the man that Haqib found disquieting. Perhaps it was his swagger – the way he strutted around Listerhills, driving his father-in-law's car, talking to the kids. He was a dealer. Haqib knew that because Naveed had tried to recruit him. Mindful of his previous experience with drug dealers, Haqib had refused – even when Naveed's grin had sent shivers up his spine, he'd held firm. It hadn't been easy, but Haqib had learned to play his trump card. 'You wouldn't want me, anyway. My auntie's a pig and she has all the pigs monitoring me. I'd attract too much of the wrong attention, Naveed.'

Haqib had felt bad for dissing his auntie, but better that than being forced into doing Naveed's bidding. Naveed had slapped him on the shoulder amicably enough, but his tight lips and insincere grin made Haqib want to go home and shower.

Jolted out of his reverie, Haqib jumped when Naveed glared at him, taking a step towards him. 'What the fuck you looking at, you little Hindu half-caste boy?'

'Nowt.' Haqib began walking to Charlie's house, his hands trembling. He'd like nothing more than to land a punch on Naveed's nasty, smirking face, but he valued his life too much. Who the hell was he to call him racist names? Haqib was neither Hindu nor Muslim, but that wasn't the point. Naveed had used the fact that his parents followed two different religions to taunt him, and Haqib had suffered enough of that shit all his life. With a snort, Haqib realised he'd much less trouble imagining Naveed wielding a machete than he did Fareena's brothers.

Hefting his schoolbag onto his shoulder, he watched as the car containing Fareena pulled away, before walking up the path to his auntie's house. He'd no sooner stepped into the hallway than Charlie was in his face. 'You're soaked, Haqib. Is she bloody worth it, that Fareena?'

Despite wanting to defend his girlfriend, Haqib was more interested in getting a towel to mop up the water dripping from his hair. 'Hey, cuz, can I borrow some hair product?'

Charlie rolled her eyes. 'Yes, but be quick. I don't want to miss the bus.' As Haqib rushed upstairs, Charlie hummed 'You're So Vain' under her breath, making him grin. At the top of the stairs, he turned. 'Hey, Charlie …' When she looked up, he raised the middle finger of one hand in her direction before stampeding into her room in search of gel.

Back downstairs, shortly afterwards, his Auntie Nik wandered out of the kitchen, yawning and holding a coffee cup as if her life depended on it. All teen concern and no tact, Haqib's eyes widened and his mouth fell open. 'God, you look like crap, Auntie Nik.'

When his aunt raised her eyebrows and glared at him, he realised he'd been less than tactful and tried to back pedal. 'Well, like. You know, when I say crap … all I mean is erm …'

Lips twitching and her dark eyes full of mischief, Charlie slapped his shoulder. 'You for real, Haq? Course she looks tired. Unlike you, who had full advantage of your beauty sleep – and let's face it, you need it – my mum's been up all night working on Maz Khan's abduction.'

'You mean he in't come home yet? Fu …' Haqib's cheeks flushed as he met his aunt's gaze.

'You were saying, Haqib?' His aunt lasered him with dark eyes that saw everything. Shit, he'd put his foot in it now.

'Nowt, I wun't saying owt. I mean it's crap, yeah. All this stuff going on with the machetes and whatnot is just …'

'Crap …?' asked Nikki, her smile showing she was teasing him. 'If you two want, I'll give you a lift to school in the new Parekh-mobile.'

'You got new wheels?' Haqib could scarcely contain his disbelief. He'd thought his auntie would never give up her Fred Flintstone Zafira. Visions of a posh Jaguar, like Saj's, had him grabbing his backpack and heading for the door. 'Come on, Charlie, let's rock 'n' roll! Thanks, Aunt Nik.'

Hefting the bulging schoolbag onto his shoulder, Haqib picked up the morning's mail and stopped short when he saw a hand-written envelope addressed to Nikki with a foreign postmark. 'Hey, Auntie Nik, who do you know in Thailand?'

His auntie grabbed the envelope, eyes flashing. 'Nobody. I don't know anyone from Thailand. It'll be junk mail.'

Haqib frowned. Why the hell was she acting all weird? His eyes narrowed as she stuffed the envelope into her handbag, eyes darting upstairs as if she didn't want anybody to witness her hiding it. He shrugged. Auntie Nik was allowed her secrets, and he wouldn't tell anyone ... not even Charlie – hell, *especially* not Charlie.

On the kerbside, Haqib looked up and down the street. He couldn't see a posh car anywhere. Maybe his aunt had parked it further up the road? Then, the chirrup of a door unlocking, and the flash of orange lights from a boxy black seven-seater family car drew his attention. Open-mouthed, he studied the vehicle. 'You bought a *Touran*? Why didn't you go for a Maserati or a Jag or summat cool? That's an old lady's car! It's the sort of thing LallyMa would buy.'

Charlie pushed him. 'Shut up, Haq, you're gonna upset her.'

Shit! Haqib glanced at his auntie to see if his mention of his grandma had agitated her, but other than a slight smile, Aunt Nik looked her usual self. He shrugged. 'Sorry.'

Nikki ruffled the hair he'd just carefully gelled. 'We can talk about LallyMa, you know? It's important we do and you're right, she'd have loved this car.'

Haqib couldn't help wondering what his aunt was thinking. She had money – his mum was always going on about how Auntie Nik had spent none of her share of the proceeds from his grandma's estate – and she'd opted for ... boring ... boring, dull and plain. She'd have been as well sticking with the Zafira. 'But why that one?'

'Duh, let me think about that, brainbox … I've three kids and their mates to drive around, plus I use it for work. Do you know how long a Maserati would last in some of the places I visit?'

Haqib yanked the door open and got in. 'Good point – it's just, it's, well, dull. You could've gone for red … or gold … or …'

'Yeah, I get it … anything but black, eh?'

A gasp from Charlie, who was slouched in the back seat, scrolling online, interrupted their conversation. 'Haq, you seen the newest post from **#WhatsWrongWithThisShit** blog?'

Haqib scrolled through his mobile whilst Charlie handed hers to Nikki. 'You should see this too, Mum. Everyone knows about Maz's ear being chopped off and delivered to his mum now. It's on this blog.'

Ignoring her daughter's incredulity for a moment, Nikki grabbed the phone and scrolled down. 'I did, but it was supposed to be kept under wraps. This isn't good news.' She clicked her seatbelt in place and checked her mirrors. 'Send me the link, please, Charlie. Now, come on, let's get a wriggle on, for I need to drop you off. Then me and Marcus are meeting with Saj.'

Chapter 36

On the drive back to Listerhills to pick Marcus up, anxiety plagued Nikki, and she knew she'd have to pull over and open the damn letter. Certain it contained yet another postcard from her father, Freddy Downey, Nikki didn't want Marcus to see it. If he did, he'd march her right down to Trafalgar House and insist Archie start an investigation involving the Thai authorities. What was worse was she'd have to come clean about the other five post-cards she'd received since her mum died. And Marcus would be so angry with her for not confiding in him.

Truth was, she was well aware that she should have told him already, but when they first started arriving, she'd no energy to deal with both Marcus's rage and her own, so she'd shoved them in a shoebox in the back of her wardrobe and only looked at them when Marcus was at work. She hadn't wanted to deal with the range of emotions each postcard elicited – but now she was recovering, she would have to deal with them.

Pulling into a McDonald's car park, Nikki parked as far away from other vehicles as possible, took a deep breath and punched her fists on the steering wheel. Why did the bastard have to intrude on the things that made her happy? She'd looked forward to driving her new wheels, safe in the knowledge that no wayward drips would find their way down her neck and that the heating would work. Now the bastard who'd contributed only half her DNA and most of her heartache had tarnished this – just like he tarnished every damn thing he came into contact with.

Glaring at a van that drew into the spot right next to hers, Nikki yanked the offending letter from her bag and, ignoring all forensic protocol, ripped the envelope open. Inside was, as expected, a postcard, written in the same scrawl as the name and address. Uninterested in the picture, Nikki read the terse message. It was the same one every time.

I'll be back. Your choice – who's next, you or your sister?

Her hand trembled as her fingers stroked the scar around her neck. This was a constant reminder of just what the man was capable of. Her chest tightened and her throat constricted as she fought to control her panicked breaths. In … Out … In … out …

When her breathing settled, she returned the postcard to its envelope and thrust it to the bottom of her bag. Then she grabbed her phone and, unshed tears threatening, hit a number she'd hoped not to have to use. 'Dr Mallory. It's Nikki Parekh. I need to see you. Today if possible.'

With an appointment for later that morning, Nikki brushed away the wetness from her eyes and started the car. The decision to confide her secret made her feel better – still shaky, perhaps, but definitely better.

Chapter 37

The Honourable Fixer

Anticipation is always a good thing. Especially when based on the knowledge that plans have been made and are ready to go. I can't wait for this evening. To observe the results of my planning first-hand will be deliciously satisfying. Fruits of my labour and all that. I don't usually get to be up close and personal with the actions I've set in motion, but tonight will be different. Under the cloak of my very public presence, I'll watch as the events I've planned unfold. It'll be like being at a 3D movie – or a 4D. The forecast is for a chilly breeze, after all. No matter the weather, I'll be there and no one will suspect me of being complicit in the fun and games. It'll be a grand opportunity to see close-up the response of the mighty Bradford police. I open up the files stored under layers of encryption and flick through them, drinking in the candid photographs of them, flicking through the notes I've made. First up is DC Sajid Malik – all posh clothes and little substance. Gay. His partner's the pathologist – that bodes well for interesting bedroom antics. I grin at the thought. The more recent pictures of him show that he's lost weight – not much – but some of his suits hang off him a tad. Poor sod's missing his mentor. I flick to my file on DS Nikita Parekh. She's one tough cookie, but she's also a crumbling cookie. I access her referral to the police-appointed psychiatrist. It details her disintegration at a crime scene a couple of months back. She's not been at work since! Maybe she'll never return. Still, I'll keep tabs on her progress, for she's got balls of steel and the tenacity of a Rottweiler. If she returns to work, she could be a threat to my operation – not a deadly threat. Even so, best not to underestimate my opponents.

When my Headhunter phone buzzes, I sigh, but pick up. 'Tell me everything is under control.'

'Y-yes. Everything's in place exactly as you requested. We're all g-g-g-good to go.'

I pause and wonder for a moment if Headhunter is deflecting. 'You okay?'

His voice comes across stronger and more definite despite his persistent stammer. 'Y-yes. Everything's sorted. Everyone's briefed. We're all aware of our responsibilities.'

'And …' I wait, knowing he'll be wracking his brains to work out what more I'm after. It sinks in.

'Oh, Maz? He's okay. We went back l-l-l-last night, and I cleaned him up a bit. Left f-f-food and painkillers and stuff.'

'You took precautions, I hope?' Again, I'm met with silence for a moment. The idiot thinks I'm talking about condoms and can't fathom out why – thicko! 'I mean, you hid your identities?'

'Oh, y-yes.' He sounds relieved. 'Wore balaclavas and hoodies. None of us spoke to him. He were out of it, anyway.'

Well, that's a relief. Seems Headhunter is getting better at covering his tracks. 'Well, you know what to do, don't you? After the vigil?'

'Erm, 'bout that – I'll let Maz go, l-l-like you said, but the others?'

'What about them?'

'Well, y-y-you said …'

'I'm perfectly aware of what I said. Is that a problem?'

'N-no … no, there isn't.'

'Good. Then we're on the same page. I'll expect to see two press announcements soon. One covering the safe return of poor abused Mazin Khan and the other regarding the tragic deaths of two more machete killer victims.' Before he has a chance to argue, or worse, plead with me, I hang up.

Today is turning out to be an excellent one.

Chapter 38

Situated just down the street from Trafalgar House police station, the Lazy Bites café was a haunt of many of Nikki's colleagues, and she'd rarely eaten there since her breakdown. When she and Marcus entered, the aroma of freshly brewed coffee and bacon butties made Nikki's stomach rumble. For the first time in ages, she was energised and able to shake away the residual lethargy caused by her persistent insomnia and, it seemed, her appetite had also returned. Isaac, the lad she now considered her surrogate son, bustled out of the kitchen and threw himself at her. 'Nik, Nik, you're here. I've missed you.'

Nikki inhaled the scent of cooking from his hair as she returned his embrace. After her mum's death, she'd been remiss in maintaining contact with Isaac, leaving Marcus and the kids to make up for her inability. She should have been there for him. A voice sounded in her ear, another Malloryism from her therapist – '*you can't undo what's done, but you can do better …*' Still, Isaac had needed her – he'd lost his LallyMa, and had to adjust to moving back into the residential flats for adults with learning disabilities. 'Love you, Isaac.'

He extricated himself and grinned, doing a slow pirouette. 'What's not to love?'

Nikki laughed. 'Funny. Now, you going to chat all day, or can Marcus and I have bacon butties and coffee? We'll be over there at Saj's booth.'

Isaac saluted her, clicking his heels together like a soldier. 'Yes, sir.'

Still smiling, Nikki joined Sajid and Marcus. They normally sat at the booth furthest from the door because it offered privacy. However, it was also the table where Nikki's dad had confronted her, and it was from here that she'd last seen her mother alive. Marcus caught her eye. 'We can move, Nik?'

She shrugged off her coat and slid into the seat. 'Nah – can't avoid the memories forever. That's what messed me up in the first place, isn't it?'

Despite her bravado, she sent a surreptitious glance round the café and was relieved that no work colleagues were dining there. She wasn't up to that right now – baby steps. 'We have a leak, Saj.'

She handed her phone to her partner and played with the sugar sachets whilst he scrolled down.

'What the …!' Sajid's face went redder and redder as he read more. 'Who's leaked this and who the hell is this damn blogger?'

'We were chatting about that on the road over. It could be someone from Ali's side or …' Marcus looked at Nikki.

Nikki's lips tightened. If there was anything she detested, it was bent coppers. 'Yeah, or one of ours.' She paused. 'Or maybe the blogger's involved in the attacks. Doesn't sound like it from the tone of their posts – either way we need to find out.'

'Forward the link and I'll have one of the techy geeks track down the owner and I'll send Anwar and Williams – they're asking for you by the way – to re-interview Ali's men, see if they know anything about it.'

Isaac deposited bacon butties and coffees on the table and, in ultra-professional mode, left them to it after another quick hug with Nikki. Between slurps of coffee and bites of her food, she asked Saj for an update.

'We've interviewed Maz's mates, his ex-teachers from school, that Michelle Glass girl – she's a piece of work, isn't she – and nobody's saying a damn word. The kids were either nervous, rude or mocking – but that's no surprise. They've seen four of their peers macheted to death and now another one abducted – they think we're not acting fast enough and who can blame them?' He dragged his fingers through his short hair. 'I spoke to Ali earlier, and he says he's still had no ransom demand.'

Nikki snorted. 'He wouldn't tell you if he had, Saj. He'd just go after the abductors himself. You know what he's like.'

Saj nodded. 'Yep, and that's why I've put a tail on him and Haris; although Haris has been on the move – mainly taxi business – Ali's stayed with Jane so far.'

'Talking of Jane – did you realise she and Ali were a couple?'

Saj looked at her, eyes wide. 'What, you mean you didn't? For God's sake Parekh, call yourself a detective?'

Saj winked at Marcus and Marcus laughed. 'She's oblivious to that sort of stuff, Saj. You know that by now.'

Nikki glowered at them. Neither of them had known, had they? Sensing the conversation was getting away from her, she placed her roll on the plate. 'Focus, you two, there's a missing kid and a sea of murdered teens to get justice for. What's next? How can we help?'

'We need to work out if the murders are linked with Maz's disappearance. Time's running out and if Ali's telling the truth about the ransom demand, then we might be looking for a corpse before long.'

Nikki nodded. 'I wanted to talk to you about an idea I had last night. Remember that mugging gang – I think you were still a PC when they were doing the rounds ...'

With a click of his fingers, Saj smiled. 'Yeah, I remember them. Didn't they take turns targeting their next victim and notch up points depending on how much cash they stole? You thinking our killers are doing something similar? Killing as a game?'

172

Nikki shrugged. 'It's just a thought, but the forensic evidence proves that there may be multiple killers. Stranger things have happened, haven't they?'

'You can say that again.' Saj wiped an imaginary fleck off his sleeve. 'And there's nowt queerer than …'

'Folk.' Nikki grinned. 'Nowt as strange as you, anyway.' Grinning, she prodded her partner. 'I'm going to talk to Amar Akhtar again. He was banging on about infidels and people not adhering to Islam. He might have something more to offer. Besides, he worked with Maz, didn't he? Who better to know Maz's secrets? I'm also going to drop in on Ali. Make sure he's got nothing planned that we need to be aware of. You?'

'The Dark Knight pretty much wants me glued to his side for the rest of the day, oh joy of joys. Think he gets off on bossing me around. We're re-interviewing Ali and Jane and retracing all the work I did yesterday. I thought Archie was bad with the micro-managing, but Ahad's proving worse. We're also heading down to Forster Square arches to talk to the rough sleepers there …' Sajid's lips drooped, making him look like a clown without the make-up.

'Aw, there, there, Malik. Now you appreciate how easy you had it working with me, eh?' Before he could reply, Nikki jumped to her feet. 'We've gotta go, Saj. I've got an appointment and you don't want to keep your new partner waiting, now, do you? See ya at the vigil.'

With a wave, she and Marcus headed for the door. Nikki blew a kiss to Isaac before they left. 'Mr Fashion in the corner will pay ours today, Isaac.'

Chapter 39

Maz woke up shivering and throbbing all over, despite the duvet they had given him and the warmth coming from the cranky old central heating system. He'd never felt so ill before, and he suspected his ear was infected. The pain was worsening, and Maz was tempted to succumb and swallow a couple of the Naproxen his captors had given. He'd still have plenty left over if he needed them. Though he wasn't sure how many of the cocktail of pain-killers he would need.

He'd lost track of time. It must be morning, but it *could* be afternoon, and he had to make a decision. How much longer should he give his dad before he took matters into his own hands? He couldn't escape. Hell, if he could, he'd have tried already, but that wasn't an option – not with his knackered leg. The only alternative was to do the unthinkable. He was damned if he'd allow those bastards to hack him to death, like they had the others. His mum would be in bits, no matter how he died. At least an overdose would be prettier for her. She'd know he hadn't suffered as much as those other kids. Well, except for his missing ear and the other cuts which still seeped blood if he moved.

He'd no idea when his captors would return, but he was sure they would. He tried to arrange his thoughts. The vigil? Had it happened already, or would it be tonight? Yes, tonight. That's when it would be. He decided that if he wasn't rescued by night-time, he'd have no choice. The Eyes would kill him anyway, sooner rather than later. Were they aware that he knew more than he should? Probably, and that was his own fault. He should've kept schtum when he overheard Amar talking to that bloke he called Headhunter. But that wasn't all he'd heard. Maz could identify the Headhunter. He'd overheard him talking to someone called the Fixer. Until then, Maz had assumed that it was all a load of daft kids playing vigilantes. That had been bad enough. He'd known a bit about that, too. They'd wanted him to inform on some of his friends and, because he wanted to find out more, he'd pretended to be into it. When they'd asked him to join, he'd been all too eager. His dad kept him on a tight leash and they'd made him feel like an adult. He hadn't realised the sort of stuff they did – how they hurt people. It was all meant to be a bit of harmless fun. Besides, the extra dosh had come in handy. Now, word had got out, and the Eyes were actually getting paid to do shit ... bad shit. He wasn't sure where Headhunter or this Fixer character fit in to it all. He suspected the Fixer pulled the strings, though. It all seemed to involve kids being killed to order for doing crap their folks didn't like. Rumour had it that their families paid for it. With the amount of cash being splashed around, there was plenty of big bucks in it. In his current predicament, Maz kept going over and over how stupid he'd been to confront Headhunter. The guy could be vicious and he also had many 'friends' who would do anything for him. If Maz had gone to his dad and not said owt to anyone else, he wouldn't be here minus an ear and thinking about topping himself. He needed to focus, so he swallowed a couple of pills and tried to think.

Some of the Eyes had plans for the vigil and they'd offered Maz 500 big ones to join in, but he'd refused. There were plenty of other Eyes with no morals who'd be happy to hack off someone's ear for a couple of hundred. Maz was sure that he'd be safe till afterwards. So, he'd wait, praying that his dad would come soon and – if not – Plan B. When he heard his captors return to the house to end him, he'd swallow the fucking lot of the pills and that would be that.

Chapter 40

So as not to worry Marcus, Nikki told him that Dr Mallory had offered her an extra appointment after a cancellation. She hated lying to him, but with everything that was going on and all the things she needed to do, she couldn't afford to be distracted by a protracted discussion about Freddie Downey, followed by a detour to hand over the postcards to someone in Trafalgar House. She'd laid her soul bare to her colleagues before, and she didn't want to have to do it again. Besides, when it came to it, *she* would deal with Downey in her own way. There was too much at stake for her not to.

With the familiar aroma of Dr Mallory's perfume filling her nostrils, Nikki allowed the super cosy chair to engulf her as she studied the woman opposite. In true Mallory style, she wore a bright orange skirt, a lilac top that revealed a fair amount of impressive cleavage, and a matching feathery thing that bundled her hair into a messy bun, leaving only a few purple tendrils hanging down. Mesmerised by the cacophony of colour before her, Nikki's eyes followed the doctor's glittery amber nails as they tapped against her pen. The pen had a fluffy plume sticking out the top, which momentarily distracted her from the purpose of her trip. Did normal people buy that kind of stuff?

Mallory pushed her specs back up her nose and quirked an

eyebrow. 'Well, *you* asked for this appointment. You going to just sit there and ogle my pen? Beautiful though it is, I wouldn't have thought it was your sort of thing.'

Ice broken, Nikki grinned at her. 'I'm not sure it should be anybody's sort of thing. It's … well, it's …' She shrugged. 'Actually, words defy me.'

She lifted the envelope from her bag and thrust it at the doctor. 'This arrived today. You can open it.' Although Nikki had discussed Freddie Downey's role in her mother's killing and his relationship to her, she hadn't told Mallory about the postcards. Now she had no option. She had to talk about them with someone, and Anika and Marcus were out of the question, as were Saj and Archie.

Mallory looked at the address written on the envelope before opening it and extracting the postcard. For a moment she studied the image on the front – a sandy beach on Krabi Island with an expanse of blue sea surrounding it. The caption read 'Visit Thailand'. 'The postcard arrived inside the envelope? Why didn't the sender just post the card?'

Nikki rolled her finger, telling Mallory to turn it over. The doctor read the short inscription, pulling her eyebrows together as she absorbed the threat behind it. 'Who sent this to you?'

Taking a deep, steadying breath, Nikki spat out the name. 'Freddie Downey … my fa—'

'Father … Oh my God, Parekh. Have you told the police?'

The doctor's words brought a fleeting smile to Nikki's lips. 'I *am* the police, Dr Mallory.'

'Oh, you know what I mean. The person dealing with the investigation into your mother's murder needs to see this, surely?' The doctor looked at Nikki's bowed head and exhaled. 'This isn't the first one, is it?'

'No.'

'For goodness' sake, DS Parekh. You should have shared this with me earlier, but also – more importantly, you should have handed this over. It's evidence.'

Mallory's use of her title wasn't lost on Nikki. This was the doctor's way of reminding her that she was a police officer and that, by not handing evidence in, she was in effect, committing a crime – obstructing an investigation. Nikki's fingers drifted up to her scar as she waited for the next salvo.

'How many? How many of these have you received and what did they say?'

Voice low, Nikki focused on the carpet. 'Five. Always in an envelope, always to my home address and always with a Thai postmark and …' She shifted her gaze to meet the doctor's eyes. 'Always bearing the same message.'

'Okay, give me a moment to think.' Dr Mallory got to her feet and approached the cooler in the corner of the room. She poured two glasses of ice-cold water and, returning to her seat, offered one to Nikki before speaking. 'I recommend that you take all the postcards to the appropriate officer. They need to know. Perhaps they can involve Interpol or …' She waved her hand in the air as if the name of another organisation would occur to her, then gave up. 'I strenuously suggest you do that, Nikki. In fact, I'm surprised Marcus didn't …'

Nikki's hand jerked, spilling a droplet onto her jeans.

'Oh no … you haven't told Marcus either, have you?' When Nikki shook her head, the doctor continued. 'Again … you should. However, my chief concern is your mental health and I assume that's why you wanted to see me. Tell me what happened.'

Nikki took a long gulp of water. Its iciness focused her thoughts and she described the anger she'd felt in the car earlier. Dr Mallory listened and then together they practised mindfulness exercises. By the time the session was over, Mallory had extracted a promise that Nikki would tell Marcus about the postcards and submit them as evidence. As she left the building feeling less tense, she convinced herself that although she'd promised to do the two things Mallory suggested, she hadn't agreed on a timeline for completion of said promise.

Chapter 41

Nikki found Ali Khan at his taxi firm on Toller Lane. She'd phoned first to make sure there was no danger of running into Sajid or the new DI. That was a meeting she'd be happy to avoid for a while. Besides, neither she nor Saj wanted to broadcast her involvement in the investigation into Maz Khan's disappearance and she didn't want to land her partner in hot bother should Ahad work it out.

Instead of sitting in the back office where he usually worked, Ali was pacing up and down at the front, mobile clenched to his ear. The few taxi drivers waiting for pick-ups darted worried glances in his direction, but he was oblivious to them. As he paced, he spoke in Urdu, and it didn't take a genius to deduce that he was venting. Whilst she waited for him to wind up the call, Nikki noted his changed appearance. His lower face was a black fuzz of stubble, and his forehead was pulled together in a frown. He wore the same clothes he had worn when Nikki last saw him, and despite it being only twenty-four hours since then, he seemed skinnier. When he hung up, he cast a glance in her direction. 'If you've no good news, I've no time for you, Parekh. I need to find my lad and your lot prioritise a fucking gora junkie over my boy.'

He strode past her, and Nikki struggled to keep up with him.

She understood his anger. The press had taken up the mantle for the West Yorkshire mayor's son, and the appeals for information about Maz's abduction had been relegated to the back burner. However, that wasn't the police's choice – it was yet another sad indictment of the way journalists prioritised their news, and it irked her almost as much as it did her friend. 'Wait up, Ali. I want to help. You know I'd do anything for you. I'm not here as police, I'm here as your mate. I can help you find Maz, just like you helped me when Charlie was snatched.'

Her words seemed to mollify Ali, for he paused. Nikki stepped close to him and thrust out the Greggs coffee and cheese and onion pasty she'd bought for him. 'You tell me where to go and I'll drive whilst you eat. You look like you need some nourishment.'

Despite his grief, a smile flashed across his face. 'In your heap? No damn chance, Parekh.'

Nikki walked past him into the forecourt and, arms wide, presented her new car to him. 'Ta da. Got myself some hot new wheels. Get in.'

Mumbling, Ali crossed to the car and slid into the passenger seat, already opening the bag containing the food whilst Nikki awaited instructions. 'Where we heading?'

'I'm trying to find that stupid kid, Michelle Glass.' He chewed for a moment and swallowed before continuing. 'Amar said she was hanging around the garage, all tarted up in a hijab.'

His use of 'tarted up' and 'hijab' in the same sentence amused Nikki, but Ali was in no mood for jokes, so she repressed her quip.

He snorted. 'Like any of us are going to forget her brother was a racist little fucker, because she wears a hijab. Like there's not a lot more to being a good Muslim than what you wear on your head. That Amar told me she hangs out with Chas Choudry – You got any ideas where?'

Nikki didn't, but she knew someone who might. 'Give me a mo to make a call.'

Seconds later, she was speaking to DC Farah Anwar. 'Hey,

Farah, it's Parekh here. You any idea where to find either Michelle Glass or Chas Choudry? Saj told me you were reaching out to your contacts on the street.'

After a brief conversation, Nikki looked at Ali, a triumphant grin on her face. 'Got eyes on Chas Choudry. He's dodging school and Anwar saw him not five minutes ago in Broadway.' Before she'd even finished updating Ali, she'd tossed her phone into his lap and was driving out of the taxi lot, heading towards the Broadway shopping centre in town. 'Anwar sent me an image of him so he'll be easier to identify.'

They parked in the multi-storey Broadway car park. Ali strode off, forcing Nikki to run to keep up. This made conversation difficult, so Nikki focused on keeping him in sight. When they entered the complex, Ali looked around, uncertainty clouding his face. 'Where the hell shall we start?'

In her experience, teenagers gravitated towards either Primark or the Food Court. How the pair of them were going to find either kid in Primark was a mystery. She'd rather they spotted them in the mall itself. Relieved that it wasn't too busy, Nikki headed in that direction, leaving Ali to follow. They were nearly at the Primark store when Nikki noticed a crowd of kids loitering just beyond the entrance. So much for gaining an education. At the very least she'd tear a strip off them for not being in school. Veering towards them, Nikki scoured their faces, but had identified neither the girl nor the boy, before a youngster, hoodie concealing his face, broke away from the group and started running. Unsure whether it was Choudry, Nikki recognised suspicious behaviour when she saw it, so she took off after him, yelling at Ali to circle round the other way to block the boy's exit.

The lad didn't have too much of a head start, so Nikki forced herself to run faster as he darted ahead, dodging some shoppers and banging into others. Seeing the commotion, the shoppers peeled away to the sides of the walkway, creating a clear space. Nikki, taking her chance, pumped her arms and increased her speed. Fortunately, the boy wasn't very fast, for within seconds she'd closed the gap. However, he was approaching an exit, and there was no sign of Ali. If he got outside the mall, there was no way she'd catch him. So, with a last effort, Nikki flung herself at him, grabbing the back of his hoodie with the tips of her fingers. It was enough to slow him down, which allowed Ali to bulldoze in from the other side and knock him to the floor.

Catching her breath, Nikki left it for Ali to yank him to his feet and pull the hood from his head. Still panting, she cursed. It wasn't Chas Choudry. Ali, recognising that fact, released his hold on the lad and growled at him. 'Why the fuck did you run?'

Breathing heavily with pink cheeks, he raised his chin in Nikki's direction. 'She's Five-O, in't she?'

Nikki stepped forward. 'Yep, you got me. I'm Five-O – minus the sun and the Hawaiian shirt – but Five-O nonetheless and you're nicked.' Nikki didn't have her warrant card and certainly had no jurisdiction, but she hoped the kid wouldn't be savvy enough to question her authority. 'What are you carrying? Drugs …' She took a step closer. 'Or a machete?'

The boy paled. 'No machete – no weapons. Shit, you're trying to pin that white kid's murder on me. No, I had nowt to do wi' it. Honest.'

Nikki gestured behind to the empty area where his friends had been. 'Well, you've got nobody to vouch for you. Your so-called mates scattered and left you to take the blame. So, what's your name?'

Nikki almost felt sorry for him – almost, but not quite. He was small for his age, with a bit of bum fluff on his chin and a badly executed Celtic tattoo spreading up his neck, that he would – if he had any sense – regret in later years. The lad looked round, as if hoping someone from the crowd of interested bystanders would come to his aid. Ali towered over him and the boy tried to edge away, so Nikki closed the gap and crowded him from the other side. 'Name?'

'Noor. Noor Ahmed.'

'Right, Noor Ahmed, spill your pockets.' As Nikki expected, he had a couple of bags of weed and a few Es. Enough for her to reprimand him, but having apprehended him unofficially, she had to let that go. However, she could use it to exert pressure on him. 'You know Chas Choudry?'

A nod.

'Michelle Glass?'

Another nod.

Talk about blood and stones. 'You're going to give us more than a nod, Noor! If you don't, I'll have to take you in now, won't I? Believe me, I don't want to spend the afternoon filling in paperwork because you didn't share what you know about Chas Choudry and Michelle Glass.'

Noor's shoulders slumped, and Nikki knew they had him. She exchanged a smile with Ali. 'Go on, then. Where can we find them?'

'I dunno. Honest I dun't. Saw Chas here a while ago, but he and Michelle left. Said they had to lie low for a few days. No idea why.'

Nikki pondered this. It seemed both her and Ali's instincts about Glass had been right. 'And where would two teens go to lie low for a few days, eh?'

'Told you, I dun't know.'

Nikki waved the drug bags in front of his face. 'Oh, I think you do, Noor. I really, really do.'

'Fuck, you're gonna get me killed. I can't tell you.'

Ali took a step closer and put his hand on Noor's arm, his whitening knuckles betraying the pressure he applied 'You better, lad. For your own sake, you better. Now spill!'

A tear rolled down the lad's cheek and his lower lip trembled as he tried to escape Ali's pincer grip. 'You never heard this from me like.'

Nikki nodded. She'd happily lie to the little scrote if that meant they got the information they needed.

'There's this bloke – no idea who he is, but they call him the

Headhunter. He's got places all over Bradford. Maybe they've gone to one of them.'

'Headhunter? Whose head does he hunt?' Nikki's antennae quivered. She'd not heard the name before and she pretty much knew all the lowlife in Bradford – well, the ones who mattered anyway.

'I dunno. You just hear stuff, but I'm not one of his crowd. Not even sure Michelle and Chas are …' He shrugged. 'Honest, Miss, I dun't know owt else.'

This lad, she was certain, had nothing more to offer them. Still, he'd given them a starting point and Nikki was pleased with that. She nodded to Ali, who released him with a shove and a, 'Don't fucking mess with drugs again, you little tosser.'

Soon as they got back to her car, Nikki phoned Saj with the update and a request that he get someone on monitoring the CCTV to track where Glass and Choudry had gone to.

As she was about to hang up, Saj halted her. 'Nik?' His tone was the one he used when he'd found something important. 'Is Ali in earshot?'

Her heart skipped a beat as she walked away from the car. Ali was inside now, so he wouldn't hear, but she didn't want her expression to reveal anything. She had the horrid sensation that whatever Sajid had to share was bad. Had they found Maz Khan's body? 'Go on. He's in the car and can't hear me.'

'We matched some prints.' Saj paused and Nikki wished he'd get on with it.

'Fuck's sake Saj, just tell me.'

'We matched Maz's fingerprints to a bottle the CSIs found in the bushes after Molly Cropper's fake acid attack. We didn't have Maz's prints in the system till now …'

'And?' Sajid's tone told Nikki that the bombshell he was about to deliver would not make Ali Khan happy.

'The bottle contained traces of vinegar. It seems …'

'Maz was the kid who traumatised that poor girl. Fuck's sake!'

If Nikki had the lad in front of her right then, she'd have shaken him. Why did kids have to do such stupid, crappy things? It would devastate Ali and Jane. This one malicious act would tarnish all their treasured memories of their 'perfect son'. She could only hope they found Maz alive, so he could make up for his stupidity. Nikki sighed and glanced into the car. Ali dozed in the passenger seat, and Nikki was grateful for the reprieve.

'Exactly!' Saj hesitated. 'Will you ...?'

Nikki's heart thundered against her chest. She owed it to Ali to be upfront with him, but this would break his heart. Ali would know that it put Maz under suspicion for the machete attacks. Shit, shit, double shit and crap. 'Yeah, don't worry, I'll tell Ali. See ya later.'

Chapter 42

#WhatsWrongWithThisShit?

DON'T FORGET THE VIGIL
POSTED BY BFDLASS#WWWTS NOVEMBER 26TH 14:32

With all the crap going on in Bradford right now we need to unite. We need to show that we are in solidarity and that no matter how bad things get we stand together.

#JusticeForAqsaAndJusveer

Come to the peaceful vigil tonight on the steps of City Hall.
Come and show that despite everything we still stand together.
Come and show your support for their families.
Come and show the world that even when Bradford is in mourning for our murdered friends, we still care about injustice.

#JusticeForAqsaAndJusveer

Views: 103 Shares: 15

COMMENTS:

JakeK4292: *Sod that! Got better stuff to do!*

Karryann3: *I'll be there #RIPAqsaAndJusveer #JustiveForAqsaAndJusveer*

ZainK: *Me too – see ya there*

Jazzygirl3: *I'm too scared to come – and my mum won't let me out of the house after dark. Soz. #RIPAqsaAndJusveer #JustiveForAqsaAndJusveer*

LazyJayz04: *Waste of time, worrying about them … What about Jamie Jacobs? #RIPJamieJacobs*

   MayLee: *@LazyJayz04 you make me want to vomit. You racist AH. #WhereIsMazKhan?*

   Jazzygirl3: *@LazyJayz04 What about the machete attacks in Bradford? Not going to talk about them? #WhatsWrongWithThisShit #RIPAqsaAndJusveer #JusticeForAqsaAndJusveer #WhereIsMazKhan?*

ILuvCurry: *Can't 2nite. POS – Thinking of you all. #WhatsWrongWithThisShit #RIPAqsaAndJusveer #JusticeForAqsaAndJusveer #WhereIsMazKhan?*

Chapter 43

The Honourable Fixer

Decision made; I feel like celebrating. I've had such a good day that it wasn't too hard to talk myself into attending the vigil. For all these months I've kept my distance, seen the consequences of my machinations second-hand on TV or social media or via the journalists on the ground, picking up the street vibes. It's never been an option for me to be anywhere near the action and till now, that's been fine. But this vigil is a completely different plate of paella. There will be such a crowd that I won't stand out. In fact, perhaps I'd be more notable by my absence given the day-to-day persona I perpetuate.

I pour myself a finger of whisky – enough to celebrate but not enough to loosen my tongue. Not when I've still got a few 'day job' clients to see. It's unusual for me to drink on the job, and it has the effect of making me feel reckless and freer than I've ever felt before in this charade I've cultivated. It's a strange sensation, but not an unpalatable one.

I down my shot in two swallows and prepare myself for the rest of my boring old afternoon, happy knowing that although my day might be dull, my evening promises to be a lot more electric.

Chapter 44

Haqib wandered round the school cafeteria, looking for Fareena. They'd arranged to meet in a spot under the stairs near the lockers, but Fareena hadn't showed and now lunchtime was nearly over. She still wasn't answering his texts, and he wondered if she'd either lost her phone or, worse, had someone from her family confiscated it! In an attempt to control his concern, Haqib decided he'd do another round of the school to see if he could find her and then if not, he'd be forced to ask one of her mates if they'd seen her. Since the Eyes had become more militant and after the fake acid attack, he and Fareena had agreed not to involve their friends in their relationship.

The machete attacks had only made them stick to that decision more firmly. No way did they want to expose their classmates to any sort of potential violence. They weren't even certain that the machete attacks were linked to the Eyes. All they knew was that fear had replaced the initial bravado of his mates. Increased vigilance and frequent school assemblies focusing on personal safety compounded their worry. Nobody spoke about the tension in the air, but it was there. His mum, similar to many other parents, had imposed a curfew on him. As for Auntie Nik? Well, she'd always been quite strict about stuff like that, but even so, she'd ratcheted up the rules. Charlie was always moaning about it – not that she really minded. Even his take-no-hostages cousin was unsettled by everything going on. As Charlie said, 'If we identified what made these kids targets, we'd be able to avoid putting ourselves at risk.'

Still unable to find his girlfriend, Haqib circled back to the canteen and was about to approach Fareena's friends when he saw her waving from across the room. Where the hell had she been? Battling his way through the groups of kids, Haqib followed Fareena as she headed to 'their' cupboard. He prepared himself for more tears, but when he stepped in and closed the door behind him, she flung herself into his arms and kissed him long and hard.

He pulled back and studied her. Not a tear in sight, but what unsettled him was the anger that tautened her entire face. Her lips were sculpted into a tight line, a pulse throbbed at her temple, and her cheeks were flushed. She appeared feverish, yet when Haqib drew a finger down her cheek, her skin was cool, almost icy. 'What's wrong?'

Fareena blinked and exhaled. When she spoke, her tone was cutting. 'You want a list?'

She began counting off on her fingers whilst pacing the confined space of the art closet. 'One, I'm worried sick about Attiya. Some of her clothes are missing and she's still not active on social media – not anywhere. Two, I've had to hide my phone and say it's lost, because that tosser Naveed suggested we monitor it in case Attiya contacts me – so I'm on my own at home, completely on my own.' She flung herself onto a box filled with paint bottles, a little less fraught now. 'Three, Naveed's a sleazy git, and yet the menfolk think he's some bloody guru or something. Dad's always asking him for advice about stuff. It's like they're all just pretending he's not a bloody drug dealer.'

Haqib opened his mouth to offer a platitude, but Fareena glared at him and he snapped it shut again as she continued. 'Four, the damn FMU people have arranged with Mrs Brick to meet with me after lunch in her office and I don't know what to tell them.'

Mrs Brick, the head teacher, was okay. She'd take care of Fareena, Haqib was sure. But word could still get back to Fareena's family if she spoke to them – and that would put her at risk.

'I want you to come with me, Haqib. I prefer someone I trust there when I speak to them.'

That was the last thing Haqib expected. Normally, he was the one needing help, and it was strange for him to be in the supporter's role. Still, it felt good. He sat next to Fareena on the box, determined to meet her expectations. 'If that's what you want, then it's fine. I'll be there for you. We'll tell them everything we can about Attiya – all the gossip, and the crap that's kicking off at your house, all of it – and they'll find out what's happened to Attiya.'

The school bell rang, signalling the end of lunchtime, and they waited for a few minutes to let the crowds of pupils making their way to their various classes die down before leaving their sanctuary.

At first Mrs Brick was uncertain of including Haqib in the meeting. She was the designated adult there on Fareena's behalf, and she saw no genuine need for Haqib's presence, but Fareena insisted. The officers from the Forced Marriage Unit were happy to include him and so Mrs Brick brought an extra chair for Haqib and placed it next to Fareena's and the five of them sat in a small circle in the corner of her office.

When the two officers introduced themselves, Haqib studied them with interest. Apart from his aunt's colleagues, Haqib had little experience with law enforcement, and they intrigued him. The woman seemed senior, for she took control of the meeting, leaving the older man to take notes whilst she made introductions. When Haqib heard their ranks, he realised he'd been mistaken, and Mr Note Taker was actually in charge although he deferred to Ms Earnest But Kind, probably to make Fareena more comfortable.

Ponytail swinging, as her head bobbed back and forth to include both Haqib and Fareena, Ms Earnest But Kind, reassured Fareena. 'This isn't a formal interview or anything, Fareena. We just want your help to locate your sister, Attiya. We spoke with your parents the other day and they said Attiya had left home, which, of course, she is perfectly entitled to do. She's eighteen and an adult. Normally this wouldn't even be on our radar, but Attiya approached Safer Bradford and although I'm not at liberty to reveal details of her conversation – communications are confidential – her disclosure resulted in her being referred to our unit. Since then she hasn't responded to our attempts to contact her and her phone is switched off, with its last known location being your address. We want to make sure Attiya is safe and well. Do you understand?'

Fareena reached over and gripped Haqib's hand, her fingers squashing his. She nodded.

Ms Earnest But Kind smiled. 'We're going to ask a few questions and your answers will be treated in confidence, okay?'

Fareena's grip tightened, but she agreed, her gaze never leaving the older woman's face.

'Do you know where Attiya is, Fareena?'

Fareena's voice cracked when she tried to respond, so she slugged from her water bottle before trying again. 'No. I've no idea and I'm worried about her too. She's not active on any of her usual social media platforms and that's sooo not like her.'

'She's definitely not at your home?'

With flashing eyes, Fareena shook her head. 'I've just told you that. We don't know where she is. She's taken some of her things from her room though.'

'And you have no clue where she might have gone? Who she could be with?'

Fareena glanced at Haqib with a slight nod. Haqib squeezed her fingers and cleared his throat. 'There's been rumours, like. You know, probably not true or owt, but …'

'Go on, Haqib. If you've heard something it might help us locate Attiya.'

193

Reluctant to speak ill of Fareena's sister, but aware that her disappearance was a serious issue, Haqib, head bowed, revealed everything. 'Some folk say she's got a boyfriend – some older bloke. We were joking like, saying it could be a teacher.' His voice faded off as he remembered where he was. Flushing, he glanced at Mrs Brick. 'I mean – we were like larking about – she won't be going out with a teacher – well, I don't think she would.'

Mrs Brick took pity on him. 'Just tell the officers what you know, Haqib. All of it.'

To avoid eye contact with his head teacher, Haqib looked at Ms Earnest But Kind. 'She had a bust-up with her friends a few weeks back. Everyone was talking about it, calling her a right slag and a cow. Then they were all saying she were pregnant, like.'

He peeked at Fareena. Although he'd already shared this with her, it wouldn't be pleasant hearing it again. But Fareena, despite the blush of red on her cheeks, nodded for him to continue. 'It were like she were a pariah – suddenly everyone hated her. The Eyes made sure nobody spoke to her and then she wasn't around anymore.'

Ms Earnest But Kind exchanged a glance with Mr Note Taker. 'The Eyes?'

Haqib's stomach curdled. He hadn't meant to bring the Eyes into the conversation, and now everything was spiralling out of control. There was no way he could tell Mrs Brick or the police about the Eyes. The spark of interest on Ms Earnest But Kind's face told him it would be difficult to back pedal, but that was his only option. He gave, what he hoped was, a genuine laugh. 'I just mean her friends and that. You know what girls are like when they fall out?'

God, but he was glad Charlie wasn't here to witness him saying that; she'd have his balls if she found out he'd said that. But it wasn't Charlie he was concerned with right now, it was Ms Earnest But Kind and the look she sent his way told him he hadn't convinced her one iota. She stood, followed by her partner, and smiled, first at Fareena and then at Haqib. 'You've both been very helpful and we won't keep you.' She offered a small rectangular card to each of them. 'If you remember anything – anything at all, if you see anything or if Attiya contacts you or if you're worried about anything, contact us.'

She then headed for the door after thanking Mrs Brick for the use of her office. Before exiting the room, Ms Earnest But Kind swung round. 'If you could just spend a few minutes with Mrs Brick compiling a list of Attiya's friends – even the ones she'd fallen out with and of course, 'the Eyes', Mrs Brick will make sure we receive it.'

The tension dissipated with the exit of the Forced Marriage Unit officers, and Haqib heaved a sigh of relief. Then he turned to Mrs Brick, and her determined expression pushed the pressure up again. No way was he or Fareena getting out of the head teacher's office without making that list.

Chapter 45

When Nikki entered Akhtar's garage, the only difference was that the two older Akhtars were nowhere to be seen. Mohsin, on seeing that Ali was with her, extricated himself from the innards of a car and wiped his hands on a rag that hung from his overall pocket. 'As-Salaam Alaikum, Ali. How are you? We've been praying for Maz. Any word?'

Ali returned the greeting, 'Wa-Alaikum-as-Salaam.'

As the men hugged, a flicker of guilt worried at Nikki's stomach. She hadn't told Ali about his son's involvement in the fake acid attack, preferring to get this visit to the Akhtar's out of the way first. He deserved to know, but Nikki wanted him focused for this. She needed Ali's bulky presence when she interviewed Amar Akhtar. From her experience at school with Amar, she was well aware he'd respond better to a Muslim man, and whilst this wasn't normally a consideration in Nikki's interviewing strategies, today it was. Time was of the essence, and the longer Maz was missing, the less likely his chances of escaping alive became. Besides which, if Amar was responsible or was hiding something, he'd find it much more difficult to lie in the company of Maz's dad.

When Mohsin turned to her, his hand raised in greeting and

a smile on his face, Nikki stepped forward. 'It's actually Amar we're here to chat to, Mohsin. He about?'

'Amar – you've got visitors!'

The sounds of someone moving in the car pit alerted Nikki to Amar's whereabouts, and a moment later his head poked out. On spotting Nikki, a frown furrowed his forehead and his lips curved in a supercilious snarl. 'What do you want, Parekh? I'm busy.'

The abrupt change in his demeanour when Ali moved into his line of vision was almost comical. The frown disappeared and an over-bright smile lit up his face. 'Hi, Ali. You with her?'

Just as he and Nikki had planned earlier, Ali stood, arms folded across his chest, dark eyes thunderous between gathered brows. Ali nodded, allowing his brooding silence to dominate the other man. Using her hand to hide the smirk that twitched her lips, Nikki observed the speed with which Amar vacated the car pit and approached them. With a head jerk intimating that Amar should follow him, Ali strode towards the vacant office, whilst Amar, Mohsin and Nikki trailed after him.

Once settled – Ali behind the desk, Nikki on her feet beside him, leaving the other two men to sit in the lumpy visitor's seats – Nikki began. 'Just wanted to ask a bit more about Maz's disappearance, Amar. Seems you were close with him so it stands to reason you'd know anyone who might want to mutilate the boy.'

Amar shrugged, but before he could launch into a denial of all knowledge, Ali butted in. 'Don't even think about weaselling out with an "I don't know owt". I've got ears on these streets and it wouldn't take me long to find out things I'd feel obliged to share with DS Parekh here. That, of course, is only if you don't help us.'

Arms stretched out, Amar glared at Nikki. 'Aw come on, Parekh. We were at school together. You know me, I'm pure as the driven snow.'

Nikki snorted and looked at Mohsin. 'I'm sorry, Mohsin. I know you dote on Amar, but to tell the truth he was always a bit of a holier than thou Muslim. Even all those years ago he'd spout the sort of crap he spouted the other day, and now I'm wondering if he's got something to do with Maz's disappearance or even the machete killings. We've profiled that we're looking for a male in his age bracket, who does manual work and has access to the victims. We're aware he's become close to Maz since the lad started here. Maz's mum said you were his mentor.' None of this was true. They didn't have enough evidence to compile a profile and anyway they weren't the FBI, but Amar didn't know that. Nikki was getting used to working outside the remit of her badge, and this newfound freedom was growing on her.

Mohsin jumped to his feet, scowling. 'What the hell? I thought you were a friend.'

Nikki shrugged. 'I'm Ali's friend and his son's missing, and word has it that your son knows something about it. You see where I'm going with this, Mohsin? We mean no disrespect, but Ali's desperate and, well, I'm not sure how much longer I can keep him with me. You know how many contacts he has on the streets. How many people owe him favours? If I was you, Amar, I'd spill the beans and tell us about this Headhunter and Maz's disappearance – before Ali loses his temper big time.'

Again, as rehearsed, Ali puffed his chest out, glowered at Amar and with a growl said, 'I want my boy and nobody will escape unscathed if they've kept something from me.'

Amar's face darkened, and he jumped up, his mouth curled like a petulant child's. 'This fucking sucks. I know nowt about your Maz other than the sun didn't shine out of his shiny half-caste arse like you think it did. Oh, and one more thing.' He paused and glared right at Ali. Despite sensing what Amar was about to say, Nikki was powerless to prevent it. How she wished she'd told Ali about her earlier conversation with Saj.

'It was your precious Maz that threw vinegar at that girl in July. That's how bloody innocent your brat is. Came babbling to me like a baby, scared that he'd be caught.'

He threw his oil rag onto the table, stripped off his overalls, chucked them on the floor, and marched out of the office. 'Thanks a lot, Pops, for defending me. Maybe if you spent more time at the mosque than down the pub or screwing that posh bint of yours, you'd have more faith in me.'

The other three watched as he stormed past vehicles in various states of repair and through the concertina doors into the street. When Nikki turned to Ali, his eyes were narrowed. 'You knew, didn't you? You knew Maz had done that?'

Shoulders slumping, Nikki kicked herself for not telling him earlier. 'I'm sorry.' But her apology fell on deaf ears as Ali pushed past her and left the garage. Nikki turned to Mohsin, but he wafted a hand at her. 'Go. Just go. You've done enough damage for one day.'

Chapter 46

The Forster Square arches, despite it being daytime, were as putrid as they had been last time Sajid had visited. Here in this underground burrow of poverty, abuse and decay, the disenfranchised festered in their own decline, away from the eyes of the city. Sajid's sphincter muscle tightened against the barrage of overwhelming emotions: pity, anger and helplessness that confronted him. No one should have to live like this. No one should have to *die* like this. Where Nikki had shown compassion and a certain affinity with the folk who inhabited this dark hole, Ahad's dismissive scorn reverberated through each harsh word and every threatening gesture as he moved through the huddles of people fighting to stay warm and dry against the inclement November weather.

'You! Get the fuck up. Do you recognise this man?' Ahad thrust the photo of Jamie Jacobs under the addict's streaming nose, his lips curled in supercilious distaste, his tone accusatory.

The old man, cataracts making his dilated drugged eyes seem almost alien, stared at the image, shaking his head and twitching as he did so. Sajid wanted to pull Ahad to the side and challenge him. They were more likely to gain information by sweetening the questions with a hot coffee, a fiver or a bag of chips than a glowering glare and cuss words. As Ahad trailed through the crowds,

Saj dropped back behind him, trying to dissociate himself from his boss, shame and anger churning his stomach as he watched Ahad in action. Why exactly had the DI bothered coming here? They wouldn't pick up any leads about Jamie Jacobs using his methods. Surely this wasn't the DI's first foray into the world of the homeless – rough sleepers, self-medicating on whatever drug they could get their hands on and vulnerable to every pimp, dealer and bastard out for their own ends.

More tainted by his boss's attitude than by the stench that engulfed him, Sajid drifted away from Ahad, and wandered deeper into the tunnel, all the while looking for a semi-familiar face, someone whom either he or Nikki had spoken to before. Finally, he found a group of women, sitting on their haunches beside a rusty old tin bin that served as a fireplace. They cackled and mithered at each other like hags round a cauldron, as they fed bits of rubbish to keep the meagre flames alive. Aware that in his Armani suit and mohair overcoat, he didn't present the same approachable, down-to-earth image that Nikki did, Sajid tried his dazzling smile. They looked up as he approached. He recognised one of them from last time he'd been here – Nancy? Or maybe Natalie? No, definitely Nancy.

She tugged on the sleeve of her friend's too thin anorak. 'Ooooh, we got a bit of meat here – not sure he'll be man enough for us, but we can break him in, can't we?'

Sajid's grin widened as the women shot flirtatious glances in his direction and reached out to smooth their mucky hands down his coat. Inside, he cringed, picturing Langley's laughing face when he revealed why his clothes stank of smoke and filth. He only hoped the dry cleaners could work miracles. Squashing the icky thought that he had no idea where those fingers had been, he tried to radiate humour and honesty. 'Well, gorgeous ladies, I'm wondering if you can help me?'

The four women guffawed, and embarked on a competition to see which of them could make the lewdest comments.

'Help you? Hell, I'd do you for free, son.'

'Don't mind her, son, you want an experienced hand.' Amid giggles, the familiar woman, Nancy, made the universal gesture for masturbation whilst wiggling her eyebrows.

Meanwhile, her friend edged closer to him, pursing her mouth in what she probably meant to be a Marilyn Monroe type gesture, but in reality was more gargoyle-like. 'Never mind hand relief, I got the best chops for a blow job.' And she opened her mouth wide, allowing Sajid to see her toothless and ulcerated gums before slapping her lips together in a sloppy sound that made Saj want to retch.

'Now, now ladies.' Saj cringed, yet kept his tone light. 'I'm not after that, I'm after information.'

He waited as they continued their lurid, ribald gestures – hips thrusting, hands pawing, lurid winks and lewd comments, all part of a routine they frequently danced. When their ribaldry faded, he took out the photo of Jamie Jacobs and handed it to Nancy. 'If you can tell me about this lad, there'll be something in it for you.' As the winking and nudging started up again, Saj pulled a fiver from his pocket. 'Now, now ladies, you've had your fun, let's cut the crap.' He waved the note just beyond their grabbing hands. 'I've brought plenty of these to exchange for genuine information.'

Nancy, all trace of mischief replaced by a knowing mercenary glower, snorted. 'A fiver. Just a bloody fiver … you a cheapskate or summat, lad? We're worth more than that. You know what folks say around here, lad – "You don't get owt for nowt!"'

Grin pinned on his lips, Saj shook his head and winked at her. 'Good try, but I'm happy to pay. I'll be fair with you, if you've got decent info on this boy.' He paused and studied the quartet of emaciated wretches as they exchanged glances and nods. They knew something. The way their eyes flicked back to the photo told him that, so he waited, hoping that they'd feel compelled on a promise of a few quid to share their information. What a way to live. It gave the saying 'hand to mouth' a much more poignant meaning. None of these women had come here voluntarily. They'd each have their own heart-breaking tale of their road to destitution – he'd heard many over the years. But now they'd been here so long, the likelihood of them escaping this lifestyle was non-existent. Many salved their consciences by maintaining that they chose to dwell here in the sewers rather than take advantage of the shelters, but Saj was all too aware of the risk of exploitation, coercion and physical violence in some of those places. At least here, in their small friendship groups, there was a modicum of safety.

Hands on hips, Nancy assumed the role of spokesperson for her little group. 'We want your scarf and those posh gloves and the dosh.'

Saj would have preferred to give them cash instead of his scarf and gloves, which cost a hell of a lot more than the amount they stood to gain, but looking at them – emaciated and shivering in the paltry heat from their mini fire, he agreed. 'Fair's fair. Information first, then your reward.'

Nancy shrugged, wiped the snot-covered sleeve of her torn anorak over her face, and grinned. 'Deal.' She looked at her friends, and after receiving a nod from each of them, she began. 'Jamie's a regular here. He's a good lad. Sleeps in a box by us because we don't let the pervs near him. They bandied the poor soul about from pillar to post till he met us. Not seen him for a while.' She turned to her friend. 'You remember when we last saw Jamie?'

'Was the other night. He said he were gonna stir up some shit at the sleep thing in City Park.'

This was news to Sajid. There had been no mention of Jamie being at the sleepout, but he would check it out. 'Did he say why he was going there?'

Nancy shrugged. 'Said he wanted to show up the bastards who'd left him like this. Wanted to make a stir. There was someone there he really hated, and he were gonna make him pay.'

'Did he give a name?'

Again with the shrug. 'Not to me.'

The other women shook their heads and turned back to feed their little heat source with bits of wrappers. That was his dismissal. If they had more information, they weren't prepared to share it right now.

So, sticking to his deal, he handed a fiver to each of them, unwrapped his scarf from his neck and handed the soft angora to the nearest of the three, yanked his gloves off and gave them to a second woman. He was about to turn away, having kept his side of the deal, when he noticed that one of them wore only a summer jacket. She hadn't contributed to the earlier ribald comments, so Saj had paid her scant attention. She was young, barely as old as his niece and although emaciated, her skin hadn't yet developed the unhealthy sallowness that the other women had and her eyes were clearer, although fear-filled. Her skinny body trembled and her gaze darted around, as if seeking any potential threats.

Before he could reconsider, Saj slipped off his coat and handed it to her. Eyes wide, she accepted it, but not without a surreptitious glance to Nancy, as if asking her permission. Saj ignored Nancy and smiled at the younger woman. 'Take it. I think you need it more than I do.'

Unable to meet his eyes, the girl shrugged it on, wrapping it round her frame, sinking into the residual warmth, and darted a fleeting smile at him, before turning back towards the fire. Saj nodded and backed away. He had only taken a couple of steps when a quiet voice reached his ears. 'He's dead, isn't he? That's the only reason any of you lot ever come down here. You only come when someone's dead.'

Saj turned. The girl, dwarfed in his coat, looked at him, eyes filled with an expression Saj couldn't interpret. He nodded, knowing there was no way to sugarcoat it.

A trembling sigh escaped her lips as she wrapped the flapping sleeves of Saj's jacket round her waist. 'It were his old man that did it, then? He told me that his dad were after him and that if he turned up dead one day, it would be him what did it.'

Saj studied the girl's expression. Something else replaced her initial sadness – despair? Anger? This girl didn't fit his expectation of the poor souls who inhabited the arches. She didn't share the drug-twitch of the other women, nor were her eyes glazed. He frowned. 'Thanks – I'll follow up on that. If his dad had anything to do with Jamie's death, then I promise we'll bring him to justice.'

The girl snorted. 'Yeah, so you say. Nobody bothers keeping promises to the likes of them.'

The use of the word 'them' wasn't lost on Sajid. Was it that she was still in denial of her new circumstances? Interesting. 'I do. I keep my promises. I'll come find you when I discover what happened to your friend, and that's a promise.' Sajid paused before pulling a business card from his pocket. 'Here. Take this. You need anything or if you hear any more about Jamie's death, contact me.'

He met her gaze, willing his eyes to express his sincerity. The young woman hesitated, then plucked it from his fingers, stuffing it into her pocket before he had the chance to withdraw his empty hand. 'My name's Sajid. Sajid Malik and if you need help, I know some safe shelters. Shelters that will look after you – not like the ones Nancy and her friends spoke about. These are harder to get into, but I can pull strings.'

She bit her lip and glanced at the other women who were debating how to spend the money Saj had given them. References to Voddy and K told Saj that nourishment wasn't a priority for them, so he took another note from his pocket. 'Get yourself some food. Your friends' idea of nourishment comes in liquid form and I think you could do with a meal.' He hesitated, not wanting to push his luck and scare her away. 'What's your name?'

She glanced round to make sure no one was listening. And when she spoke, it was so softly that Sajid almost missed it. 'Attiya. My name's Attiya.'

Saj smiled and in an equally soft tone said, 'Ring if you need help. I mean it, Attiya. You don't have to be here.'

A voice barked through the arches. 'Malik. We're done here. Time to go and take a long hot shower to get rid of the stench of this cess pit.'

Saj raised a hand to acknowledge he'd heard Ahad, but when he turned back, the girl had slipped into the shadows. Damn! At that moment, Sajid wanted to yell at his boss. There was no call to be so objectionable – so cruel. With a last glance around, Saj walked towards Ahad.

'For fuck's sake, Malik, you've been had big time. Can't believe you gave that little whore your coat. Did she give you some important information?'

As Sajid studied Ahad's narrowed eyes, he made a decision he hoped he wouldn't regret. 'No, they didn't recognise the lad.'

Ahad snorted. 'And still you gave them your coat. You on a promise or something? You heading back later on for a shag?'

Sajid walked past his boss, eager to return to the car and out of the chill air. 'It's called charity, sir. Zakat? You understand the concept of that, don't you?'

Aware that his tone verged on insolence, Sajid kept walking, schooling himself not to say anything else that might come back to bite him on the ass.

Chapter 47

Centenary Square was buzzing and despite the cold nip in the air, the vigil had gathered a good crowd. By the time Nikki and her family arrived, the steps of the town hall were already filled with flowers and lit candles, and she was pleased to note that the small police presence maintained a respectful distance from proceedings. With her scarf rolled several times round her neck and pulled up to obscure the lower part of her face, and a cap angled down over her eyes, Nikki hoped that none of the officers on duty would recognise her. She wasn't ready to confront anyone from work yet, and even coming to this event in such an open and crowded space had been hard for her. Marcus, dressed similarly, had his arm flung lightly over her shoulder, offering his reassurance, whilst giving her the room to extricate herself from him if she needed to. Nikki recognised one officer – lazy sod who she'd crossed swords with on many occasions. She prayed he wouldn't spot her, for he'd more than likely take great delight in ridiculing her. To the dark side, close to the Mirror Pool, Nikki spotted Williams and Anwar and although they would never ridicule her, she wanted to avoid their pity, or worse, their doubt in her ability to recover. Near the In Plaice fish and chip shop she spied a tall man who also, despite being in plain clothes, had the air of a copper about him. It was probably the way he held himself apart from the crowd. She didn't recognise him, but then there were always unfamiliar faces at Trafalgar House.

Sunni pulled at her hand, desperate to make sure he got one of the glow sticks being handed out by those in high-vis jackets. She released him, but kept a watchful eye as he approached the organiser and accepted his neon light before returning to her side. Although the atmosphere was upbeat, with a group of dhol drummers accompanied by a sitar player filling the air with a soft beat, Nikki sensed an underlying tension in the way parents watched over their kids and how the teens seemed to stay in groups.

Charlie and Ruby had wandered off to be with their friends near the front, but content to remain on the periphery of things, Nikki and Marcus held back. Nikki's copper's eyes made regular surveys of the surrounding area. As a police officer, she'd been to many of these peaceful events and was all too aware of how quickly the atmosphere could turn from peace to violence. Eyes scanning the throng, Nikki frowned and tried to see past Marcus. Had that been Amar Akhtar? What the hell was he doing here? She'd have thought he'd rather be down the mosque being ultra-virtuous than supporting a vigil for the victims of honour killings. There he was again, sidling up to some lad she didn't recognise, but then the two men walked away from the crowd and towards the Interchange. He'd probably only used City Park as a meeting spot, not realising there would be a vigil. Still, the knot that had tightened in her stomach when she saw him, relaxed as he disappeared out of sight. It was then she spotted DS Springer loitering near the front of the crowd. Nikki traced the other officer's gaze and saw that she was tracking Amar Akhtar's progress with his friend. When she pushed herself away from the City Hall wall and made to follow them, Nikki frowned. Hadn't Saj told her Springer was always going AWOL? It didn't seem like the other woman to follow the likes of Amar Akhtar without back-up. But then, Springer veered right towards the Mirror Pool and was swallowed in the crowds. Perhaps she was just showing willingness and there for some low-key crowd control. Nikki snorted – if Springer was involved, it would be very low key. She was never one to want to get her hands dirty at the best of times and if Saj was right, her heart wasn't in the game at the minute anyway. Someone nudged her, and she was about to step away, allowing the person space to move in front of her when she recognised Sajid with his partner Langley. She grinned and nudged Saj back before hugging Langley. 'Good to see you both.'

'Yeah, well, it's this sort of event that takes some of the sting from the senseless honour crap that goes on. The bastards who killed Aqsa and Jusveer got caught, so now it's time to remember the victims.'

As Sajid spoke, he focused on something to Nikki's right. She stood on tiptoes and followed his gaze to the group of women on the periphery who were using the opportunity to beg from the crowd. 'Who are they?'

With a shrug, Saj shook his head. 'Just some of the rough sleepers I spoke with under the Forster Square arches earlier. There were four of them, but I can only see three now.' He thrust his gloveless hands into his pockets and shrugged. 'Went down there with the new DI to see if any of them recognised Jamie Jacobs. He was a right dick.'

Head tilted, Nikki smiled. 'Jamie Jacobs?'

'Nah. DI Ahad. It was like he hated them.' Saj's gaze moved over the cluster of figures. 'I saw him earlier hanging out, watching the crowds. No idea why he'd be here. I left him at Trafalgar House and he told me he was working there till late.'

Still watching the begging women, Nikki shrugged. 'He probably needed a change of scenery and thought he'd get a feel for Bradford by coming here.'

Langley nudged him. 'Forget about DI Ahad. What I want to know is if the lass you gave your very expensive winter coat too is here?'

'What? You telling me that not only did Mr Sartorial Elegance go down the arches, he *actually* gave away his Armani coat?' The teasing note in Nikki's voice made Langley laugh.

'He came home minus coat, gloves and scarf to be precise.'

'Shut up, you two. They were freezing down there.' He grinned. 'And they're wearing my scarf – look.'

Two of the women had wrapped his scarf round both their necks as they worked the crowd, but Sajid still wore a frown.

Nikki spotted his concern. 'You okay, Saj?'

'Yeah. Just wanted to be sure that the girl's still okay. She was only young and …' If he'd been going to expand on his worries, he got no opportunity because a magnificent vision in purple and orange approached. 'I wondered if I'd see you and your delightful family here tonight, DS Parekh.'

Nikki grinned at the way Saj's mouth fell open. Truth was, she too was quite overwhelmed by Dr Mallory's fluffy two-bobbled aubergine coloured hat and the brightness of her orange coat. She introduced the psychiatrist to Langley and Sajid, enjoying the way Sajid eyed her flamboyant apparel. If she was being honest, she thought the mauve scarf complete with carrot-orange pompoms was a bit much – but her eccentric dress sense was one reason she liked Mallory.

The metallic shriek of a microphone rent the air and all eyes turned to the steps of City Hall. A slight drizzle peppered the air, and the wind had picked up. Still the mood remained optimistic as a minute's silence began. Before the minute was up though, a dull chanting from near the Wetherspoons pub became audible. Initially, Nikki assumed it was part of the vigil, but when it got louder the words became clearer.

No Honour in Dishonour!

No Honour in Dishonour!

Was she hearing this right? Nikki glanced first at Marcus, then at Saj and Langley, and saw from their shocked faces that she had heard correctly. The three men, all much taller than Nikki, craned their necks to see over the swarm that had gathered behind them. 'What's going on?' Nikki gripped Sunni's hand and jumped up and down, hoping to glimpse her daughters near the steps. All around her, people edged backwards, craning their necks to see what was happening. The wind carried their disquiet through the square. The atmosphere had flipped in an instant.

From nowhere, a series of bangs erupted, and the crowd began to scatter as hysterical screams of 'Bomb!' vied with the threatening 'No Honour in Dishonour!' chants.

'Marcus, we need to find the girls and get the hell out of here.' Nikki was already pushing and shoving through the stream of dark figures towards the town hall, dragging a tearful Sunni behind her. Other people had a similar idea, and they thwarted her progress at every turn. She glanced back, but could no longer see Marcus, so she pushed her way to the side, hoping to escape the crush, skirt it and reach the steps by a less congested route. As she stumbled out of the throng, she couldn't believe what she was seeing. Her heart stopped for a moment, then she thrust Sunni behind her as masked figures, four or five metres apart, dressed in oversized black hoodies, circled the crowd. Each brandished a machete and chanted, whilst corralling the vigil attendees into a huddle at the steps of City Hall.

No Honour in Dishonour!

No Honour in Dishonour!

Eyes fixed on the masked figures that seemed to encircle the entire group of fifty or so people, Nikki edged back into the crowd with her body in front of Sunni's. Her heart hammered and her breath came in short panting gasps. Tears flowed down Sunni's cheeks but one quick glance told her he was physically all right. Then from nowhere, Sunni was snatched from her. Nikki yelled his name as loud as she could, 'Sunni …' and began battling with the figure who had taken her son before realising it was Marcus.

No Honour in Dishonour!

No Honour in Dishonour!

211

'I have him, Nik. Come on, Saj and Langley have the girls. Let's get into the middle where it's safer. Saj says back-up is en route.'

Fingers latched onto the hem of Marcus's jacket, Nikki allowed him to bulldoze a path for them to the centre of the crowd and that was when things got really bad …

Chapter 48

As soon as the chanting had started, Sajid had got his phone out. Two groups with conflicting ideologies converging in City Park would require back-up. As he spoke, he scoured the crowds, absorbing as much as he could, checking out the positions of the uniformed officers in relation to the aggressors. The figures in black continued their approach like a skilfully coordinated SWAT team. Their taunting, hateful chants filled the air, replacing the dhol and sitar strains.

The emaciated girl he'd given his coat to lurked on the periphery of the hoards. Her eyes darted around and even in the half-illuminated park her fear was palpable. She hunkered further into his coat, pulling the collar up round her face, and edged away from the cornered crowd nearer to the far side of City Hall. As she sidled away, she cast furtive glances towards the dark forms that pushed closer to the flock of people.

No Honour in Dishonour!
No Honour in Dishonour!

Saj released a long breath as she skirted the building, then gasped as a vast form moved in front of her and grabbed her shoulders. He thrust through the streams of people towards her, but had only taken two steps when she raised a knee and aimed a well-placed hit to her captor's groin before thrusting him away and darting off. Now that she was safe, Saj focused on his own situation. Langley grabbed his arm and pointed at Charlie and Ruby, who were trying to reach them. He glanced around and saw Nikki and Sunni pushing their way through the crowd in the opposite direction.

No Honour in Dishonour!

No Honour in Dishonour!

Everything had happened in less than a couple of minutes as emotions heightened by adrenalin and fear splintered the celebratory atmosphere. In the distance, sirens blared as they approached, but Sajid had seen the machetes and knew that they could still do a lot of damage before his colleagues arrived. Anwar and Williams, extendable batons at the ready, had placed themselves between two masked forms and the vigil attendees. Other uniformed officers moved to flank the machete wielders and Sajid focused on making sure he reached Nikki's girls. They were his family, and neither he nor Langley would let anything happen to them.

No Honour in Dishonour!

No Honour in Dishonour!

Ruby threw herself into Langley's arms and Charlie quirked an eyebrow at him, her fear betrayed only by her pallor and the way her eyes darted around the crowds. 'Oh, you're here, Saj. Those bastards could have macheted me and the Rubster before you got here.'

Saj tried to work out a plan to reunite the girls with their parents and Sunni. That was when he saw Nikki dwarfed by three dark forms towering over her, one with his machete raised.

No Honour in Dishonour!

No Honour in Dishonour!

214

Chapter 49

The scarf tightened round Nikki's neck, forcing her to release her hold on Marcus's jacket. Desperate fingers clawed at the wool, her eyes bulging as the pressure against her throat intensified, constricting her air flow and making her dizzy. Coldness flooded her body, and she visualised herself as a youngster, scrabbling at the rope cutting into her skin, her father's eyes wild and blazing as he yanked her backwards, enjoying her ever weaker gasps as the breath left her lungs and her throat closed over. She was right back there, only this time it was an unknown masked assailant, not her father. All around her people screamed, sirens blared, and the crowd surged forward and consumed Marcus and Sunni. At least they'd escaped.

She wasn't a child anymore though, so she wrenched her body sideways, hoping to loosen her attacker's grip, but he held firm. Instead of pulling against him, Nikki lunged backwards, satisfied to hear the clunk of her skull on his chin and a surprised yelp leave his masked face. His hands loosened from her scarf and she gulped in air, but his grip tightened and he jerked her towards his body. Using the momentum, Nikki spun on her heel, thrusting her elbow into his stomach with the same anger she saw reflected in his eyes. Before she could repeat her attack, he pushed her aside, loosening his hold on the scarf. Losing her balance, Nikki toppled sideways, her head clattering onto the concrete. What little breath remained poofed from her lungs as she lay there, stunned, looking up into her attacker's eyes.

Beside him stood two figures, each carrying machetes. One was taller and broader, whilst the other was of a slighter stature. Was that one a woman? Nikki had no time to plan, for the larger man raised his booted foot and slammed it into her side. The force of the impact threw Nikki into the air sending a spiral of white heat through her ribs and up into her shoulders before she reconnected with the ground, her shoulder slamming onto the hard surface. She tried to roll into a ball, but again the boot connected with her body and both her attackers were upon her. All she could do was lift her arms over her head to protect it, although the ringing in her ears and her double vision told her she was injured. As the barrage of violence unfolded, her attackers' taunting chant became more frenzied.

No Honour in Dishonour!

No Honour in Dishonour!

Someone grabbed her hands and yanked them behind her, twisting her wrists. Pain burned across her shoulders, radiating down to her fingers, and she yelled. She couldn't take much more of this. Testosterone, anger and adrenalin fuelled these men, and her body was too fragile. They wouldn't stop till she was dead. Someone seized her ponytail and used it to drag her further away from the crowd. Nikki attempted to dig her heels in, forcing her body to become an uncooperative deadweight. But there was nothing of her. She'd lost muscle mass over the last few weeks, and her passive resistance was futile. Her assailant continued dragging her, and her scalp burned – but then every inch of her body also throbbed. As dizziness washed over her, she was ready to pass out.

No Honour in Dishonour!

No Honour in Dishonour!

She had one last chance – she reached up and dug her finger-nails into her attacker's wrist. Searching for skin, she felt only the leather of his gloves, but she persevered, scraping the cuff of the glove down till she connected with his flesh. Wishing her nails were longer, she pressed them into his fleshy wrist and dragged them down. When they found her body, Sajid and the team would have a chance at identifying this big bastard from the DNA under her fingernails.

No Honour in Dishonour!

No Honour in Dishonour!

Releasing her ponytail, the man cursed, then slapped her across the face before dropping her to the ground. Nearby, Nikki could see the Mirror Pool. They'd only moved about fifteen yards from the crowd gathered at City Hall, yet in the chaos nobody was aware of what was happening to her. He placed one heavy foot on her belly, pressing down hard, bringing acid to Nikki's throat as the contents of her stomach forced their way upwards. All around them that ominous chanting continued – loud and abrasive.

No Honour in Dishonour!

No Honour in Dishonour!

The sirens stopped and yells of 'Police – stop!' echoed through the park.

The man took his machete from the belt around his waist and tucked the tip under her chin. 'Bitch pig. You need to learn your fucking place.'

No Honour in Dishonour!

No Honour in Dishonour!

A dribble of blood oozed round the blade and rolled down Nikki's neck, soaking into her scarf. This was it then. This was the end for her. One quick slice across her throat and she'd bleed out in seconds. Images of her kids and Marcus floated into her mind, and her heart contracted as tears poured from her eyes. They'd be okay – better without her, in fact. They all would. Saj and Langley would be their support system. Nikki realised she was repeating the same mantra she'd tried to convince herself of months ago when she'd considered taking her own life, and anger flooded her. She'd fought back from the brink of suicide. She'd got help, she'd done it for her family and now this fucking bastard who'd invaded a peaceful vigil was going to take her life. No way. No fucking way.

No Honour in Dishonour!
No Honour in Dishonour!

From somewhere, Nikki found the energy and focused every ounce of it in her leg. He stood above her, straddling her, unable to hide his sneer behind his mask and Nikki allowed her eyes to flutter, her upper body to go limp and then with everything she possessed she lifted her knee and rammed it as hard as she could into his balls.

His screech made her smile. *Serves him right. Serves him fucking right.* Then he landed half on top of her, his knee landing on her chest as he tried to control the pain in his groin. *Good luck with that mate*, thought Nikki, as she attempted to roll to her side to escape his weight. Again, dizziness flooded her and this time she *was* going to pass out, but before she did, a slash singed down her cheek followed by warm liquid.

'Take that, you little bitch. Take that.'

Just before she passed out, Nikki saw two figures hefting her attacker to his feet and scurrying away towards Great Horton Road.

218

Chapter 50

The Honourable Fixer

Who would believe the thrill of seeing the results of your endeavours pan out so beautifully right before your eyes? It's so much fun to be here in the chaos, able to savour it in all its glory. When AntiVigilVirgil first requested my assistance to disrupt the Bradford vigil, I expected it to be a bit of a damp squib. Not that I'm complaining. Why would I? In addition to receiving my Bitcoin, seeing my plan executed so successfully is a job well done.

What really makes this special though is being here in person to taste the cordite from the flashbangs exploding, to hear the chants in stereophonic and witness the terror etched on everyone's faces. With my scarf pulled up over my mouth, nobody can see my grin as I meander through the screeching crowd. Beautiful, absolutely beautiful. My team are flawless in their execution – carrying out my directions exactly as I imparted them to the Headhunter.

No Honour in Dishonour!
No Honour in Dishonour!

What a fabulous little chant – threatening and rhythmic in equal measure. Something's going on near the Mirror Pool and as I edge my way closer, a bubble of excitement lightens my

219

steps. Never in my wildest dreams could I have anticipated my satisfaction at seeing my team go off-script. Perhaps if it hadn't been DS Nikita Parekh at the centre of the ad-libbing, I would have been angry, but in this particular instance I am prepared to let it slide. Her presence could cause me problems, so making sure she's got other things to think about can only work in my favour. It's not that I dislike her. It's that I won't make the mistake of underestimating her. I know just how clever she is and her imminent return to work could make things harder. Best she's dealt with now, before she can do any real damage.

She's on the floor, and one of my protégés is laying into her. I inch nearer, trying to look inconspicuous as I hear running feet approaching from behind. There's blood dripping onto the concrete and my minion– not sure which one it is, but I'll ask the Headhunter and pay the man a bonus for this – lifts his machete. I inhale and absorb the intensity of the rage and bloodlust, anticipating a grand finale and – here it is – a flick of the wrist and DS Nikki Parekh will have another scar to remind her of her troubled present as well as her tortured past.

For a moment I think he's going to be caught, but the other groupies grab his arm and drag him away as the police arrive. I keep my distance – only a concerned observer, as the Eyes escape into the darkness of the city. She's lying there … motionless. Her little boy flings himself at her, tears streaming down his face but, just in time, his dad grabs him. 'Mummy, Mummy, wake up.'

Oh my God, but this is so much better than watching telly. His dad, an enormous brute of a man, catches him and hoists the child into his arms whilst the paramedics work on her. With increased police activity all around City Park, I back away. The vigil has been well and truly disrupted and AntiVigilVirgil and his friend's message has been delivered. Which means ker-ching, ker-ching, ker-ching for me! As I head back to my vehicle, I chant under my breath.

No Honour in Dishonour!

No Honour in Dishonour!

It's quite a catchy little mantra. Not that I necessarily believe it – but hey – as someone famous once said, 'You gotta do what you gotta do.'

Chapter 51

Maz enjoyed the company of the radiator as it creaked and groaned, spewing heat into the bedroom he considered to be little more than a cell. It was dark, and he'd no idea how much time had elapsed, but he sensed it was approaching midnight – OD time.

Feverish shivers rattled through his body despite the fever, and dull throbbing pain escalated to stabbing agony at the slightest movement. He'd suffered enough – more than enough. Any expectation of his father finding him had diminished as the night pressed in on him and with all hope shrinking, the inevitable resolution to his captivity approached. There was no way they'd leave him alive. No way! He knew too much, which was why they'd grabbed him in the first place. That and the fact that he was all set to confide in his dad. He should have kept his mouth shut about his doubts. If only he'd been stronger, less gullible. His dad always told him never to be a sheep – to think for himself. Yet what had he done? Gone and got himself embroiled with the Eyes, and there was no way out.

Trying to ignore his discomfort, he inched to the edge of the torn, stinking mattress and fumbled about under it. The tablets were there, thank God. Tears streaming unheeded down his cheeks, he grabbed a bottle of water from the bedside cabinet and with trembling fingers, he eventually managed to turn the cap.

Flinging a couple of pills into his mouth, he gulped and swallowed. Then another two – and another – and another. He was so caught up in the rhythm of overdosing that he registered neither the footsteps thundering upstairs nor the sound of the bedroom door being thrust open.

Two figures, panting like the hounds of death were after them, stood in the doorway. Maz still had a handful of pills, and their presence had foiled his plans. Surely they'd stop him if they spotted him knocking back the meds with gulps of Lidl's finest water. He moved his hand so that it was hidden under the manky sheet and waited, eyes half closed as he pretended to be asleep. Shit, this wasn't good!

They'd not even glanced in his direction yet, but they would. He could be sure of that. It was a moment before he realised that they no longer wore masks. It took a further second to register the tears rolling down her cheeks and the way they slammed the door shut behind them before locking it from inside and a final moment for him to realise that he recognised them.

'What we gonna do, Chelle?' Chas Choudry's voice shook as he paced in front of the bed, running his fingers through his cropped hair as he did so.

Slumped on the floor, cross-legged, Michelle, hands covering her face, sobbed. 'Fucked if I know. Why did I listen to you, Chas? They're gonna kill us. He told us they would. What'll we do?'

Maz strained to hear their words. As he thought about it, he realised, they were the same build as his anonymous captors. The third captor – the one who cleaned his wounds – wasn't here. Where was he? Was he already dead? Had his dad found him and killed him? He hoped so, because that would mean his dad was on his way. Now he wished he hadn't taken those pills. He was woozy, and his stomach churned. Had he swallowed too many? Was he going to die just when his dad was about to rescue him?

It was hard to focus, and he knew he really had to. It looked like Chas and Michelle had kidnapped him. Why the hell would they do that? They were supposed to have his back. He knew why, though. They didn't want to be in bother for all the crap they'd done – and they would be. Maz saw that now. They'd done far worse things than him and they didn't want to be punished, didn't want to go to prison – plus they liked the dosh. Not many jobs in Bradford that paid as well as the Eyes. They ignored him, more interested in blaming each other. Maz grinned weakly. They were in bother now and it served them right.

Chas joined Michelle on the threadbare carpet, their eyes fixed on the locked door. Maz almost felt sorry for them – almost, but not quite. The bastards had taken his ear off and beaten him to a pulp. They deserved everything that was coming to them – every damn thing. And with a small smile on his lips, Maz drifted into unconsciousness.

Chapter 52

**THE ONE WITH THE VIGIL AND THE MACHETE GANG
POSTED BY BFDLASS#WWWTS NOVEMBER 26TH 23:08**

> *Picture this – a peaceful vigil in City Park. Lit candles on the steps of City Hall, kids with neon glow lights, people playing dhols and sitars. The crowd are peaceful – families of all ethnicities, religions, ages, all gathered together to show their collective support for the families of Aqsa Mahmood and Jusveer Khatri. All gathered together to express their condemnation of so-called honour killings. All gathered together in unity and peace.*
>
> ### *Then, what do we see?*
>
> *Dark cowardly figures in balaclavas carrying machetes surrounding the vigil*
>
> ### *#WhatsWrongWithThisShit?*
> ### *What do we hear?*

Views: 223 Shares: 93

COMMENTS:

Karryann3: *OMG! Can't believe this! I'll never be allowed out again. Who was hurt? #WhatsWrongWithThisShit?*

> **JakeK4292:** *@Karryann3.You shouldn't be allowed out without summat over your head – like them Darth Vaders you see all round town LMAO* 😄😄😄

Karryann3: *@JakeK4292 Get a life AH*

> **JakeK4292:** *Chillax bitch. Can't take a joke, eh?* 😛

ZainK: *Wanker! @JakeK4292 It was scary you know. All that freaky chanting and the machetes and all. I'm grounded till I'm 40! It was a Five-O that got hurt. She looked dead to me. #WhatsWrongWithThisShit?*

Jazzygirl3: *FS! B*****ds. Why do they do this shit? #WhatsWrongWithThisShit?*

MH616: *The police officer's ok – well I think she is? #feeling-scared #WhatsWrongWithThisShit?*

LazyJayz04: *She's a Paki – Nikki Parekh – in't her daughter at our school? She's a half-caste #servesherright #stickwithyourownkind*

226

MayLee: @LazyJayz04 You're one sick F****R You racist AH.

Jazzygirl3: It's all gone to fuck! #NoonesSafe #WhatsWrongWithThisShit

ILuvCurry: @Jazzygirl3: IK 2 FS! #WhatsWrongWithThisShit?

27TH NOVEMBER

Chapter 53

Half past three in the morning and it had finally stopped raining. Nikki wasn't bothered either way – she wasn't going anywhere, not now she was home. It had been touch and go whether BRI would release her, but a combination of her fierce insistence that she was fine and Marcus's promise to watch out for concussion had worn the harried doctors down. She'd downplayed the ache in her ribs – two broken – but neither had pierced her lungs, so she could live with the throbbing and the restricted movement for a few days. She'd managed before, hadn't she? A black eye and a swollen, but unbroken nose made her face tender but, the bruises under her clothes were the worst. Her breast looked quite colourful and Nikki fully expected it to host a rainbow hue by lunchtime.

The events of the previous night had not only shocked her, they had angered her, and she couldn't shake the outrage that mangled her muscles into tense knots of barely contained energy. She teetered on the edge. Not like before – not a suicidal edge, more like a raging fire bolt that needed to be expunged. It was that hyper-anxiety that stole sleep from her. That and the throbbing reminding her that, only a few hours earlier, she'd taken a massive beating. She hadn't looked at the wound on her cheek yet. It had been deep and would scar her. Her fingers traced the dressing, her eyes flashing. Another mark on her body caused by a violent man. When would this sort of crap stop happening to women?

She stood by her bedroom window, the curtains parted only a crack so as not to wake Marcus. Moonlight and the white glow from the streetlights below, her only illumination. She didn't know how long she'd been standing there, in her shorty pyjamas. In fact, she'd no recollection of changing from her blood-soaked clothes, nor of making the epic traipse upstairs to bed. The last thing she remembered was lying on the couch downstairs, dizziness washing over her and a brass band playing inside her skull. She'd closed her eyes to block out all the talking because, despite her discomfort, she had to think. She was certain of something – she was ready to return to work. Not at that precise moment, of course. She'd taken a physical beating, but mentally – she was raring to go. This was *her* city, and the crap that was happening had to stop. It had gone too damn far. This wasn't the Bradford she wanted her kids to grow up in. Bradford was better than this – stronger than this – more caring than this. However, she was unsure how to broach the subject with Marcus.

Behind her, Marcus, mouth open, one arm flung over as if seeking out her body to spoon, snored. Movement in the street interrupted her recollections of how much his snoring annoyed her – the way she'd teased him, the time she'd recorded it as evidence. The flash of blue lights in the road outside alerted Nikki to the arrival of police cars. She pressed her forehead against the glass, savouring its coolness and counted them; not one, but three of them pulled to a halt outside her house. What the hell was going on?

As officers got out, more vehicles arrived, lights flashing, sirens off and double parked beside the others. Something big was happening, and an unfamiliar stirring of annoyance gripped her. Why had no one told her something was going down on her turf? Was this to do with the vigil? Her lips tightened. If someone on her street was responsible for the violence in City Park, then she wanted to be involved in bringing them to justice. There was no place here for terrorist activity. As she observed, the officers congregated around a tall, plain-clothes officer who looked familiar. Her interest was piqued, and it had been a long while since she'd felt this degree of engagement. True, the machete killings had engaged her heart, but combined with the insidious attack on the vigil, this had become personal!

A dark figure darted from next door's gate and approached the familiar officer. Nikki sighed. *What's Haqib up to?* Couldn't he just keep his daft head down for one bloody minute? Whatever the discussion was about, it involved expressive gestures fuelled by suppressed anger. *Oh, Haqib!* Once Nikki might have suspected her nephew of being caught up in gang-related crap like many other disenfranchised youngsters, but he'd changed. He wasn't the silly, petty drug dealer he had once been. His father being imprisoned, and losing his grandma had sobered him up. Haqib was different nowadays, which was why it surprised her that he was challenging a police officer. She was on the point of turning away to get dressed when the detective grabbed her nephew's arm, twirled him round, and jerked it up towards his shoulder blade before pushing him up against a squad car. What the hell? He'd over stretched. No way was this acceptable behaviour for a police officer.

Without thinking, Nikki spun from the window and hurtled downstairs, pausing only to shove her feet into Charlie's trainers before careering out the front door into the frigid night air. Cheeks burning, adrenalin making her immune to the cold, Nikki stormed up to the man who was handcuffing Haqib's arms behind his back and grabbed his shoulder. 'Leave him alone. He's unarmed, and he didn't lay a finger on you, so get those fucking cuffs off him. Now.'

The tall detective turned, a sneer marring his handsome face. 'Well, well, well, what do we have here? You this scrote's mum, are you? Looks like you've been banged about a bit.' It was only when his eyes raked over her that Nikki remembered she wore only a pair of shorts and a vest top that left little to the imagination. Chin jutting, Nikki forced her arms to remain by her side, determined not to give the pillock the satisfaction of covering her chest. With a glare, she all but spat her next words at him. 'Name and rank. Right now!'

Aware that she was attracting the attention of the other officers, Nikki refused to avert her eyes. Still, she saw Haqib's grin and heard his mumbled, 'Go, Auntie Nik.'

The officer's smirk widened. 'Well, *Auntie Nik*, perhaps you should move your arse out of my way before I cuff you too.'

Nikki gawped. It had been a long time since she'd witnessed such provocative behaviour from a detective. She'd hoped this sort of copper was long gone, but it seemed not. With her feet planted right in front of him, she stepped closer, maintaining eye contact. Just as she opened her mouth to vent her anger, a not-so-subtle throat clearing made her glance behind. DCs Williams and Anwar, worried frowns on their faces, approached and Anwar spoke to the man. 'DI Ahad, this is DS Nikki Parekh, she's …'

Ahad's eyebrow quirked. 'Aw yes. I've heard all about you, DS Nikita Parekh.' His drawl was full of the sarcasm that flashed in his eyes and Nikki's hand itched to slap him across his face, but he wasn't worth risking her job over. Instead, she forced a smirk to her lips. This sort of bullying only worked if you let it!

Unfazed by her lack of response, Ahad winked at her. 'Not satisfied with contaminating a crime scene, you appear to want to fuck up my arrest too?'

He stepped closer to her, using his bulk to intimidate her, but Nikki had taken enough intimidation for one night and stood her ground. 'Back off and release my nephew, before I get on the phone to DCS Clarke.'

Anger churned in Nikki's stomach, and after the events of the previous evening, she was in no mood to play nice. She was about to blast him with a few home truths when Marcus appeared and wrapped a duvet round her. This small intervention was enough to ground her, and in icy tones, she repeated her earlier request. 'Release my nephew.'

With a careless wave of the hand, Ahad indicated that Anwar should release Haqib. He then looked at Williams. 'Come on, detective. We've got nasty little men to arrest. I'll catch up with this one later.'

The urge to retaliate flooded Nikki as she moved closer to Anwar as the younger detective released Haqib. 'What's going on here, Anwar? Who is he arresting?'

However, her question was pointless as Ahad marched across the street flanked by four uniformed police and Williams and pounded on Fareena Mushtaq's door. Barely giving the family the chance to respond, Ahad hammered again, this time louder and longer. Lights flicked on in the front upstairs bedrooms and within moments, Mr Mushtaq had opened the door, only to be brushed aside as Ahad and his entourage entered.

'Is this about the vigil, Anwar?'

Farah Anwar shook her head as the Mushtaqs' door slammed shut. 'Nope. It's about a call that came in from the Forced Marriage Unit earlier on today. One of the Mushtaq sisters has gone missing after reporting her family for attempting to force her to marry someone from Pakistan.'

Nikki turned to Haqib, who, with Marcus, was listening to the exchange. The lad's reaction was instantaneous. 'You know about this, Haqib?'

As her nephew shuffled his feet and avoided meeting her gaze, Nikki waited. Haqib couldn't stand the silent treatment and always caved before either Charlie or Ruby. Exhaling, he thrust his hands into his jeans. 'It'll be about Attiya. Fareena's middle sister. She's gone AWOL. The Forced Marriage officers spoke to her about it yesterday at school.'

Nikki frowned. 'So, if there was cause for concern about Attiya's whereabouts nearly twelve hours ago, why has it taken Ahad till now to respond?'

Anwar's inelegant snort made Nikki smile. She enjoyed working with the younger woman and was well aware that Farah Anwar was a straight shooter. 'Like to share?'

'Too right I do. We should've been here at teatime, but that ...' She bit her lip, her eyes flashing. 'I mean, erm, DI Ahad suggested that a night-time sweep would ...' She cleared her throat before continuing, 'I quote, "blow more smoke up their asses and get the bastards to talk".'

'Wow.' Nikki could think of nothing else to say. She wouldn't have dealt with it like that. If the FMU called in for an assist from her team, then they acted pronto. Particularly if the safety of someone was in doubt. These types of delaying tactics were, in her opinion, irresponsible and had the potential to result in deadly consequences.

The Mushtaqs' door opened. Mr Mushtaq, his unkempt beard the only sign that he'd recently wakened, flanked by two officers, was ushered down the steps and to the nearest squad car. Seconds later, the Mushtaq brothers and the brother-in-law were also escorted and deposited in separate vehicles. As they drove into the night, the figures of three women, each wearing niqab, huddled in the doorway.

This was unacceptable. Whether the Mushtaq men were guilty or not, this wasn't how things should be done. 'Did Ahad give any other instructions, Farah? Did he direct uniforms to look for her, issue a BOLO, talk to any of her friends?'

Face flushed, Anwar shook her head. 'No, he didn't. I suggested asking DCI Hegley for more resources or even to divert this investigation to another team. We've got so much on at the minute with the machete deaths and now the vigil stuff. DC Williams and I thought a different unit should deal with this, but he refused.'

'What about Saj? What were his thoughts?'

'He doesn't know.' Anwar scowled. 'We were on direct orders not to involve DC Malik in this.'

Nikki glanced at Marcus, whose smile told her he was on the same wavelength. 'It's time for you to go back to work, Nik. You can't let this Ahad bloke fuck things up.'

Grinning, she moved into his arms and with a wave to Anwar and Haqib, she and Marcus went indoors. 'First thing in the morning …'

Marcus looked at his watch. 'In about three hours, that is …'

'Yep, then … I'll phone Mallory for an emergency appointment and force her to sign me fit for work.'

'Eh, Nik …' Marcus's tone was thoughtful. 'Don't you think she might have reservations. I mean, apart from anything, it was only a few hours ago that she witnessed your attack, and, well – your injuries aren't exactly hidden, are they?'

Nikki snorted. 'Shit, Marcus, the fact that I fought the bastard off is proof that the old Nikki is back. Bring. It. On.'

Chapter 54

Without warning, the door crashed open, reverberating as it hit the wall. The clatter shattered the silence of the mouldy bedroom and was accompanied by screams and the hustle of bodies skirmishing. Maz wakened, his head still groggy from the pills he'd taken earlier. Through a fog, Maz tried to make sense of the scene unfolding before him. He blinked, then blinked again, squinting at the figures who'd burst into the room but everything was blurry and happening in slow motion. Initially, he'd thought he was back home, his mum wakening him for work, but that wasn't right. His bedroom might stink of old socks sometimes, but it never smelled as bad as this. His eyes flickered as he tried to get his bearings to ground himself.

He tried to prop himself up so he could call out, but his throat was dry and even after a few gritty swallows, he only managed a faint squeak. He squished his eyes shut, held them closed for a second, then opened them. If he could just … but then his vision cleared. Three dark figures, their faces covered and machetes in their hands, laughed and whooped as they knocked the paltry furniture to the floor. One grabbed Michelle by the hair and dragged her screaming across the carpet. The figure responded to Michelle's squeals by yelling something, but Maz couldn't decipher the words. Then the tallest lifted his machete high and glowered at the other two. 'It's time. Let's do this!'

The others followed suit, each raising the arms which held their weapons. Maz realised that a masked figure stood over him next to the bed where he lay, and as he looked into the hooded figure's eyes, he knew he would never see his parents again.

The tall one, voice hoarse and high-pitched, grunted and glared at Chas Choudry, who cowered on the floor. The sudden stench that consumed the room told Maz that Choudry had evacuated his bowels. Michelle's squeals faded to anguished sobs as she accepted her fate. Time slowed and, refusing to show weakness, Maz stared at the man who held his life in his hands.

'After three!' The yell was coarse and wavery, as if the antici-pation of bringing those machetes down was too much to bear. 'One … Two …'

Chapter 55

The Honourable Fixer

Who'd guess that merely disrupting a vigil would result in more clients than all the previous fix-its put together. Seems there's an appetite for subtler ways of getting a message across. The dark web's been buzzing like crazy. My services have never been so popular. It's not a problem, I'm happy to meet market demand and I can skim off more of the profits this way. I've drawn the attention of several criminal enterprises and I need planning time to work out how to cope with the increased desire for my services. I'm only one person after all, and the beauty of my operation has always been my anonymity. My business model requires me to keep layers of separation between myself, the Headhunter and the Eyes. Of course, I have background information on all my minions, and that makes me efficient in sanctioning their punishments. Shame I'll be losing two, so will also need to think about recruitment. It's hard to find good people.

Besides, clients don't want to know who's filtering through their filth. They don't want to put a face to the person solving their problems. However, they are mistaken in their assumption that if *they* can't identify *me*, I can't identify *them*. Still, it is flattering that some of the terrorist cells operating in the UK have identified a niche for my particular brand of activity. It's not only terrorists though – trafficking and paedophile rings have struggled to infiltrate my encryptions to find out more about me, but I've blocked them every time. And each time they've sought to breach my security they've revealed a bit more about themselves. All of which I've stored safely. Sometimes I feel like a hibernating squirrel storing away nuggets of information in preparation for the lean days.

The downside of joining forces with any of these organisations is that they'd expect a bigger stake in my business. No more anonymity, no more picking and choosing, no more retiring on my own terms. So, my strategy is to keep them hooked – keep them onside whilst blocking each of their devious attempts to infiltrate my security and learn my true identity. It would be much easier to just give them a wide berth and not engage with them, but I'm a pragmatist. Every iota of intelligence I garner now is knowledge I can cash in if the need arises. Not that I anticipate that any of them are smart enough to catch me out – or at least not before I've skipped the country leaving a tangled web of false leads to track. Not Nikita Parekh and her little band of merry detectives. Not Ali Khan and his super thugs. Not any of the big government acronyms – no one. Not a sodding one of them can catch me.

Chapter 56

Maz had never been a devout Muslim, and had stopped going to mosque school yet, during the masked attacker's countdown, the words of long forgotten Dua sprung to his lips. He closed his eyes, raised his palms upwards in supplication, and prayed as he waited for the machete to strike.

He was so focused on making peace with Allah that the change of atmosphere didn't immediately register. Then, hearing the thump of a body falling to the floor and a yelp like a wounded animal, his eyes shot open and a rush of relief swept over him because his prayers had been answered. The room was in chaos, filled with harsh-voiced men issuing orders in Urdu and English. Maz strained to identify the newcomers, but like the previous three, they wore balaclavas, but instead of knives, they carried guns. Heart pounding, Maz wondered if he'd been rescued from one fate only to face another deadlier one, and he cursed his mangled leg and the residual wooziness that made his movements clumsy.

He wanted to yell out and ask the gunmen to name themselves, but he was too scared to draw their attention. Four of them jabbed their guns into the stomachs of the first attackers, indicating they should lie down on the stinking floor. Not so brave now, they whimpered like babies on the floor, hands behind their backs. When their masks were snatched off, Maz strained to get into a position so he could identify them, but before he could do so, one of them ran to his side, whipped off his mask, and gathered his broken son into his arms.

His dad had found him. He was glad he hadn't swallowed the rest of the drugs. Tears seeped from his eyelids, but he didn't care. He was safe now.

'Dad!' Maz's shaking fingers traced his father's face. A face he'd thought he'd never see again. 'I knew you'd come. I knew you would.'

Ali, with a gentleness that was at odds with his huge frame and usual manner, pulled Maz to him, his familiar scent cocooning him like a safety blanket allowing him to release the tears and fear he'd struggled to keep in check during his captivity. It seemed like he wept forever, but when Maz finally stopped and looked round, he realised it could only have been a short time, for his dad's friends were still tying up Michelle, Chas and the three attackers. 'Let me see them. I need to see the people who were going to kill me.'

Ali helped his son swivel into a sitting position on the edge of the bed and, one by one, his men, still masked, dragged Maz's oppressors over.

First up were Michelle and Chas Choudry. Neither was capable of protest or even coherent sentences. 'Those two brought me here. That's Michelle Glass and the other one's Chas Choudry.'

Ali nodded. 'We followed them, but we lost them in the vigil's chaos. That's why we were late reaching you.'

A lot had happened whilst Maz had been held captive, but he was too tired and sore to hear the story. 'They attacked me with machetes when I was on my way home from work.' He cast feverish eyes in his dad's direction. 'I wanted to talk to you, Dad … I need to …'

Ali placed a hand on his son's shoulder. 'I know all about the vinegar attack, Maz. We'll discuss that later. Just remember that although you did an awful thing, I'm on your side. I love you. We'll work through that together.'

Maz could only nod, so grateful for parents like his. He didn't deserve them. He really didn't. He'd done bad things so he could afford a pair of overpriced trainers. He didn't deserve their support. He looked at the whimpering figures on the floor. Choudry stank of shit and Michelle Glass was doing her best to edge away from him. Fear and trembling lips replaced the fervour she'd displayed when she attacked him. A lump formed in his throat as the memory of what they'd done to him hit home. He'd never have his ear back and who knew what other damage they'd inflicted on his body. A rotten stench rose from his fetid flesh, and he flashed her a look of hatred. 'She cut off my ear, and he kept slashing me and kicking me and …'

Maz could not continue. His adrenalin had ebbed and all he wanted was to go home. But Haris, his dad's right-hand man, was dragging another unmasked figure forward. Maz gasped. 'You?' He frowned. 'You were going to kill me, Amar? How far would you go for the Eyes? You'd kill for them? Did you …?' His words trailed away because the idea that Amar Akhtar might be responsible for at least some of the machete killings didn't seem so outlandish anymore.

Amar's chin jerked up and his lips curled. 'You're such a dick, Maz. No balls. That's your trouble – Daddy's little good boy, Mummy's little wimp. Course I was going to kill you … and what's more I'd have enjo—'

He didn't get to finish the sentence as Haris's steel-capped boot connected with his shin, sending him crashing into the wall. Instead of howling in pain, Amar just laughed – a hysterical eerie cry that reverberated round the room, making the wound where Maz's ear had once been smart. Haris planted a forceful fist on Amar's temple, and the hateful noise stopped abruptly as Amar's eyes rolled back in his head and he collapsed.

Haris lugged the other men forward. In contrast to Amar's almost manic reaction, these two were subdued, their eyes downcast, their faces drained of all colour. They couldn't have looked further from killers if they'd tried. Maz recognised them and pointed to the smaller figure on the right. 'That one's Taj Jhuti. Molly Cropper were his girlfriend. Shit, man. What the hell are you doing joining the Eyes? You were going to kill us?'

Taj's only response was a numb head shake. Haris jerked the lad's head up for Maz to see his face, but there was nothing there. His eyes were blank, as if he was unaware of his whereabouts. Maz couldn't understand it. If he'd made a list of possible Eyes, Taj Jhuti would have been behind even Haqib Parekh, and that was saying something. Maz wondered why Taj hadn't steered clear of them after what had happened to Molly. He turned to his old man. 'They must have something on him, Dad. No way would Taj have done this voluntarily. Not after what I did to Molly.'

'Maybe, maybe not.' Ali paused. 'I'd never have had you down for that sort of stunt either, kiddo. Sometimes kids just do awful stuff without thinking of the consequences. Parekh says it's to do with a part of your brain not being fully developed – she might have a point.' He sighed. 'Tell me who this last guy is and we can head up to BRI.'

Maz frowned. The last lad must have struggled with his dad's men, as his right eye was swollen shut and his lip was cracked. It took him a moment to recognise him. 'That tosser calls himself Mally. He's been hanging around the garage, but he's older than me – Mohsin sometimes works on his car for nowt.'

Pausing, Maz looked at his dad. 'What's going to happen to them? What're you gonna do with them?'

With a shrug, Ali hefted his son to his feet, putting one arm round his shoulder and gesturing for one of his men to take the other side. 'Haris will finish up here and later I'll give Parekh the heads-up. Come on, let's get you seen to. Your mum's waiting.'

Chapter 57

Saj couldn't sleep. His nerves jangled and the after-effects of the adrenalin rush that had overtaken as the vigil unfolded made him shaky. Langley had fallen asleep like a baby, and Sajid envied him his ability to switch off like that. No matter how hard he tried, though, Saj couldn't erase the image of that machete swinging down and slicing Nikki's face. She'd coped with the necessary interviews and the hospital attention with as much grace as she could, but Saj worried that this might be what made her turn her back on policing.

That thought brought him onto his current worry – DI Ahad. He'd been prepared to give him the benefit of the doubt, but his behaviour at Forster Square arches the previous day had been off. He'd taken a call from Farah Anwar, which had made his blood run cold. It wasn't only Anwar's account of the Dark Knight's flagrant abuse of protocol outside Nikki's house, or even the unnecessary run-in with Nik and Haqib that unsettled him – it was the missing girl's name: Attiya. If Ahad had only told him about the FMU referral before they'd gone to the arches, he'd have been aware that the girl was on the missing persons radar. He would have glanced through the FMU report and connected it with the waif-like girl. Like Anwar, he would have recommended passing the investigation to another team, but at least he'd have been able to help Attiya. Why Ahad hadn't done so, he couldn't fathom.

Which was why at 5 a.m., Sajid was driving into town. No matter how bleary-eyed he was, he wouldn't settle until he'd checked out Forster Square. He'd seen Attiya fleetingly at the vigil, and now the memory of that looming figure grabbing her became more ominous. He had to check she was okay.

With the beginnings of daylight making their presence felt, the arches carried a different aura. The undercurrents of sound were muted, as if wary of wakening the sleeping underbelly. Scattered around the damp ground, shadowy lumps of clothes, boxes and makeshift protection showed the number of rough sleepers placing themselves in direct combat with the elements, the predators and the temptation to lose themselves in the fog of addiction.

As dawn broke, the figures awoke, their drowsy movements beneath their meagre coverings slow and leaden. Sajid tiptoed around, squinting into the faces of those whose heads were visible. He wanted to find Attiya, but would settle for Nancy or indeed any of the trio he'd met yesterday.

The further under the arches he progressed, the darker it became, and instead of just peering at the almost lifeless bodies, Saj shook them and shone his phone torch on them. How many people were under here? Still, he continued, bundle by bundle, heap by heap, studying each person, grimacing at the stink that erupted each time a sleeping figure moved under his touch. He wasn't sure which was worse – the acrid metallic odour of the drug addict, the stale brewery smells of the alcoholics, or the revolting stench of the great unwashed. Each carried its own story and as desperation set in, Saj's hope of finding Attiya again waned.

Chapter 58

'You don't recognise me, do you?'

The woman who sat opposite Nikki was Fareena's mum, and Nikki assumed she'd come for advice on what to do about the arrest of her husband, sons, and son-in-law. After Marcus left the room, she removed her niqab and glared at Nikki, her eyes filled with disgust as if Nikki had pissed in her chai. Nikki frowned. Granted, she wasn't the most popular person on earth, but to her knowledge she'd done nothing to warrant this reaction from Mrs Mushtaq. Especially since she'd gained entry to her home on the pretext of asking for help. Mindful of Haqib's illicit relationship with the other woman's daughter, Nikki opted to swallow her scalding retort and instead kept her tone neutral, but polite. 'I'm sorry, should I recognise you?'

Whilst sipping the spicy chai that Marcus had made for them, Nikki studied the woman. She looked familiar, but Nikki had initially assumed that it was her likeness to Fareena that had triggered that thought. Now, she realised that the similarity between Haqib's girlfriend and her mother was slight. So, where had she encountered her before? She doubted it had been during her work. Fareena's mum didn't seem the sort to be in trouble with the police. In fact, according to Haqib, she hardly left the house.

Still, there *was* something about her. Nikki tried to look beneath the fat rolls under her chin and the wrinkled forehead. Still, she couldn't remember when she'd met her before. The Mushtaqs had lived opposite for years, yet the most they'd shared was a wave in passing. She must be mistaken.

Mrs Mushtaq's glare deepened, her mouth widening into a sneer, and again a tingle of recognition stalked the recesses of Nikki's brain.

'You'll have to tell me, I'm afraid.' Nikki kept her tone flat. She'd no intention of matching the other woman's animosity. Her mind was already buzzing, and this drop-by visit was unexpected. All she wanted was for her neighbour to ask her questions and leave. In fact, if she didn't change her attitude fast, Nikki wouldn't give her the chance to ask anything. Instead, she'd escort her back onto the street. How dare she come into her home, accept tea from Marcus, demand help from her, then treat Nikki like this? Nikki wouldn't stand for that crap. No damn way.

'Hmph. So, Nikita Parekh's got a short memory. That won't help in your chosen profession, will it, Miss Perfect Parekh?'

The 'Miss Perfect Parekh' brought a frown to Nikki's forehead as recognition dawned. She'd not heard that name since high school, and it left a bitter taste in her mouth. A group of older girls had made her life miserable, bullying her because she refused to take part in their childish shenanigans. 'Rabia Ishmail? *You're* Rabia Ishmail?'

The overweight woman sitting opposite bore no resemblance to Nikki's recollection of Rabia. She'd been skinny to the point of anorexic. With concave legs and no tits, she'd compensated for her lack of stature with her larger-than-life nastiness. She'd been a goth back then – all dark eyeliner, lipstick and clothes, with piercings along her eyebrows and in her nose. In crop tops with plunging necklines and skintight jeans, she'd bared more flesh than would be acceptable for her current religious viewpoint. It was little surprise that Nikki failed to recognise her. She was sure her sister hadn't made the connection either, because Anika, being a gossip monger, would have shared this news with glee. What had transformed the rebellious teen into this stalwart of the Muslim community?

Rabia smirked. 'Mushtaq now. Respectable married woman, I am. Wondered how long it would take you. Not so Perfect Parekh anymore, are you?' And she wafted her hand around Nikki's busy kitchen. 'Living in sin with a gora and three bastard half-castes to your name, eh?'

Nikki jumped up. No matter how much she wanted to glean inside information into the arrests of the male members of Rabia's family, she wouldn't stand for being racially insulted in her own home. 'Get out. You were a bully at school, and you still are, Rabia. But I'm not Miss Perfect Parekh anymore and I've got the scars to prove it.'

Rabia struggled to her feet, grabbing her niqab as she did so. With a snarl, Nikki stepped right up to her. 'Get the fuck out of my house and take your racist crap with you. I won't help you even if you come back begging.'

Nikki grabbed the larger woman by the arm and using every ounce of strength, she dragged her protesting carcass to the front door, yanked it open and shoved her out, not bothering that she barely managed to keep her footing as she stumbled down the stairs. In the street, the few reporters who'd caught wind of the previous evening's arrests turned their cameras to Nikki's house as she uttered her parting words. 'I hate racists and I hate hypocrites too. Utter a racist comment in my hearing again and I'll have you arrested, got it?'

Heart hammering, Nikki slammed the door shut. Her breath was constricting her chest, her broken ribs making breathing difficult and painful. She knew what was coming, so she twanged her wrist twice, before realising her daughters and Marcus were at the living-room door. They were grinning like she'd just told them they were off to Disney World for a week, then they clapped, surging round her.

'You dissed that bitch, Mum,' was Charlie's summation as she grabbed Nikki and pulled her close. Rubster, in hushed tones, said, 'Bloody awesome. You kicked ass.'

Nikki glanced at Marcus, who continued smiling, his eyes full of pride, and instead of being engulfed by panic, Nikki was supported by the love of her family. That old bag didn't deserve one iota of her stress. 'Any idea what that was all about?'

Marcus shrugged. 'None. She must have seen us outside last night when her family was taken away. That doesn't explain why she came here and was so nasty.'

The sound of someone clearing their throat by the kitchen door made Nikki turn round. 'Haqib? You know something about this?'

Her nephew shuffled his feet and backed into the room. 'Any more tea, Marccy?'

His upbeat tone seemed strained to Nikki's ears, and his pretend nonchalance did not fool her. 'Spill it, Haqib. I've no time for your coyness. What's going on?'

Before he could answer, a quiet rap sounded on the back door, and relief flooded Haqib's face as he jumped over to open it for his girlfriend. Fareena yanked off her niqab as she entered and hugged him before addressing Nikki. 'I'm sorry about that, Mrs Parekh. I sneaked into the back alley without my mum knowing. It's my fault. I insisted she ask you for help because my dad and brothers have engaged a solicitor and he won't tell us owt.' She glared at the floor, her next words spat into the room. 'Probably because we're women. Sexist old tosser.'

Nikki frowned as she studied the two lovebirds. 'What am I missing? Your mum said she wanted help, then vented a load of racist crap. What's that all about?'

Fareena sunk into a chair; Haqib following suit sat beside her. 'My middle sister Attiya has gone missing, and we don't know what's happened to her.' She looked at Haqib. 'Didn't you tell your auntie about Safer Bradford and the FMU?'

Haqib shrugged. 'Forgot – besides, my auntie was beaten up last night. Didn't want to hassle her.'

Nikki concealed her smile. Haqib was definitely growing up. 'Look, I've got ten minutes now. Tell me what's going on.'

'Attiya told Safer Bradford that she was being forced into a marriage she didn't want in Pakistan.' Fareena turned to Haqib. 'Zara told me that was true this morning.'

Turning back to Nikki, she continued. 'Zara's my oldest sister. She says Attiya's disgraced the family and the men are sending her to Pakistan. That's when Attiya went missing and the Forced Marriage Unit think we've had her killed off or summat.'

She spread her hands out before her. 'As if we'd do that. I know they're strict and all, but sending her to Pakistan to get married is one thing, killing her is another thing entirely.' She glanced at Haqib and grimaced acknowledging her earlier uncertainty about what her family were capable of. 'We didn't know what to do, so I sent Mum over.'

'That went well.' Nikki smiled to take the sting from her words. 'She didn't get round to asking for help. Instead, she vented a lot of racist crap.'

A tear rolled down Fareena's cheek. 'I'm so sorry about that, Mrs Parekh. I really am. I didn't know she had beef with you till Zara told me. She hated you at school. Said you were a stuck-up cow. If I'd known, I wouldn't have made her come here. I guilt-tripped her saying if she cared about the family, she should ask for help.' She shrugged. 'That's the trouble with my family. They're too damn strict. Too many secrets, too much worrying about what the "community" will think and not enough trust.'

As tears gathered in Fareena's eyes, Nikki made a decision. After her meeting with Dr Mallory, she hoped to be signed fit to work, and she'd be able to find out what was going on with the Mushtaq men and hopefully a bit more about Fareena's sister too. 'Okay, Fareena. I can't make promises, but I'll see what I can find out.' Nikki had worked similar cases with the FMU before and knew the results could be unpredictable. Family secrets and so-called honour could cause dire consequences and extreme actions from even the most placid of families. 'Just be prepared, Fareena. This might not turn out as you'd like.'

Fareena paled, but her nod was firm. 'I've had enough of this crap. I need to know what sort of family I'm part of, and I want to find my sister. That's all.'

Chapter 59

Sajid jogged through a thin drizzle along Smith Lane to the rear entrance of BRI. To say he was angry would have been an understatement, and not all of it was due to lack of sleep. He'd been cold and worried by the time he'd returned home to shower and change from his foray to the Forster Square arches. No matter how hot the temperature, he couldn't seem to expunge the stench from his nostrils, nor could he wash his ever-increasing concern about Attiya Mushtaq down the drain with the soap suds. Then, the phone call from DC Williams telling him that they had admitted Maz Khan to BRI early that morning. Relief that the lad was safe conflicted with outright anger at not being notified earlier. This wrath increased when he found that Ali hadn't told Nikki either. With resentment bubbling in his chest, he exploded through the hospital doors, ready to challenge Ali Khan to a gunfight at dawn. He and Nikki had risked their jobs to help their friend, and Ali hadn't had the courtesy to inform them his son was back.

As he headed past the Costa coffee shop near to the lifts, he bumped slap bang into Ali Khan, who was exiting the café, two takeaway coffees in hand. Not bothering to contain his rage, Saj prodded Ali in the shoulder. 'What the fuck, Ali? Why are Nikki and I the last to know Maz is safe?'

Ali's brows furrowed, and for a second Saj wondered if the larger man would have punched him had his hands not been full. 'Aw piss off, Malik. My son's been through hell. He's been beaten and minus an ear and you, you self-absorbed little turd, expect me to have you on speed dial? You can fuck right off.' The huge man nudged Saj none too gently as he passed and carried on towards the lifts.

This wasn't like Ali – not at all. It was as if the taxi driver was trying to divert Saj's attention by inviting an angry response. Ali's greying stubble and sunken cheeks mollified Sajid a little. However, he was going to do his job. Ali may well be upset and irate – who wouldn't be in his situation? The lad's abductors were still at large, and valuable time had been wasted. If Maz could identify his attackers, then Saj wanted to bring them in ASAP – before they had a chance to dispose of anything incriminating or even skip the district. He needed to know where Maz had been held and, at present, only the boy could tell him that. There could be forensic evidence there and CSIs should process the scene before it degraded. There was also the question of why they'd released the lad. Had he escaped or what?

Although finding Maz's captors was Saj's priority, there was still the issue of Maz's fingerprints on the bottle of vinegar used in Molly Cropper's fake acid attack. That matter would have to be addressed, and he would ask some hard questions regarding Maz's probable involvement in the spate of machete murders. Sajid followed Ali into the lift. 'We've lost precious time because *you* failed to mention that Maz was back, Ali. I'm not prepared to waste any more. He's going to talk to me.'

A pulse throbbed at Ali's temple as he glared at Sajid. 'You don't think he's been through enough?'

Saj studied his friend for a moment. What was he missing? Why was Ali not out there looking for the culprits? That wasn't like him. 'You're not telling me everything.'

Ali snorted and took a sip from the drink. 'He needs to rest, that's all. He's in pain and an infection has set in. He's the victim.'

'Hmm – what does that make Molly Cropper?' Saj was hitting below the belt with those words, but he didn't care. Maz's recovery was a consideration, but so was catching the perpetrators and working out where Maz's abduction fitted into the other murders and Molly's attack. Maz Khan had information, and Saj was damned if Ali's dickish behaviour was going to prevent him from extracting it.

Ali's face blanched and something flickered in his eyes. Sajid found it difficult to interpret, but he had more pressing matters to deal with. He was going to interview Maz, and Ali would have to put up with it. In silence, the two men stared straight ahead till the lift opened on the third floor. Saj followed Ali along the corridor, through a set of doors that required authorised admission from nursing staff and into a side room occupied by Maz Khan and three other patients. Jane slumped in an armchair, but her eyes lit up when Ali offered her a drink.

Her exhaustion was clear from her wan complexion, the enormous bags under her eyes, and the lines that had formed across the bridge of her nose. She didn't speak, and Saj was grateful for that, as he yanked the curtains closed to afford them some privacy, and dragged a chair over to the bed. He wanted to focus on the boy. Taking his time, he studied Maz Khan. He had a drip attached to his hand via a catheter and a dressing round his head showed which ear was missing. Numerous cuts and bruises were visible on the boy's face and arms, and a cage kept the covers from touching Maz's leg. The boy returned Saj's gaze with a worried, almost haunted one of his own, but remained silent. It was hard to believe the youngster was old enough to have left school, never mind hold down a job. Saj summoned a smile to his lips. After all, the lad had been through hell, and Saj's beef with his old man didn't warrant taking it out on Maz.

'You up for a few questions, Maz? We need to catch these bastards.'

Maz's eyes found his father's, and the silent exchange between them wasn't lost on Sajid. These two shared a secret, and Maz was clearly double checking with his dad. Ali nodded and moved round so that he was now within his son's gaze, but not visible to Saj. Saj exhaled and turned, first to Ali and then to Jane. 'As Maz is an adult, it'd be better if I interview him in private.'

Whilst Jane got to her feet straightaway, Ali stepped towards Saj. His bulk would have threatened another man, but Saj kept smiling. 'I'll let you know when we're done, Ali. Shouldn't take too long. He looks tired, so we'll come back later for a more detailed statement.'

Scowl furrowing his brow, Ali opened his mouth, but didn't get the chance to reply because Maz interjected. 'It's fine, Dad. Honest.'

Ali studied his son, then gave an abrupt nod. Without looking at Saj, he left the curtained-off area.

'Parents, eh? Always worrying, aren't they?' Saj winked and shrugged. 'Later on, we'll go over how you were abducted, Maz, but because you look exhausted, let's focus on who your abductors are, where they kept you, and how you came to be released, okay?'

Maz flinched and another wave of sympathy rolled over Saj. The sooner this initial interview was over, the better for everyone. 'Did you recognise your attackers?'

Maz, eyes focused on his hands, which rested on the bed covers, shook his head.

'You didn't recognise them? Hadn't seen them before, interacted with them?'

Maz hesitated. 'Not sure. They wore balaclavas. Didn't see their faces.'

Observing with interest the rush of blood to Maz's cheeks, Saj probed a little more. 'Did they speak to you? Perhaps you recognised their voices.'

Again a head shake.

'Maybe their stature? Were they tall, short, fat, thin?' This time, a shrug rewarded his efforts, so Sajid tried a fresh approach. 'I know you're scared. Hell, I would be if I'd gone through what you did. However, the best way of keeping you safe is to catch the people who did this.' He allowed his words to sink in. 'How many were there? Evidence retrieved from your abduction site shows there was more than one attacker – two?'

This time, Maz considered his response, then nodded. 'Yah, two I think.'

'Okay, so where did they keep you after they took you?'

'Dunno. It was a bedroom. They locked me in a bedroom with crappy old furniture, but I don't know where it was or owt. I was unconscious and only woke up after they left.'

This was progress, yet Sajid was wary. It seemed that this particular answer had been rehearsed because the words flowed so quickly with none of the pauses or antsy body language of his previous replies. A nurse popped her head through the curtain and frowned when she saw Sajid there with his tablet out, taking notes. 'If you want to interview him, you need to come back later. He's been through a massive trauma and he needs surgery on his leg soon.'

Saj suspected Ali was responsible for the nurse's appearance. He'd wanted more time before being evicted, but there wasn't much he could do about it. 'One more question, and I'll leave.' Without waiting for her acquiescence, he turned to Maz. 'How did you escape? Did they let you go?'

Eyes wide, Maz swallowed hard. 'They dumped me outside my house and my mum phoned the ambulance.'

'They dropped you off in a car?'

'Yes …'

'Really – how did they get you in a car with your leg so badly damaged?'

'I … eh … I don't …'

'That's enough, detective.' The nurse's voice brooked no

argument. 'You need to leave now. You can speak to him again tomorrow if he feels up to it.'

With a shrug, Saj nodded at Maz. 'Good luck with your op. We'll be back to take an official statement later. In the meantime, chillax, okay?'

Before his eyes, the boy seemed to sink further into the pillows propped up around him and his voice shook. 'You've got more questions for me?'

Aware that he was turning the screws, Saj was unrepentant, for he was becoming more and more certain that Maz Khan wasn't telling him everything. 'Course I'll be back. We still need to talk about your role in the attack against Molly Cropper' He moved to the curtains. 'And what you know about the machete killings.'

Blood drained from the boy's face, and Saj wondered if he might faint. Maz knew a lot more than he was sharing.

Chapter 60

'Well, I'm not sure you're ready, Nikki. Not sure at all.'

Nikki's heart plummeted when she heard Dr Mallory's words. She'd been certain that Mallory would agree to her return to work. She was always banging on about Nikki's progress, and had even reduced her therapy sessions. It was unexpected that at the last hurdle, Mallory had put a downer on things.

Dr Mallory steepled her fingers on her lips and studied Nikki across her desk. Nikki looked at her therapist with a resolute expression, hoping this would cover up the fact that she wanted to yell at her. Nikki was certain that she was fit for work and to have Mallory react like this was puzzling and upsetting. 'I thought you'd be happy.'

Mallory gave a small tinkling giggle that grated on Nikki's already frayed nerves. How had she not noticed the woman's annoying laugh before? The psychiatrist got up, walked around the desk and leaned on it. Her purple corduroyed skirt, complete with orange edging, would normally have elicited a smile from Nikki, but not today. Today Nikki was fierce and determined. No way would the doctor's eccentric dress sense sway her from her mission. 'I am pleased, Nikki. Of course I am. However, being pleased that you think you're ready and being concerned that you might be over-reaching are two very different things.' Again with the tinkling laugh. A worried frown pulled the doctor's brows together. 'I mean, look at you. You're all bruised and who knows what damage, both physically and mentally, you sustained after that beating last night. Remember I was there. I saw what happened to you. No one, not even Nikki Parekh could escape from that beating without some trauma.'

'But that's just it. I've been beaten, yes, I agree. But that made me realise that it's time for me to take the next step in my recovery and *that* step involves returning to work.' She was thinking off the top of her head. Despite Marcus's misgivings, Nikki hadn't anticipated any real issues. They'd both considered this meeting with Dr Mallory a formality and it was *so* frustrating that the doctor wasn't on the same page. With crossed fingers, Nikki took a deep breath and offered her final argument. 'Besides, I spoke to DCI Hegley this morning, and he thinks it would be a good idea for me to return to work. He's got a plan of action all worked out to ensure I get the support I need and space to recap directly with him. My team will do most of the heavy lifting and, I'll work from Trafalgar House mainly.'

Nikki hadn't spoken with Archie and nor did she have any intention of being confined to the incident room, but she was prepared to do anything to convince Dr Mallory to sign her fit for work form – even if it meant lying through her gritted teeth. She was sure that between them, she and Sajid could convince Archie that it was in his best interests to support her return, but hopefully she wouldn't need to involve him in this. With any luck, her fib would convince Mallory, and she'd sign her off. 'Of course, I'm happy to increase my therapy sessions with you whilst I'm settling back in and obviously if you had any concerns we could always think again.'

This was all Nikki had left. If that last concession wasn't convincing enough, she didn't know what else she could do.

With a parched mouth and sweaty hands, Nikki smiled at the therapist. She was aiming for a 'look at how in control I am' vibe, yet she wasn't sure how long she could hold it. 'Please, please, please, let me back to work,' thudded through her skull in time with her heartbeat as she awaited Mallory's response.

The other woman pushed herself away from the edge of her desk and with a sigh returned to her chair where she picked up the horrible feathery pen from her pen pot. Nikki didn't dare hope that this was a promising sign. Her face muscles were aching, and she just wanted the signed form in her hands so she could relax her mouth and cheeks. Mallory exhaled exaggeratedly, telling Nikki that she felt coerced. She pulled a pad towards her and scribbled something on it before ripping the top sheet from it and passing it to Nikki. 'This is against my better judgement, DS Parekh. You know that, right?'

The psychiatrist kept hold of the paper until Nikki offered a grudging nod. 'I expect to see you twice weekly and expect to receive a detailed, and I mean detailed, report of *any* possible triggers you encounter in your working life for us to work through at each session. I will review the situation afterwards, but in the meantime, do not overdo it! Don't make me regret this decision.'

When she released the fit-to-work note, Nikki leapt from her chair and headed for the exit with a 'You won't regret it. This is what I need.'

She'd already yanked open the door when Mallory delayed her relieved exit for a second. 'Oh, and I will expect DCI Hegley to email me details of his "plan of action" ASAP.'

Caught out, Nikki could only nod. *Shit.* Now she'd have to cobble something together and hope that Archie would go along with her deceit and pass it off as his own idea. In the elevator, Nikki replayed the session. She could not get her head round why Dr Mallory had been so obstructive. Yes, she had been beaten and, in fairness to Mallory, Nikki supposed that she had to question her state of mind. That was no doubt why she'd forced Nikki to justify her desire to expedite her return to work. Nikki could barely keep the grin off her face. She was coming back to Trafalgar House, and they'd better be ready for her. She took out her phone and called Archie to tell him the good news.

Chapter 61

#WhatsWrongWithThisShit?

**THE ONE WHERE THE LAD RETURNS MINUS ONE EAR
POSTED BY BFDLASS#WWWTS NOVEMBER 27TH 10:22**

So, the lad whose ear was sliced off and sent to his mum is in hospital.

He's in a stable condition and despite many injuries he'll survive!

The question is, will he recover?

Who knows what happened to him in captivity? Who knows how this will affect his future?

Beaten, kidnapped, tortured and thrown out on his mum's front lawn like a pile of garbage!

#WhatsWrongWithThisShit?

But let me ask you this. Whilst the police are all over Jamie Jacobs's murder, what are they doing about Maz Khan's abduction?

Are they scouring the streets looking for his attackers?

264

> Or are they running round in circles as Bradford spirals out of control?
>
> **#WhatsWrongWithThisShit?**

COMMENTS:

ZainK: *#JusticeForMaz #WhatsWrongWithThisShit Bradford police need to get their fingers out of their anuses and do summat.*

> **Karryann3:** *@ZainK WTAF! My parents will never let me out again. #WhatsWrongWithThisShit but there's plenty of police around. Saw loads outside school yesterday. When's this crap gonna end?*

JakeK4292: *need to lock everybody up. Heard a nasty rumour about @MazKhan03 – he's not the innocent you all think*

> **Karryann3:** *You can't just keep us hanging, man. You gotta spill. What do you know?*

JakeK4292: *@Karryann3 That's for me to know and you to find out. I'm not a grass. Just let's say he's got his coming to him 😂😂😂*

> **Karryann3:** *@JakeK4292 You're just winding things up. AH. Things are bad enough without you stirring it. #WhatsWrongWithThisShit #JusticeForMaz*

Jazzygirl3: *I'm with you on this one @Karryann3 POS all the time these days. No freedom. I Can't breathe! ☹️☹️☹️ #WhatsWrongWithThisShit #JusticeForMaz*

> **MH616:** *@Jazzygirl3 #WhatsWrongWithThisShit #JusticeForMaz*

Chapter 62

In an adrenalin slump after her meeting with Dr Mallory, Nikki took time to ponder what she would face on her return to Trafalgar House. Archie had been gruff, but pleased to hear she was coming back, which tempered Saj's over-enthusiastic response. Her team – Anwar, Williams and Saj – didn't concern her though. It was the other detectives. The new detective, Ahad, with his supercilious look, came to mind. She wasn't looking forward to working under him, especially not after their heated disagreement the previous night, but Saj would provide a buffer – he always did.

As she drove to Trafalgar House, enjoying her car, she popped the radio on to catch the local news.

'… *lad, Maz Khan, who was abducted three days ago, is, according to one source, recovering in Bradford Royal Infirmary. However, with the abrupt end to yesterday's peaceful vigil where off-duty police officer DS Nikki Parekh was …*'

Hearing her name, Nikki switched it off. Fuck, fuck and double fuck … who the hell had released her name to the journalists? The low-key return to work she'd anticipated was now damn near impossible. When she pulled into Nelson Street, Nikki stopped. A small group of reporters hovered about outside, holding takeaway cups hosting the Lazy Bites logo, their heads jerking towards the entrance every time someone exited the building. Nikki grabbed her baseball cap and pulled it on, tipping the peak down so it put most of her face in shadow. Not the best disguise, but enough to divert the ever-alert journos whilst she entered the car park through the automated gate.

As she sailed through the gates, barely allowing them to open, Nikki glanced in her rear-view mirror. The reporters had been too slow and now huddled together, gazing after her as the bars slid closed behind her. Thank God. If they'd recognised her, they'd be attacking her with a barrage of probing questions involving her last case, which had ended tragically, her sick leave and the reasons for it, as well as the attack she'd sustained at the vigil the previous evening. Nikki wanted none of that. She wanted to focus on everything that was happening without being hounded by irrelevant crap.

Nikki twanged her wrist band as she exited the Touran – just the once and not too hard. It was a reminder of her coping strategies before entering the building she hadn't visited in almost two months. Despite a weird, wriggly sensation in the pit of her stomach, it was as if she was coming home. Spine straight, she took a deep breath, jutted her chin out and entered the building, only to find a welcoming committee gathered by the door. Her chin relaxed and a grin spread over her face as Williams, Anwar, Saj and Archie fell into place on either side of her, like ferocious Dobermans on protection duty as she weaved her way through to Archie's office. Once there, Anwar and Williams returned to work, whilst Sajid and Archie sat down and waited for her to sit too. Words failing her, Nikki glanced round the room, avoiding eye contact with Archie, until the silence grew heavy, punctuated only by Archie's bronchial breathing and the odd creak as Saj shuffled on the chair beside her. 'Good to be back.' That was all she could manage, the understatement breaking the mood, and Sajid chuckled.

Archie studied her, his eyes filled with concern. 'Ye look …

267

well … you look … colourful – like ye've had yer proverbials slapped. You sure yer okay to be back, Parekh?'

Nikki hesitated. Should she tell him about her little white lie to Mallory? She glanced at Saj for help, but his wide grin and shrug told her she was on her own on this one. 'Yes, of course I'm ready. I wouldn't come back otherwise.' On catching her boss's eye, she held contact. 'I'm fine, Boss. Honest, I am.'

Archie snorted and slurped from a water bottle labelled The Boss. It had a picture of Archie taped over what she presumed was the original Bruce Springsteen image. 'And Mallory's okay with you coming back?'

Nikki was about to nod, but something in Archie's tone alerted her to the trap a blithe response would tip her into. Instead, she shoved the signed fit-to-work note across the table with a shrug. 'Well, she took a bit of convincing if I'm honest, but …'

'Aye, ah ken. Ye took the proverbials, didn't ye, Parekh.' Archie moved his computer mouse to activate the screen and scanned the content. 'Seems, she's expecting some sort o' action plan frae me, eh?'

Beside her, Saj chuckled again. Bastard! Nikki groaned. Mallory must have contacted Archie as soon as Nikki had left her office. 'Well, erm …'

Archie waved a dismissive hand. 'Hold your proverbials, Parekh. Ah've worked wi' ye long enough to ken that aw I'm going to get from you right noo is a bunch o' excuses.'

With a nod, Nikki averted her eyes and waited for whatever judgement Archie was about to pass. The big man heaved himself to his feet, shaking his head as he moved round to the front of the desk. What was it with everyone she met today, leaning on their desk before her as if she was a naughty kid? 'Here's what's going tae happen.'

Nikki's head jerked up to meet his gaze. 'Malik will work with you like before and will filter any interactions between you and DI Ahad. I heard about his stunt last night and Aah'm no best pleased. However, that's a different matter. You and Malik will focus oan the murders and the Khan kid's abduction, and Ahad will work the Mushtaq missing persons case.' He pushed himself away from the counter and waddled back round. 'Oh and FYI, ah've cobbled together an "action plan" based on one ah did for Springer's return tae work. I've emailed you – you better read it so we're on the same page wi' it when ye meet wi' Dr Mallory again. Noo off yes go. Ah've work to dae.'

Chapter 63

The Honourable Fixer

Something is wrong! All morning I've been trying to get hold of the Headhunter, but either the little bastard has lost his phone – for which he will be punished – or he's avoiding me – again a punishment would be in order. I don't enjoy feeling twitchy like this. I prefer regimented order and this is not orderly. My extensive contacts inform me that Maz Khan is in hospital. That's good, for it's exactly what I demanded Headhunter do. However, he should have confirmed the task's completion, yet I've heard nothing. Not a damn thing, and that is unconscionable. Not only had I ordered him to free Maz Khan, I also told him to dispose of the two rogue Eyes and I still have no confirmation of that.

I find it hard to shake off the disquiet. Various things have marred today and unease infiltrates my every thought. Things have not gone to plan and I can't tolerate that. I whip off a flurry of emails cancelling the rest of the day's appointments and head to my flat. I need peace to gather intel, and reaching out to my extensive sources is best done where I won't be interrupted and where my security system is in peak condition.

It's been so long since I've felt this uneasy, I can barely

remember it. Everything had turned out peachy after a few tense days, involving a bit of back-tracking and a lot of pruning. Even if my current unease is justified, everything is in place to deal with unforeseen problems. All I have to do is double check things and remain calm. I ring Headhunter's number one last time and when he still doesn't pick up, I hook my burner phone up to my PC and fry it. If it should fall into the wrong hands, there is no chance of it being traced back to me. That done, I can relax. Cutting Headhunter loose hadn't been in my imminent plans. Still, it feels good to do so. Now, for added security, I will issue an order to dispose of Headhunter, and also Chas Choudry and Michelle Glass if he hasn't done so already. Best to be safe because sorry isn't in my vocabulary. And Nikki Parekh is back in the game. Seems like she's tougher than I imagined, so I'll need to make sure she's too preoccupied to do her best work.

Chapter 64

Despite being told that Attiya Mushtaq's disappearance was DI Ahad's domain, both Nikki and Saj agreed that they should, at the very least, cast a quick eye over those reports before focusing on the case they'd been assigned. Nikki wanted to have something to tell Fareena. When a young person – usually female, but not always – was referred to the FMU and subsequently disappears, the first step was to investigate her family whilst ascertaining if they'd left the country. Thankfully, Ahad had actioned that very thing. Nikki was interested now in seeing the transcripts of the interviews with Attiya's male relatives, but other than a shed load of 'No comments' from all four men, she gained nothing. Ahad had since released them, but he'd authorised for them to be followed in case they could lead them to Attiya.

That Sajid had met Attiya was interesting. A young Muslim girl from a traditional family wouldn't voluntarily spend time down the arches. Saj had filed a report of his sightings of Attiya, and having seen her only the previous night at the vigil, it seemed unlikely that they had sent her abroad. Her current whereabouts were a major cause for concern, but, theoretically, it wasn't Nikki or Sajid's worry.

Saj updated Nikki on his interview with Maz Khan and Ali's

strange behaviour. 'Ali was being a dick. I've never seen him like that before. He's usually amenable, but he was bang out of order today ... made me wonder ...'

Nikki waited for Sajid to continue, but he shook his head, as if dismissing whatever thought had sprung to mind. 'It's nothing, Nik. A niggle that I can't shift. Let me think about it for a while, eh?'

Allowing thoughts to develop organically was something Nikki liked to do. 'Okay, just let me know if anything strikes you.' She sighed. 'It's a pity that CCTV around Jane's home is so sparse or we might have seen who dumped Maz. That would make our job a hell of a lot easier.'

Eyes narrowed, Saj clicked his fingers. 'That's what's pissing me off. We'd only *just* stood down the officer who was stationed at Jane's house round the clock. With the attack at the vigil, we needed all hands on deck here, so they diverted everyone to City Park. Very convenient for whoever dropped the lad there – almost as if they knew they wouldn't be observed.'

'Mmm. You thinking they're local?'

'Yeah, or ...'

'Or ...?' Nikki imitated his thoughtful tone, her senses igniting at the prospect of an enlightening moment.

'Nah, ignore me. Just ... well ... It's strange that Ali had no one stationed there. He's got plenty of manpower for that. You'd think he'd enlist his men to protect Jane.'

Sajid was right. Ali would have battened down the hatches in the light of his son's disappearance. His priorities would be locating his son and keeping Jane safe. He'd make sure someone was watching her – just in case. 'Ali tell you where he was last night, Saj?'

'He said he was at home with Jane.' He paused. 'You're not suggesting he snatched his own son and amputated his ear, are you?'

Nikki thumped him on the shoulder. 'No, course not. But ...'

Saj caught on. 'Perhaps he or his men followed up on the leads you got yesterday afternoon. Perhaps Ali found out who took his son and maybe Maz wasn't returned by his abductors, but was rescued by his dad.'

'That would explain Ali's behaviour at the hospital …'

'Nik?' Saj frowned. 'You don't think …?'

Nikki exhaled. Sajid didn't need to finish his sentence. The same thought had occurred to her. 'I don't know. Ali's not a killer. No way. But … well, Maz is his son, isn't he? Who knows what someone would do to protect their child?' Nikki would do anything for her own kids and wondered how far she would go if they'd been hurt.

She jumped up, grabbed the last few crisps and, stuffing them in her mouth, she set off towards the door. 'Looks like we've got to interview a man about an alibi.'

Chapter 65

The Honourable Fixer

I don't recognise the number, but the call is to one of my burner phones. I activate a location diversion app and ensure my voice distortion is on before I reply. 'Yes.'

'It's me …'

My relief is palpable. Even the glass of red hasn't reduced my anxiety, but now, with Headhunter back in action, I can breathe again.

'Had to get another burner phone. My other one wouldn't work.'

I nodded – that was because I'd spliced it to make sure that if it landed up in someone else's hands, it couldn't be traced to me. 'Hope you paid cash and went out of town for it.'

There's a moment's hesitation before Headhunter responds, and I'm positive the idiot didn't have the sense to cover his tracks. Never mind. Soon as I end the call, I'll deal with that, the same way I dealt with his previous mobile.

'S-S-Summats going wrong. Three of the Eyes are AWOL.'

His voice wobbles and I sense he's very near the end of his tether. Time to end him, but not until he's tied up the loose ends. 'Locate them!'

'I've tried. C-can't find them. Don't know where they are and …'

A foreboding prickle looms as his tone becomes gruff. He's teetering on the edge and I need to draw him back – for now, anyway. 'There's nothing we can't solve, Headhunter. We're a team, you and I. We can sort anything. So, tell me everything.'

'They were supposed to … d-d-d-dispose of Michelle Glass and Chas Choudry, and dump Maz Khan somewhere he'd be found.'

I already know this from my sources, but I let him continue. 'Maz's dad took him to BRI, but I can't find the others. They're not picking up and neither are Glass and Choudry. No bodies have been reported …'

'Have you been to the safe house? The one where they kept Maz Khan captive.'

'N-n-n-no.'

I swallow my frustration – you can't get quality help these days. 'Well then, Headhunter. You know what your next move should be, don't you?'

My PC's beeping like there's no tomorrow, so I hang up and pull up my private message board.

Veed32: *I paid you good money to get the job done, but it isn't done yet. Need a refund or proof of death.*

I always thought Veed32 was egotistical, but this surpasses even my perceptions of his arrogance.

TheFixer: *The job will be finished. Be aware that I have much more information about you and where you've dipped your dick than you know.*

I don't usually taunt my clients like this, but it's been an arduous day so, for good measure, I attach one of the less salubrious images I have of Veed32 and await his response. When it comes, it exceeds my expectations of his stupidity.

Veed32: *You're dead. You're fucking dead. How did you get that photo?*

The Fixer: *Happy to organise a double hit, for no additional charge. You and your little floosie? How would that suit? I'd watch your tongue, Veed32. I know where you live and I'm happy to arrange for a cat to take your tongue if you don't show respect.*

I wait for a full ten minutes, savouring my wine and contemplating my next moves, but he doesn't respond. That's good. One less rogue to think about. However, it does seem that I might require that ticket to Venezuela sooner rather than later. The rollercoaster is racing too quickly for my liking and I need to hop off.

Chapter 66

'I'm scared, Haqib. Really scared. I've done something I shouldn't have, and I need to hide. They'll kill me if they find out.'

Haqib hadn't seen Fareena look so anxious before. This wasn't the same as when she cried over Attiya. Or even like when she was stressed about speaking to the Forced Marriage cops. This was something else entirely. Her whole body trembled and, although they'd snuck into his bedroom, she kept glancing round as if she thought someone was about to jump out from the shadows and attack her. Her disquiet was contagious, and he was beginning to feel uneasy too. 'What's happened, Fareena? Shall I get Auntie Nik?'

But before he'd finished uttering his suggestion, she jumped to her feet, shaking her head. 'No. No. We can't involve anyone else in this. It's too dangerous.'

'Come on, Fareena. You're shitting me up now. You've got to tell me what's going on!'

She looked at him from her perch on the side of his bed. 'Oh, Haqib. I know where Attiya is ... and I know why she went missing.' She reached out and grabbed his hand, holding his fingers so tightly the blood flow almost stopped. But Haqib didn't care. Fareena needed him, and he was determined to be there for her. 'I'm listening.'

'He's put out a fatwa on her.' Fareena's voice trembled as she uttered the last word. 'Like we're in the fucking Middle Ages or something. A fatwa, can you believe it, a fucking fatwa?'

Haqib frowned. He'd no idea what a fatwa was, but he suspected it wasn't a good thing. 'Fat What..?'

'Well, it's not really a fatwa. I mean, it's nothing official. Not like an official Islamic ruling from a Hafis or owt. Sensible Muslims wouldn't issue fatwas.' She looked at him, her brown eyes earnest and pleading, 'But it's almost as bad, yeah?'

Haqib was no wiser, so he shrugged.

'He's put out a hit on her, Haqib. The bastard's put out a hit on Attiya. That's why she ran away.'

Haqib's lips twitched. Fareena was having a laugh at his expense, but now he got the joke. 'Yeah right. Pull the other …'

'Shit, Haq. I thought you'd get it. Thought *you'd* be on my side. I'm not joking. This is serious and now I've stolen this, I'm in big trouble too.' She held a phone out to Haqib. 'Take it. You've got to hide it. If he catches me with it, he'll kill me. It's evidence.'

Haqib looked from the phone to Fareena and back before taking it from her. In silence he switched it off, took the battery out and then carried it to his wardrobe. Haqib had watched enough detective films to know how to make a mobile untraceable. After rummaging, he produced a battered old shoebox and put the phone inside. 'Right. Now you need to tell me everything. Who's ordered a hit on Attiya, and why, and who the hell is going to kill you? Who does it belong to?'

Fareena took a deep breath. 'Attiya texted me. It wasn't from her phone. She said she'd borrowed one from some druggie in town. She's been sleeping rough, Haq. Can you believe it? My sister sleeping rough under Forster Square arches. Anything could've happened to her.'

Shit. This was bad. Haqib had heard his auntie talking about the crap that went down under the arches. No wonder Fareena was petrified for her sister. But that still didn't explain about the phone he'd hidden or the death threat. 'Go on.'

'Attiya said a bloke grabbed her at the vigil and told her he'd been paid to kill her. She escaped, but only just. She's terrified.' Fareena's eyes welled up, but she brushed the tears away with a swift brush of her fingers. 'She's pregnant.'

Haqib tried not to look too satisfied that he'd got something right.

'But it's not a boyfriend's kid. She was raped ... the bastard fucking raped her and he'll rape me next if I don't get away. You have to help me, Haqib. You need to help Attiya and me escape from Bradford.'

Haqib wasn't sure how to respond, but before he got the chance, someone hammered on the front door. Scared eyes darted in Fareena's direction.

'It's him, Haqib. It's him. Don't answer. Please don't open the door.' Her fingers trembled as she plucked at his bedding.

However, Haqib had no choice, because his mum had already opened the door and was talking to someone. He strained his ears, but could only hear his mum's side of the conversation. 'Yes, he's upstairs. Come in.' Then a yell up the stairs. 'Haqib, you got a visitor!'

As heavy footsteps pounded up the two flights of stairs leading to the attic bedroom, Haqib bundled Fareena over to the small storage space under the window, yanked open the hatch and helped her crawl inside. He'd only just concealed the entrance and thrown himself back on his bed when the door burst open.

Chapter 67

'I really don't get where you're coming from, Ali.'

Nikki, Sajid, Ali and Jane stood outside Maz's hospital room to allow the woozy boy to rest. Nikki had assumed that after the success of Maz's operation, Ali would be in a better frame of mind. The truth was, she'd taken Sajid's description of Ali's unreasonable behaviour with a pinch of salt. Ali was always amenable, friendly and open. Of course, she made allowances because he'd been through so much and must have been worried sick. But this degree of hostility towards both Saj and herself was out of order. She'd done everything she could to help him – hell, she'd even risked her job by going off piste and this was how he thanked her?

Ali had the grace to avert his sneering gaze, but Nikki wasn't finished. Not yet, anyway. She moved closer, invading his personal space, forcing him to look at her. The smell of sweat rolled off him, showing that he'd not yet left his son's side. She couldn't blame him for that. She'd be the same if one of her family lay in that bed. Beside him, Jane's frown deepened as she studied Ali and Nikki. 'You two should sort this out. Ali, we've got Maz back, and I know Nikki helped you. Why are you being so hostile? At a time like this we need our friends around us.' She tugged on his arm, her voice softening. 'Those bastards are still out there, Ali. Nikki can help us find them.'

During Jane's speech, Nikki studied Ali. Head bowed, he'd flinched at Jane's final words. *Oh Ali, what have you done?* Nikki didn't speak her thoughts aloud, because she didn't want to worry Jane. Instead, she lasered Ali with a penetrating glare that demanded his full attention and jerked her head to the exit before strutting down the corridor and into the hall outside the ward. A multitude of thoughts hammered in her brain, but foremost was the apprehension that Ali had taken matters into his own hands. Ali wasn't a killer, but Nikki had witnessed first-hand how far someone would go in extreme circumstances and, despite her loyalty to him, she wondered if he'd gone over to the dark side.

Ali waited for a group of visitors to enter the ward before glaring at Nikki. 'Get out of my space, Nik. I know you mean well, but I need to focus on my lad.' He extended his palms, placatingly, and his next words were less abrasive. 'Don't worry about me. I'm fine. I promise.'

If it hadn't been for the bulbous vein throbbing in his neck, Nikki might have been mollified, but she knew him too well. He was obfuscating, and Nikki would not be distracted from finding out what had happened to Maz. Again, she moved close to him, her pugnacious chin angled upwards, eyes flashing as she prodded him in the sternum. 'You're lying to me, Ali.' As he opened his mouth to respond, Nikki prodded him again. 'I know you are, so don't bother trying to deny it.'

She inhaled, long and slow. The tension across her chest resulted from frustration and anger, and if she was to avoid exploding, she had to dispel it. She turned and kicked the wall, her Doc Martin boots preventing any actual damage to her foot. Although the wall was too hard to be affected by the kick, she attracted concerned glances from some visitors who were waiting to be admitted into the ward. Ali remained silent, his stubbly taut jaw and blazing eyes the only indication he'd been affected. 'If …'

She went back over to him and recommenced her prodding. 'If you've done something to Maz's captors, you need to come clean, Ali. If you delay telling us, things will go badly for you. You know I'll do everything I can to protect you, but …'

Ali sneered and brushed past her. 'Just fuck off, Nikki. Fuck right off with your "goody-two-shoes, I can save the world" attitude.' Before Nikki could stop him, he re-entered the ward without a backward glance. His words still reverberated around the small area when Saj joined her. 'No luck, I take it, Nik. Ali's face looked like a slapped arse and even Jane gave him a wide berth.'

After a surreptitious twang of her elastic band, Nikki exhaled. 'He knows something and I'm worried that he's done something to Maz's abductors that we won't be able to protect him from.'

'So … we take him down to the station?'

Nikki's smile was grim as she shook her head. 'So … we put a tail on him and one on Haris. If we're going to find out what they've done, one of those two will have the answers.'

'Anwar and Williams?'

'A uniformed officer here for Ali. I'm not sure how far he'll move from his son's bedside, so we only need an alert if he's on the move. Anwar and Williams can take Haris – I suspect he'll be the one cleaning up any mess that might have resulted from Maz's rescue.'

Ali's strange behaviour had convinced Nikki that Maz's abductors hadn't returned him to his parents, and the only question now remaining was what Ali had done to ensure his son's safe recovery.

Chapter 68

Nikki forced herself to push all thoughts of Ali out of her mind. There was nothing more they could do. He was under surveillance, as was his second in command, Haris, and with Maz still recovering from his op, they had to wait to re-interview him. Nikki was convinced they'd be able to wrangle the truth from the lad, but that would have to wait till later, when he was more comfortable.

Instead, she and Sajid turned their attention to their assigned task – narrowing down leads on the machete killings and working out whether Maz's abduction was linked. In her element, now that she was in an incident room with a full-size board to peruse, Nikki plonked herself in front of it and began thinking aloud. 'Maz was abducted on the same day Jamie's body was found. Coincidence? I think not.' She shook her head. 'Assuming that we link the fake acid attack to the machete killings, can we be sure Maz played no part in the other killings? Was Molly's attack the catalyst for the others? Did the fact that they got away with it lead to an escalation?' She sighed, yanking on her ponytail to tighten it. 'I keep coming back to motive. We know hatred or disapproval of her relationship with a Muslim boy motivated Molly's attack. Could something similar have motivated the others?'

284

'We've been going round like this in circles since Shabana Hussain's attack.' Sajid glowered and popped open a bag of crisps. 'There were rumours of her having a non-Muslim boyfriend, but that lead dried up when her family and friends closed ranks and denied it. She was a glowing example of the good Muslim girl and even a couple of follow-up interviews couldn't shake anything else loose.'

'Well, the murders aren't random, are they? They can't be a series of disparate attacks with nothing linking the victims.' Nikki ignored her partner's moans, and grabbing a handful of crisps, stuffed them in her mouth.

'You reckon we should focus on Jamie Jacobs for now, Nik? His murder is the most recent and you haven't been able to go over the details of that yet.'

Nikki nodded. 'Sounds like a plan. Attiya told you that Jamie was going to confront someone at the sleepout in City Park. Do we have any CCTV to confirm that he ever arrived there? It was probably his dad, judging from your observations. Maybe we'll get that confirmed. Mr Jacobs is alibied to the hilt, but who knows, we might spot something significant.'

The pair moved over to the vast screen designed for scanning CCTV footage. When divided to show different angles of the same scene, each image was as clear as it could be. Nikki remembered how, as a new police officer, she'd spent hours trying to focus on grainy images. Despite some of the younger officers nowadays moaning at the tedium and headache-inducing monotony of scouring CCTV, technological improvements made it all so much easier. Saj brought the images of City Park up. The number of streetlights combined with additional illumination from the town hall's tower, the Wetherspoons and the Mirror Pool fountains which had been lit up for the charitable event, made visibility clearer than she'd expected. It was easy to fast forward to the time just before the hooded figures appeared, chanting their ominous chant. A shiver raced through Nikki's body at the memory. It had been so chilling to hear such hatred amid a positive event, and that was before she'd noticed the machetes. But before that, Nikki wanted to survey those present, hoping to spot a signal between attendees or something equally ominous. There had been a lot of attendees, and Nikki remembered thinking she'd spotted Amar from Akhtar's garage there. Perhaps other dubious characters had also been in the vicinity and might have valuable information.

Saj slowed the footage, and they studied it frame by frame from the point when folk gathered. There were four cameras focused around City Hall. One from the row of buildings facing the town hall, which included Sunbridge Wells, City Library, Starbucks and Wetherspoons. The second covered the area from the Alhambra side of the park from the mound above the Cake 'Ole café. The third was angled away from the city to the park and offered only a rear view of the hooded figures. The last one recorded activity from City Hall itself and showed a panoramic view of the masked figures converging on the vigil. It was by far the clearest option, so they focused on that as they scrolled through each frame, trying to identify possible suspects. Their technical analysts were sifting through all footage in order to track each of the machete wielder's movements to a point prior to them pulling on their balaclavas. However, that would take time – a commodity they were rather short of.

With a notebook beside him, Saj jotted down names of anyone they recognised from the crowd. It was a thankless task and because it had been so cold, many attendees had wrapped up with scarves and hats covering their features, making them impossible to identify. An hour in and their list was growing, but inconclusive. When Saj pointed out Attiya to Nikki, she bounced up and down on her chair. 'The guy who's hassling her is Amar Akhtar, I'm sure of it. He's a bit of a tosser and it's likely he'll know Attiya's brothers – although they'll be younger than him. Amar is around my age.'

Another few frames further on, Saj paused and gestured to

286

a figure approaching City Hall from the Mirror Pool. 'That's Taj Jhuti. He was Molly Cropper's boyfriend. Good to see him attending the vigil.'

Nikki agreed. The poor lad's girlfriend had dumped him after the attack. Nikki recognised him because he was Haqib's friend. With a growing list before them, Nikki's eyes tired and she was on the point of suggesting they head to Lazy Bites for a break when she spotted Dr Mallory. With a grin, she pointed her out to Saj. 'Look, there's Doc Mallory.'

Saj laughed. 'Well, at least with the footage being in black and white, I won't need to grab my sunglasses. What is it with her and bright clothes?'

'What's she taking photos of, Saj? It's not the vigil, or the Mirror Pool or the town hall. It's something off towards the shops.' Nikki wasn't curious about what the doctor had found of interest. Bradford had many colourful characters living on its streets and the varied architecture was always something to admire, so a reflection on a building had probably attracted Mallory. However, spotting her taking photos gave her an idea. 'Have we requested camera and video footage of the vigil from the attendees?'

'Yeah, and we got heaps of it to trawl through. The techies are pulling their hair out.'

'Well, maybe if we spot something of interest, it will narrow down their viewing time to a few frames … fingers crossed, eh?'

Nikki was distracted now. She'd followed the doctor's line of vision and saw that whatever Mallory had intended to photograph also included a figure drawing on a balaclava. 'Zoom in on that, Saj. Look. Whoever that is, they're pulling on a hood and their build looks very similar to that of the guy who attacked me. Can we catch their face – get an identity?'

Saj played about with it, but couldn't enhance the image, so instead, he froze it on the screen, noted the details and emailed the tech team requesting they prioritise that section. Whilst he did that, Nikki, noticing that Dr Mallory wasn't on the list of attendees who'd forwarded their images, shot off a text asking her to email hers over. Saj faffed about and then brought up the image of Nikki's attacker beside a grainy image of the man pulling his balaclava on.

'Zoom in, Saj. There may be an identifying mark, a clothes brand … anything we can use.'

Saj zoomed in on both images. Apart from the figure being male and with a shaved head, there was nothing useful on the frame. Tired and frustrated, Nikki and Sajid agreed to take a break and were heading out of the station when Saj's phone rang. 'Yep, Williams, whassup?'

Saj's smile faded, and Nikki's stomach muscles clenched as a frown appeared across her partner's forehead. By the time he hung up, she'd gleaned what the call was about. 'Another murder?'

Sajid stepped into the elevator and pressed the down button before responding. 'Yep. Chellow Dene again.'

Nikki's heart pounded. *Please don't let this be anything to do with Ali.*

Chapter 69

Charlie took one look at Haqib lying on his bed, face flushed and a startled expression in his eyes, and groaned. 'Aw yuck. You weren't, were you? You'd think you'd lock the damn door, Haq. What if your mum had walked in?'

Haqib jumped to his feet, all too conscious that Fareena could hear every word his cousin uttered. 'Fuck's sake, Charlie. I wasn't wan—'

Charlie raised a hand in the air. 'TMI! I don't want to know about your masturbatory habits.'

'I told you, I wasn't wan—'

But he couldn't finish his sentence because a loud bang made both cousins jump. 'What the hell, Haq? What was that?'

Eyes wide, Charlie scanned the room, looking for the source of the banging. She jumped again when she heard a faint voice accompanied by another bang. 'Let me out, Haqib. There're spiders in here and I hate spiders.'

As Haqib pulled the chair away from the wall and yanked open the hatch beneath the window, Charlie looked speechless for once … but not for long. 'WTF, Haq? You kidnapping women now or what?'

When Fareena climbed out, shaking her limbs and scraping her fingers through her hair to dislodge any lingering insects,

Charlie groaned again. 'You two are idiots, you know that. If your brothers catch you in Haqib's house, never mind in his bedroom, they'll slice you both limb from limb and dispose of you in suitcases on the moors.'

'Aw shut up, Charlie. For once, can't you just hold back on the wise cracks. Fareena's in trouble and we need help, not you and your stupid damn jokes.'

It wasn't often Haqib retaliated to Charlie's endless teasing, but when he did, she knew he'd had enough. That combined with his pallor, and Fareena's tear-stained face, told her something serious was going on. Without a word she locked his door, then sat on the chair, leaving the bed for the other two. 'Spill.'

Half an hour later, after a convoluted explanation of what had brought Fareena here, Charlie thought she had a handle on things, but summarised in case she'd misunderstood anything. 'Your sister, Attiya, was raped. She's pregnant. She says someone put out a hit on her and she's accusing your brother-in-law of all the above. Is that right?'

The two lovebirds, fingers entwined, nodded in unison.

'Your parents know she's pregnant and were trying to make her marry a bloke in Pakistan ...'

'An old bloke,' added Haqib. 'He's at least twenty-five.'

Charlie ignored him and continued. 'The Forced Marriage Unit says Attiya has gone AWOL, you've stolen your brother-in-law's phone and ...' She spread her hands before her to show that she was reaching the finale. 'You're scared for your life and don't know what to do.'

Fareena and Haqib exchanged a glance, then turned back to Charlie, their faces hoping she'd sort everything out for them, and repeated their earlier synchronised nod.

'Are you both fucking mad?' Charlie jumped to her feet and began pacing the room. 'You two are the most stupid couple I've ever met. This is big. B.I.G. Big. Too damn big for you to handle on your own. Got it?'

Fareena's eyes welled, and Haqib released her fingers to place a reassuring arm round her shoulders. Charlie shook her head and exhaled. 'You've got two options – well, three actually, but the last one isn't really an option. One, you contact the FMU like they told you – duh? Not rocket science, that one, is it?' She counted off the next option on her fingers. 'Two, you tell my mum all of this and let her deal with it … again not rocket fucking science. Or three … you hang around here moping and do nothing and then we're back to my earlier scenario involving amputated limbs and suitcases … What's it to be?'

Chapter 70

Like old times, they travelled in Sajid's Jaguar. Nikki was grateful for the heated seats, not because she was cold, but because the familiarity was comforting. It was rare that they attended two crime scenes in the same area, never mind in such a short space of time, and Nikki wasn't sure what she made of that. It seemed too coincidental that her first crime scene back on the job was at Chellow Dene, where she'd suffered her meltdown. A glance at Saj's tense chin told her he felt the same. To distract herself, Nikki shot another text off to Dr Mallory, requesting her images from the night of the vigil. The woman was busy, still, Nikki had expected her to acknowledge her earlier message.

'You gonna be okay, Nik?' Saj glanced her way as they turned off Haworth Road into the Chellow Dene reservoir car park where two CSI vans, a couple of police cars and Langley's van were already parked up and crime scene tape fluttered around the perimeter of the small car park, creating the outer cordon.

'Trying to consider this a baptism of fire, Saj.' Nikki winked at him. 'If I can survive this, then I can survive anything.' Despite her light-hearted words, Nikki twanged her band as her heart rate sped up. She hadn't been looking forward to her first meeting with those who had witnessed her breakdown, and she definitely hadn't expected it to be at the same site, and this alone increased her anxiety. She took a moment to ground herself with a few breathing exercises before joining Saj near the cordon. No matter how hard she tried, she couldn't stop thinking that people wouldn't be able to see past her behaviour at the last scene. It was okay for Mallory to talk about the detrimental effects of transferring her personal anxieties onto others and assuming that she'd judged their feelings accurately, but the doctor didn't have to go through this. Only Nikki did. As she stepped forward and Saj fell into place by her side, she corrected herself. She wasn't on her own. Saj was here and Langley was probably with the body right now, too.

She and Saj signed themselves through the cordon, donned the crime scene apparel and wended their way down the muddy path towards the bustle of activity. Although cold, it wasn't raining like last time and there was no fog – either in her brain or swirling around them. About a hundred yards short of Liaqat Ilyas's crime site and to the left, she noticed the white tent that had been erected to encompass part of a ramshackle shed. Before them stretched an expanse of water-logged, uneven land dotted with now barren trees. A further few yards beyond that was a newly built housing estate with gardens sprawling towards the marshy ground and the rickety building. Hedges that hadn't quite had the chance to sprout and grow enough to provide a barrier, bordered them. The shed looked out of place next to the new build. It was strange that they had left it standing.

Both she and Saj cursed under their breath as they took their first step into the boggy ground. Although Nikki's feet sank around two inches into the quagmire, her sturdy DMs protected her from the worst of it – *thank you, Marcus, for replacing the leaky old ones*. Sajid fared less well and boy, did he make a fuss about it by lifting his muck-covered shoe up and hopping about on the other, trying to shake off the mud before repeating the pointless action with his other foot. 'Get a grip, Saj. Your Primark chinos and shoes are destined for the bin.'

She paused, head to one side, and slammed her palm against her forehead. 'Oh shit. I forgot, you don't do Primark, do you? That's a shame.'

Although Sajid scowled, his lips twitched, but another voice drowned his reply out. 'Just so we're clear, Parekh, you're not welcome at my crime scene. Not after the last time. You really fucked us over with that carry-on and I don't need a repeat performance. So, I'm only gonna ask you this once. *Are* you able to conduct yourself professionally or not? I will have no hesitancy in barring you if there is even a remote possibility of a repeat performance.'

For a moment, Nikki froze. Whatever she'd expected from Gracie Fells, the crime scene manager, it hadn't been this level of hostility. She and Gracie had a reasonable working relationship – each respecting the other's professionalism. She'd anticipated intense scrutiny – a sense of 'all eyes on her' – but this was unexpected. This wasn't the first time someone had compromised a crime scene. It happened occasionally – they were only human after all.

Gracie stood, hands on hips, like some vengeful Amazon warrior. Saj took a slushy step towards her, but Nikki put out her hand to let him know she had this. Although the level of toxicity was unexpected, Nikki and Dr Mallory had role-played a few scenarios like this one. With a deep breath, Nikki walked towards the other woman, maintaining eye contact as she moved. 'Firstly, Gracie, your disrespectful attitude has been noted and will be written up on my return to Trafalgar House. Secondly, I think you'll find that as SIO it is *my* crime scene not yours and you have no authority.'

Gracie pulled her mask down from her mouth, ready to respond, but Nikki stepped even closer, her eyes sparking in contained anger. 'I find your attitude repellent. I expect better from you. I had a mental breakdown which resulted in minor – I repeat minor – disturbance of a crime scene which offered little evidence, anyway. I wonder if your reaction would be the same if I had compromised your scene by slipping on a slick piece of earth as you did a few months back. Or, if I'd been on crutches like another of your colleagues, who accidentally messed up tyre tracks. It's like you relegate my mental health to the "excuses, excuses" box – the "if-you-can't-see-it-it's-not-real" box. The "I-don't-give-a-fuck-if-you're-in-mental-agony" box. Frankly, that is crap and it stops right here and right now.'

Nikki made to walk past the CSI, then hesitated before turning back. 'Oh, by the way, thanks for welcoming me back to work – your support gives me warm and fuzzy flutters in my stomach. I was expecting sharp and prickly – but hey, good to be proved wrong. It makes all the difference to know that my colleagues have my back.'

They used the metal treads the CSIs had placed as they walked closer to the tent, leaving an open-mouthed Gracie behind. Sajid released a long, low breath. 'And she's baaaack …'

Despite her trembling legs and fluttering heart, Nikki snorted. She'd coped with the first 'return to work challenge' but it hadn't been easy. Still, no need for Saj to know that. 'Damn right I'm back …' Before she could add to her triumphant statement, she slapped a hand over her nose. 'Oh, for God's sake, didn't anyone tell you we had a raw one?'

The smell of a decomposing body was distinctive, and Nikki prepared herself to view this one. At least it wouldn't resemble anyone she knew this time. Pulling aside the tent flap, she poked her head through and saw a figure in a coverall kneeling before their corpse. Although covered up, she recognised Langley. 'Hey Langley, can we come in?'

He turned to her, his eyes crinkling. 'You sure you want to, Nik? It's not a pretty sight.'

With Saj following, Nikki entered, taking care to follow the steps. She couldn't afford to compromise another scene. She ignored the slither of whispers circulating among the CSIs and took a few moments to study what was left of the body whilst Langley worked. Although Nikki had witnessed similar scenes, she was still both horrified and mesmerised by the destruction caused by exposure to the elements and wildlife activity. It was the circle of life and would have been marvellous had the corpse not been the victim of a violent death.

'What can you tell us?'

Langley shrugged. 'I assume you don't want all the detailed stuff about autolysis and putrefaction, so I'll just skip that. None of this is conclusive, but it might give you a starting point. I'll know more when I get this lad to the mortuary.' He stood up and winked at Saj, which was the only sign that their relationship was more than professional. He stepped away from the body before speaking. 'The shed offered some protection from the torrential rain we've had off and on combined with low temperatures – near freezing at some points during the last few weeks – anyhow, this makes it hard to determine with any accuracy time of death without doing a post-mortem. However, decomp is advanced and getting an initial ID on this lad might have to rely on his possessions and clothes for now. I'll check his pockets as soon as I get him in the morgue.'

'But he's male?'

'That's a best guess at the moment, Nik. The skeleton will confirm that, but again …' Langley waved his hand, not bothering to finish the caveat with, 'we'll have to wait for the PM results.'

Eyes focusing on everything but the decaying mass, Saj shuffled his feet. 'Time of death … or cause of death …?'

Langley shook his head. 'On time of death, I can't be more specific than more than a month, less than a year. I suspect the PM will confirm that he's been slashed.'

He moved closer to the body, Nikki close on his heels, and pointed to the unidentified boy's hands. 'You can see that these bones are visible because of decomposition of the skin. Well, I'm almost certain that these marks on the side are because of some sort of knife attack.'

'Machete?' Nikki asked, more in hope than expectation. The state of the body made it impossible to say until Langley had worked his magic. Still, it seemed a logical assumption.

'Aw Nikki, I'm good at my job, but I can't tell you that. Let me finish up here and get him back to the morgue. You'll have my report later on today, okay?'

Farewells said, Nikki left the tent, lifting a hand in greeting to the few CSIs who acknowledged her presence. Nikki limited her interactions at crime scenes to the scene manager or fellow officers as, with thoughts whirling in her brain, she worked on autopilot. Moving back towards the trail before turning round to survey the scene, Nikki pondered on the information Langley had offered. The wounds on the dead boy's hands and arms looked like defensive ones, and it seemed likely that the weapon was a machete. Which led to the question, why had he been dumped in a more secluded spot than the other bodies? Had he been killed there? Nikki looked around. There were two routes to the dilapidated shack – one was through the new estate and the other was via the path she and Saj had just used. She turned to Saj. 'What are the odds that they killed him the same night as Liaqat Ilyas? Timeline might fit. Get someone to check out missing persons reports from after Liaqat's death. I know the parameters are wide until we have more info from Langley, but I don't want to sit on this.'

Saj gestured for a nearby officer to approach. 'You're thinking they were killed at the same time?'

'Could be. Perhaps this victim and Ilyas were together when they were attacked. This victim may have escaped with defensive wounds. The timeline sort of fits and it feels right. He might have hidden in the shed and ...'

'... died there?'

Instead of responding, Nikki retraced her steps to Saj's car, her thoughts filled with sympathy for the needless loss of yet another life. She was eager to return to Trafalgar House and go over Liaqat Ilyas's file with fresh eyes.

Chapter 71

Exhaustion swept over Nikki, and mindful that she needed to pace herself, she left Trafalgar House before Sajid and headed for home. She was exhausted, yet her mind couldn't stop running over everything that had happened that day. She hadn't written Gracie Fells up, prepared instead to let her words stand for themselves. She had too many other battles to fight, and Gracie Fells's issues with mental health weren't top priority.

Langley's post-mortem report was delayed because of a double-booking at the mortuary suite, but that hadn't stopped her from going over Liaqat Ilyas's file to link the new body with his death. Nothing conclusive had come up, but Anwar was on the case, re-interviewing Liaqat's friends. Nikki hoped that the passing of time might have also loosened some tongues. Missing persons had supplied a list of reported missing persons from that date onwards, and Nikki and Saj had narrowed it down to a single likely candidate. Of course, that all depended on whether Nikki's proposed scenario of two boys being together was accurate. She might be off the mark with that. The lad they had identified as a likely candidate was a Graham Moorhead. He was sixteen, from the Eccleshill area of Bradford and although he and Liaqat didn't go to the same school, a deep dive through his social media revealed he knew Liaqat and had been in communication with him. They'd requested access to Moorhead's accounts, but suspected that, like Liaqat's, any data discovered would be inconclusive, any communications would be vague.

Slamming into her house with a loud, 'I'm home!' Nikki was met with silence. Although surprising, it wasn't unheard of, so she wandered through to the kitchen and stopped short just inside the door. There on the table was the box where she'd hidden the postcards from Freddie Downey. Cold sweat spotted her forehead as she stared at the offending item. Marcus had found them! Marcus had found the fucking postcards from her father before she'd had the chance to tell him about them. Her eyes spun around, looking for signs that Marcus was around, but there were none. No pan on the hob with a Bolognese simmering in it. No dishes piled up near the sink ready to be washed. She darted back through the hallway. Not only were Marcus's coat and shoes gone, but so were those belonging to the kids. 'Marcus! Charlie! Ruby! Sunni!' She clattered upstairs wrenching each of her kids' bedroom doors open to be met by silence. Up the next flight to Charlie's room and more silence.

She ran downstairs and on reaching the hall, sank onto the bottom step, her heart hammering, her face clammy and tears pouring down her face. What the hell had she been thinking? Mallory had told her to confide in Marcus. But Nikki had ignored the doctor's expert advice and had brushed the lot under the carpet. This secret – the only one she kept from Marcus now – had been one too many for him to bear. He'd gone, taking the kids and leaving her.

She didn't know how long she sat there wallowing in her grief, berating herself for her prickliness and wishing she could rewind the clock to when the first damn postcard had arrived. The sound of the front gate creaking open roused her, and a deluge of footsteps tramped up to the door. Jumping up, she wiped the tears from her face and waited, pale faced and wide eyed, for it to open.

It swung inwards, clattered against the wall and ricocheted back. All three kids and Marcus tumbled in amid a flurry of limbs and laughter. Marcus took one look at her and held up the bag he was carrying, a frown furrowing his brow. 'Got takeout for tea to celebrate your return to work.'

Sunni bounced forward, unaware of the tension, and thrust another bag at her. 'And ice cream. We got Ben and Jerrys and …' As he marched through to deposit his treasure in the freezer he yelled over his shoulder, 'Charlie's got the wine and Rubster's got the flowers.'

Relief made her weak, and Nikki slid back onto the step she'd just vacated. 'I thought …' She gestured through to the kitchen.

'What …?' Marcus nudged her to the side and joined her on the step. 'You thought I'd left you because you didn't tell me about those damn postcards? Don't you know me by now, Nik? I ain't going nowhere. I only found them because I was looking for my old Bradford City scarf. We'll deal with them together. But right now. We're celebrating.'

28TH NOVEMBER

Chapter 72

Nikki started awake, her heart hammering and, struggling to free herself from the duvet, she wakened Marcus.

'Nik, Nik. It's okay. I'm here … what's wrong?'

She lay on her back, watching the moonlight cast its shadows over the bedroom ceiling, allowing Marcus's soothing words to watch over her. Something had roused her, but she didn't know what. As her breathing slowed, she focused on the noises in the house. The gurning of the central heating, the creaking floorboards and the sound of rain on the windows of her Victorian terrace. Everything seemed normal. She relaxed. No sounds of a marauding man charging up the stairs, so all was good. Then, a blue light flashed across the room before it was gone again.

Marcus sat up. 'God's sake – not again.' Nikki jumped out of bed, hurdled the box of postcards they'd left shoved on the floor after perusing them the previous evening, and dragged the curtains apart. 'Ahad! He's at the Mushtaqs' door and …' She swung round, grabbed Marcus's hoodie and pulled it on. 'Haqib's standing out there watching with his arms round Fareena Mushtaq. Whatever's going on, the silly bugger's going to end up getting a beating from the Mushtaq boys. What's he thinking?'

With Marcus close behind, she ran downstairs, shoved her

feet into her eldest daughter's trainers and was outside in the rain before she could consider her options. After a few seconds of relentless drizzle, she was thankful that Marcus had brought the huge golf umbrella with him. Frantic, she approached her nephew. 'Haqib, what's going on?'

Bouncing on the souls of his feet, Haqib seemed unaware that he was being drenched.

He glowed with excitement, and his reaction was reflected in his girlfriend's face. 'Hey, Auntie Nik. You're just in time.'

Nikki paused and inhaled sharply. What the hell was the silly fool talking about? Just in time? Like they were waiting at a bus stop in the middle of the day rather than standing in the pissing rain in the dead of the night. She nudged him with her bony elbow, but he didn't appear to notice. So, Nikki diverted her attention to the police cars that were lined up outside Fareena's home and from there onto the tall figure – DI Ahad – who was hammering on the door, flanked by two officers from the Forced Marriage Unit. 'What's going on, Haqib? You and Fareena shouldn't be out here in the middle of this. You know you shouldn't. If her brothers see you holding her like this, they'll beat the crap out of you.'

Haqib's snort, if it hadn't been so high and girly, would have showed an 'I don't care' attitude. However, he dropped his hand from around Fareena's shoulder and moved closer to his aunt. Nikki exchanged glances with Marcus and shook her head. In so many ways Haqib was growing up, yet he was still the wriggling, wailing, defenceless baby she'd first clapped eyes on moments after his birth. He turned to Nikki, his eyes gleaming. 'They're gonna arrest him. That's why they're here. They're gonna arrest him and …' His bouncing increased in tempo, making Nikki wonder if he needed the loo. 'It was me and Fareena who got it all … sorted.'

Even more puzzled than she'd been earlier, Nikki realised that, with all the excitement of flashing police car lights and officers hammering on doors, she would not get any sense from her nephew. Instead, she slipped her arm through Marcus's and together they huddled under the brolly, watching as events unfolded. This must be to do with Fareena's sister, Attiya. When she'd left the station, there was no progress on locating Attiya, and Ahad had sloped off into a meeting with Archie, the FMU officers and DCS Clark. Since then they'd received more intel – enough to make an arrest? She was intrigued that Haqib seemed to know what was going on. What had the lad been up to?

Ahad and the other officers entered the Mushtaq house, and before the door closed, Mrs Mushtaq's bulky frame loomed in the doorway. Behind her, someone flicked on a light and Nikki realised the woman was staring straight at her, her uncovered face a screwed-up ball of animosity and anger. 'What the fuck do you think you're looking at, Miss Perfect Parekh? You need to get the fuck out of my family's lives. How we deal with our own is nowt to do with you.' She turned to glare at her youngest daughter. 'As for you, you little slut. You and your sister can rot in hell …' She would have continued her vengeful tirade, but someone dragged her backwards into the hall and the door slammed shut.

Eyebrow quirked, Nikki studied the drenched teen couple with interest. Haqib stared at the sodden ground and his adrenalin-fuelled bounce had stopped, whilst Fareena, her eyes wide, stared at her home, gripping his arm as if it was the only thing keeping her upright. 'You two care to enlighten us now?'

Haqib looked up at her. 'Aw shit, Auntie Nik. I think I've fucked up.'

'Aw, Haqib.' Nikki wrapped her arms round his shoulders and pulled him to her chest. He towered more than a foot taller than her, yet he relaxed into her protective embrace, almost toppling her with his weight as he leaned into her. 'What's happened?'

Nobody wanted to leave the street till whatever was happening inside Fareena's home was resolved, so Marcus headed indoors and grabbed a couple of towels, some coats, and another umbrella. Meanwhile, Haqib, interrupted by Fareena, told his auntie all about Attiya and her brother-in-law and the 'hit' and how they'd taken Charlie's advice and contacted the FMU. Whilst wishing that Charlie had confided in her, Nikki took a moment to savour her pride in her daughter's common sense. Charlie was a star! Haqib, his tone indignant, finished up. 'That pervy brother-in-law has done it before, you know? He's already married – twice according to the stuff we found on his phone. Plus, there're images on there that are just sick ...' Haqib shook his head, disgust flashing in his eyes. 'There's evidence on there that he contacted someone called the Fixer to arrange for Attiya to be killed. How sick is that?'

Shoulders slumped with the enormity of witnessing so much depravity first-hand, Haqib exhaled. Poor Haqib! It seemed he was destined to flit around the outskirts of violence and immorality – after all, his dad was one of the worst criminals Bradford had ever seen. He paused for a moment, then unable to comprehend the inhumanity – or perhaps just unwilling to let it into his heart – he shrugged and a huge grin spread over his face. 'Anyway, DI Ahad is on the case. He'll get it sorted. They'll track down this fixer bloke and that Naveed will be banged up forever.'

With raised eyebrows, Nikki smiled. 'DI Ahad, eh? He your best friend now, is he?'

The lad shuffled his feet, a slight flush burning his cheeks. 'Well, he's not as bad as I first thought.' The flush deepened, and he avoided meeting Nikki's gaze. 'I called him a wanking bastard that night, Auntie Nik. He had a right to be angry with me.' He sniffed. 'Anyhow, that's in't past. He says he'll put in a good word for me when I sign up for police training.'

There was no time for Nikki to be gobsmacked right then, because the Mushtaqs' door opened and officers guided three figures down the steps to the waiting police cars. Nikki's mouth fell open. Naveed Mushtaq, Attiya's brother-in-law, was first in the line. Cuffed and in his usual jeans and hoodie, he strutted into the street, glaring insolently at the crowd, which had increased in numbers since the Mushtaq door had first slammed shut behind the officers. Fareena's father was next, and despite his benign expression, he struggled against the officer all the way to the car. But what surprised Nikki was the identity of the third person. Last in the trio of arrestees was Rabia Mushtaq, now wearing her niqab, but identifiable by her size. Despite only her eyes being visible, her glare scorched the bystanders, and as the officer helped her into the police vehicle, she glared at Nikki. 'Watch your back, Parekh. There's plenty of folk I know who'll do me a favour and off you and your bastard kids.'

Fareena cowered between Marcus and Haqib as her mother yelled at her. 'As for you, you spawn of the devil. Insh'Allah, you and your sister will end up in hell. Allah Akbar!'

Stunned, Nikki's little group could only watch in horror as the cars drove off, leaving the FMU officers and DI Ahad behind. Ahad walked over and, hand extended towards Haqib, he grinned. 'You did good, lad. You did good. Now, don't forget what I said about signing up. We could do with honest lads like you in the police, couldn't we, Parekh?'

Seeing her nephew grow three inches at the praise, Nikki met Ahad's gaze, her expression stony and untrusting. 'If you say so.'

Ahad nodded and shrugged. 'A word, Parekh?'

Grudgingly, Nikki joined him a few feet away from the others and waited.

'We got off to a poor start and I'm sorry about that.' He frowned, his dark eyes clouding over. 'This has been a difficult few weeks for me,' and seeing Nikki roll her eyes, he gave a humourless laugh. 'I'm not expecting sympathy and I'm not making excuses. I was a dick the other night. Your lad acted up and I overreacted. I'm sorry for that.'

He held out his hand, but Nikki wasn't ready to forgive and forget. He'd been out of order – well out of order – and, according to Saj, not for the first time. He retracted his hand and ran his fingers through his hair before lowering his voice so only she could hear. 'My wife and child died three months ago. Childbirth.' He swallowed. 'Ours was a love marriage, and we lost our families over it. We moved north because her dad had paid some fixer or other to kill us both …' He stopped and shrugged. 'You get what I'm saying?'

Nikki looked into his eyes and saw the depth of his grief. She understood that sort of pain. Losing her mother had been bad, but to lose Marcus or any of her children would be intolerable. She reached out to squeeze his arm, then hesitated. A pulse throbbed at his temple. 'The other day was her birthday and the last place I should have been was at work. I really am sorry. I won't make those mistakes again.'

This time Nikki reached out. 'Apology accepted. I know a bit about dysfunctional families, loss and grief.'

He nodded and made to move towards his car. 'Oh, Parekh …?'

She smiled, understanding what he was about to say. 'Don't worry. I don't gossip. What you just told me is between you and me only.'

Ahad laughed. 'Actually, I knew that already. What I was going to say was, get some sleep. I expect you bright and early tomorrow – it's going to be a long, long day.'

Chapter 73

The Honourable Fixer

'What the hell's going on?' The words leave my mouth and echo round the space, mocking me. Rage smothers me, but I have nowhere to direct it. I pick up a vase of flowers and smash it against the wall. Water splashes everywhere, dripping down the lilac walls before soaking into the carpet amid ceramic shards and bruised petals. The anger stays with me, though, and I'm soon back to pacing the room again. Round and round and round. That vase cost three thousand and now, just like that, it's gone. I look at the pile of passports lying on the coffee table and some of my frustration dissipates. It's not like I can take the damn thing with me, is it?

I had muted the notifications on the PC, but now it's time to check out the damage. I delve deep into the dark web and enter my website – The Honourable Fixer Fixes What You Can't. First up, I check my security measures and encryptions, and rage threatens to engulf me again. There have been numerous attempts to bypass my security – all unsuccessful, of course. But the very fact that they're out there, like a bunch of zombies, seeking entry, a way to take over my operation, a way to insert themselves above me in the pecking order, makes me glad that I've used pre-emptive viruses that will backfire on them.

If I step away from my business, it won't pass to some rogue using a back door to effect an amalgamation. It'll go to the highest bidder and *that* won't be you, *PrincessesForSale*, nor you, *KnifeForHire*, and it's most certainly not going to be you, *DeathByTheDime* – tacky or what? I send the details of each cyber-attack to an encrypted file. I don't have time for this crap right now, but I'll circle back to it – probably when I'm sitting with a cocktail on a Venezuelan beach – and punish them. Using an incognito program, I trawl through their websites before I put the matter to bed. The despair and degradation these people plunder turns even my hardy stomach. However, their particular brand of evil is not my immediate concern. I access my private message board and infiltrate various meeting rooms – you'd think the idiots would take their griping off site. But no, they think because it's labelled private that it's safe from my prying eyes. Lots of discussion going on about whether I have a handle on things. Some cold feet trying to back out, asking how to exit the site, leaving no crumbs. I grin. The only person able to leave the website without leaving a trace is me and each of their sorry backsides is going to be sent on platters to the police. I laugh; it's my civic duty after all.

Chapter 74

#WhatsWrongWithThisShit?

THE ONE WHERE THE GIRL GETS RAPED AND THE FAMILY COVER IT UP
POSTED BY BFDLASS#WWWTS NOVEMBER 28TH 09:22

#WhatsWrongWithThisShit?

So, when your daughter gets raped, what do you do?
   a. Chop the rapist's balls off?
   b. Report it to the police?
   c. Send the girl off to Pakistan to get married?
   d. Make sure your daughter gets all the help she needs?
If you answered anything other than a, b, or d, then you're a shit and you're part of the problem.

#ForcedMarriagesMustStop

This story is all too familiar and it happened in my family. My sister was raped by our brother-in-law and somehow that's her fault?

#WhatsWrongWithThisShit?

*Instead of protecting her, my parents, for fear of 'Dishonour',
opted to arrange a marriage for her with a man she's never
met … in a country she's never visited.*

*Instead of chucking my brother-in-law out of the house
and setting the law on him, they funded him when he hired
a hitman to kill my sister.*

*My other sister, the scumbag's wife, is destroyed by all of this.
This is not honour, this is illegal and it is barbaric.*

#WhatsWrongWithThisShit?
#ForcedMarriagesMustStop

Views: 98 Shares: 12

COMMENTS:

*Karryann3: OMG! This is awful. Are you okay? This is crap.
Don't know owt about forced marriage but it sounds awful
#ForcedMarriagesMustStop*

JakeK4292: Fucking pakis – they all do this shit …

*MH616: @JakeK4292 WTAF! You for real? Forced Marriage
isn't Islamic. Shari'ah law does not support this and nor do
most Muslims, but as usual when something like this hits
the news, we're all tarred with the same brush and the racial
slurs come out. You don't know what you're talking about.
#WhatsWrongWithThisShit #BeBetterThanThat*

*JakeK4292: @MH616 What do you know? I live next door to
some pakis and they had a forced marriage for their son …
bloody racket in the street it were.*

*MH616: @JakeK4292 Duh? There's a huge difference between
Forced, Arranged and Love Marriages #FactCheck AH! In*

Islam all marriages should be consensual – what's the problem with that? Oh let me think – yeah it's skin colour that bothers you not who we marry. #RacistScum

Karryann3: @JakeK4292 Why don't you just sod off? @BradfordLass#WWWTS Can't you block him? Things are bad enough without him stirring it. #WhatsWrongWithThisShit

BradfordLass#WWWTS: @Karryann3 He's blocked. Thanks for your support.

BradfordLass#WWWTS: *Thanks for all your support and shares. I'm closing this account today, so you won't hear from me again. I have my sisters to think about now. But rest assured all your support fills me with hope. Keep fighting the scumbags* **#WhatsWrongWithThisShit #BeBetterThanThat #ForcedMarriagesMustStop**

Chapter 75

The next morning, Nikki, with Marcus as back-up, approached the Mushtaq home. Every room was lit and a Family Liaison Officer had entered the house a short time ago. A CSI team would go over the house whilst the rest of the family would remain in the front room or perhaps the kitchen, whilst they worked. At first, no one answered, but after a second attempt, the door inched open a crack and a pair of eyes glared at her through the gap. It was one of Fareena's brothers, but Nikki didn't know which. 'Whaddya want?'

Nikki wasn't sure why she'd reached out. She supposed it was the thought that these three kids, barely out of their teens, had suffered a traumatic experience and her conscience wouldn't let her rest till she'd offered her help. Her mother would have done the same, after all, they were neighbours. Haqib had hinted that the brothers were very protective of the girls. Whether they'd been party to Naveed's behaviour was unclear. Then there was Zara, Fareena's older sister. She'd learned that her husband was not only a rapist, but he'd ordered her sister's murder. Who knew how she felt right now?

Nikki grimaced. 'I don't want anything, just wanted to check you're okay. I mean …' She waved her hand in the air. 'All of this must be a shock to you.'

The door opened a little wider and the lad, who Nikki now recognised as the older brother, Kam said, 'You here as a pig, cos we've already got one inside?'

Nikki smiled back when the lad gave a rueful smile, as if to take the sting out of the word 'pig.' 'No, I'm here as your neighbour and as a friend of Fareena's. Nothing more. Do you need anything?'

He looked across the street to Nikki's house and wiped his arm over his nose. 'Fareena okay?'

'She's in shock – like you are. She doesn't know what will happen to her or …' Nikki paused, unsure whether she should utter the next words, but unable not to put the subject out there. 'Or if she's lost all of her family.'

Her brother gave a sort of combined nod and shrug. The action was so like one Haqib would make that Nikki's heart contracted. 'And Attiya, she okay? She really pregnant?'

Nikki could only nod. Kam already knew Attiya was pregnant, but was still processing the details of her rape and his parents' and brother-in-law's actions. A muscle in his chin contracted as he tried to keep hold of his emotions. 'I'll kill that bastard. Fucking kill him.' He sniffed and blinked, as if to stop his emotions from getting the better of him. 'We were fine till they made Zara marry him. Me and Farooq knew he were bad news but they wouldn't listen …' He banged his brow lightly on the door. 'Fucking bastard. Now I've got two sisters, each of them carrying his kid … fucking bastard!'

Nikki hadn't realised that Fareena's older sister was pregnant too, and this complicated an already complicated situation even more. She made a mental note to ask Mallory for a referral for the Mushtaq kids when she deigned to reply to Nikki's messages. She glanced at Marcus, who gave a slight nod. It was time for them to go. They'd reached out and they would do so again over the coming weeks, but they'd done enough for now. The Mushtaq kids needed a chance to process what had happened. 'You need anything, anything at all, you just come over.'

315

They turned and made their way down the concrete steps to the path and had just opened the gate when Kam spoke again. 'Tell Fareena and Attiya to give us a few days. We're going to be tied up with your lot for a while and the officer …' He jerked his head behind him to show he was talking about the FLO. 'Says we've not to talk to Attiya or Fareena till we've given our statements.'

He exhaled and washed his palm over his face. 'This shit should never have happened. Don't know what the parents were thinking.' He looked right at Nikki. 'It was my mum more than my dad, though. I'd bet anything on it. She was always a bitch. Handy with her fists. Me and Farooq spent more time in that cellar than was healthy for a young kid. She deserves everything she's got coming to her.'

Hand on the gate, Nikki hesitated until she was sure he was done. 'You're not on your own. We'll look after Fareena for now and when you're ready come over.'

Chapter 76

Fuelled by an ongoing sense of excitement, feverishness almost, Haqib arrived early. His Auntie Nikki had taken Fareena to BRI to visit her sister before dropping her back off at school. Attiya was recovering well. She was dehydrated and in shock, but other than that, she and her baby were physically fine – whether it made her loopy, like his Auntie Nik, he didn't know. Attiya had a lot of decisions to make over the next few weeks, and Auntie Nik had promised her the support she needed.

It was weird to see Fareena without her niqab outside school and wearing Charlie's clothes. She was pale, her eyes dull, but she smiled when she saw him. However, there was something on his mind and he couldn't hold it in. 'Shit, Fareena, all that **#WhatsWrongWithThisShit** stuff was you?'

Since he'd put two and two together after her last blog post, Haqib wondered what other secrets Fareena was keeping from him, but then, he had secrets too. Like his plan to have a gap year with Charlie before applying to join the police. 'Why didn't you tell me? In fact, why did you do it? Some of that stuff you got from me, didn't you?'

Fareena flushed. 'Sorry. I didn't want you to get in trouble if anyone sussed out it was me. I …' She shrugged. 'I didn't want you getting hurt. If the Eyes found out – or Naveed – or my parents, anything could have happened.'

The pair of them sat together in the assembly hall, their fingers entwined as they conversed in whispers, so the other pupils, most of whom were casting curious glances in their direction, wouldn't overhear. Things had kicked off big time. Fareena, Charlie and Haqib had given statements about the Eyes and their suspicions about the group's involvement in Molly Cropper's attack and Maz Khan's abduction. Then, soon after registration, the police converged on the school. Officers shepherded the most aggressive Eyes out to waiting police cars and although Haqib didn't regret naming them, a prickle of fear lingered. Were there others who hadn't yet been named? Others who would realise his role in the arrests of their friends? What they would do to him didn't bear thinking about. He'd just have to watch his back till things settled down.

The head teacher and DI Ahad were at the front of the hall, ready to make an appeal for information regarding not only Molly and Maz's attacks but also about the machete murders. His auntie had told him that another unidentified body had been discovered yesterday. According to Auntie Nik, various schools throughout Bradford had been found to have an Eye's presence and were also being visited by senior police officers. As DI Ahad stepped forward and began his appeal, Haqib sat up straight in his seat. Pride in his part in exposing the Eyes, flowed over him. He hadn't considered following in his auntie's footsteps until recently, but now that he had, he felt a sense of purpose. A sense of self-worth that overrode his guilt at the things his father had done. He was his own man, and he didn't have to live in the darkness of his father's shadow. He would do what his auntie did and blast his way through the darkness by putting the bastards away.

Chapter 77

Nikki had been on the go all morning, leading the investigation into the murder of Graham Moorhead. The boy's identity had been confirmed from a student bus pass found in the pocket of his jeans. Exactly how they'd extracted the information from the soiled ID was something Nikki didn't need to know. Sajid and Williams had notified Graham's parents, and now Williams and Anwar were focusing on building up a picture of the lad's interests and friendship groups. The parents were devastated, which was to be expected, yet, according to Saj, they'd already reconciled themselves to never seeing their son alive again when he didn't turn up or contact them after a few days.

They and the rest of their small extended family were desperate to help and had already provided a list of their son's friends. Graham was gay. Saj's smile was tinged with sadness when he told Nikki that Graham's dad had proudly described his son as 'out and proud.' Saj could never expect that sort of support from his own family, and it hurt. No matter how caring Langley's parents were, Saj had little contact with his family, and it saddened him.

As Nikki fell into her chair with a cuppa and a sausage sandwich, she realised that she'd need to pace herself for the rest of the day. Her time off and the trauma of her breakdown made her less robust than before, and her body and mind needed time out.

'PM report's in.' Saj peered over the top of her computer, startling her. 'Check it out. Langley confirms time of death as between four and six weeks ago. He also matched the marks on the bones with the machete used in Shabana Hussain's death. Think that about confirms that they're all linked.'

Nikki rolled her neck, feeling the creaking of sinew and muscle as she did so. Boy, was she tense. 'Anything else notable?'

Saj sat down and mumbled to himself as he scrolled through the report.

'Nothing much. A lot of stuff about ...' He paused and then his head popped up, his eyes sparkling with excitement. 'Cause of death! It wasn't blood loss because of knife wounds. It was hypothermia. Poor soul must have been knifed before he escaped.'

'Perhaps he wasn't their primary target? Perhaps he was with Liaqat Ilyas when they attacked him?'

'You still going with the assumption that the two lads were together?'

Nikki grinned. 'Well, I've been skimming through the interviews with the Eyes – stupid fucking name that – very *Handmaid's Tale*, isn't it?'

'Eh?'

'Margaret Atwood – dystopian series about ...' Nikki paused when she saw Sajid's eyes glaze over. *Uncultured git.* 'Never mind. I'm just saying it's a strange coincidence for two kids to have been found dead in the same proximity at around the same time. These bullies are naming names and making accusations. However, we can't locate the ringleaders they're dobbing in.'

'Oh, and who are they?'

'The usual suspects – delightful bunch. The ones we picked up on the CCTV at the vigil – Michelle Glass, Amar Akhtar, Chas Choudry.' Nikki rammed the last of her lunch into her mouth and got up, grabbing her coat from the back of her chair as she did so. 'Come on, Boy Blunder – it's off to work we go.'

Mumbling about the rare likelihood of being both vertically challenged *and* a Boy Blunder, Sajid grabbed his coat and ran after Nikki.

Waiting for the lift to arrive, he doubled back to a conversation from earlier. 'So, she said she wanted me to visit?'

Nikki nodded. 'Her precise words were, "Can you get that dopey bastard who gave me his coat to drop in so I can tell him how stupid he was?"'

'Piss off, Parekh.' Sajid frowned. 'I'm only asking because she must be traumatised. I mean, it's not every day your parents finance your brother-in-law's attempts to have you killed off, is it?'

Nikki took pity on him. 'Saj, Attiya appreciated your kindness. It came when the only people on her side were addicts with a memory span of ten minutes. Besides, she needs as many friends as she can get.'

'Reckon we'll get to the bottom of this? Find out who the Fixer is?'

The kids who'd been interviewed talked about some anonymous person called the Honourable Fixer or the Fixer for short. Honourable was a word that had no place in the same sentence as the Fixer. This Fixer character kept their own hands clean by paying dumb kids to do the dirty work. Nobody had been able to ID him, and Nikki wondered if they ever would. Most of them were spilling information like jellybeans to minimise their punishments for various misdemeanours – carrying a weapon at the vigil and being part of the fake acid attack and beating kids up at school for supposed 'honour' violations. So far, Maz Khan was implicated only in the fake acid attack and Nikki's fingers were crossed that Ali's son hadn't got himself in any deeper than that. The consensus was that the Fixer's right-hand man – a bloke called the Headhunter – had hired the youths.

'We'll keep the investigation open till we find the Fixer bloke and the Headhunter. Maybe when we catch up with Glass and Akhtar, they'll lead us to their doorstep – but we need to locate the little scrotes first.'

It could take months to sift through, double check and corroborate all the statements, but Nikki wasn't holding her breath that they'd find either the Headhunter or the Fixer soon. From what she gathered, The Fixer had created carefully constructed layers that distanced him from the violence. How much money did this Fixer have? Naveed Mushtaq had paid him to kill Attiya, but he'd clammed up as had Attiya's parents, their only response 'no comment'.

Nikki's phone beeped, signalling a text, so she held up a finger and glanced at the content. Seconds later, she jabbed her finger on the lift button, cursing under her breath. It was an unknown number, but in Nikki's line of work, that was hardly surprising. She often received tip-offs from her sources on the streets. What intrigued her with this one, though, was that it came with an attachment.

'Whassup? Something happened?'

'Just got a text and a damn photo. Someone's yanking our chains and I think I know who it is. That bastard's been holding out on us. Come on.'

Chapter 78

In the end, Nikki decided not to wait for the elevator and instead hightailed it downstairs, Saj at her heels. All the while, she cursed the texter *and* her sore ribs *and* the stairs *and* the inefficient lifts in Trafalgar House. Saj followed in silence, allowing her to vent. When she reached the car park and wheezed her way towards Saj's Jag, her arms folded round her body as she dragged air into her tortured lungs. She glared at him. 'Open the damn door, I need to sit down.'

Breathless, after their unexpected sprint, Saj rummaged for the keys in his pockets, panting as he did so. His fumbling became more frantic as Nikki leaned against his car, eyebrows raised. 'Don't … just don't … tell me … you've …?'

With a triumphant whoop, Saj held the keys aloft, ignored Nikki's irritated glance, and opened the door. Groaning, Nikki lowered herself into the seat, berating herself for not waiting for the damn lift. In the end, they'd only gained seconds – if that. She'd pay for her foolishness later and she'd nobody to blame for her pain but herself … and Ali, she added, cursing him again under her breath.

'So?' Saj switched the ignition on and glanced at her. 'What the hell made you think you were up for a marathon after weeks of doing little more than a bit of light housework? Care to tell me where we're going?'

Nikki raised her middle finger, then rummaged about in her own pocket for her phone, every move pulling on her fragile ribs. 'See for yourself … Bloody idiot!'

Saj took her phone and read the text aloud. '*Present for you! You can thank me later!*' He opened the attachment and his mouth fell open. In the image, five bruised and beaten, blindfolded figures slumped against a nondescript wall, their hands and feet tied with cable ties which looked to be biting into their flesh. 'Shiiiiit!'

'Exactly. Shit! Any guesses who they are?'

'I'd guess we've found Glass, Akhtar and Choudry – not sure about the other two, but fucking hell, Nik, are they even still alive?'

'For my anonymous texter's sake I hope they are.'

'It's Ali, isn't it?' Saj glanced around as he spoke, as if expecting someone to have creeped into the car with them.

'That'd be my best guess. The idiot's smart enough to use a burner to give himself deniability. I assume this was the reason he was being such a dick. These scrotes must have been responsible for what happened to Maz and—'

'—he took his revenge. But are we sure it's him, Nik? It could be anyone?' Sajid's tone had a hopeful lilt to it.

Nikki was quick to dash his hopes. 'Don't be soft. Course it's him. You *know* it's him. It could only be him.'

Banging his fist on the steering wheel, Saj exhaled. 'Any idea where they are?'

'Shit yes, sorry, cotton wool brain. He sent another text with the address.' She typed it into the satnav, and Saj drove whilst Nikki contemplated what awaited them at the end of their journey. Ali wasn't an evil man, but his only child had been mutilated, and that meant he was unpredictable. Would he have killed five kids? She doubted it – or rather, she *hoped* he hadn't. The Ali she knew wouldn't have done such a thing, but those kids looked in a bad way. Surely if he'd killed them, he would have dumped the corpses where they'd never be found. Ali had contacts all over and she didn't doubt that, if he wanted, he could have arranged the clean disposal of the bodies. She clung to that thought as they drove, for that was the only way Ali giving her the heads-up on their whereabouts made sense. Why he'd taken so long to contact her, however, was beyond her.

'Should we call it in? Paramedics, CSI, more officers for back-up?'

Nikki hesitated. Whatever she decided could have consequences on her being able to continue at work. If she called it in, there was no way she could ensure her friend's anonymity. Could the victims identify him? She snorted at her own stupidity. Of course, none of them had seen Ali, or so they said. He'd have made sure of their silence. She suspected Haris would have been responsible for the state of the captives. If she didn't call it in and those kids were dead, she'd be sacked. Exhaling, she shook her head. 'I trust Ali. He wouldn't have left them in a critical condition, I'm certain of it. I'll call the paramedics, but we won't need back-up. Ali wouldn't lead us into a trap. I know he wouldn't.'

'I hope you're right, Nik.' Sajid's sombre look and morose words made her doubt herself, but only for a moment. Ali had had her back more times than she cared to remember, and now she would have his. Sometimes Ali could achieve things she couldn't, and she suspected this was one of those times. She phoned emergency services and requested an ambulance and then studied the image of the five captives, using the zoom mechanism to focus on different areas.

Satisfied, she turned sideways, ignoring the pull at her ribs. She needed to see Saj's face when she asked him for his silence. 'Saj, I think Ali has done us a favour. I think he tracked down the kids who took his son and I think he exerted just enough pressure to extract information about who's behind it all. I zoomed in on each of them and the blood smeared over their faces looks staged. He's mocked up a horror show so that we act quickly. They must

325

have told him something, but rather than dispose of them, he's handed it over to us – to the police. These kids might help us break this case wide open and might identify the head honchos.'

Sajid said nothing for a long moment, then gave an abrupt nod. 'You're asking me to say it was an anonymous source. To leave Ali out of it.'

Nikki exhaled. 'Only if you're comfortable with it, Saj, and definitely only if those kids' injuries are minor.'

'Fuck, Nikki, things were never this quiet whilst you were off. With you, police work is sooo simple and straightforward ...' He grinned 'Besides, it *was* an unnamed source. We don't know for sure Ali's behind this.'

She allowed herself a smile, appreciating Sajid's sarcastic attempt to ease the tension that had built up between them in the car. She owed her partner big time ... and so did Ali Khan.

Chapter 79

The Honourable Fixer

I'm picking up all sorts of chatter on the internet and none of it's good. It's time for me to go – leave whilst I'm ahead. I can easily paint my last strokes from Venezuela. I frown; the sweet scent of the flowers wilting on the carpet irks me, but I make no move to clean it up. That's someone else's problem now.

My real issue is Parekh. She's got her finger on the pulse and she seems to be everywhere. She's there at the recent crime scene and God knows what she's thinking. Then she's there when Veed32 gets arrested. I underestimated her, and that grates on me. I thought she'd have another breakdown. Or be too knackered to do any good, particularly considering the injuries she sustained at the vigil. But the stupid bitch is up and at 'em like she'd never freaked out. It's just not natural. I'll make sure she pays. Maybe I'll meet up with her daddy. I know where Freddie Downey is and could easily strike up an alliance with him. Of course, it would only be temporary. I do my best work solo, and there's no way I want a partner.

It's not only her, though. The Headhunter forgot to tell me about that little loose end in Chellow Dene. Not a damn peep about a second body from him, and now the bastard's ignoring me again. I don't care if the Eyes acted without authorisation. It's still his fault and I will ensure his punishment. Not because it makes me safer, but because it gives me pleasure.

I've already chosen my new identity – Lalita Parekh – how good is that? My flight's booked, my transport secured and in ten hours it'll be 'Bye bye Bradford. Bye bye UK, bye bye rain and ... Hellooooo sunshine.'

Chapter 80

Saj had barely parked up before Nikki threw open the door, narrowly missing a cyclist. With a 'sorry' thrown over her shoulder, she crashed through the dilapidated gate and into the unkempt garden of a Victorian terrace in Bradford Three. Someone had thrown a *For Sale* sign onto the overgrown lawn amid a heap of other discarded items, which Nikki had no intention of studying further.

She hesitated at the rotting door and waited for Sajid to join her. As eager as she was to go inside and determine what had happened to the five captives, some part of her wished herself far away from the sordidness of it all. With a tentative hand, she pushed the handle down. As expected, she gained immediate access to the foul-smelling premises. Whilst Saj sought a light switch, Nikki strained to hear any noise through the ominous silence.

The light springing on startled her. A pile of junk mail and old letters – mostly bills – was haphazardly piled on a rickety table where a phone had once stood. Dust motes shimmered in the air and the entire house seemed to yell 'let me die'. They split up and checked the downstairs – a living room with broken furniture and a poxy unsanitary kitchen. Once the downstairs was clear, Nikki pointed upstairs and when Saj nodded, she began her ascent, trying to avoid any creaking stairs as she crept. Although she knew Ali wouldn't have led her into a trap, all of her senses were on high alert as she swung her head this way and that, as per her training.

'Which room?' Sajid's whisper made her jump. They were on the landing and faced with three doors. Nikki studied them. The first was ajar and revealed a stained porcelain sink. Each of the others was closed, but only one had a lock with a shiny new padlock positioned just above it. 'That one?'

Saj nodded and before Nikki could stop him, he braced his arms on the walls of the narrow hallway, raised a foot and slammed it into the wood. It shattered, and the remains of the door burst inwards. A double bed with blood-soaked sheets lying in disarray faced them. Her gut contracted. Was this where they'd held Maz Khan? No wonder he'd needed strong antibiotics to combat his wound infection – this place was a quagmire of bacteria. Eyes watering in reaction to an overwhelming smell of excrement, she coughed, covering her nose to the stench, and glanced round at the five cable-tied figures slumped against the back wall. They were gagged and their eyes – the ones that weren't swollen shut, anyway – were wide and fluttering, fear emanating from each blink. Blindfolds lay discarded on the rotten carpet. It didn't take a genius to work out why four of them had attempted to shuffle away from Choudry. His once grey trackie bottoms were now sodden and brown.

A sigh of relief escaped Nikki's lips as she approached and began to cut their binds. Thank God, they were alive. A kernel of doubt that she'd misinterpreted Ali's capabilities had niggled her on the drive over. However, now her faith in her friend was restored, she wanted to both hug and berate Ali at the same time. All five of them remained in place, leaning against the wall as if it was more than their lives were worth to move. Nikki made a cursory assessment of their injuries – apart from some yellowing bruises and a few cuts, their wounds appeared to be minor.

She recognised Amar Akhtar straight away. His right eye was swollen and his jaw had a massive yet fading bruise, which was an older wound. She studied him for a moment, her mind going through the list of people they'd identified in the vigil's vicinity. With narrowed eyes, she stepped closer to him, imagining him upright rather than sprawled in an ungainly heap. Her mouth widened into something halfway between a snarl and a sneer. 'It was you, wasn't it?'

His eyes darted around the room, anywhere but in Nikki's direction. She nudged his foot with her boot. 'You gave me this.' She pointed to the wound on her cheek. 'You, you slimy little bastard, were going to kill me that night.'

Amar's head moved from side to side in silent denial, but Nikki wasn't done. She remembered the few injuries she'd inflicted on her assailant and, with no pity at all on her face, she sent her fist into his ribs – precisely where she'd slammed into him during the fight. He paled, and a whoof of pain exploded from his mouth.

'See, you do remember.' Nikki's smile was wide, as if she was congratulating a wayward child for some minor achievement.

'All right, all right, it was me … I admit it. Just don't do that again. Please d-d-don't …'

His pathetic pleading angered Nikki more than the fact that he'd scarred her. She'd been scarred before and had worn her wound like an amulet – a symbol of her survival. She'd have respected the idiot more if he'd owned his misdeeds. With a 'tut' that made him flinch, she moved down the line to the next person.

Michelle Glass, head down, hijab nowhere in sight, avoided Nikki's glare. *What is it with these kids?* Glass's injuries were minor too. Her wrists, where the cable ties had been, had no marks. Nikki was right, Ali had staged the scene.

'Why are you here, Michelle? Who did that to you?' Nikki pointed at the girl's bruised face and the scratches on her arms. Michelle shook her head, but Nikki noted that she angled her body away from Amar. *Interesting.*

The lad sprawled to Michelle's left was Chas Choudry. As soon as she'd released his bound wrist, he'd folded his arms across his chest and focused on the floor. Nikki skipped him for now. He would be easier to break in an interview room on his own. It took her a moment to recognise the next lad. Not because he was beaten beyond recognition, but because she was used to seeing him immaculately dressed, his hair gelled in a similar style to her nephew Haqib's. Now, his lustrous hair was replaced by a shaved head and heavy stubble, both of which altered his appearance almost beyond recognition. 'Taj?'

Nikki shook her head. Why the hell would Taj Jhuti be here with the bunch of headbangers responsible for attacking his girlfriend? It made no sense. Her eyes fell to his trainers. She recognised those. They were the same ones that Maz Khan had bought with his ill-gained earnings. It fell into place. 'You hooked up with these idiots for the money?' She didn't bother to hide her incredulity. Why should she? She'd just identified the weakest link in the bunch and, later on, she and Saj would exploit that.

The final captive, Mally, hadn't been on either Nikki or Saj's radar until then. He was a bruiser though, and she was sure he'd have a record. His chin jutted upwards in insolence and as his eyes kept steady contact with hers, his lips curled, making no secret of his hatred for them. Deciding not to give him the satisfaction of giving smartass responses to her questions, Nikki turned and walked back to the beginning of the line and addressed Amar. 'What happened?'

The five cast worried glances at each other, and then Amar said, 'We're going to come clean to you.' His gaze went to the floor as if hoping it would offer some guidance, but when none appeared, he looked at Nikki. 'The game's up and we know we're in big shit, but there're others that have done worse things than us. We're only kids.'

'Eh …?' Nikki pointed at the other four. '*They're* kids, Amar.

You, on the other hand, well, you're the same age as me and that makes you an adult.'

He shrugged. 'But I'm not well …' His words trailed off and his lips tightened. Nikki realised that Ali had used Amar's ill health as a carrot to get him to talk. She decided to back off for now. The last thing she needed was to undo any of the good work Ali had accomplished. That was when Saj attracted her attention.

'Nik?' Sajid was grinning. 'Looks like someone had the presence of mind to make recordings.' His smile widening, he looked at the row of battered people. 'Wonder what juicy confessions you made on this.' He pointed to the iPhone mounted on a tripod and facing them.

Michelle Glass began to weep, her head bowed. 'It's all your fault, Amar. You and your old man's.'

It was then the sound of the ambulance approaching filtered through the dodgy double glazing. Nikki grinned at them. 'Soon as you're all patched up, we'll interview you. For now though, we've got this to watch.' Extracting gloves from her pocket, she took the iPhone from its stand and put it in an evidence bag. 'Hope you've got your stories straight or …' She wiggled the bag in their faces as the first of the paramedics entered the room. 'We'll know if you're lying.'

Chapter 81

After the captives had been taken to BRI to be assessed, Nikki left the house in the safe hands of three rosy-cheeked uniformed officers. DI Ahad was waiting for Nikki when she and Saj returned to Trafalgar House. 'A word, Parekh.'

Keen to go through the files they'd found on the iPhone before the five suspects returned to Trafalgar House for interview, she had no time for DI Ahad. Still, she rolled her shoulders and then gave a single nod. 'Yes, boss.'

'You too, Malik.' He marched through to the incident room, which was quiet for once, and gestured to a couple of chairs, whilst he remained standing, his face masked.

So, this was why Sajid called him the Dark Knight – he was the impenetrable Batman with dark secrets and the desire for revenge, not the slap, bang, bosh Batman of the comic strips. His eyes were hooded, their expression hidden. Yet, if she could see into them, Nikki was sure thunder clouds would roll over them. Simply put, she and Sajid were in deep shit and, if she was honest, she couldn't blame him for being annoyed. All things being equal, she should have called it in. In fact, she would have, except the anonymous text and her suspicions about its origins had tilted the balance in another direction. She braced herself for the rollicking she sensed was heading her way – after all, she was used to being harangued for her rogue behaviour. Over the years, these episodes had become water off the proverbial duck's back.

However, when he spoke, Ahad's tone was measured and calm, which left Nikki frustrated with nowhere to vent the tension she'd gathered. Hell, he was even smiling. 'Didn't think of giving us a head's up, eh, Parekh?'

He stood up and walked over to a desk in front of her and rested on it, one foot dangling whilst the other, flat on the floor, balanced his body. The smile was gone and thunder clouds crashed right over Nikki. 'You know, to tell us that whilst we were pulling out all the stops to find your little band of sociopaths, you'd been sent the location already?'

Dark eyes lasered into Nikki's, evoking the sensation of being skewered, ready to be placed on a well-heated barbeque. Aiming for nonchalance, she offered a one-shouldered shrug. 'Thought it was a hoax, if I'm honest. Didn't want to waste everybody's time on an anonymous tip-off.' She tried a smile for size, but got no response. 'It was my decision. Saj said we should call it in – just in case.'

The DI exhaled, then clapped his hands on his thighs. 'Sod it. I've no time for a pissing contest right now, Parekh. Consider yourself told off.' He moved his gaze to Sajid. 'As for you, Malik, now that you've passed your sergeant's exams, I expect a bit more independent thinking from you. That's if you want a good reference from me when you apply for jobs elsewhere.'

Whilst Nikki's head spun round to her partner, Saj's hung down, avoiding her gaze. 'You passed your sergeant's exams? Why didn't you tell me?' The news had stunned her. She'd been nagging at him for months about it, but he'd always said he wasn't ready and now he'd gone and sat the damn thing without telling her. Then came the tremor of anxiety. The solid normality of work that she'd returned to was fast becoming quicksand. A new DI and the possibility that Saj would end up working elsewhere – not on her team. *Shit!* Realising her selfishness, she reached over and poked her partner's shoulder. 'Jammy little shit. You've more brains in there than you let on. Congratulations.'

'Yes, yes, yes.' Ahad turned to one of the PCs. 'Time for that later. The techies have sent copies of the files from that iPhone. Wonder what they'll turn up? I'm assuming you want to watch them before the unholy quintet return from BRI.'

Pushing her fear about Saj moving on from her team to the back of her mind, Nikki pulled her chair over to the PC so the three of them could watch the video files together. Sandwiched between them, Nikki hoped Ali had had the sense not to be visible in any of the frames. She couldn't protect him if they caught him or his men on camera. Her next worry was the content of the videos. She hoped that whatever they were about to witness would be worth all this angst.

Whoever was at the helm of the recording was no Steve McQueen. That respected director would have had a few tips for their cameraperson. After a shaky start, where the only thing in view was the curtained window, the cameraperson zoomed in on a figure sitting on a chair, their hands and feet both tied. The first video was of Michelle Glass, and as she launched into an account of her activities over recent months, Nikki exchanged a glance with Sajid. Someone had rehearsed this and the cable ties binding her would no doubt make it inadmissible in court. Sajid noted down every admission the girl made during her coerced confession. They moved on, doing the same with each of ten-minute snapshots. As she watched confession after confession and witnessed the lack of remorse for their victims, Nikki's stomach churned. By the end of it she was both sickened by their selfish whining and determined to throw the book at the little scrotes.

With all five vignettes viewed, Ahad insisted they take a quick break to clear their minds, and Nikki was grateful for it. The overall sense of them being driven by greed and entitlement drummed into them by some higher order that told them that these kids deserved to die, was chilling. They'd spurred each other on. The dynamics of being part of a nasty little group, almost a cult, but not quite – fuelled their own warped understanding of righteousness. Throw in large amounts of money and it only took a fractured mind to be all in. The desire to go home and shower in the hottest water she could was strong and, judging by the tension in her colleagues' faces, they felt the same way.

It was now that the hard graft would begin. They had to work out a strategy for interviewing the five. Nikki suspected the perps were too stupid to realise that their video confessions were inadmissible and, providing they didn't lawyer up, they might get a more official confession from them during the interview. It didn't matter that much though because they had attained warrants to search each of their homes and, in addition, Amar Akhtar's garage. Nikki was convinced that they weren't lying about where they'd hidden their weapons and illegally gained earnings. It was only a matter now of dogged police work, supported by forensic evidence and skilful interviewing to make things stick.

As Nikki grabbed a drink, her head fuzzy with thoughts that she couldn't quite isolate, Ahad approached. 'Ali?'

Although he smiled, Nikki detected an edge to his tone. She continued adding sugar to her drink and stirred it before replying. 'Ali?'

'He's your source, isn't he? He's the one who got those confessions, yeah?'

Her laugh sounded forced even to her own ears, but she hoped that the fact that she and Ahad didn't know each other that well would prevent him detecting it. 'It was an anonymous source, sir. Besides, from what I hear, Ali Khan has been glued to his son's side up at BRI since he got him back.'

Ahad grinned and walked away. 'That's true.'

Nikki thought she'd got away with it until he stopped in his tracks, his back still to her. 'Tell him thanks when you see him. It helped blow this wide open.'

Shutting her gawping mouth, Nikki added another sugar to her coffee. Just when you thought you had someone tagged, they went and surprised you.

Chapter 82

During their break, Ahad had called in the rest of the team and had pinned summaries of the crimes each of their suspects had admitted to next to their photos on a new big board. For now, they had moved the victims board to the side where it stood as a constant reminder of what was at stake.

Ahad began, his voice carrying over the room and demanding instant attention. 'Our lovely little group confessed to many of the unsolved crimes on our books. I'm convinced that the searches of each of their homes and work premises will elicit more evidence, and I suspect more victims will come forward in due course. In summary … Michelle Glass admitted to being involved in the fake acid attack against Molly Cropper, to the murder of Shabana Hussain, to the abduction, torture and mutilation of Maz Khan, and threatening behaviour at the vigil and the carrying in public of an illegal weapon.'

He paused for a second to allow the gasps and mutters to subside. 'Amar Akhtar confessed to the murders of Liaqat Ilyas, Graham Moorhead, Jamie Jacobs and the attack on Parekh at the vigil, as well as carrying a prohibited weapon in public. Chas Choudry admitted to being present when they attacked Ilyas and Graham Moorhead, but denies killing either victim – we'll rely on forensics to tie him in more tightly on those two. He also admits – in collusion with Michelle Glass – to the torture and mutilation of Maz Khan as well as threatening behaviour at the vigil and carrying an illegal weapon in public. Taj Jhuti, who was Molly Cropper's boyfriend at the time of her attack, admits to taking part in the homicides of Shabana Hussain and Parminder Deol, whilst Mally Ibrahim confesses to being complicit in the murders of Parminder Deol and Jamie Jacobs and being part of the assault on DS Parekh. He has a scratch on his arm, and I'm sure DNA will confirm his involvement courtesy of our own DS Parekh. We knew already that Maz Khan took part in the attack on Molly Cropper, but to date we have no evidence linking him to any other crimes.'

For a long while, the room remained silent. However, it wasn't long before the impact of Ahad's words caught up with the team, and a flurry of questions peppered the air. Ahad held up his hand and silence returned. 'One at a time. This is hard for us all to process and I know you have questions. Anwar?'

Anwar had been bouncing on her seat, arm raised almost from the moment the DI had started speaking. 'I'm puzzled about motivation, sir. Why would a group of teens and one older adult perpetrate such crimes?'

Ahad gestured to Nikki, who stood up. 'The recorded confessions are available in the file now; I suggest you take the time to watch them when you get a chance. However, to answer the question …'

Nikki inhaled and focused. 'Two unidentified adults utilised their thirst for money to recruit young people to an organisation called the Eyes. This has been corroborated by these five' – she wafted her hand towards the board – 'and also by interviews carried out with teens from various Bradford schools earlier today. Apart from greed, their primary motivation is a warped sense of superiority fostered by the adults who have manipulated them. They have been policing schools, hassling anyone who they think doesn't fit their morality code.'

Nikki turned and gestured to the board. 'For example, Michelle Glass is a recent convert to Islam. With her history of involvement in a local racist organisation, a record of minor crimes from shoplifting to minor affray, combined with an alcoholic mother and a recently murdered brother, she was a ripe candidate for recruitment. The attack on his girlfriend traumatised Taj Jhuti, and his trauma was exacerbated when Molly dumped him. He became vulnerable for recruitment to the Eyes, who convinced him that interracial relationships were bad. Which is why he became involved in Shabana Hussain and Parminder Deol's deaths. He denies killing them, but is adamant that the motivation behind their murders was their illicit relationship. In his words: "*Muslims and Sikhs should stick to their own.*"'

Seeing her horror reflected in her colleague's eyes, Nikki continued. 'Liaqat Ilyas and Graham Moorhead were killed because of their sexuality. Someone from Ilyas's family arranged for the hit. We are investigating that intel right now. Moorhead wasn't a target but was meeting up with Liaqat in Chellow Dene when Amar Akhtar and Chas Choudry attacked.'

'I still don't understand why they abducted Maz Khan or why they cut off his ear.' Williams, ever earnest, stared at Nikki.

'Yes, well spotted, Williams. Apparently, Glass and Choudry got wind that Maz was going to come clean to his dad. Both of them admit to working together to abduct and beat Khan. We now know that their actions backfired, for they ended up being targeted for punishment ...' She smiled. 'Most of their injuries resulted from a conflagration between Maz's abductors and the other three.' Her grin widened. 'Of course, I can claim responsibility for some of Amar Akhtar's older injuries – I got a few hard kicks and punches in at the vigil.'

This earned her a snicker of laughter, which was a welcome release in the tense room.

Nikki stepped down, leaving Ahad to take over. 'I know this is a lot to digest, but there's more that you need to be aware of. Some of you may have already joined the dots, but I want everyone clear on this.'

Frowning, those thunder cloud eyes doing their job and Dark Knight persona in place, Ahad continued. 'We have confessions from these five. I'm certain the expedited forensic evidence will add substance to our cases against them when we take it to CPS. However, there are still two dangerous and predatory criminals out there, operating in the shadows, using layers to distance themselves from the actual crimes. We must catch them and fast, because they have the ability to cut all ties with the crimes and leave these people to take full blame. Make no mistake, these two anonymous figures are equally culpable.'

He turned another board to face the room. It was divided in two, each section headed by a name. He pointed to the first name. 'The Fixer is the head man. None of the Eyes we have in custody, nor the five idling in the interview rooms downstairs can identify this person. He is the one with the money – he finances the entire operation. The anonymity surrounding this character is absolute. The only thing we have to go on are rumours and hearsay. But this is what we have. The Fixer is employed by people, who as their title would suggest, want things fixed. His clients are prepared to pay big bucks to ensure that happens. This Fixer character, according to Amar Akhtar, has cornered the market on honour killing stuff, but is happy to take on any project so long as it pays. With this in mind, I want the financial history of each of our victims' families revisited. We're looking for unusual expenditure – a trail we can follow. Akhtar also revealed that the Fixer operates through the dark web and uses burner phones to communicate. A team from the cyber unit are working on identifying this Fixer's online presence.'

Pointing at the other name on the board, Ahad continued. 'The Headhunter – again not an original title, but effective none-theless – is the man on the streets. He recruits the foot soldiers

342

for the Fixer and initiates them into the Eyes. He arranges and coordinates the attacks ordered by the Fixer. We hope to catch a lead on this character soon. In the meantime, go out and get the information we need to catch those bastards.'

Chapter 83

The Honourable Fixer

I'm attempting to maintain a semblance of normality. My smiles come automatically for the neighbours as I leave. The greeting on my work answerphone and email is a cheerful 'Taking a few days off to get rid of the lurgy. Catch up when I'm better.'

I don't have a sense that they're closing in on me and I doubt they will be able to. However, my carefully constructed network on the ground has, on the whole, become defunct. In a moment of madness, I considered waiting it out, but only for a split second. The pleasure of having a front-row seat and maybe even being called in to consult by the police is outweighed by the risk factor. So I cash in my chips and retreat to safety. Thinking yourself indestructible is a flaw, and I've seen many fall that way in the past. In fact, I reaped the benefits of moving in on some of my competitors when they became complacent. I won't be one of those rotting in jail. No, far better to retreat and watch their farcical attempts to unravel the tangled webs from safety. First step in my plan was to have my stolen getaway vehicle delivered to an area I could get to without being under surveillance by Bradford's insidious CCTV – talk about big brother and all that.

In my toned-down attire, chosen to blend in with the crowd, I stand in a remote corner of an otherwise bustling Morrisons car park and examine my escape vehicle. The Ford Fiesta is a nightmare. What in hell prompted me to select such an ordinary car? I suppose it carries its own irony. A cunning and successful criminal would usually choose a flashy, posh car, but I'm too savvy for that. If you want to escape rather than go out in a blaze of glory, you opt for low key, blend in, proletarian travel. I'll just have to put up with it. I'd already jammed the single camera that covers this area of parking and it doesn't take long to swap registration plates, both front and back, under the pretext of searching for my keys and dropping them and faffing about. Nobody even glances my way, and why would they? It's raining and cold and everybody's busy doing their own thing. The anonymous online supplier encouraged me to upgrade, but I remained resolute – a low cost, older vehicle with 'new' licence plates was what I wanted, and that's what I got.

As I work, I smile, anticipating the look on Nikki Parekh's face through the hidden camera in my flat when she finds the message I've left for her. I almost didn't leave it because it served no practical purpose, but in the end I couldn't resist. Everyone needs something to look forward to, after all.

Donning gloves, I retrieve the key from the wheel arch as arranged, lock my bags in the boot and I'm ready for the off. Not a long drive to the airport. I can suffer the cramped, strange-smelling car for the shortish drive. Then, a few hours drinking wine and lunching in one of the better airport diners before lift-off and from then on out it's bye bye Bradford, hello Caracas!

Chapter 84

Nikki and DI Ahad observed Naveed Mushtaq through the two-way mirror. Nikki was sure he was crucial to finding out more about the Fixer, but the smug little rat was digging his heels in and refusing to cooperate. Everything about him rubbed Nikki up the wrong way. His similarity to Freddie Downey was alarming. They didn't share a physical resemblance, but they each carried a common arrogance and lack of empathy – a deadness in their eyes that was chilling in its intensity. Nikki had been on the receiving end of her father's violence and she was convinced that Naveed Mushtaq was guilty of equally horrific actions.

'I want you to go in, Parekh. Catch him off balance. We know he hates women and one like you will really piss him off. Maybe we can use that to our advantage.'

Nikki let the 'a woman like you' comment slide. Ahad wasn't slotting her into a category. He was acknowledging all the differences between herself and the sort of women Mushtaq liked to bully and rape. She was okay with that. Still, she hesitated. 'Hmm …'

'You worried you'll kill him?'

Nikki studied the way Mushtaq swung backwards on the chair, and she wished he'd lose his balance and clatter to the floor.

'Maybe … no … What about Anwar? He might be more pissed off to be interrogated by a female Muslim officer.'

She could feel the DI's gaze on her, and she flushed. She wanted to get her hands on Mushtaq, she really did, but she was emotionally invested in this because of Fareena and Haqib. A burning desire to obliterate the slimy bastard was festering in her stomach, and she wasn't sure she'd be able to hold it in check.

'You go rogue occasionally, Parekh. I'm aware of that, but …'

Was that a twitch of a smile on his lips? Nikki wasn't sure, but she was intrigued to hear the 'but' part of his sentence. 'I have ultimate faith in you. You won't let that dick provoke you or get under your skin. He won't beat you and …' Now the smile was more than a twitch. 'More to the point, you won't lay a finger on him. You'll break him using intelligence and instinct. I know you will.'

His words extinguished some of the fire in her belly and at that point she realised how good it was, after her colossal blunder a few weeks ago, to be told that someone believed in her. Oh, she knew her family and Marcus had faith in her – even Dr Mallory had – but this? This felt so damn good. 'Okay. I'll do it, but let him sweat for a while longer.'

Thinking of Dr Mallory gave Nikki an idea. The psychiatrist was a consultant to the police and often advised on strategy. Perhaps her experience could be useful in developing a strategy to break Mushtaq? Mallory's phone had gone straight to answerphone – '*taking a few days …*' – when Sajid burst into the observation room – face flushed, wide grin – looking as if he should be sporting a wagging tail to round off his excitement.

'Got a whole load of crap we can use to exert pressure on Mushtaq.'

Nikki took the tablet from Sajid's hands and flicked through the information the technical team had forwarded. They'd done a deep dive on Naveed Mushtaq's background and some very interesting stuff had come up. A grin spread across Nikki's lips and she high-fived Sajid, and refrained from repeating the gesture she and Malik had made their own with DI Ahad. 'I think Mushtaq has sweated enough, don't you?'

Moments later, Nikki, armed with Malik's tablet and a box file filled with blank paper, slammed into the room. Her abrupt entrance startled Mushtaq, who grabbed hold of the table to prevent himself from clattering to the floor. Nikki contained her grin as she raised an eyebrow at Malik, who had accompanied her. With the ease of old partners, they'd agreed on a well-practised strategy for the interview – one that would play into Mushtaq's attitudes.

Whilst Nikki plonked her stuff on the table, Malik went over to the recording equipment and faffed about getting it up and running.

'I told you to get the equipment ready beforehand, Malik. What have you been doing?' Nikki glowered at her partner as she snapped the words at him, well aware that when she turned away, he'd quirk an eyebrow and indulge in a shoulder shrug. 'Ready now, are we?'

Malik scurried over and took his place by Nikki. 'Yes ma'am.'

Mentally, Nikki cursed him. Malik knew that the word 'ma'am' made her want to laugh, and he was pushing her buttons. She snorted and flicked through the tablet, allowing the silence to grow. When she was ready, she stared at him. 'Make the formal introductions, Malik, why don't you? Or do I have to do everything myself?'

Words running into one another, Malik introduced those present for the interview, re-cautioned Mushtaq and offered him the use of a solicitor, which he declined. The older Mushtaqs, to distance themselves from their son-in-law, had refused to pay for a separate solicitor for Naveed. Since the police had attained a warrant to freeze Naveed's assets, he had no access to money he had squirrelled away, and he was only entitled to a duty solicitor.

'Well, well, well. You're a popular man, Mr Mushtaq.' Nikki looked straight at him, her face unsmiling.

'Noooo coooomment.' Mushtaq again swung on his chair, his lips twitching as his eyes raked up and down her body. He slowly wet them with his tongue – sexual intent written all over his face.

Placing the tablet back on the table, Nikki smiled and leaned back in her chair. 'I don't believe I asked a question. Did I ask a question, Malik?'

Biting his lip and fidgeting ever so slightly, Sajid shook his head. 'No. No, you didn't. No question, ma'am.'

Under the table, Nikki kicked his ankle, warning him not to repeat the 'ma'am' thing. 'In fact, Mushtaq, I don't want to ask a question right now. I want you to listen, then we'll give you a little while to think.' She flicked through a few screens on the tablet, nodding to herself, then leaned forward, arms on the table. 'Let me tell you a story.' Without awaiting a response, she continued.

'Five years ago, a young Kashmiri man by the name of …' She made a show of consulting the paperwork in the box file. 'Jamal Suleman flew to Syria and became a member of ISIS.'

She turned the tablet so Naveed could view the grainy photograph of a younger, bearded version of himself standing next to a kneeling man about to be executed. 'Whilst in Syria, Suleman got married and fathered a son who died during childbirth. His wife was fourteen-year-old Rehana Al Abadi, whom he divorced, leaving her to be raped and murdered by his ISIS friends. He then seemed to tire of terrorism because three and a half years ago, he escaped Syria – our intel shows Suleman was on a mission to gain new recruits, but instead, upon touchdown in Pakistan, Suleman went underground and took on his mother's family name …' Once more Nikki turned the tablet to show an image of a clean-shaven man. 'Mushtaq … and Naveed Mushtaq was born. According to our anti-terrorist team, it seems ISIS contacts in Pakistan are keen to locate him. However, Mushtaq holed up in his family's village in the Kashmiri foothills where he married thirteen-year-old Gazala Anwar.'

Mushtaq's chair clattered on its four legs and a pulse throbbed at his temple. Ignoring the racket, Nikki turned to Malik. 'I'm seeing a pattern here, aren't you?'

Malik nodded, and still in role, avoided Nikki's gaze. With a 'be like that' shrug, she continued. 'When Gazala tried to run away after being beaten by Mushtaq, he threw acid in her face and left her in agony by the side of a road. A rickshaw driver rescued her.'

All the while Nikki spoke, her stomach churned, and it was only her determination to make this child rapist, terrorist and murderer suffer that prevented her from bursting into a tirade against him. Instead, she kept her face expressionless, aware that when she got home, the pressure she'd bottled down deep inside her to get through this interview would erupt. Thankfully, Marcus would be there to ease her through it.

'So, with his uncles and ISIS after him, Naveed had no choice but to steal gold and money from his family and head to the city. There in Islamabad, he set up a lucrative drug dealing business. Things got a tad too hot for him there when his enemies closed in … and that was when he sought his estranged relatives in the UK – more specifically in Bradford. Twenty-five years previously, Abdul Mushtaq, your mother's brother, had done the same thing you had. Greedy and determined to escape Pakistan, he stole, not only from his extended family, but from the rest of the village and from his employers where he duped customers into making investments over several years. He came to the UK with a sizeable amount of cash in his pocket and was able to legalise himself as a citizen when he married.'

Nikki smiled and exhaled. This was her final thrust, the one that would open wounds and give them a way to get Mushtaq to open up. 'You, on the other hand, arrived in the UK on a visitor's visa. So, the point is, what do we do about that? The Pakistan government is eager to have you extradited on various counts – eighteen I believe – of crimes ranging from murder, to extortion, to rape, to …' She looked up. 'Well, you get the drift. I've heard Pakistan prisons aren't quite the soft option our UK prisons are. Strip-searches twice a day, guards turning a blind eye to most things, including nightly conjugal visits by fellow inmates, unsanitary facilities.' Nikki had no idea what conditions were like in Pakistani jails, but she didn't care. Her aim here was to frighten Mushtaq into giving them the information they needed. Her ploy was working. Mushtaq's arrogance faded to uncertainty.

Nikki grinned as she looked down at her tablet once more. 'My colleagues have done remarkable work, and in such a short time! I wonder what else they have found? Oh yes, I remember … On the upside for you, if we agree to extradition, you'd be held in a prison where many of your acquaintances are housed – let me see, you'd be sleeping next to, erm, one, two … five, no, *six* senior ISIS members, several of the drug dealers you dobbed in for cash *and* your uncle – the father of the girl you threw acid on.' She smiled, spreading her arms wide before her. 'I'd love to be a fly on the wall at that reunion, wouldn't you, Malik?'

'Bitch! You fucking bitch.' As she talked Mushtaq's face had drained of colour, but now with her last thrust, all the blood had rushed there. Spit flew across the table as he jumped to his feet, but no sooner had he done so, than an enormous uniformed officer entered the interview room and pushed him into his seat before cuffing him to the loop in the middle of the table.

With one hand behind her ear, Nikki angled her head towards him. 'Was that a "*no comment*" I heard there, Naveed?'

Eyes glinting, he strained against the cuffs, and Nikki's smile widened. 'So, here's what you need to consider. What information can you give us to make sure we're not tempted by any pressure from the Pakistani government? Easy, isn't it?'

Chapter 85

Stretching her neck muscles, Nikki sat in the observation room watching Naveed Mushtaq sweat. She and Sajid had done their jobs, but maintaining her composure had been hard. The red welts on her wrist bore testament to what it had taken out of her. Now it was Malik's turn to close the deal. Between them, they'd set him up as the sympathetic detective, the one downtrodden by the ballsy female and it was Sajid's job to use that relationship to convince Mushtaq of their shared antipathy towards Parekh, hoping to cajole information from him.

Ahad had authorised more techies to work the dark web angle. They'd advised that the site was so encrypted, it had to be accessed via a series of dark websites, each using secret access codes and each taking you a little deeper into the murky world of crime. Just when they thought they had tugged a nugget loose, an army of Trojans descended, thwarting them, challenging them to armed combat in order to evade viruses and destruction. The entire team was pulling their hair out. It seemed like the dark web was a battlefield, with their team on the side of good and the Fixer's team on the side of evil … so far the good side was losing, and Nikki was a sore loser.

The desire to head over to Lazy Bites for a top-up of goodness in the form of Isaac conflicted with her inability to move. So, when Williams burst in with a 'Techies have found something about those five tossers next door!' she was relieved to have the decision taken from her.

Although the five tossers were actually down in the cells, Nikki knew what he meant. However, his next words puzzled her. 'Not sure you're going to like it though, ma'am ... I mean erm Nik ... erm, that is DS Parekh.'

Still reluctant to move, Nikki waved a hand at him. 'Spit it out, Williams. By the way, Parekh's fine. Can't abide "ma'am" – I'm not in my damn nineties, although right now it feels like it.'

With a nod, Williams took a deep breath and spat it out. 'Each of those five were assigned to Dr Mallory via My Wellbeing College after self-harming or suicide attempts.'

As she digested William's information, Nikki frowned. She wasn't sure what this meant, not really. A glance at Ahad told her he too was deep in thought. 'You got more details?'

'Well, erm, yes.' Scowling, he looked through his tablet and cleared his throat. 'Michelle Glass attended counselling when her teachers noticed she was self-harming after her brother was murdered. Amar Akhtar and his dad both received counselling via My Wellbeing College after Amar's diagnosis with kidney failure. He then attempted suicide and his dad blamed himself. They both did a three-month course of therapy with Dr Mallory starting in January this year. They recruited Taj Jhuti after his girlfriend dumped him, resulting in a suicide attempt. Chas Choudry started self-harming after being sexually abused by his stepdad and Mally Ibrahim ... was referred for anger management after being beaten by his dad.'

Energised, Nikki began pacing the room, trying to make sense of the jigsaw pieces that jostled for attention. Mallory linked to all five of the kids involved in the machete murders. But she'd also been Nikki's saviour in her darkest hour. Surely this was coincidence; Mallory couldn't be involved in any of this? Not quirky, fun-loving, colourful Dr Mallory. Nikki had almost convinced herself of this when other thoughts pushed themselves forward.

Mallory had been at the vigil … but then so had many others. If she was involved, would she have attended? She might have. It was a well-known fact that criminals liked to see the fruits of their labours first-hand. Then she'd been really reluctant for Nikki to return to work. That had surprised Nikki. She'd thought her therapist would be keen to see her ready for work. Nikki frowned and looked at Ahad. 'Dr Mallory has returned none of my messages or calls since I've been back at work. She was supposed to set up extra sessions for me. In fact, she was insistent on that, yet …' She grabbed her mobile and dialled, setting her phone to speaker phone, and held up a finger. 'Wait a moment …'

Mallory's phone rang out for a bit, then her answerphone kicked in. 'Taking a few days off to get rid of the lurgy. Catch up when I'm better.'

Nikki grabbed her jacket and headed off out of the room. 'Get Anwar to observe Sajid's interview with Naveed Mushtaq. But before that, get a trace on Dr Helen Mallory's phone and get a team of officers sent to her work address and her home address.'

Shaking his head, Ahad grabbed his own jacket, pointed at Nikki and said, 'What she said.' Before chasing after her with a 'You do know I'm the senior officer, Parekh?'

As they hit the car park, Nikki looked round, realising that for once they couldn't take Saj's Jag. Ahad caught up with her, keys in hand, and a black BMW SUV was already flashing its light to show it had been unlocked. 'You don't think we're being premature, do you?' His tone was conversational rather than confrontational; still, it made Nikki pause as he overtook her and approached his car yanking the driver's door open. 'Come on!'

Nikki hesitated, but only for a moment, before dashing round to the passenger side and throwing herself into the seat just as Williams's text arrived with Mallory's address. She typed the postcode into the satnav. 'If she answers the door with a snotty nose and a Lemsip in hand, then we'll at least know she's not involved. On the other hand …'

Nikki let the sentence drift off. She didn't want to visit the 'other hand' scenario, not yet. She'd trusted Mallory, attributed her recovery to the doctor, and she didn't want that marred by the possibility that she was some horrific Fixer character. However, even as she thought this, a niggle of doubt persisted. Mallory was a computer whizz – she'd shared that with her, laughing at Nikki's Luddite approach to technology. Not that being a dab hand with PCs was conclusive. Still, Nikki couldn't shake the idea that someone able to get inside their heads had manipulated those responsible for the machete attacks. Someone who could hide their digital footprint. Who better to do that than a respected psychiatrist who knew computers? The blood drained from Nikki's face as that thought sunk in. Dr Mallory had got into *her* head space. She'd been privy to so many of Nikki's deepest, darkest secrets and … *No, don't go there. Not till you know for sure, Nik.*

Her phone ringing was a welcome distraction from her dark thoughts and she flicked it to speaker, so Ahad could hear. However, the distraction didn't last long when she heard DC Williams's words. 'We have found Mohsin Akhtar dead in his garage. He committed suicide – gassed himself using a pipe from the exhaust of a car he was working on.'

'Shit!' The expletive left her lips, splintering the shocked silence in the vehicle. She glanced at Ahad. 'I wanted to interview him – he was our next logical port of call after Mallory, don't you think?'

'Ma'a … I mean Parekh, that's not all.'

Nikki exhaled. Of course that wasn't all. Why would it be? Today was turning into a day of surprises all round. 'Go on, Williams, what else have you got?'

'He left three burner phones and a suicide note. Well, actually it was more of a confession. Seems he was the …'

Nikki finished the sentence for him. '… The Headhunter.'

'Yes, how did—?' Nikki hung up on Williams, whilst Ahad pressed his foot on the accelerator.

Chapter 86

Dr Mallory's flat in a beautifully refurbished Victorian building in Little Germany offered an enviable view of the city. At any other time, Nikki would have drunk it in. However, what had been waiting for her in Mallory's apartment had left her reeling. The door was unlocked, so she and Ahad donned gloves and entered. Even then, Nikki still tried to keep hold of the smallest shred of hope that she'd blown everything out of all proportion and that Mallory was innocent, but that hope was blown when, after finding the flat empty, she discovered the psychiatrist's parting gift.

The large-screen TV which dominated the living room was hooked up to a laptop – the purple one that Nikki recognised from her therapy sessions. But it wasn't the laptop which arrested her mid-step. It was the image projected on a flat screen. Freddie Downey, head averted, dressed in a winter coat, sat with a coffee cup in front of him at an outdoor table with a heater beside it, like the ones Nikki had seen when she and Marcus had visited the Christmas markets in Europe one year. A sneering smile covered his face, and it looked like he was ogling a young girl with long blonde hair sitting alone at the next table. Although the sight of her biological father shocked Nikki, sending her fingers up to touch the scar on her neck, it was the date at the bottom corner of the screen that had her scrambling onto the sofa before her legs gave way: 27th November.

Ahad spoke to her, but his words were distorted as Nikki's breath heaved in her chest, and even the twanging of her band couldn't ground her. In his haste to reach her, Ahad bumped into the desk and his motion activated a carousel of images of Downey engaged in a series of activities – none of which were in the Far East. Thankfully, the movement on the screen grounded Nikki, and after a couple of forced slow breaths, the dizziness receded. Disappearing for a second, the DI returned with a glass of water, which he forced into Nikki's trembling hand. She took a sip, and another. Then, not removing her eyes from the screen and uncaring that she was talking to a superior officer, Nikki spoke. 'That bastard is dead and so is that bitch Mallory.'

Whilst she watched the photos flit on and off the screen, she was aware of Ahad calling in a forensics team, more officers and a tech team to dissemble whatever Mallory had set up. Instructions in place, he gestured to the TV. 'I'd turn it off, but if Mallory's as devious as we think, who knows what we could lose if we tamper with it.' Nikki got to her feet and rubbed her hand across her nose, then nodded. 'Yeah. You're right. I'll search the bedroom if that's okay.'

Away from the claustrophobic living room with its larger-than-life images of Downey, Nikki took a moment to ground herself before looking round Mallory's bedroom. Flashes of the sessions she'd shared with the other woman, the secrets she'd confided, her broken, tortured weeping … all of those share memories flitted in and out of her mind. Nikki allowed them in, willing them to fuel her anger, and it worked. At that moment, her phone rang. It was an unknown number, and Nikki wondered if it might be Ali again. She almost switched it off, then reconsidered. Ali wouldn't ring for no reason. 'Yep?' She heard the tremor in her voice, but hoped Ali wouldn't.

A brief silence, then an all too familiar voice came down the line. 'How do you like my bedroom, Nikki?'

Nikki froze. Her eyes darted round the room, then to the window, but the curtains were closed and the room was empty. How in hell did Mallory know she was in her bedroom? Nikki, phone glued to her ear, backed out. 'Where are you, Mallory?'

'Oh dear, now that would be telling, wouldn't it? Did you like my surprise? Daddy dearest is closer than you think.'

Nikki waved at Ahad, trying to attract his attention as he searched the desk drawers. 'Say hallo to DI Ahad, sweetie. I think he'll find what he's looking for in the bottom drawer. Bye now. Take care of yourself. Speak soon.' And the line went dead.

Realisation dawned as Nikki glanced round. The bitch had somehow set up cameras in her flat so she could get off on seeing them search. Unsure whether Mallory could hear them, Nikki grabbed Ahad by the arm and dragged him from the apartment. She refused to speak until they'd gone down two flights of stairs. Once sure they wouldn't be heard, Nikki explained what had happened. They agreed that the tech team should sweep the flat for bugs and cameras first, but in the interim, he ordered for Nikki's phone to be monitored at all times in case Mallory phoned again.

As they awaited the various teams, Nikki checked in on Saj. He would have finished his interview with Naveed Mushtaq by now and she was keen to hear what he'd found out. After bringing him up to date on what they'd discovered in Mallory's flat, Sajid gave his update. 'Mushtaq gave us enough info to ensure he and the Mushtaq parents go away for a long time. Although he used a burner phone to contact the Fixer, the silly git kept it and both his burner and the ones we found with Mohsin Akhtar's body are spewing a load of leads – well, according to the techies. I doubt we'd have anything to go on if it wasn't for them, Nik. Bottom line is they retrieved the deleted browsing history from both phones, which has allowed them to locate the Fixer's site on the dark web. The site has since been shut down. They're totally in awe of her skills – say she's a genius at covering her tracks, but our lot are better. Nothing's ever deleted completely, so they're sifting through stuff and are confident they'll be able to follow her trail soon.

'We need to catch her, Sajid. She's dangerous. We really need to catch her.'

Chapter 87

I hadn't intended to contact Parekh. Not yet anyway. I'd anticipated settling into my new life, maybe setting myself up in another
little business – maybe a more art-based one this time – but
when the alert came in that they'd entered my flat, I couldn't
resist watching it in real time. After all, there's not much to do
in an airport, especially when your flight's been delayed. I know
it's pure indulgence, but working with Parekh, seeing how many
people she had on her side, her family, her partner, her friends …
maybe it made me see how alone I am. Not that I'm jealous. On
the contrary, I savour my privacy, but there's something soooo
annoying about Parekh and her 'boo hoo my mum's dead, boo
hoo my dad's a paedophile' that I just wanted to turn the knife
a bit. Not for money – just for sheer enjoyment – just because I
can. Just because she needs to know that I own her.

She's done herself proud. I expected it to be over a week before
they dotted I's and crossed T's but Parekh is smarter than she
looks – uneducated maybe, but she's got the street smarts of her
breed of survivalists. I've seen it before. I wonder if they've found
poor old Mohsin yet. It was such a lovely experience guiding him
through his suicide. There was little need to cajole him. During
our therapy sessions we had built up quite a rapport – especially

during the private ones in my bedroom. He likes – oops, I mean liked – a bit of the Dominatrix. Tragically, for him, he hadn't sussed out that coincidences – at least serendipitous ones – just don't happen. Finding a sexual therapist cum psychiatrist – I grin at the thought of 'come' with a 'u' – and a money-making opportunity at the same time, can't be coincidental. Poor, simple Mohsin – simple, but ever so athletic.

Even when my alter ego the Fixer directed him to enrol various teens, he didn't see the link. I'll miss him – for a short time. I look back to my screen. Parekh's sussed out the camera situation. What a shame that she's dragging the dishy DI out of my flat before she finds my last little treat. After logging off, I order another margarita. I'd have loved to witness her reaction to that. I shouldn't have phoned her so soon – I blame my celebratory mood and the cocktails.

Chapter 88

The tech team didn't take long to find and disarm the cameras which Mallory had positioned all over her flat. It took them less time, using various gadgets and a whole load of nerdiness, to deactivate the 'destroy all' precautions that were on the laptop.

'Half-hearted effort' one tech said as they packed up the equipment to take back to their lab in the dungeons of geekiness.

The team were hardly out the door before Nikki rushed to the desk. 'She said bottom drawer.'

Nikki had no idea what she expected to find and had braced herself for the very worst. So, when she yanked it open and saw only a USB stick lying there, in an otherwise empty drawer, disappointment flooded through her. She sent a desperate glance round the room as if expecting a computer to appear, then she began a dart towards the door to call the techie kids back, but Ahad grabbed her arm. 'We can't use any of her equipment because until it's been checked we don't know what tricks she's installed. We should take it back to Trafalgar House and let the experts check it out.'

As Nikki's face fell, he paused, closed his eyes and exhaled exaggeratedly before scowling at her. 'You're rubbing off on me, Parekh, you know that?'

It took a second for understanding to dawn, then she grinned. 'We're going to look at it first?'

Ahad headed to the door, issuing instructions to the officers present to arrange a canvas of the neighbourhood and to treat the flat as a crime scene till the CSIs had finished with it. 'My Samsung tablet has a USB port, we'll use that. Come on.'

Once in the car, and logged onto the tablet, Nikki's fingers shook so much that Ahad had to insert the USB into the port. There was one file on the stick which, when opened, directed them to a Cloud storage facility. Nikki looked at her boss. 'Should we? I mean ... who knows what we'll find?'

Already clicking the icon, Ahad snorted. 'Not getting cold feet now, are we?'

The screen flickered, then they had access – no password required – to an unnamed folder. Unable to contain the nervous energy surging through her, Nikki waited as Ahad opened the folder. For a moment Nikki stared at the list of documents. All, except one, were recordings and all were titled only with a date. The other one was a Word document with a single word name: Parekh.

Exhaling through her nostrils, Nikki nodded for Ahad to open it.

Dear Nikki,

    If you've come this far, you might expect a confession, but alas you will be disappointed. I'm not the confession-cleanses-the-soul sort of gal. Instead, my present to you is all the recordings from our sessions. I can visualise you now, mouth open – agape, I think, is the better word. I know, I know, I should have told you I was recording, but you must forgive me my little foibles. I've had such pleasure reliving your darkest moments in the comfort of my flat that I felt it only fair to share those moments with someone else who would derive pleasure from them too.

Is that bad of me? Oh, I don't think so … As soon as you walked through my door after your little breakdown at a crime scene I was responsible for (oops, you tricked me into that small confession didn't you?) I knew I wanted to break you. People like you are designed to be broken. People like you are designed to be pawns in more intelligent people's games.

So, consider this my final gift, (only until I get bored again, you understand.) I know how important family is to you, so … you'll love this … I've sent your files to Daddy Dearest – Isn't that kind of me?

Best Wishes,
Until next time
Helen Mallory

'Noooo!' Nikki's fingers once more flew to touch the scar, then seeing Ahad eyeing her action, she grabbed the tablet, trying to get to the other files, tears streaming down her face, but she didn't care. These were tears of anger, not anguish. Finally, the list of files was on the screen. Nikki clicked on one of the early ones. It loaded quickly and there she was in Mallory's office, a waif-like figure with sunken cheeks. Nikki barely recognised herself. Her voice was robotic as she spoke about the things Freddie Downey had done to her. Frantic and uncaring that Ahad was with her, she closed that file and clicked open another. Here she looked a little more animated. She was reflecting on her love for her first husband Khalid.

She was about to open a third file when her phone rang again. Unknown number. She showed it to Ahad and then on speakerphone, she accepted the call. 'I see you've accessed my little parting gift, Nikki. Daddy dearest accessed his copy yesterday. I'm sure he'll reconnect with you soon.'

Before Nikki could reply, a familiar sound hurtled down the line – and then it was cut off. Grinning, Nikki looked at Ahad to see if he'd recognised the sound too – an airport tannoy announcement.

Without a word he turned the ignition. 'Manchester or Leeds-Bradford airport? Which one do we want to take?'

'Definitely Manchester, but we should send a team to Leeds-Bradford just in case. Foot down, DI Ahad, we've got the Fixer to catch.'

Chapter 89

Whilst Ahad, having attached a blue flashing light to the roof of his car, drove like a racing pro along the M62, Nikki worked her phone to alert the Manchester police and the airport officials that they believed a criminal was attempting to leave the country. There were so many unknowns and Nikki knew they were clutching at straws. After she made initial contact with the airport authorities, DCI Hegley took over coordinating the flow of information between the various parties involved. He'd also extended Mallory's possible exit point to include all the other airports that had international travel.

The frustrating thing was that they had no idea if Mallory was flying under an alias or where she was heading. There was nothing to confirm she was still in the UK. For all Nikki knew, Mallory could have been phoning from Barbados or Australia, but she couldn't allow herself to believe that. She had to focus on the here and now and that involved building up any information that might help. 'Williams, can you get someone to mess around with Mallory's image to incorporate a variety of disguises – you know change of hair colour, style and so forth.'

'On it, boss, One more thing though. I've pinged you a list of flights leaving Manchester airport in the next few hours and, assuming she'll opt for a country with no extradition treaty with UK, I cross-referenced that information to narrow it down. Oh, and Malik wants a word.'

Nikki was impressed. Williams was really thinking outside the box. 'Brilliant, Williams – I hadn't thought of that. Put Saj on now.'

After some shuffling of phones, Sajid came on. 'Hey, Nik, Kevin the techie has unearthed recent activity suggesting Mallory researched flights from Heathrow to Thailand.'

Nikki let that sit for a moment. Maybe this trip was a waste of time. Maybe Mallory had opted to go south for her escape? It was so frustrating. The woman could have left the country hours ago. The last sighting of her was that morning, who knew where she could be by now. She glanced at Ahad who shrugged. 'You know her best, Parekh.'

Nikki nodded and made her decision. 'It could be a red herring, Saj. It all seems a bit too convenient that she left that information and my gut says if it was so easy to discover, then she intended for us to find it. We're continuing to Manchester. Keep us updated.'

Twenty minutes later, Ahad abandoned the car, leaving a police sticker on the dashboard. Manchester police and the airfield security were searching the airport. On the journey over, Nikki had narrowed Mallory's destination down to three possibilities: a flight to Venezuela that had been delayed already and was on the runway ready to leave – airport security had tried to delay it further, but with no warrant in place yet, it was going to be tight to stop it from taking off. The second flight was to Belarus and was boarding, whilst the third flight to Kazakhstan was already in the air. As Nikki headed inside the sprawling building, desperation drove her forward. Would they be able to halt the Venezuelan flight without proof Mallory was aboard? If they delayed it and she wasn't on board, would they have missed their chance of searching the Belarus flight? They did not know her new identity, but Nikki knew that whatever passport she was using, it would be flawless. Nikki knew time was trickling away but despite wracking her brain, she couldn't come up with any ideas to speed things up. Her phone rang. 'Williams, speak!' Nikki barely managed to pant the words out as they dodged idling passengers, flashing their IDs at security personnel, one of whom jogged along beside them to grant them more rapid access through security checks.

'It's the Venezuelan flight, Nikki. I just checked the flight manifest and one of the passengers is registered as Lalita Parekh. It's got to be that flight.'

Rage burst up through Nikki's aching lungs. How dare that bitch use her mum's name? How dare she taunt her like this? 'Venezuelan flight. She's using my mum's name. Let's go.'

With public announcements reminding fliers that this was the last boarding call for various flights and travellers dawdling, whiling away the time till they could board, Nikki, gasping for air, fought to keep up with Ahad who had overtaken her and was heading for the Venezuela flight departure gate. The airport security officer was still running with them, working his walkie-talkie, requesting assistance and trying to convince air traffic control to delay the flight.

Ignoring the disgusted looks of the passengers she crashed past, and more than once, tripping over stray luggage as she ran, Nikki kept pace with her boss. *Come on. Come on.* They had to get there in time. They just had to catch her.

The boarding desk was shut when reached the gate, and Nikki's heart plummeted. How could this be happening? She couldn't be too late, she just couldn't. Not sure what her intention was, Nikki pushed through the barriers which squealed in protest with flashing lights and a noisy alarm. Within seconds, two security guards approached, and gripping Nikki by the arms, pulled her away. All she could do was watch through the enormous windows as the plane moved. The guard who'd been running with Nikki and Ahad, signalled for his colleagues to release her at the same moment as a team of officers from Manchester police converged on the area. All around them passengers and staff watched the excitement, a few of them recording it and some snapping images. With purpose, the Manchester police, one by one, approached the spectators and demanded they remove their recordings from their devices. Nikki couldn't care less. She ran to the glass, Mallory's sneering face planted in her mind as she visualised her watching the proceedings from one of the plane's small windows. Clattering her palms against the safety glass separating her from the retreating plane, Nikki swore. 'Fuck, fuck and crap.'

'She might not be on that flight, Parekh. She could be elsewhere.' But Ahad didn't sound convinced.

'No, she's gone. She's on that plane and we fucking let her escape.' She turned her attention to the airport security. 'Get in touch with Schiphol Airport. I want that flight delayed there and we need to be on the next flight to Schiphol. This woman is responsible for at least five murders and probably a damn sight more and I'm damned if she's getting away.'

The familiar sound of her mobile rang out and, leaving Ahad to apologise for her abruptness, she took it, her voice weary. 'We missed her, Williams, the bitch got away. We were seconds too late.'

'Eh, that's just it, boss. I don't think you were too late – well actually, you were. You were three hours too late.'

Nikki collapsed on to one of the uncomfortable metal chairs and pressed two fingers on the bridge of her nose. 'I'm exhausted, Williams. You spit it out. I've no idea what you're on about. I saw the plane leave, just this minute.' She looked up. A trail of smoke lingered in the dull sky showing that the flight to Venezuela via Amsterdam was indeed on its way.

'She booked tickets for Lalita Parekh from every major UK airport going to different international destinations and leaving at different times today. The only flight manifest that shows that the seat booked in the name of Lalita Parekh was utilised was one from Birmingham that took off three hours ago. She's just left Schiphol and their next stop is Caracas. You were too late anyway.'

Chapter 90

'Can I get you another margarita, Mrs Parekh?'

I smile at the flight attendant. It's rather good being Lalita Parekh. Makes me feel closer to Nikki. 'Thank you, that would be lovely.'

Settled down, I savour the luxury of first-class travel. With a soft blanket pulled right up under my chin I imagine poor, stupid DS Nikita Parekh trying so hard to catch me. Did she really think I would be so dumb as to head to Manchester airport? I laugh aloud, drawing an amused glance from the dishy businessman in the next seat. As soon as Parekh accessed the USB stick and clicked on the files, she was mine. The tracking app is now installed on whatever device she used and following her frantic dash to Manchester amused me no end.

Although Parekh doesn't realise it yet, I have tabs on her wherever she goes and I will know whatever she does. Not just her either, but her entire family. It was so easy to plant remote access technology on that stupid little #WhatsUpWithThisShit blog. Not that I'm tracking everyone who logged onto it. No, only those who can be of use to me. Parekh might think she's seen the last of me, but boy, does she have a huge awakening coming. I'm not done with her yet and Venezuela isn't so far away, not when you have technological expertise behind you.

I sip my margarita, already anticipating my next little message to DS Parekh.

Chapter 91

By the time Nikki arrived back at Trafalgar House, her entire body protested against the day's unaccustomed activity. She had spent the return journey with her eyes closed, letting Ahad assume she'd dozed off, because her sense of failure made her want to scream and lash out at everyone. She had learned strategies to deal with this sort of situation over the weeks of therapy with Mallory. But when a Malloryism sprang into her mind, she thought she might vomit. Hurt was compounded by anger at being duped, yet she tried not to let the pain take hold. She could cope with betrayal and self-condemnation at being duped. But not hurt. Hurt made her into a victim and Nikki Parekh was done with that. She was no victim and she most certainly was no victim of Dr Mallory's.

The knowledge that her most private thoughts – her darkest moments – had been shared with Freddie Downey was hard to bear. She had little doubt that he'd lap it up like a cat with the cream, and it sickened her. The only way she could get past this was to make sure they punished both Mallory and Downey for their crimes. Right then, Nikki didn't care what form that punishment took. In her mind, prison was too soft an option and was no compensation for the misery those two individuals had caused.

On entering the investigation room, Nikki wanted to disappear behind her desk and lick her wounds in peace, but Sajid jumped to his feet and taking one look at her face said, 'You look like crap, Parekh.'

His levity belied the concern in his eyes and Nikki could have hugged him for being there for her. He was her best mate, and she doubted she'd manage without him by her side. That was a thought for another day, though. 'Really? I'm surprised because I feel great.'

Saj studied her for a moment and when Ahad joined them, he pointed to DCI Hegley's office. 'Big boss wants us in there. Wants to update us before he sends us all home for a break.'

Nikki groaned. Everyone involved in Mallory's organisation or those who had enlisted her services had been identified. However, Archie was already standing by his open door, gesturing for them to enter. When his gaze landed on Nikki, his expression projected fatherly concern and, reluctant to show how much his concern affected her, she kept her head down as she filtered past him and sat down with the others.

'Aye well. This has got everyone's proverbials in a damn lather, ye ken. The media are sniffing around, the politicians are up in arms, and DCI Clark's walking about like a bloody womble on acid.'

He placed both spade-like hands palm down on the table and lasered Nikki with a penetrating gaze. 'First of all, Parekh, hen. You have mah sincere apologies. I never should hae sent you …'

Nikki's head jerked up, her expression fierce. 'Don't you dare apologise. You did your job. I needed help, and you got me it. Nobody knew Mallory was …' Unable to find the words she needed, she wafted her hand in the air and exhaled. 'She's the one to blame. Not us. Not *any* of us. Just her.'

Ahad and Sajid averted their gazes as she and Archie surveyed each other. Archie plonked his heavy frame into his chair. 'You've all done splendid work here. We suspect the repercussions from

Mallory's online enterprise will be far-reaching. The tech team has been doubled in size to accommodate the extra and they've already uncovered evidence to ensure prosecutions of various people. This includes digital, financial and paper trails to support the forensics already in place against the three Mushtaqs and the five bad bastards you two brought in.'

He pointed a finger in the space between Sajid and Nikki before continuing. Then signalled to Sajid. 'Go on then, laddie. You dae the honours.'

Saj cleared his throat and began. 'Mallory's little enterprise started off over a decade ago as an art fraud scam involving selling on stolen artwork. It soon progressed to human trafficking for donor organs before moving on to her current little scheme. Who would have thought being a Fixer could be so lucrative? We have evidence of the Fixer being employed by many national and international businesses to infiltrate and discredit business competitors. These will be investigated and there are implications for many political leaders who have links with some of these illegal activities.' Saj looked at his iPad.

'Her "fixes" range from bringing down minor organisations, to destabilising governments. A few terrorist organisations have paid for her services … and lots more. All of that will be taken over by national and international law enforcement. However, we have kept permission to progress our case against the Eyes and the murders she coordinated in Bradford. Seems she enjoyed playing God on a local level – think she viewed her actions like a massive chess game with her directing every move, whilst keeping her hands clean. Or perhaps she wanted to personally see the effect of her work, to enjoy the misery she created, and she could best do that in her local area.' With an expression of utter contempt, Saj stopped speaking.

Whilst interested in the broad strokes of Mallory's crimes, Nikki wanted to understand the specifics. Although she was glad that they'd rounded up those who'd wielded the machetes and

374

killed the kids, she needed to know who had paid for it. 'Who paid her to organise the deaths of those kids?'

Sajid's frown deepened. 'Even that's much wider reaching than we first thought. The Fixer, according to Mohsin Akhtar's written confession, took over an international honour killing website because it was being run "inefficiently". Although he was never aware of the Fixer's identity, Akhtar was employed to deal with publicising the Bradford branch of the operation via word of mouth. Seems families have many reasons to have their members killed off, and the Fixer gave them immunity by arranging for their dirty work to be carried out for them when they could establish watertight alibis. We've handed over details of transactional murders to police in other major UK cities. So far, the team have identified over twenty similar murders, spanning the last few years.'

'Machete killings?' Nikki frowned. How could that number of deaths by machete not have set off an alarm?

'No, a variety of methods. In Bradford the machete is the weapon of choice. It's already used in gang and drug disputes on the streets. As we speak, teams are en route to bring in the following people for questioning in relation to the deaths of their family members: Shabana Hussain's uncle – a family elder ordered her death because of her relationship to Parminder Deol. A relationship the couple's family had tried very hard to keep secret after their deaths. Not content with killing his niece, he paid for the lad to be killed too. We already knew that Liaqat Ilyas's death was ordered because he was gay. It was his brother, Shames, who was behind that, because his prospective bride's family wouldn't have tolerated Liaqat's sexuality. Jamie Jacobs's dad did the honours there and his motivation was the advancement of his political career. Seems that he couldn't tolerate having a drug addict for a son ...'

Sajid sat down and Archie took his place. 'As mair and mair evidence is recovered, our case against these people will become

375

stronger. They'll be punished for their behaviour, but alas that will nae bring back the poor bairns who've died because of them. This has been a bad one for everybody, so go home, spend time wi' yer families, reboot yer batteries.' He smiled. 'Tomorrow's time enough to dot the I's and cross the T's.'

As everyone stood and headed for the door, Archie added one last thing. 'Once we've got these bastards hog-tied and ready to deliver to the CPS – then we'll go after that Mallory woman. She made a mistake when she made this personal, and mark mah proverbials – we'll get her. Nah doubt aboot it. She's going doon!'

Chapter 92

'She dumped me, Charlie.' Haqib, slouched in his auntie's living room with his cousin, was still trying to work out how he felt about Fareena's surprise announcement.

'She did?' Charlie threw the Xbox controls at him. 'Your go, bozo.'

Haqib nodded and lifted the controls, but didn't activate his avatar. 'I mean, I was worrying about dumping her, you know? I mean after all she's been through – her *and* her family and that, but ...' Placing the controls on the sofa between himself and Charlie, he turned so he could look at her. 'I, like ... I ...'

'You're such a *boy*, Haq. You really are.' Charlie grinned at him as if he should agree with her, but he didn't know what she meant, so he gave a half-hearted shrug. Of course, he was a boy, what had that got to do with owt?

'Her sisters and brothers are moving to Burnley. She's got relatives there and they're gonna rent them a house. She says she wants to leave all of this behind her, for Attiya and Zara's sakes.'

'She's probably right. I mean if she stays in Bradford, they'd always be *that* family. Yep, definitely the right thing to do.'

'Still ...' Haqib picked up the controls and weighed them in his hand as if unsure how to operate them. 'I wanted to end it.

Now that I've got a career path to follow, I need to focus. It's hard work being a copper and I've got loads of training and stuff to do in Wakefield – I need to concentrate on getting fit and stuff. No more girls for me.'

Rolling her eyes, Charlie nudged him in the ribs. 'Like I say, Haq, you're such a damn *boy*. Now are we gonna play this game or not?'

SIX WEEKS LATER

Epilogue

'As more and more evidence is uncovered implicating many respected politicians, business owners and celebrity figures both locally and nationally in the "Blood for Hire" scandal that has rocked our nation, the woman Dr Helen Mallory, dubbed the Fixer, remains at large. A source close to West Yorkshire Police confirm she is currently residing in a country with no extradition treaty with the UK and negotiations are in place to reach an agreement that will bring the mastermind to justice for her many crimes. Ex West Yorkshire mayor, Robert Jacobs, who we can see leaving Trafalgar House as I report, has been charged with, among other crimes, accessory to murdering his drug addict son, Jamie, many counts of subverting the course of justice and charges pertaining to illegal actions resulting in his election to public duty ...'

As the reporter on the wall-mounted TV droned on and on detailing a litany of crimes that Nikki and her team were still untangling, Nikki and Marcus studied the rectangle on the kitchen table as if it had the power to injure them. It wasn't the card that could hurt her or her family though. It was the monster who had sent it. As if the image of the White Cliffs of Dover wasn't enough of a warning, the inscription on the back made Nikki's knees tremble.

I'm back. Your choice – who's next, you or your sister? It's make your mind up time!

This was the third card she'd received from Downey since Mallory had poked the bear by sending him recordings of Nikki's therapy sessions. Each of the recent cards had been from Europe and carried a picture of a French landmark: Disneyland, Paris; the Louvre; Notre Dame Cathedral. This was the first postcard with a UK scene and postmark. He was getting closer. Nikki could almost feel his breath on the nape of her neck. 'He's coming after us, Marcus. What are we going to do?'

In other news, a teen boy, Mazin Khan, who was involved in the fake acid attack against Molly Cropper earlier in the year, has received a suspended sentence and community service for his role in the attack. His evidence against the Eyes – the group of rogue teens under the control of the notorious Fixer – has helped to strengthen the CPS case against those youths involved in the killings of Shabana Hussain, Parminder Deol, Liaqat Ilyas, Graham Moorhead and Jamie Jacobs.

Distracted by hearing Maz's name, Nikki looked up. An image of the lad stared from the screen. He'd got off lightly, largely because of his compliance and because she'd convinced Archie to step in on his behalf. Her friend Ali also had avoided anything more than a slap on the wrist from DI Ahad. That was because he'd covered his tracks so well and forensics found no evidence implicating him. No one was listening too closely to tales from the five killers about masked men forcing their confessions. She understood the rage that had motivated Ali's actions for she herself was experiencing something very similar. She'd arranged for Maz to have counselling via My Wellbeing College – and although she couldn't quite shake the distrust Mallory's betrayal had instilled in her, she was sure that the NHS wouldn't have another Mallory working in their ranks. After all, lightning didn't strike twice, did it?

As if on cue, her phone rang, and she answered without checking caller ID.

'Parekh here.'

'Hallo, DS Parekh. You don't look so well, and what is that Marcus is holding? Another one of your postcards? Daddy dearest up to his old tricks again, is he?'

The sound of Mallory's voice brought ice to Nikki's veins. Then the impact of her words hit her. Marcus had indeed lifted the postcard and was scrutinising it. The bitch had remotely accessed one of their devices … again.

Nikki glanced round the kitchen, then saw Ruby's laptop open on the counter where she'd left it after showing Nikki that hilarious YouTube clip at breakfast. The green camera light flashed tauntingly. Nikki ran over and smashed the screen closed, yelling into the phone. 'Nowhere is too far for me to come for you, Mallory, nowhere.'

'Aw, but, Nikki, don't you think you'll need my help to catch Daddy dearest?' Mallory's laugh came down the line, chilling her, making her want to slam her mobile at the wall. Arms folded around herself, Nikki glanced round the room as if expecting her two worst nightmares to appear in person before her.

'I don't need anyone's help, Mallory. Don't you worry, I'm more than able to take care of both of you.' She disconnected the phone, lifted Ruby's computer and allowed it to clatter to the floor before she stamped on it, allowing her rage to lessen with each satisfying stomp.

Then, she turned to Marcus and grinned before striding over to the doorway and yanking the door open, she yelled down the hallway, 'You get that, Fred?'

The cybercrime expert employed by Interpol strolled through and once again, Nikki marvelled at how unlike a detective he was. Barely in his teens, casually dressed in jeans and a Hozier T-shirt, Fred O' Reilly had been posing as Charlie's boyfriend since Archie had been approached by Interpol regarding Mallory's cyber activity since she'd fled the UK. Apparently arranging death wasn't the Fixer's only illegal activity – art theft, money laundering and hacking into and clearing her competitor's bank accounts was another of her specialities and it was these activities which had put her on Interpol's radar. Unfortunately, she'd been smart, and they hadn't been able to pinpoint her location. That was when they put their heads together and realising that at some point she'd feel the need to make contact with Nikki again, they'd set up a trap for her on Ruby's device. As soon as she'd activated the dormant function on Ruby's laptop, it had jump-started a series of ultra encrypted actions – none of which Nikki understood. The upshot was, that they offered a heavily encrypted and an almost completely undetectable back door entry into Mallory's PC should she try and spy on Nikki again. In effect it was a cyber battle of humungous proportions between Mallory's expertise and the entire weight of the Interpol tech team, and hopefully Mallory wouldn't see them coming till it was too late.

Before he'd even had the chance to sit down at the kitchen table and open his laptop, Nikki crowded him. 'Did it work? Did you manage to trace her?'

Fingers flying across his keyboard, Fred grinned before he replied, his soft Irish accent gently teasing. 'Chill, Nik. Course I did. That was the aim, wasn't it? We'd already tracked her to Venezuela and now we know precisely where she is, I'll let the dogs loose. Watch.'

Nikki and Marcus gathered round him peering at his screen, waiting to see what would happen. Within two minutes the dark, silent screen was replaced by blue sky and a buzzing sound. As the image moved, Nikki saw that the drone, activated by Interpol on receipt of Fred's information, hovered above a still, blue swimming pool in the grounds of a balconied white painted mansion. A sunlounger with a parasol sat next to the pool. The drone dived down and zoomed in until Nikki could see a figure on the lounger. One with red hair, wearing a purple swimsuit. Nikki's grin widened across her face and she gripped Marcus's fingers tight in her own. 'Won't she hear the drone?'

'No way. This drone's nearly a mile away from her. It's top of the range. All you have to do is confirm her identity and my team in Venezuela will move in.'

As the drone got closer, Nikki saw Mallory raise a cocktail to her lips, take a long sip before setting it back on the table beside her and settle back rubbing sun lotion into her arms. Anger froze Nikki for a second. This woman had contributed to so much desolation and here she was lazing by a pool whilst they were picking up the pieces after her. When Nikki spoke, her tone was taut. 'It's her.'

Fred typed, then sat back, a satisfied smile on his freckled face. 'Now we wait and watch.'

The drone retreated till Mallory and her pool were no more than a speck on the screen, then it held its position. Tension spreading over her shoulders, Nikki watched, barely remembering to breathe as they waited. Within twenty minutes, ant-like figures began to crawl across the screen from all directions. Fred issued instructions to the drone, which moved in closer to capture the entire scene in close-up. For long moments, Mallory, ear buds in, huge purple sunglasses obscuring most of her face, lay basking in the sun, oblivious to the danger she was in. Then, something must have alerted her, for she jumped to her feet, knocking the table and shattering her cocktail glass on the pristine tiles as ten armed soldiers approached, guns directed straight at her.

Nikki wondered if she'd make a run for it, but instead of running, Mallory grabbed her glasses from her face, flung them at one of the soldiers and dived into the pool. Within moments, two soldiers dived in after her and after an undignified scuffle in the water, dragged her to the side of the pool. Another two soldiers dragged her from the pool, where she lay like a bedraggled purple puddle.

Nikki, exhaled and, her voice barely a whisper, said, 'Gotcha.'

Acknowledgements

With just about every other author over the past eighteen months, writing has been a strange and wonderful experience, sometimes a good one and sometimes not. *Blood Games* started off as an exploration of honour killings and became something a bit different as it explored the wider meanings of honour and family expectations in the context of multi-cultural, multi-class, multi-faceted society. It also took Nikki down a very dark route, which in many ways was a reflection of everyone's struggles recently.

Of course, my family played a huge part in easing the way for me to write *Blood Games* and they have both my gratitude and my love for that. The online book groups that kept me sane, provided entertainment and general support, filled the void of social mixing. Huge thanks to everyone at UK Crime Book Club and Crime Fiction Addict.

As ever, my editor, Belinda Toor's, support was second to none as we navigated the tricky waters of mental health blips, isolation issues and adapting to new ways of working and that goes for the rest of the team at HQ Digital who did a stellar job in editing, designing covers, responding to queries and all the myriad of other stuff they do on a daily basis. Huge thanks to all of you.

Rachel Gilbey as Rachel's Random Resources worked hard to create a blog tour that helped me get *Blood Games* out there, thanks so much.

My friends and in particular Toria Forsyth Moser (my first reader), my generous ARC group and writing buddies (too many to mention) all supported me through this and I love them to bits.

Lastly, you, the readers, are the ones who deserve the most thanks, for without you there would be no point in this journey. You generously read my books, invest your time into leaving reviews, support, share, follow and retweet the love and keep a smile pasted on my face. I hope you enjoyed *Blood Games* as much as I enjoyed writing it.

Thank you all so much!

Keep reading for an excerpt from
Last Request …

Prologue

1983

Her hand, scaly and trembling, reaches out. The flash of shocking-pink nail varnish that I'd applied with painstaking care whilst she'd been sleeping is incongruous against her yellowy skin. The stench of death hangs heavy around her, as if she's rotting from the inside out. I take her hand, careful not to grip too tightly. Every worm-like sinew, every frail tendon, every arid vein a braille pattern against my palm. Still, she flinches, the pain flashing in her milky eyes. A sheen of sweat dapples her forehead. Her nightdress is soaked with perspiration that mingles with fetid pus and piss, creating a cacophony of odours that make me want to retch. Her pink scalp shines through matted hair. Her cheekbones, jutting against paper-thin skin, bear raw scabs.

The room is dire – stinking and filthy. I should clean it, but I don't know how. That was never one of *my* jobs – cleaning up, keeping things neat, tidy. That had always been her job. Her eyes look heavy. Soon, once the morphine kicks in, she'll doze off. The dim light from the bedside lamp illuminates the layer of dust that covers the cabinet top. We don't use the main light anymore. It hurts her eyes. With the curtains drawn against the outside world, we are cocooned in this hell hole together … slowly disintegrating … decomposing like two worthless corpses thrown on an unlit pyre.

The carpet's gross. I've spilled more piss on there than has made it into the bedpan and that's not mentioning the stains where she's thrown up. No matter how much Dettol I use the overwhelming stink of vomit still hangs in the air.

When she drifts off into an uneasy sleep, I switch the television on. Casting anxious glances her way, I wait. Today's the day. The court hearing. It's like the entire country is on tenterhooks waiting for the verdict. I've tried telling myself I'm imagining things – the looks, the surreptitious glances, the whispers every time I go to the shops – each one a piqueristic experience of both pleasure and pain. Each one grounding me in the reality of what *he's* done to us. Deep down I know that everyone – the postman, Mr Anand at the corner shop, Mrs Roberts two doors down – everyone in the entire fucking world is waiting, holding on to their bated breath, with the heightened anticipation of an illicit orgasm.

They barely noticed me before this. Now it's as if, in the absence of my mother's presence, I've been thrust into minor celebrity status, my every move scrutinised. At least the paparazzi have slung their hooks, for now. Not before Mum had to face them though. When the story first hit the news, she was forced to run the gauntlet, her head hung in shame, her eyes swollen and red, her gait unsteady. It took its toll. Well, that and the shit that he'd infected her with. It all combined to drag her down, drain her.

The recording I've seen so many times, the standard one they played on endless repeat when the shit first hit the fan, flits across the screen. He looks so suave, sophisticated. All spruced up in his suit, beard trimmed, sleazy smile playing around his lips. Like he'd done nothing. Like none of this was *his* fault.

I daren't put the volume up so I flick to subtitles …

'Three more students under the care of Professor Graham

Earnshaw have come forward, with accusations of rape. This brings the total number of victims to fifteen. Professor Earnshaw's solicitor still maintains his client is not guilty and as the trial enters its fifth day, the court heard how Professor Earnshaw is alleged to have infected not only his wife, but four of his victims, three male and one female, with the HIV virus. It looks like this case could run into its second week, if not longer.'

The camera flicks to the front of Leeds Court and after a quick glance to make sure Mum is still asleep, I pull forward to hear what the Dean of Social Sciences is about to say about my father.

'... and the department has responded to student concerns as quickly as possible. We are doing our best to support our ...'

A groan from the bed and I press the remote. The screen goes dark and I look round. She's holding her hand up in front of her, a slight smile tugs her thin lips into a toothless grimace. 'Thank you. I like pink, always have.'

I lean over, tuck the sheets around her emaciated frame, ignoring the wafts of decay that hit my nostrils. Her frail hand grips my arm and I pause, turning my head towards her. 'What, Mum? What is it?'

Her smile widens, and I try not to flinch at the bloody cracks at the corner of her mouth and the gaps inside. She nods once and swallows. I go to lift the half-filled glass from the bedside table but she shakes her head – a painful movement that pulls a frown across her forehead. When she speaks her voice is low and raw. 'Promise me.'

I lean closer, hardly able to hear her words.

'My last request – you've *got* to promise that you'll do it. Live your dream. Do *everything* you always planned to do before this.'

Her hand gestures towards the TV. She saw it. I haven't been quick enough.

I bow my head and promise her. I'd promise her anything right now, but still, I keep my fingers crossed. I curse my carelessness but there's no point, for when I glance back her eyes are closed. She is on her final journey and, as if on cue, my entire body responds to the smash of a train hurtling through my core, pummelling me to the ground and, as she gasps her last breath, I cower on the floor hugging my knees tight to my chest. My heart shatters into a jigsaw of fragments that can't ever reconnect; a sense of relief coddles me like a woollen blanket and guilt and anger swamp me.

*

Days pass with those whose slurs had previously scorched us, now offering platitudes. Each false word drips like acid, as I take in the detritus that is my life from here on in, and all the time her last request plays in my mind like an annoying jingle.

There's nothing else for it. I'll have to do something about that.

Monday 15th October 2018

Chapter 1

Dour rain pummelled the cobbles that ran between the two rows of houses on Willowfield Terrace, making them sleek and dangerous underfoot. Except for the oppressive, grey clouds that promised more of the same, the alleyway was deserted. The air hung heavy, waiting to embrace the latest drama involving the Parekh women as Detective Sergeant Nikita Parekh flung open the back door and stormed out. Anger emanating from her every pore, she flew down the steps into the yard and out the gate, followed by her daughter. Leather jacket flying loose, she ignored the spatter of mucky water that her trainers kicked up the back of her jeans. With a plastic bag looped over one wrist, she raked her waist-length hair back into a ponytail and slipped a scrunchie round it. She was on a mission and nothing would deter her.

'Mum … Mum! Wait up.' Charlie, a foot taller than her mum, ran behind, hitching her schoolbag onto her shoulder. Unlike her mum, she tried to avoid the puddles created by the worn cobbles.

But Nikki was already pushing open the back gate of the neighbouring house and striding up the steps. Using her fist, she brayed briefly on the door before turning the handle and pushing it open, not waiting for a reply. Entering the kitchen, she glanced at the hijabed woman cooking a fry-up in a huge frying pan on the cooker. 'Where's Haqib?'

The woman puffed her cheeks out in a 'what's he done now?' expression and, shaking her head, pointed her spatula towards the kitchen door. 'Front room.'

Stopping only to grab a bite from a piece of buttered toast on a plate on the worksurface, Nikki marched out of the kitchen, through the small hallway and into the living room. The room was in semi-darkness, with just the light from an Ikea tabletop lamp and the TV illuminating the area. She went straight over to the large bay window and swished the curtains open, allowing the scant light from outside to penetrate.

'Oi!' All angles, acne and attitude, Haqib, slouched on a bright red leather sofa, TV blaring, remote control in his hand, bare feet balanced on top of a glass-topped coffee table. 'What d'ya think you're doin'? Can't see the telly, can I?'

Nikki turned with her hands on hips, and glared at him, the spark in her eyes forcing him to back down.

Charlie panted into the room, the knot on the top of her head wobbling as if it might fall off, her cheeks spattered with raindrops. 'Mum, if you'd just hang on a minute.'

Nikki extended her hand, one index finger raised to her daughter, just like her own mother had always done, '*Chup kar.*' She rounded the bulky couch and positioned herself right in front of the TV.

Charlie folded her arms under her boobs, one hip extended towards her mum, pure sulk dripping from her pursed lips.

Haqib bobbed his head, first to one side and then to the other, trying to see the TV, his tone a little less confrontational this time. 'Can't see.'

Nikki bent over and swiped his feet off the table.

'Hey.' He glanced from his aunt to his cousin, his hands splayed before him. 'What's up? What've I done now? You can't just come in and do that, you know?'

Nikki snorted before tipping the contents of the plastic bag she was carrying onto the table where Haqib's feet had been. Haqib stopped, mouth open. If Nikki had been in a better mood she'd have laughed, but right now she was fuming. Really fuming. Haqib's eyes moved from his aunt's stern face to the bags filled with multi-coloured pills, then up to Charlie. The pills with their smiley faces, love hearts and winky eyes incensed Nikki. Over the past few months she'd seen umpteen cases of kids in the city taking E and landing themselves in Bradford Royal Infirmary. This new batch was potent – three deaths and a brain damaged kid testified to that. It made Nikki's piss boil. She snatched the remote from her nephew and switched off the racket that boomed from the speakers. 'Spill!'

Haqib clipped his mouth shut, then opened it, before once more closing it like a minnow about to get swallowed by a shark. That analogy appealed to Nikki. All she wanted to do was to swallow the lad up, chew him till he squealed and spit him out.

'I … erm, I …' He looked at Charlie as if expecting her to bail him out.

Nikki moved closer, breathing heavily, her anger exuding from every pore. 'You selling MDMA to my 14-year-old, are you? Got a death wish, have you?' Another step and Haqib was trying to mould his body into the leather couch.

'You all right in there?' Nikki's sister, Anika, called from the kitchen.

Nikki glowered at Haqib. 'You'd better start spilling before your mum comes through.'

'For God's sake, Mum.' Charlie, her face perfectly made up, eyeliner on point and her school skirt too damn short, flounced forward and flung herself onto the sofa beside Haqib, sliding her schoolbag round till it rested on her lap. 'If you'd give me half a chance to explain. Haqib didn't *sell* me it.'

Nikki glared at the lad, eyebrows raised. 'You *gave* them to her? You *gave* your 14-year-old cousin E? That's no better. In fact, that's bloody worse.'

He ran the back of his hand across his nose and glanced at Charlie. 'I didn't. I wouldn't – she …' He glanced at Charlie and shrugged.

Charlie elbowed him in the ribs. 'Tell her then – you might as well …'

Head bowed, looking like a 2-year-old in trouble for stealing the Easter eggs, he mumbled something.

'What?' Nikki's voice was sharp. She'd thought Haqib knew better than to bring drugs of any sort near her family, near her home or even onto the damn estate. What the hell had he been thinking?

Clearing his throat, Haqib tried again. 'She' – he jerked his thumb towards Charlie – 'confiscated it.'

'You *what*?' Nikki looked at her eldest daughter who was all sulky indignation and 'I told you so'.

'What? So, you thought I'd *buy* Es? I'm not a loser, you know!'

Nikki grinned and scooped the bags up. Charlie wasn't a loser. Definitely not. Nearing the sofa, she leaned over and kissed the top of her daughter's top-knot head. 'No, *you're* not.' She leaned over further and cuffed Haqib's head. 'You, on the other hand, will be, if you don't stop with the damn drugs. Now I've got to bail you out, yet again. Not good enough, Haqib – not fucking good enough.'

She could just about put up with the weed that was rife on the estate – turn a blind eye and all that – but *this*? Once this shit got a grip on the estate it'd spread like wildfire bringing with it crime and violence and despair. She'd seen it all before on other Bradford estates and she was buggered if she'd allow it on hers. But what was she to do about Haqib? She was tempted to turn the little scrote in – let him see what it would be like – but deep down she knew she couldn't do that to her family or to this runt of a boy.

Haqib rubbed his head. 'I don't take them, Auntie. It's just …' He sighed.

Charlie broke in. 'What he's trying to say is that Deano's back.'

A talon curled its way round Nikki's heart and squeezed, hard and sudden. If Deano was back, then that meant his drug lord boss Franco was too … and he was an evil sod. 'I'll deal with this.' She hung the bag back over her wrist and chucked the remote control at Haqib, making sure it whacked his head. 'Don't be late for school, you two.'

When she re-entered the kitchen, Anika handed her a mug of steaming coffee. 'Weed? Again?'

Nikki sighed. Anika took a pragmatic approach to her son's weed consumption. Personally, Nikki would rather he didn't smoke the stuff, but then she knew how many alternatives there were out there, so she let it pass. She could tell her sister the truth, but what purpose would that serve? Anika would wail and moan and threaten to ground him and Haqib would do what he always did and ignore her.

She'd deal with it and they'd move on with her keeping a closer eye on the little turd. 'Yeah, summat like that.' She shrugged. 'Deano's back … and Franco. Don't worry, I'll sort it though.'

Anika nodded and went back to the fry-up she was cooking. 'He's trouble, that lad, but I've heard Franco's worse. Sort it before it gets out of hand – like last time.'

Nikki munched the remains of the toast she'd started on her way in. She enjoyed spending time in her sister's kitchen. It was homely. Filled with clutter and love. Kids' schoolbags by the back door, shoes kicked off in a huddle next to them, well-tended plants on the windowsill, a series of sentimental 'There's No Place Like Home' plaques and cutesy pictures of cats. Her own kids were always telling her to get some plants and put some pictures on the walls. Truth was, Nikki was as green-fingered as weed killer and the only plant that had been able to flourish in her home was the cactus Charlie had given her three Christmases ago. As for the sentimental crap? Well, that was *so* not Nikki. She liked things streamlined – no clutter. That way she knew if her space had been infiltrated. That way she felt safe and in control. As she watched her sister, something niggled at her. Something was different. When she realised what it was, she smiled but her heart sank. Why did Anika have to be so needy? 'You can't have it both ways, Anki.'

Anika frowned. 'What you on about?'

Taking a sip of coffee, Nikki pointed at her sister's head. 'You can't wear the hijab on one hand and fry bloody bacon and sausages on the other, now can you?'

Anika's face broke into a grin. She flung her head back, laughter bubbling out of her like warm fuzzies on a winter's day. 'Just as well I'm not wearing it on my hand then, innit?'

Covering her sigh with a smile, Nikki nursed her coffee, observing the warm flush across her sister's cheeks. Anika was happy … for now. 'Take it *Yousaf's* back an all.'

'Aw don't be like that. I love him. Maybe he'll stay this time.'

Nikki wanted to shake her. Make her wise up. 'You know he'll never leave his Pakistani family. 'Specially now he's a "councillor".' Nikki made air quotes round the last word and crossed her eyes for effect, pleased that her silly actions seemed to have taken the sting out of her words when Anika laughed.

'He loves me and he loves Haqib.'

Nikki groaned and stuffed more toast into her mouth, chewed, swallowed and then spoke. 'Come on! When's the last time he bought Haqib owt – or you for that matter? Yousaf's a loser. You keep taking him back every time he turns up for a booty call and he'll get you up the duff again and leave you. The likes of us – working-class, dual heritage and Hindu to boot – are *not* good enough for well-off businessmen-cum-councillors and especially not for married ones. He won't leave her.'

Anika's eyes welled up and Nikki could have kicked herself. Maybe sometimes she should just learn to shut her big mouth. She jumped to her feet and moved round to put her arms round her sister, hugging her tight. 'I'm sorry. I know I'm bitter and twisted, but I just don't want you getting hurt again.'

'Not everyone's like you know who, Nikki.'

Nikki sighed. Anika was right. Just because she'd had a bad experience didn't mean Anika would. But the truth was Yousaf just was not good enough for her sister. She only had to convince Anika of that fact. The sisters hugged until, smelling something beginning to burn, Nikki wheeled round, turned off the cooker and yelled through the house, 'Breakfast's ready.'

Haqib and Charlie appeared from the living room as Nikki knocked on the wall that adjoined her house and yelled. 'You two, Auntie Anika's got breakfast ready. Shift it.'

Faint yells of, 'I'm starving' and 'Hope it's a fry-up' filtered through the walls and within seconds, Nikita's younger two children, dressed in school uniforms, faces all rosy and clean, ran into the kitchen and plonked themselves down at the table, grabbing their cutlery and looking like they'd never been fed in their lives. As Nikki grabbed another slice of toast, she felt her phone vibrate in her pocket. Pulling it out, she saw it was a text from her boss, DCI Archie Hegley. She circled the table to drop kisses on each of the kids' heads in turn. 'Work. Gotta run. Be good and, Charlie, change into trousers. Your skirt's too damn short.'

Driving down Legram's Lane in her clapped-out Zafira, windscreen wipers going like the clappers, Nikki wondered if she had transferred her wellies from the pool car back to her own. She had a sinking feeling she hadn't. Every so often a drop of water landed on her head and Nikki cursed. She really needed to get a new car, but the kids seemed to have an endless stream of requests for stuff that was never free. The car would have to wait. A new drip splatted on her head, rolled down her forehead and landed on her nose. She wiped it off with her sleeve. Maybe after she'd done her Inspector's exam and got a promotion, she could treat herself to a car that didn't leak – or maybe she'd have to repair the leaky tap in the bathroom and the thermostat on the central heating and double-glaze the kitchen window before its old wooden frame rotted and released the pane.

After taking a right at Thornton Road, Nikki joined the trail of commuters. A few hundred yards and she could already see the telltale police vehicles and crime scene vans. She abruptly took advantage of a gap in the traffic and bounced her car onto the opposite kerb. Ignoring the hoots from cars travelling in the opposite direction, she got out and turned her collar up against the rain. Typical! Weeks without a suspicious death and then you choose the day when it's pissing down to reveal yourself. She jogged the last few hundred yards, hoping the crime scene tent would be up and she could get some shelter.

Dear Reader,

We hope you enjoyed reading this book. If you did, we'd be so appreciative if you left a review. It really helps us and the author to bring more books like this to you.

Here at HQ Digital we are dedicated to publishing fiction that will keep you turning the pages into the early hours. Don't want to miss a thing? To find out more about our books, promotions, discover exclusive content and enter competitions you can keep in touch in the following ways:

JOIN OUR COMMUNITY:

Sign up to our new email newsletter:
http://smarturl.it/SignUpHQ

Read our new blog www.hqstories.co.uk

🐦 https://twitter.com/HQStories

📘 www.facebook.com/HQStories

BUDDING WRITER?

We're also looking for authors to join the HQ Digital family!
Find out more here:

https://www.hqstories.co.uk/want-to-write-for-us/

Thanks for reading, from the HQ Digital team

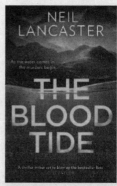